OBSIDIAN SOULS

MICKEY MARTIN

MMH PRESS

 A catalogue record for this
work is available from the
NATIONAL
LIBRARY
OF AUSTRALIA
National Library of Australia

National Library of Australia Catalogue-in-Publication data:
Obsidian Souls/Mickey Martin

ISBN: 978- (Paperback)
ISBN: 978- (Ebook)

GLOSSARY OF TERMS

VEINS – Mortal Enemy of the Soul Keepers
Once a magnificent species created by a powerful being, their greed, as they feed of death, chaos and destruction, has turned them into parasites.

SOUL KEEPERS
Both Elemental and Heavenly Soul Keepers have the power to protect and nurture Mother Earth.

They restore her declining biodiversity, and protect her innocent pure-souls that the Veins destroy and feed on in their all consuming hunger for power.

PURE-SOULS
Animals *and* Humankind. Mundane, no special gifts, but their presence on Earth is required for balance to flow in harmony.

GLOSSARY
ITALIAN TO ENGLISH

La Stella – Star

Si – Yes

Bellissimo – Beautiful

Vigliacco – Coward

Fratello – Brother

Compagno – Partner

Maledetto Inferno – Bloody Hell

Sanguinante – Blood – Bloody

Caro – Dear

Bella – Beautiful (Female)

Bello – Beautiful (Male)

Finalmente – Finally

Bene – Okay/Good/Well

Stronzo – Arsehole

Zucchero – Sugar

Pazzo – Mad

CHAPTER ONE
SAMANTHA

Stars above, why does he wear anger so well?

Maxwell Black raised frustrated green eyes to glare in her direction. The anger only enhanced his handsome, dark features.

Samantha Storm averted her gaze and forced herself not to one, cringe at his disapproving glare and two, flush with desire. A flashback of him poised over her naked body several months prior as he'd worshipped her ignited a steamy memory she knew they would never revisit. Well, according to *him*.

She looked at her coffee and sighed. She stirred in another scoop of sugar after reaching for an ornate spoon decorated with the Glenormiston College emblem. The comforting lunch time noise of the cafeteria helped drown out her misery of wanting a man who didn't want her. He'd told her as much a week ago when he'd returned from Italy that what they'd once shared was and would always be nothing but a fond memory.

"Hey, you, it's cold enough this time of year without you freezing up the only place that's warm at lunchtime." Angel Cloud, Sam's once soul-sibling and now sister-in-law by pure-souls standards, slid into the chair opposite her. Sam grinned at the pretty woman who'd been a sister to her since the day they were born.

"Sorry, didn't realise me trying to ice out my heart would freeze the entire room too." Sam took a deep breath and focused on returning the cafeteria to its normal temperature, noticing a few students and professor rubbing their arms.

Angel shook her head, her tone sympathetic when she said, "It won't always be this hard, Sam."

"Won't it?" Sam folded her arms as she met Angel's steady gaze. "I thought when Max came home, things would be different. That he would have had time to heal. Time to want me again." She raised a dark eyebrow, offset by her blonde waves as Angel released a humourless chuckle.

"Oh, he still wants you, Sam. Count on that."

"Oh yeah? Then why was the first thing that came out of his mouth when he saw me after eight months away was to state that he was glad we could still be friends and nothing but friends? Tell me that?"

Angel shook her head. "I can't tell you what's going on in that mind of his." She looked over her shoulder towards Max, who was sitting with his mates, Eddy and Gary, before meeting her sister's gaze. "But what I can tell you is this; that man loves you still."

"Yeah, well, he has a funny way of showing it." As the bell rang, indicating lunch was over, Sam shoved her chair back and grabbed her mug. "I'll see you this afternoon," she called over her shoulder as she headed to dump her mug on the return counter and on to a lecture on national soil strategies.

MAXWELL

Maxwell Black sped past the mansion's axed bluestone and wrought-iron gates and along the driveway lined with agapanthus and jonquils. Ancient elms stood guard, their twisted limbs casting shadowy arms above him as he pulled into the old carriage house. He didn't bother locking the sports car before heading towards the 1873 Classic Revival mansion. He waved as the last of the tradesmen drove by him. The site manager, Jason Binery, waited for Max at the front.

"We're all finished up, Mr Black," he said, passing an invoice to Max, who tried not to cringe at the use of his despised, departed father's name. He'd stopped trying to get the workers on the property to call him Max.

"Thank you." He shook Jason's hand while peering past him, keen to get inside and have a look around.

"Building inspector approved everything this morning, so you're good to go."

"Can't wait to see it. Tell your crew there will be a bonus for all their efforts."

Jason grinned before clapping Max on the shoulder. "Have always enjoyed working for your family. If there's anything I can do for you in the future, give me a call."

"Will do. Thanks for everything."

"Yup. See you around." He waved before sauntering off towards his vehicle, whistling a merry tune.

Max sighed, grateful to be alone as he looked up at the picturesque Gothic Revival structure, enhanced with its distinctive iron veranda, elaborate gable barges and gothic ornament at its finest. He pushed the heavy, carved door open and stepped into a wide, open arched entrance, leading into a tranquil space of whitewashed walls and open-plan living. He grinned, spotting the large pool table in the main lounge and pushing his hands into his jeans pockets, strolled through the soothing interior, taking in the finished space.

Rooms, once dark and oppressive, closed off and secretive, were now open and airy. Decorative skylights in the interior walls allowed the afternoon sunlight to stream in through the floor to ceiling windows that overlooked gardens. Once overgrown and neglected, now they were abundant in springtime glory.

Black iron pendulum lighting contrasted nicely where they hung from thick wooden beams and as Max walked from once space to the next, horse carriage lights softly glowed, turning off once he'd walked by them.

He'd positioned furniture around the space for both solitary comfort and group conversations. Large indoor plants added a vibrant layer of colour as grey rugs flowed along the polished floorboards. A solid wall held a deep-set fireplace with raised hearth for seating and above it, black and white photographs framed to celebrate the area's beauty. Mount Noorat, The Glenormiston College, Terang and Camperdown's tree-lined avenues contrasted in a play of shadow and light. His favourite sat above the mantel, a scene of an apricot sky kissing five ancient elms that stood proudly in the middle of one of Quick's paddocks. He stared at it as he listened to the calm silence of the mansion, feeling at peace for the first time in months.

He sighed, content, as he ran his hand against the smooth, varnished wood of the mantel. "I'm home," he whispered.

He turned towards the open-plan kitchen, designed with a masculine touch. Black Italian marble graced the tall island bench in the middle of the spacious room, appliances tucked behind streamline cabinets. From the fridge tucked behind a cabinet, Max grabbed a cold beer before heading out the back door and stepping onto the decking. He twisted off the cap and tossed it into the fire pit, then he leaned against the polished timber railing, taking a deep swallow of the cool ale as he looked over the sprawling yard.

The deep pond, strewn with vibrant green Lilly pads, sat beside an old-as-time Weeping Willow where a new swing had been attached. He nursed his beer as the frogs began their afternoon chorus and glanced beyond his property towards Mount Noorat. Only then did he allow his thoughts to turn to Samantha Storm, and what seeing her had done to the solid wall he'd been building around his cold, broken heart for the past eight months.

He closed his eyes for a moment as her image flooded his senses. Since he had seen her last, her strawberry blonde waves had grown past her shoulders. Her eyes, always warm, amber flames, now liquid pools of honey. Her lips… he remembered the feel of them beneath his all too well. His eyes flew open.

"Jesus Christ, if you want to torture yourself, fool of a man, go for a run." He shook his head, turning to go back inside, planning on doing just that. He tipped the beer into the sink and paused by a dark wooded door in the hallway that led down to the cellar. Max pressed his palm against the carved timber, resting his forehead against it for a moment before shaking off the oppressive feeling taking over any happiness left inside his soul.

"One problem at a time," he whispered, knocking his knuckles against the door once before pushing away and heading up the staircase to the next level. He was pleased to see they'd furnished all the bedrooms ready for his guests, who would arrive soon.

He raced up another narrow staircase that twisted towards the attic, opened the door, and stepped into the sprawling space. Dark, varnished floorboards presented a room with several large gabled windows that overlooked the property and allowed the afternoon light to spill across a massive bed that sat in the middle of the room. Ivy grew along the ceiling in an elegant emerald river to drip down through the middle of an ornate ceiling rose and had entwined itself through the black chandelier. Along the walls were black and white photographs of plants and animals that looked like a national geographic photographer had taken them. Max was proud when the decorator had asked where he'd purchased these and the ones downstairs above the fireplace, as she was hoping to reach out to his supplier and use them in her staging business. Photography was a passion of his and had helped calm his racing mind when he had travelled overseas to escape his pain. He hadn't realised he had a natural talent for capturing the living world until he'd started experimenting.

Throwing on his running gear, he was determined to run off his 'Sam Storm obsession' before he had to face the Light Accords council meeting to which they'd summoned him. The second, two days in a row. He only hoped they weren't onto him as he thought about his prisoner downstairs.

"Fun times," he said as he ran downstairs, through the house, out the back door and towards Mount Noorat.

CHAPTER TWO
SAMANTHA

"Samantha?" Bowie Storm called from the bottom of the homestead's staircase as he walked in the front entranceway.

Sam walked down the corridor and leaned against the wall, folding her arms as she stood behind her brother, always highly entertained when his energy was tuned to a high volume. She'd felt his frustrated vibration before he'd even walked in the front door and was curious to hear what had set him off this time. She watched as he ran a hand through his dark blond hair and yelled her name once more.

"Sam, get down here!"

"Dear brother," she said, laughing when he jumped. "Why do you assume I'm in my room?"

He turned to face her, relief on his face that he'd located her. "Sam, something's gone down. Fletch is on his way."

"Okay." She nodded as he walked by her towards the library they often used as a second lounge room. Two long couches faced each other, a low table filled with white candles in the centre, sat opposite a roaring fire. A six-foot desk stood by a large window that opened up towards the gardens. On the desk, three feet in circumference, was a glass world globe.

Sam perched on the arm of the couch closest to the fire as she watched her brother pace by the desk. "What is it?" She frowned when he continued pacing while footsteps approached.

Sam turned towards the door as Angel and her blood-sibling, Michael Cloud, walked in, followed by Fletch, a council member from Warrnambool. His being here didn't bode well. An uneasy ball begin to roll around Sam's stomach as she stood, waiting.

"Good," Fletch began as he walked towards the desk. "Everyone's here."

"Are we waiting for Tom and Jess?" Michael asked, sounding as flustered as Bowie had. Sam frowned, noticing fidgeting movements and an unhappy scowl infiltrated Michael's usually calm presence.

Angel joined Bowie and placed a comforting hand on his arm. He smiled down at her, then slid his arm around her waist, holding her close as they turned towards Fletch. A year ago, if Bowie was anxious, it would have been his pocketknife he reached for. Now, the only comfort he needed was to be close to Angel. Sam looked away as fingers of loneliness wrapped around her heart. Shaking it off, she asked. "What's going on?"

Fletch was ever the serious man, no matter the occasion, but it alarmed Sam to see a fleeting flash of fear fill his eyes. She met Michael's gaze briefly before Fletch began.

"The council has asked me to update you on some changes that will be taking place over the next several months. As you all know, Maxwell Black has returned."

"Happy he has," Michael said.

Fletch nodded. "He will be living at the Black's mansion and is opening his home to boarders."

"A boarding house?" That intrigued Sam, knowing Max didn't need the income. His family estate and worldwide holdings made him one of the wealthiest bachelors in Australia.

"Correct."

"Why?" Angel asked, scooping a wayward hair strand behind her ear.

Fletch shrugged, uncharacteristically. "For the past eight months, Maxwell was assigned by the Light Accords to infiltrate a Vein cell in Italy where Brendan Black ran his operation."

"That would have been easy enough for him to do, considering he'd spent time there with Brendan before they came back here to abduct Angel." Bowie said, stroking Angel's arm in a soothing gesture.

"Why did the Light Accords send Max to Italy so soon after Brendan's death?" Michael asked Fletch. "The Vein activity had been close to nil after Sam and Angel killed him."

"Because of this," Fletch turned to the world globe. He stretched his arms on either side and, tapping his long fingers against the glass, he whispered, "Reveal his secrets," before throwing his arms towards the ceiling.

Sam gasped, caught unaware as the globe flew up in the air before spinning above them and then before she could blink, it stretched its circumference wide, encasing them in its transparent dome. The library walls disappeared as they turned to look around them and Sam cringed when her eyes landed on a younger version of Max's father; Rob Black, standing in his mansion, wiping the brow of a beautiful woman who was screaming in labour pain while she delivered a baby.

"*You're doing great, Rebecca,*" Rob soothed as a figure donning a black robe stepped forward, taking the baby. Rebecca's screaming continued as another contraction rippled through her and a second baby emerged. Once again, the robed figure entered and took the baby away once it slid out of the exhausted woman's body.

Sam cringed as she watched Max's father trail a lingering kiss across the exhausted woman's lips before she began moaning pitifully as another baby made its way into the world. As the third baby left its mother's warm body, it was coated in a glistening, silver liquid-like oil. Rob's eyes widened. "*The prophecy is real,*" he whispered in glee as he turned to the approaching robed figure, who swept the baby up.

"*Send Brendan in, keep this baby away from the others,*" he commanded.

The figure nodded, leaving Rob and Rebecca alone. She lay motionless and exhausted. Moments later, Brendan Black walked into the room, eyes widening when he saw the silver afterbirth flow from between Rebecca's legs before nodding to Rob.

The Soul Keepers watched on as Rob Black's eyes dilated, a macabre grin spreading across his face as he ran a hand over his wife's damp, weakened body and then open his arms wide as if to worship her.

"*Rob,*" she whispered. "*What are you doing?*" She reached for his arm, looking confused at his strange expression. "*Rob?*"

"*I loved you so, my dear, but you've served your purpose and for that, I'm grateful. Forgive me, darling.*"

"*Forgive you?*" She raised an eyebrow. "*Forgive you for what?*" She whispered, then gasped as movement rippled beneath his flesh. Her eyes widened in terror as long veins burst from his forearms and slid eerily towards her. She froze in disbelief and fear. "*Rob, what's going on? What the devil are you…?*" A desperate scream, filled with pain cut off her question when his long, sharp veins speared into her flesh, penetrating her body and sucking the life essence from her. As Rob did this, Brendan had inserted his veins into the silver afterbirth and absorbed the metallic liquid until not one drop remained.

Rob Black stood with soulless eyes as he sucked the life from his once beautiful wife until she lay motionless. As Rebecca's body deflated like a helium balloon, skin sagging across thin bones, Rob Black turned his back to her and stared with pupilless eyes in Sam's direction, causing her to cry out before the image vanished and the globe evaporated around them, returning to the desk in a snap.

Everyone in the room remained silent for a full twenty seconds afterwards. Sam's gaze locked with Angel's, who looked as disturbed as she felt.

"What the *hell* was that?" Had she truly just witnessed Max's birth and his dad suck the soul-essence out of his wife?

"That," Bowie replied, "was insanity."

"By the Angels, he killed her right after she gave birth to their children," she whispered in disbelief. "What sort of monster does that?"

"A vile one," Michael answered.

"What was that silver liquid? Blood?" She raised an eyebrow in question to Fletch, who didn't have time to answer as someone fired the next question his way.

"Max is a triplet?" Angel asked in disbelief.

"It appears so."

"Does Max know?" Bowie asked.

"Yes."

"I thought the council said Max was the only half heavenly, half Vein ever born?" Michael looked at Sam, waiting for Fletch to answer.

"We assumed that was the case until a week ago. One of our elemental Soul Keepers apprehended who we thought was Maxwell Black doing unspeakable things to a heavenly soul."

"Not Max," Sam stated, her voice solemn, "but his triplet?"

Fletch nodded. "His name is Kyle Black."

Sam rubbed her arms before waving her fingers towards the fire.

The flames surged, warming her instantly, removing the weird chill that filled the room the moment Rob Black's eyes had met hers.

"Rob Black *is* dead, isn't he?" she asked, hating that she sounded nervous.

"Yes," Fletch said.

"So, Max has siblings and one of them is clearly as evil as his father. What's the big deal if he's in custody?" Angel asked.

"Because three days ago, he disappeared from his cell." Fletch replied.

"That's not good." Bowie frowned.

"Clearly," Sam muttered before asking, "How did he manage that?"

"That, we don't know. We have never had a Vein escape our custody before."

"Going back to your earlier comment, what changes are taking place?" Bowie asked.

Fletch folded his arms. "Samantha, you are being assigned to move into the mansion with Maxwell and keep an eye on things."

Sam scoffed. "I don't think Max is going to leap at the idea of me living under his roof." She frowned as a memory of her soul ceremony, over a year ago, to Peter emerged. Max had moved out of the homestead and away from her, faster than a flash of lightning.

"Whether Maxwell likes it or not, he is being informed of the decision tonight by the council."

"Why is Sam being assigned to live there?" Bowie asked.

"Because Maxwell's new boarders are Veins."

"What?" Bowie turned to face Fletch.

Fletch ran a hand along his jaw before explaining. "I know it's unsettling, a group of Veins living so close to our sacred ground, but Maxwell has assured the council these Veins want change. That they've fought against their dark, inner cravings to destroy the living world, including consuming heavenly souls."

Sam shook her head. "It's too risky having them so close to Angel, Michael, and Jess, let alone the rest of us."

Fletch turned to Sam. "As I said. That is why you are being assigned to live with them, keep your eye on them and your ear to the ground."

"So, you're turning Sam into a spy?" Bowie frowned.

"No. Maxwell will be made aware of Sam's role and it will be his duty to keep her safe at all times."

"Well, I don't have anything to worry about. It's not like they want to suck the life out of me without risking electrocution." Sam grinned across at Angel, who returned her smile.

"That may be so, Sam," Michael said, "but you still have great power that will attract their dark side."

"Side?" Bowie snickered, his lip curling. "They only have *one side* and that is putridly evil and wanting nothing more than to cause chaos and debauchery."

"As I said," Fletch addressed Bowie. "Maxwell has stated that these Veins are no threat to us, or the community that we are protecting here."

Angel looked up at Bowie, who still wore a look of disgust on his handsome face.

"I trust Max and if he says these Veins want change, I believe him. We'll make them welcome and show Max he is still a part of our family.

Bowie's scowl disappeared as he looked down at her before dropping a quick kiss against her lips. "Okay, we'll give them the benefit of the doubt."

"The council aren't granting them access to the college, are they?" Michael asked.

Fletch shook his head. "No, not at this stage. Samantha, you'll be moving in first thing Saturday morning."

"Great," she whispered. "Just how I wanted to start my weekend."

"I'll be in touch." Fletch nodded before leaving the room.

Once he was gone, the four royal-souls looked at each other before Angel asked, "Are you going to be okay, Sam?"

"Do you mean living with a houseful of soul suckers? Or under the same roof as Max again?"

"Both." Angel sighed, crossing over to her. "Will you be okay?"

"Sure I will. If anyone looks at me the wrong way, I will kick their arse. And that includes Max." Sam grinned.

Bowie laughed. "That's my sister. Go and pack what you'll need. Michael and I will organise an early going away dinner."

"Really?" Michael looked at Bowie.

"Yep, pizza and beers."

Sam beamed. "Sounds perfect. Come on Angel, will you give me a hand?"

"Of course," Angel tucked her arm through Sam's and they headed towards Sam's room to get what she'd need to feel at home in the old Black's mansion.

CHAPTER THREE
SAMANTHA

Saturday morning came faster than Sam would have liked. She stood in front of Max's front door, blew out a nervous breath, ran her sweaty palms over her black jeans before making sure her hair was in place. Sam knew she looked good; she'd made sure of it as she'd dressed that morning. Tight jeans and an even tighter sweater clinging to curves and toned muscle. The blue scarf tucked loosely around her neck complimented her amber eyes, making them sparkle. Was she trying to make him regret his declaration of them moving forward as 'just friends'? Yes. Yes, she was.

She raised a hand and was about to give the door a good bang when it opened and her fist connected with a firm chest. A nervous laugh slipped through her lips as she looked up into Max's calm, dark green eyes, framed with thick black lashes.

"Sorry." She hated that her voice sounded breathless and that he looked mouth-watering, as always.

"No problem," he answered in his usual quiet tone before he reached past her to pick up her suitcase, as if it weighed no more than her handbag.

She caught his intoxicating scent and watched his muscles bunch under his tight-sleeved shirt as he hefted her overloaded suitcase up and turned to go inside, calling over his shoulder, "Come in."

Drawing another breath, she whispered to herself. "Get a grip, woman," before following Max into a space that took her breath away.

The feeling inside the mansion all those years ago when Rob and Brendan Black had lived there when Max was a young boy was opposite to everything he'd transformed it into. In an instant, Sam felt at home in the space Max had created.

"This is stunning," she declared in awe, as she followed him further into the open space.

"Thanks." He sounded pleased as he placed her suitcase down. "Do you want a tour of downstairs before I take you up to your room?"

"Sure." She looked across at the roaring fireplace and the captivating photographs above the wide, slick mantel before turning her eyes back to Max.

He was staring at her, hands casually in his pockets before angling his head.

"This way." He offered her a slight smile before turning to walk by the pool table and towards the kitchen.

Sam wondered if he'd felt the energy pass between them when their eyes had met and shook her head, following him. He'd claimed he wanted nothing more than friendship and she'd prove to them both she could agree to his terms without making things tense whilst they had to live under the same roof.

"Wow," she said, taking in the massive kitchen and the large dining table opposite. "This really is gorgeous, Max."

"Yeah, I think so. I had the designs sent over whilst I was still in Italy."

She watched as he looked around the room proudly.

"Jason Binery and his crew did an excellent job."

Sam paused, wondering how to bring up the subject of his siblings. They stood silently, Max watching her with ever-serious eyes.

She cleared her throat before blurting, "How do you feel about having siblings?"

He ran a hand over the back of his neck, holding it there for a moment before saying. "You know?"

"Yeah, Fletch came by and showed us your birth." She paused, wondering if he'd seen it too. "Your mother was beautiful, even in her weakened condition," she ended.

"Was she? I chose not to watch." He pushed both hands into his jeans pockets and Sam noticed a large black, ornate ring catch the light before disappearing into the denim.

Pretty. "So, you're a triplet. How do you fell about that? Are you okay?"

"Of course, nothing's changed for me. I've never had them in my life, so..." He shrugged.

She watched his forest-green eyes flash but couldn't detect the emotion behind them. She was about to ask another question when he cut in.

"Do you want to see outside?"

"Absolutely." She smiled, sensing he didn't want to talk about it anymore. She walked by him to open the back door and stepped out onto the decking, where outdoor furniture sat around a large fire pit. Stairs led down towards the pond and a small pier where a little rowboat sat amongst the lily pads. "Oh, a swing," she said, then grinned. "This space is cool."

She startled when a little boy and girl ran by, laughing as a tiny chocolate-coloured Dachshund chased them. She turned towards Max to ask if he knew who they were and gasped in confusion as a lovely red-haired woman stepped up to him and wrapped her arms around his neck before reaching up to slide her lips along his. Sam felt a flare of jealousy as Max wrapped strong arms around her waist, pulling her against him as he deepened the kiss. Sam frowned as a dizzy wave of anger threatened to bowl her over.

"Samantha?"

Sam blinked, shaking her head as the woman suddenly disappeared and the sound of the children's laughter vanished along with the yapping puppy. Max was in front of her in a flash as she steadied herself, noticing he'd reached out to grab her arm, but stopped himself just before he made contact.

"You okay? You went really pale all of a sudden."

"Yeah, um." She swallowed, tucking a silky curl behind her ear, noticing his gaze follow the path of her fingers as they trailed along the smooth flesh of her neck. "I skipped breakfast."

He stood motionless for a moment before nodding. "Come on inside. I'll fix you something."

"No, you don't have to do that, Max," she said as he was halfway to the back door. He stopped before turning towards her and she watched his shoulders rise as he pulled in a deep breath.

"Sam, we have things to discuss and I need a tea. So, let's go in. You can sit and put something decent in your stomach before you make yourself at home. Okay?"

"Your house rules, huh?"

"Yeah." His eyes darkened. "Something like that."

"Okay, thanks."

He nodded before turning around and headed inside. She shook her head, glancing over her shoulder at the magnificent yard before following him. Whatever the hell that vision-thing was, she had other things to focus on.

MAXWELL

Max grated cheese into the omelette stuffed with capsicum, tomatoes, and mushrooms, just the way Sam liked it. He slid the plate towards her along the marble island before turning to pour her a coffee and himself an Earl Grey tea.

"Thanks." She smiled at him before leaning forward and taking a deep breath as the steam carried the aromas towards her.

His gut tightened when she moaned in pleasure before picking up her fork and digging in.

"Mm, yummy. Want some?" she offered around a mouthful, raising her warm, honey-eyes towards him.

He watched her over the rim of his mug as he blew on his tea, shaking his head once. He stood opposite her as she sat on a kitchen stool and admitted to himself that he loved having her here, despite the imminent danger to her, being in a house full of Veins; some who were still struggling to control their natural instincts and urges. He'd promised the council he'd keep her safe once they'd informed him of the role she would play in keeping her eye on his guests. After his surprise late-night visitor the night before, he was more determined than ever to prove he could keep her safe. Bowie wasn't shy in informing him they'd be watching his every move, or the threat that followed if anything were to happen to Sam whilst she was under his protection.

He had a great deal to share with her and wasn't sure where to start. "I'm sure you have questions, but I'll give you what I can whilst you eat." He thought he'd make the most of her beautiful mouth being filled with food and hoped for fewer interruptions as she ate.

She paused momentarily, reaching to take a swig of coffee before nodding and scooped up more of the fluffy omelette.

"As you know, I went to Italy for several months and it wasn't just because I needed to get away."

She stopped chewing and a look of sadness swept across her sweet face. Eyes filled with unshed tears met his.

He swallowed, feeling her emotions wash over him. Clearly, she'd been as distraught as he'd been when he'd left Australia without a good-bye. It had been the month after Sam had lost her soul-partner, Peter, after Max's vicious cousin, Brendan, slaughtered him. Peter's death broke the soul-essence bond he'd shared with Sam, for the short time they'd been joined by their soul-essence ceremony. Angel had told Max at the time, that Peter's death had left Sam feeling alone in the world, confused and guilt-ridden that she hadn't been more devastated by him dying. Max should have been there for her at the time, but seeing her so distraught was almost as difficult as it had been seeing her completely happy after her ceremony.

He shook his head, forcing unwanted memories away before continuing. "I also left because the council asked me to return to Italy and see if I could locate any of Brendan's Veins I'd met previously. They wanted me to establish that, after Brendan's death, the Vein activity had, in fact, decreased in the city where the Veins ascended."

She nodded, allowing him to continue.

He sat his mug down before stepping back to lean against the kitchen counter, folding his arms as he continued. "I discovered at least two-hundred Veins had perished. Mostly the ones created from Brendan's line."

"Created?" Sam interrupted. "Have you been watching too many episodes of the Originals, Maxwell?"

Max gave a dry laugh. "Vampires aren't real, Sam."

"No? Let's face it, Veins are our version of vampires, aren't they?"

He sighed, rubbing a hand over his cheek, waiting for her to be quiet so he could continue.

She watched him back before waving her fork in the air. "By all means, continue," she said before stabbing a mushroom.

He watched her pink lips part as she slid the mushroom into her pretty mouth and cleared his throat before continuing. "Although the majority of the known cell had vanished, I did discover a group of Veins who'd been imprisoned. Some of them, like me, had lived a life without knowing their darkness even existed until Brendan discovered them and forced them to consume, destroy and kill."

He paused for a moment, recalling the fear on their faces when he'd found them locked in the Veins tower, which was sinking into the city. They'd been petrified of him, certain he'd been sent by his cousin to kill them all.

"I convinced the group to come away with me to the country, away from any temptation. For months, I did everything I could to build up their self-worth and convince them they deserved to live. But it was... difficult, to say the least. Some were consumed by self-loathing after the despicable things Brendan and his minions had made them do. Thankfully, in the end, they started to believe they didn't have to become the vile parasites they'd been branded. That they could, in fact, choose a different path."

"It sounds like you had your work cut out for you."

"Yeah, it was a busy time, considering I was also assigned by the council to heal all that I could whilst I was in Europe.

"Productive time away," she said.

"It wasn't time wasted, that's for sure."

Sam smiled. "You are a heavenly soul, through and through, Maxwell."

They looked at each other for a few moments. The longer he stared at her, the pinker her cheeks became. She dropped her gaze to her plate and scooped up the last few mouthfuls. He reached for his tea and took a few deep swallows, washing down the desire to have a taste of that mouth of hers.

"What else did you get up to?" she asked.

"I discovered Veins have the ability to absorb negative energy and can potentially aid in the healing of all that is ill in this world."

Sam looked surprised. "What? How did you discover such a thing?"

"Accident, then experimentation mostly."

"I'm intrigued." She dropped her chin in her hand and stared at him, making him forget what he had to share with her. He cleared his throat and began again.

"I took my group out on a ship for a few weeks, where the ocean was polluted and the marine life dying. I needed to get them off land and away from the pure-souls after an unfortunate incident, so that seemed like a two in one kinda deal."

"Incident?" she raised an eyebrow.

Max sighed. "A relapse if you will. One of the group killed two pure-souls in a pub one night. Drained them dry in a bathroom."

"Oh…" she whispered.

"Yeah." He nodded. "Anyway, I thought being out on the Global ocean was a safe place to isolate, and the perfect opportunity to use less of my heavenly abilities and experiment with my Vein abilities."

"How?"

"After using my heavenly abilities to begin the healing of the ocean, I became depleted after a few hours without another Soul Keeper present. It took days to fully restore my energy. So, I experimented with consuming acidification, toxins and pollutions within the ocean using my veins."

Sam stilled before asking, "You *fed* on the effects of climate change? On the filth, the poison?" She pushed her plate aside to nurse her coffee, tilting her head. Silky waves fell across her face, which she tucked behind her ear.

"I did, and I discovered that by doing so, after a few hours, I gained energy."

"That doesn't make sense?" she said. "Why would a Vein destroy and kill if they could gain energy by removing poison or disease?"

"This is my short version of the story." He couldn't give her anything else just yet or confess that consuming toxins didn't give off a nice, buzz-like-side effect, which consuming a heavenly soul did. The pleasure of that act was almost indescribable.

"Did it make you ill?"

He shrugged. "For a short while." He didn't want to elaborate on the painful, unpleasant side effects one experienced after absorbing a poisoned Mother Earth. No doubt equivalent to a pure-soul taking a mouthful of diesel oil.

"Well, I don't like the sound of you being ill, for any reason, but this is incredible, Max?"

He nodded, keeping one important piece of information to himself. One lot of secrets was enough for now.

"Amazing," she whispered before taking a mouthful of coffee.

"That's not all."

"Oh?"

"I discovered that the poison and toxicity I absorbed could kill another Vein."

"How?" she asked, intrigued.

"Mostly, we use our weapon, our *veins*, to cause pain and extract energy for pleasure, but, after absorbing toxins, they can also be used to inject poison."

"You did this to another Vein?"

"I did," was his abrupt reply.

"You consumed toxins, then inserted your veins into another Vein's flesh and injected poison into them?"

Max nodded, his eyes not leaving hers, and he watched her shift uncomfortably. She'd just described a monstrous image of the evil Veins could do.

"Okay," she said, averting her eyes, trying to get her head around this information.

"Are you judging me, Samantha?"

"No," she answered, too quickly. "No, I'm just processing, is all." She met his steady gaze.

"If it helps, the one I assessed my theory on had abused children."

"Oh." She offered him a small smile. "Well, I hope you made him suffer then."

"I did." He took a mouthful of tea, impressed she'd held his gaze without blinking after his direct answer.

Sam broke eye contact to look out the window, quiet for a few moments. "This could change everything," she mused.

"That's the plan," he said, and she remained quiet.

He waited patiently, taking his time looking at her while her eyes remained averted. She was so beautiful. Everything about her enticed him. She always had. He forced himself to look away, thinking that being under the same roof with her after all this time apart might be harder than he'd first thought.

Her hopeful gaze met his. "Imagine, Max, if all Veins discovered they could get as much of a boost from healing and absorbing the sickness in the world, instead of creating it? We could end war, murder, greed, and work together to save Mother Earth. Can you imagine it, a peaceful society?"

Max adored the passion in her voice and it echoed his feelings of hope, but he knew they had a long way to go

"Yeah," he said. "The idea is a cool one, but we have to be realistic. Many Veins desire the easy rush of death and to absorb what they shouldn't. We've a long road ahead before we can make any real impact."

"Sure, but it seems like now you have a way of eradicating those who do not want to embrace the change?"

He blew out a slow breath, thinking about killing Veins. Essentially murdering them if they didn't convert. It didn't sit well with him, but he knew what he had to do.

"Small steps can make a big difference when they're taken together," Sam offered as she drained her coffee.

"Sounds like a UN speech." He laughed. "And true enough, which is why the council agreed that I can use my home as a haven for any Vein who wants to reform and make the change."

"Reform. Do you really think that's possible, Max?"

"We have to try and at least we have a few who want the same outcome as we do." He grabbed her plate and turned to the sink to rinse it before bending to open the dishwasher, sliding her plate inside. Closing it, he turned around to catch Sam look away, a swirl of pink flooding her cheeks. His male ego chuckled.

"Well, I look forward to meeting your new friends." Sam's gaze met his as he reached for her cup. "When are they arriving?" she asked, sliding her neat backside off the seat and headed towards her suitcase.

He followed, forcing his eyes on her back and not the sway of her hips. "This afternoon," he answered, watching as she paused at the wooden door, leading down to the cellar.

She ran her hand along the intricate carvings, glancing at him over her shoulder. Sadness filled her eyes, and he knew the memory that swam beneath their honey-dew surface. The time his cousin had stolen Bowie's identity and almost killed him.

"Bowie," she whispered.

He nodded. "I remember." He said, wanting to chase that look from her eyes. "And because of you and Angel, Bowie is fine and Brendan is dead."

She blinked once before looking back at the door, removing her hand. "Did you renovate down there too?"

"I did. And it's out of bounds."

"For everyone?"

"Yes, Samantha. Everyone, including any Light Accords council member or royal soul."

She turned towards him, raising an eyebrow in question.

He sighed. "I'm sharing my space with a lot of people soon, Sam and maybe more will come. I wanted a space, just for me, that didn't include my bed."

He watched her as she looked up at him and held his breath as she took a step closer, closing the gap between them.

She placed her hand on his arm, tilting her head back, their eyes locked; he felt a ripple of electricity hum in the air, stirring lust in his belly.

"Sam…" he warned, forcing himself not to touch her. "What are you doing?"

Sam sighed, stood on tiptoe and brushed a chaste kiss across his cheek. "I'm thanking you for what you're attempting to do." She stepped back and headed towards her suitcase.

He ran a hand through his hair and followed her, lifting the suit-case before she could.

"I'm going to do everything I can to help you support your people, Max."

He headed towards the stairs. "I appreciate that. I'm glad the council chose you to stay here with me."

"Are you?" she asked.

He chuckled, looking at her over his shoulder. "Of course. Imagine if I had to have Fletch or Bowie move in." He mock-shuddered, causing her to laugh.

"Yeah, I see your point. Although, you do know Bowie loves you, don't you?"

"He didn't seem to love me last night when he threatened to light me up if any harm befell you."

"He didn't!" she exclaimed in horror.

Max laughed without reservation for the first time since she'd stepped foot inside the house. "Yeah, he did and I wouldn't expect anything less from your brother." He pushed a door open that was nearest to the stairs leading up to his room and waited for her to walk in before following her.

"Oh my stars, Max. Is every room in this house straight out of Better Homes and Gardens, country living extraordinaire?" she asked as she circled the room.

He had to admit, seeing her reaction made him happy. She ran her fingers over the four-poster bed, to the chaise lounge at its end before crossing to the window seat and peeking into the bookcase.

"I'm glad you like it," he said as he watched her race over and open a door before gasping in pleasure. "Oh, Angel is going to die! A claw-foot tub with those views." She turned to face him, shaking her head. "You'd better be careful, Maxwell, I may never leave."

He leaned against the door frame watching her, wishing he could tell her he never wanted her to leave either. Instead, he smiled and said, "Oh, I don't know. I think you'd miss Mrs McGoldrick's cooking too much."

She followed his 'keeping things light,' lead and smiled. "Yeah. You're right."

"Okay, I'll let you settle in. We've a few hours before the gang arrive. If you need anything, just yell."

She nodded. "Sure, Max, thanks."

He pushed off from the doorway and reached to close it. "You're welcome." He watched her beautiful face before he closed the door between them and released a long breath, wondering how he was going to keep up this calm charade of not wanting her.

CHAPTER FOUR
SAMANTHA

Sam spent what was left of the morning and most of the afternoon unpacking and settling in. After exploring the house more thoroughly, she changed into running gear, hoping to run off the desire to put her hands on Max in any inappropriate manner. When she returned an hour later, she headed up the driveway, admiring the splendour of the gardens as she walked by a mass of blooms that scented the air with honeysuckle. *Mm, honeysuckle… just like Max.*

Damn, that didn't work! She spied him in the doorway of the old gate lodge that was wrapped in yellow climbing roses and realised that, even if she'd run till her feet fell off, she'd still have the energy and desire to want him. She slowed her steps, tugging her earphones out, noticing a concerned crease between his dark brows. He hadn't noticed her yet, and she took her time taking in his features that tended to steal her breath away.

The light breeze swept its fingers through his silky dark hair, tossing it into forest-green eyes that stared with intensity, deep in thought. His cheekbone structure and lips belonged on a model and his apparent oblivion to his dark, good looks had always been something Sam had loved about him and made him that much more desirable to her.

She took her sweet time, appreciating every masculine inch as her gaze swept up and down before returning to his lips, which always hinted at a smile and kindness. Even when he wore a worried expression, which is what he was wearing right now.

What is he thinking about?

Within that second, his eyes flashed to hers and a moment of sweet tension passed between them.

"How was your run?" he asked, breaking the spell.

"Great. What's up?" She forced light in her question, trying to quell the never-ending desire to kiss him.

He stepped inside the lodge and said, "Take a look."

She followed him inside and it surprised her to see he'd removed every interior wall and replaced the old tin roof with a glass dome. Hundreds of species of plants lined thick glass shelving. The cement floor had been removed and fresh, composted soil lay beneath a layer of damp mulch and moss, with red gum steps pushed into the earth. She sensed the microorganisms in the rich soil bringing pure energy in the space.

"Is this your version of a greenhouse?" she asked, watching as he adjusted a string-of-hearts vine dripping from a hanging basket attached to a hook in a support beam.

"Yeah, kinda." He walked around the large space. "This will be the training area to test the abilities of healing with plants. Angel said she'd supply me with healing herbs grown from the college's sacred ground. I've got the barn prepped for animal testing..."

Her gasp cut him off. "*Maxwell*, you are *not* going to test Veins abilities on animals. You *can't*," she cried in horror, imagining the poor sweet pure-souls being tortured.

He turned towards her, raising a hand. "It's not what you think, Sam. As if I would do anything to harm a pure-soul." He shook his head. "If you'd let me explain." A small smile tugged at the corner of his mouth.

"Sure." She sighed, relieved, feeling a little foolish to imply *her* Max would do anything untoward.

"Come with me." He headed out, through the garden and towards the barn, situated to the side of the property.

She was pleased to walk behind him on the path, watching his broad back as they walked towards the huge barn. She stepped inside and noticed it was set up with clean stalls, packed with feed and cleaning equipment.

"We can house at least twenty large stock animals in here, along with pigs and sheep." He indicated to several pens, then a section screened off. "Chicken coop for night-time and free range during the day." Sam could hear them clucking outside in the sunshine on the other side of the barn, which led off to the gardens.

Max walked further in and gestured towards the stalls as he explained, "Jess has organised a delivery of animals to arrive tomorrow. Abused and heading to the abattoir. At least here, I can give them a good home whilst my... Veins." He cringed. "I really need to stop calling them that."

Sam nodded. "They are your clan, a new family. They need a decent name."

"You're right." He looked thoughtful for a moment before meeting her gaze with a smile of certainty. "Obsidian Souls."

"Black souls?"

"No. Just Obsidian." He grinned. "But clan for all intents and purposes." He didn't elaborate on *Obsidian* but continued. "At least this way my *clan* can practise healing without causing further damage."

Sam nodded. "I guess that makes sense."

"I know the council have sent you here to keep an eye on things…"

"To *help* with things," she interrupted. "Not to spy on you, Max." She placed a hand on her hip.

"Right." He looked down at the ground for a moment, marking a line in the dirt with the toe of his boot.

"Hey." She waited till his gaze met hers. "I'm here to help. Tell me you know that?"

He sighed, sweeping a hand through his hair. "I know that those are your intentions. Sorry if, for reasons of my own, I don't completely trust the council."

"No, it's understandable. They haven't always been fair when it's come to you."

He barked a humourless laugh. "That's an understatement."

Sam fidgeted with her earphones, wanting to walk over and offer him some comfort for everything the council had put him through in the past. They hadn't been fair to him at all, considering he was one-of-a-kind. Well, now it looked like one of, three-of-a-kind.

"Anyway," he said, interrupting her thought flow. "I'm going to ask something of you, Sam and I need you to listen."

"Sounds serious?"

He shrugged. "There's going to be some training that I don't want you to be a part of, for your own safety. When I ask you to stay away, will you?"

She tilted her head, her hair falling over her shoulder from her high ponytail while she regarded him. "If it's really necessary."

"It is."

"Don't you trust me?"

He shook his head. "It's not about trust, Sam. The clan's powers will be unpredictable during training. I can't risk you getting hurt."

"You know I have superpowers, right?" she joked, raising an eyebrow.

He chuckled. "Oh, I remember your skill set, Samantha. But still, there'll be times when I'll need you to stay away."

"Sure, no problem." She agreed to let it go for now. They could work things out as time passed. She didn't want to start their first day off in hot water.

He smiled, looking relieved she'd agreed to his terms so readily.

"Good. Well, they'll be arriving soon. I'm going to organise a meal and drinks by the fire."

"Sounds lovely." She matched his stride as they headed out of the barn and towards the mansion. "I'll freshen up and give you a hand if you like?"

He looked down at her as they crossed the lawn and headed towards the backdoor. "Great, you've got an hour."

"Sweet, I wouldn't mind trying out that bath with a book." She smiled up at him, her breath catching as his gaze seemed to eat her up.

He looked away as they walked up the back steps and across the deck before he opened the back door for her. "Take your time."

She breezed past him, exhaling his citrus and sandalwood scent, thinking a cool shower would serve her better.

MAXWELL

Max waited as her footsteps trailed upstairs and her bedroom door closed before leaning his forehead down on the marble bench top and released a frustrated groan, closing his eyes. This was going to be hell.

The way she'd looked in her tight, running gear with her smooth little belly exposed, a light sheen of perspiration covering her glistening skin and her eyes sparkling like warm embers from the fire. Her lips all dewy, with her attitude which begged for attention. He still remembered all too well, the feeling of her body beneath his. His gut tightened at the mere thought. How was he going to keep his promise to himself and keep his hands off her?

Well, he'd just bloody well have to. It was the one thing he *could* do to keep her safe. He straightened, glancing at the ceiling before walking over to the fridge and reaching for a beer. He downed the cold liquid in six deep swallows before reaching for another to drink in a calmer fashion. He washed up before pulling foods out of the fridge to make a few decent platters.

Thank god the house would soon have extra bodies in it and multiple tasks daily to keep any idle, sexy thoughts at bay.

SAMANTHA

Sam spent longer in the bath than expected and had dozed off for who knew how long. The sound of music and laughter rose up the stairs to greet her. As she dried herself off, she was impressed she hadn't turned into a prune.

"Casual night," she whispered, checking out her clothes she'd hung earlier as she combed her fingers through her hair, fluffing it with her solar-charged hair dryer.

"There you are," she grinned, pulling out a black, cotton dress that would cling to every inch. "Sorry Max," she chuckled, imaging his eyes falling out of his head when she went downstairs. Happy at last with her hair as it hung down her back and around her face in soft shiny waves, she popped on mascara and eyeliner and added a layer of pink lip gloss. She tugged the dress over her head, grabbed her black Niki high tops and rammed her feet into them. After checking her reflection in the mirror, she nodded. "Yep, perfect." The dress sat above her knees, short sleeved, with a heart shape cut out just above her breasts, leaving her pretty cleavage to greet the world. A dash of perfume and she was done and excited to meet and greet Max's clan.

"Here we go." She winked at her reflection before taking a steadying breath and headed towards the gathering downstairs.

The carriage and pendulum lights gave the spacious rooms a welcoming hue as Sam stepped off the bottom stair to head towards the sound of conversation. A group of five were standing about the roaring fire, holding drinks and laughing.

Just like normal people. Not evil, soul-sucking leeches. She wasn't sure what she expected. Not perfectly dressed individuals, who looked like they'd just stepped out of an Italian magazine for rich college kids. Their accents were smooth and tinged with European flavour.

"Hello there." A tall, confident looking man, with an electric blue streak in his blond hair, walked towards her. Hand held out as he looked her up and down, wearing a pleasant smile as he said, "You must be Samantha. Max has told us *so* much about you. Please, won't you join us?"

Taking his hand, she noticed it was cool and soft beneath hers. *Clearly not a farm boy.* He was dressed in a dark grey, casual suit with his shirt unbuttoned and by the way he carried himself, thought he was important.

"Thank you." She flashed her pearly whites at him as he led her towards the others. *Where is Max?*

An excited squeal had her eyes widening as a pretty, dark-haired girl ran across the room to envelope her in a warm hug.

"Samantha!" She squealed as if she were embracing an old friend. "I'm Gemma, It's so great to meet you!"

"Hi Gemma," Sam grinned, confused at her enthusiasm. "Nice to meet you too. Please, call me Sam, all of you." She looked at the others who had milled about, waiting for their turn to say hello.

"I'm Trent, by the way." The tall blond with dark brown eyes smiled charmingly over Gemma's head.

"Trent, hi."

"Oh, sorry," Gemma giggled, stepping back. "Don't mean to hog *la stella.*"

The star? Sam was confused but didn't have a chance to ask as three men stepped forward, each offering a hand in greeting.

"Daniel," A sweet, timid looking, sandy haired man, shook her hand before offering her a flute of champagne.

"Thanks, Daniel." She took the glass and smiled warmly, hoping to make him feel at ease. What had Max told these people about her?

"I'm Rick." A tall, sublimely beautiful man slid his arm around her back and led her to the fireplace.

Sam took a much-needed, deep swallow of the sweet bubbles as she nodded a hello before being surrounded by the welcoming party.

"How was your trip here?" She thought that was a safe question.

"It was wonderful. I have always wanted to see Australia." Gemma smiled, closing her eyes briefly as if savouring the fact she was here.

"Yes, it really is a *gorgeous* country." Rick agreed, his eyes raking over Sam as he said gorgeous in a meaningful way.

Sam smiled feeling uncharacteristically flustered. "It sure is. I'm glad you like it and hope you'll be happy here. Can anyone tell me where Max is? I just need him for a moment."

"Outside with Nadine." Daniel pointed to the back door.

"Thanks." She smiled, placing her empty flute down near a platter of food, which made her stomach rumble and headed out towards the backdoor. The conversation behind her resumed.

She sighed, pushing the door open. Her heart thudded at the sight before her.

Max had his head bent and his face pushed into the neck of an auburn-haired goddess, whose silky strands brushed her waistline where Max's hands rested.

Sam swallowed her jealousy down, appreciating the shape of the woman in Max's arms. She had a nice bum, Sam decided, noting how the white dress clung to just beneath her curvy bottom. Six-inch heels brought her level to Max's height, which was no easy feat as he was well over six feet tall.

Max raised his head to smile down at the woman before he caught Sam staring. He flushed before saying, "Sam, I'd like you to meet someone." He released the woman's waist.

I'm sure you would, slick. She forced a charming smile as she crossed towards them. At least now she had the *real* reason why he wanted nothing more than to be 'just friends' with her. Sam's breath caught once again as the woman turned around and she faced the woman she had seen in her vision earlier that morning. She was every bit as beautiful as she had been in the vision.

"Hi." Sam forced cheer into her voice.

"Hello, I'm Nadine." The beauty queen smiled, reaching to embrace Sam. "It's wonderful to meet you."

Caught by surprise as she was held close, Sam met Max's eyes over Nadine's shoulder.

"Nice to meet you," Sam managed as Nadine released her.

"Well, aren't you just the prettiest little thing?" Nadine smiled down at her.

Sam tried to detect if Nadine was being polite, or condescending, but she exuded warmth and honesty. Maybe Sam just got the odd vibe because the woman's crotch had recently been pressed against Max's.

"Thanks," she said.

"Shall we go inside and join the others?" Max asked.

"Sure, honey." Nadine smiled over her shoulder at him before walking by Sam, running her hand over Sam's waves before disappearing inside.

Max pushed his hands deep into his jeans pockets as he looked at Sam. His black turtleneck sweater clung to every inch of his torso and biceps, defining muscles she knew were the real deal.

"You okay?" he asked.

"Just peachy, *honey*." She flashed him her own killer smile as she spun around and headed inside after Nadine. She hoped the view of her backside tortured him as much as witnessing their embrace had tortured her.

"Fun times," she heard him whisper and felt a small flash of satisfaction before she was once again surrounded by her unwarranted fan club.

CHAPTER FIVE
SAMANTHA

"So, tell me everything. What are they like?" Angel asked the following morning after picking Sam up from the front gates.

"Well, let me see. They are charming, good-looking, polite and for some weird reason, refer to me as the, and I quote from fifty times last night… '*La stella*,'" Sam made air quotes with her fingers as she rolled her eyes.

"Well, that's true enough, you are a star." Angel smiled in Sam's direction before concentrating on the road as she steered the car towards Terang.

"Yeah, I'll take that." Sam grinned before sighing and dropping her head back theatrically against the headrest.

"What?" Angel said.

"Nadine."

"Who?"

"Nadine, Max's… *girlfriend.*"

"Oh…" Angel trialled off, waiting for Sam to continue. "What's she like?" she asked when Sam remained mute.

"She's like a blood splatter."

"Excuse me?"

"You know when bloods drips on a pristine white cloth and then before you know it, those little edges of red weave their tiny fingers into the fabric, integrating themselves deep into the cloth and no matter how hard you rinse it, it won't budge. In fact, the longer you stare at that perfect, crimson stain, it looks like it belongs there. In its own beautiful, invasive way."

"Okaaaay…" Angel looked at Sam from the corner of her eye.

Sam turned her head towards Angel, eyes flashing, "He *bloody* well told me he didn't have time for a relationship! Why couldn't he have just been honest with me and say he didn't want a relationship with me because he already had a *bloody* girlfriend?"

"Oh Sam." Angel reached across and rubbed Sam's arm which was folded tight across her chest in frustration.

"I'm just venting because I can. Honestly, I'm fine." Sam patted the top of Angel's hand as they swerved to a stop in front of the Terang Bakery.

"Well, I'm glad we have the chance to catch up, even if it is just to pick up the canteen's order for tomorrow."

"Yeah, it looks like I'm Max's 'Mrs McGoldrick' now." Sam smiled getting out of the car to follow Angel inside the bakery.

Angel grinned at her over her shoulder. "That's not such a bad thing if it gives us twenty minutes together."

"Yeah, you're right." Sam smiled before drooling at the sight of the vanilla slices.

"Hey ladies." Angela Glee beamed from behind the counter. "Here to pick up the order, Angel?"

"Yes thanks, Angela." Angel wondered over the display case. "I'll grab half a dozen of Mrs Quick's Apple slices, too."

"Good call," Sam said as Angela put a large bag of bread rolls on the counter before sliding the sweet slices into a box. "I'll grab the same and a half dozen of the vanilla slices as well, thanks." Sam's stomach rumbled loudly.

Angela laughed as she grabbed a box for Sam's treats. "Skip breakfast, did we?"

"Yeah, something like that." Sam met Angel's gaze as she fished out a fifty dollar note from her back pocket. "I'll grab half a dozen chicken and leek and two pizza pies on top of that."

"No problem. I hear Maxwell Black is back and staying at his father's estate, setting up some sort of farm stay?" Angela boxed up Sam's goodies and slid them on top of the glass counter, taking the fifty from Sam's outstretched hand.

"Yeah, his first lot of visitors arrived yesterday."

"Nice enough people?"

"They seem so."

"That's good. Please say you'll bring them into town for a meal and a game of pool one night?"

"Sure, if Max doesn't have them working around the clock."

"Ah, farmers, hey. Never a dull moment." Angela passed Sam her change.

If only she knew. Sam brushed against Angel's mind.

Angel grabbed her bag of rolls as Sam grabbed both the boxes. "See you during the week, Angela."

"Will do." Angela waved before turning to her next customer.

The trip back to Max's went too fast. Angel parked the car at the bottom of the driveway. Sam sat in the car looking through the gates, not wanting to leave the comfort of her sister's calm energy just yet.

"I wish I could come in and say hello to Max without setting off the pool of sharks." Angel sighed.

Her comment had the right effect and Sam laughed. "Well, they'd get some sort of training if they tried that."

"What, like lightning-bolt evasion technique?" Angel chuckled.

"Yeah," Sam's eyes glinted dangerously, happy as she imagined frying the beautiful Nadine until her gorgeous mane of hair turned to frizz. She laughed at her evil image. "Something like that."

A surprised squeal burst from Angel's lips as she looked past Sam. She undid her seatbelt and flew out of the car.

Turning, Sam saw Max strolling towards them, a bright smile on his face as he watched Angel run towards him. Hands that had been tucked into his jeans pockets came out to grab Angel around the waist as she launched herself at him. His laughter washed over Sam as she got out of the car and stacked the two boxes on top of the other before walking towards them.

"Oh Max, I've really missed you." Angel kissed his cheek as he lowered her to her feet.

Lucky girl.

"I've missed you too."

Angel turned to smile at Sam, hearing her thought. "Now Max," Angel turned back towards him. "Are you taking care of our Sam?"

Max looked over Angel's head and nodded, meeting Sam's eyes. "Of course."

Sam tried not to squirm under the intensity of his gaze and was glad when Angel hugged him once more, taking his focus away from her.

"I'm glad I had the chance to see you," he told her.

"Me too. I know it's not safe for me to come around at the moment, but as soon as you need me for training, I'll be ready."

"Need you?" Sam frowned, not liking the sound of that. "We are *not* using you for any training, are we, Max?"

"That's up to the council and Angel." Max reached to take the bakery boxes from Sam's arms.

Sam raised an eyebrow, placing her hands on her hips. "I don't think so."

Angel reached out and grabbed Sam's arm, tugging her towards her.

"Sam, you know I'm pretty much unbreakable, don't you? No matter what Max throws at me, I'll be fine. And I'll have you with me, so there's nothing to worry about."

Sam let out a deep breath, knowing Angel was right. She was, as far as they all knew, close to invincible, but that didn't mean she couldn't feel pain. She frowned as she looked at Max, who had his head tilted, raven hair falling into his ever-watchful eyes, waiting for her response.

"Okay, as long as I am present for *any* training involving you."

"Well, it wouldn't be any fun without you there," Angel grinned, hugging her before turning to Max. "Take care of her, brother of mine."

Max grinned as he nodded. "You know I will."

A loud honk, had them all turning to see a cattle truck heading toward them, indicating it was about to turn up the driveway.

"Better go, I'll see you both soon." Angel ran around to get in her car that was blocking the truck's entrance and tooted as she started the engine before heading towards the college.

Max took hold of Sam's upper arm to pull her off the driveway, so the truck could pass them as it ambled by. The warmth of his body when she brushed against his side had hers tingling all over. She risked a glance up at his face, her lips parting as she caught his sweet scent of honeysuckle, orange and sandalwood. His gaze locked on hers, wearing a slight frown, similar to the disapproving look he'd sent her way in the canteen the other day.

She raised an eyebrow as she tugged her arm out of his grip. "What?"

He opened his mouth to reply as a smooth, velvety voice called his name, cutting him off.

"Max, honey, the driver needs to speak to you," Nadine called from the top of the driveway, waving her arm at them. She wore white jeans, impractical high-heeled wedges and a green jumper that clung to every inch of her curvaceous figure. Sam thought she looked like the perfect country wife any man would be happy to roll into bed with at night.

She kept that thought guarded and grabbed the bakery boxes off Max. "You better take care of that." She started walking towards the mansion.

"Can you meet me in the barn once you've put those inside?" he asked following her.

"Yeah, all right," she said over her shoulder, increasing the distance between them, trying to block out the fact that his scent, his voice, every bloody little thing about him was making her feel as if she would spontaneously combust. Yet he remained unaffected by their past, as if their sexual chemistry had never existed? Hadn't she promised herself she could play the same game? She would be the *friend* that Max needed, not some pining, miserable ex who'd make him regret being tied up with her in the first place.

"Hi." Sam grinned as she walked by the auburn-haired stunner.

"Hello." Nadine beamed back with enthusiasm.

"I've got you all something tasty for lunch. Max's favourite pies." She glanced over her shoulder towards Max, who'd reached Nadine's side.

"Chicken and Leek, or Pizza?" Max asked.

"Both."

"Sounds lovely." Nadine tucked her arm through Max's as they headed off towards the barn where the driver was waiting.

"See you in a minute," she said with too much cheer, disappearing around the curved pathway lined with lavender bushes and roses. She released a deep sigh once she was alone and rolled her eyes. "You can do this," she pep-talked as she stepped up onto the back decking to find Daniel and Gemma pulling on gumboots.

"Smart choice." Sam smiled as she pushed the back door open, thinking of Nadine's wedges.

Gemma grinned as she turned to Sam. "We've got animals arriving any minute and we're going to help get them settled."

"The first lot have just arrived. I'll put lunch inside and join you after I get changed."

Gemma grabbed Daniel's arm, who was standing watching Sam with the same timid star-struck expression he'd used on her the night before.

"Come on, Daniel, I can't wait to see the furry critters."

Sam watched Gemma drag Daniel down the steps and around the corner of the house before turning inside to pop the pies on to warm in the oven and slid the box of slices into the fridge. She stood with the door open, helping herself to a strawberry, deciding what else to nibble on, when a cold draft slid under her hair to brush the back of her neck. A sharp pain, then nothing as if she'd pulled a muscle. She frowned before reaching back to rub at her cold flesh, shaking her head at her own unease. She closed the fridge and yelped in fright as a tall figure startled her, looming in her personal space. She laughed, spying a twinkle of mischief in Trent's eyes.

"Oh, I'm sorry." He smiled charmingly, not sounding sorry at all.

She shook her head as she walked the long way around him and out of the kitchen. "Don't be." She waved her hand, heading towards the stairs. "I don't usually startle so easily."

She ran upstairs before he could reply and closing the door,

51

grabbed a pair of work jeans, her Blundstone boots and a black and white flannel to pull over a white skivvy. She'd show these gorgeous Italian models what it took to be Max's right-hand man; the strange sting to her flesh forgotten.

MAXWELL

Max shook the driver's hand and watched him climb back into the cab before steering the truck back down the curving driveway. He smiled when Gemma's laugh flowed from within the barn. She'd come so far from when he'd first found her several months ago. She'd been starving and had been tortured by Brendan's brethren because she'd refused to partake in the slaughter of pure-souls. He knew she still had a long way to go, as did the others, but he could see how far each of them had come since working with him. He thought of one in particular, and frowned.

Don't go there. He rolled his sleeves up as he headed into the barn, pushing hair out of his eyes as he prepared for the hours of work that it would take to settle the animals in. Jess Callum's driver said they were getting another delivery soon and the horses could arrive at any moment.

Stalls had to be prepared with fresh hay, assorted feed and water. He'd give the clan, as he was now referring to them in his head, a couple of days to settle in and acclimatise to their new surroundings before serious work and training began.

"Oh they are so cute." Nadine crooned, keeping a safe distance away from the lambs' wiggling tails as they chased their mother about the pen, trying to get to her for her milk. Gemma climbed into the pen as Daniel stroked the neck of a jersey cow. Its large eyes widened in terror as she felt the energy of the young Vein's internal desire to inflict pain.

"Daniel, mate. Best move away from her until we can get your inner longing under control," Max called as he grabbed a blade hanging near some farm tools on the wall.

"I didn't mean to upset her." Daniel said, walking away, looking upset with himself.

"I know." Max sliced the knife along the twine of three hay bales before shoving it in his back pocket. He reached for the hay fork and scooped up the hay and filled the two wheelbarrows.

He sensed Samantha before she stepped through the doorway. Then her delectable scent of musk wrapped around him.

"I'll do that," she offered, holding her hand towards the hay fork. "The other truck's coming."

"Thanks." He looked down at her, appreciating her appropriate dress which meant she was ready to get her hands dirty. The thought of having her by his side for the next few hours thrilled him and he couldn't help the smile that broke across his otherwise focused expression.

"Where's Trent and Rick?"

"Inside."

"Nadine, can you round them up for me?" he asked, passing Sam the fork and reaching for another by the wall.

"Of course." Nadine beamed at Max before heading towards the mansion.

"Daniel, give Sam a hand, would you? I have to direct the truck to the south paddock for this delivery." He handed Daniel the fork.

"Right you are." Daniel saluted as Max caught Sam's eye before she ducked her head and forked another pile of hay.

"Be back soon," he called, jogging out to flag the truck, to catch a lift towards the paddock.

The following hours consisted of filling stalls with fresh bedding and animals allocated to their appropriate stalls and paddocks. They stopped for a break three hours in. Nadine served their warm pies and cold drinks before they continued.

It was late afternoon when they had finished for the day. Sam and Gemma seemed to be the only ones not upset about the fact they were sweaty and wearing equal parts dust and livestock manure.

Trent headed out of the barn. "After we clean up, who's up for drinks and a game of pool?"

"Count me in." Nadine said.

"What are you looking so pleased about?" Rick grumbled to Gemma who was sighing contently as Max was checking that all the stalls were locked up tight. Sam was making sure all the animals had what they needed before they headed out.

"Everything," Gemma said in a singsong voice. "And you should be too."

Rick grinned wickedly before hooking his arm around her neck. "You're right and to celebrate, how about a swim in the pond to clean off all this hard work?" he said, dragging her out of the barn and towards the back yard.

"What! *No*, it's too cold!" she cried, laughing as he continued marching them towards the pond.

"Daniel," she screamed between bursts of laughter. "*Help*."

Daniel chuckled as he ran after them.

"This I have to see." Nadine followed Daniel.

Max grinned at their playful banter, happy to see them enjoying themselves and settling in so well within the first twenty-four hours of arriving.

"What the hell?" Sam's cry of dismay had him turning towards her as she pushed open a stall door to rush inside.

He followed close behind and was alarmed to see a cow on its side, its legs stiff with pain, who only minutes ago had seemed fine. He knelt

54

beside Sam and ran a hand along its neck, trying to soothe the animal.

"What's wrong with her?" she asked, as he placed a hand over his heart and began whispering a healing incantation.

Max closed his eyes and pushed his heavenly energy deep within the cow's body, sourcing the location of her pain. When he found it after several minutes, his anger grew as he sensed the parasite lingering within her warm body, feeding off her. He pushed towards it, hoping to wrap his healing light around it and destroy it within, but it didn't budge. He knew what he had to do.

"Sam, don't be alarmed," he warned and before she could ask, twisted his wrist, causing the flesh along his forearm to split open. He felt her stiffen beside him, but ignored her discomfort and focused on releasing a long, obsidian vein from his flesh. It slid like liquid silk, falling onto the soft caramel hide of the cow before burrowing its head inside the tormented animal.

He closed his eyes once more, allowing his vein to follow the path of his heavenly energy, hoping to find the source of her pain and praying it wasn't what he feared. He located the parasite and frowned, disappointed as he sensed the Leecher, fat and filling with the cow's blood, straight from its heart.

He pushed his disappointment and fury aside. His vein struck at the Leecher, biting into its side and allowed the essence it had consumed to return to the creature. Once the Leecher was destroyed, Max extracted his vein, pulling the parasite out with it. When he heard Sam gasp, he opened his eyes, pulling his vein back into his forearm. Sam picked up the foul, twelve-inch Leecher Max had dropped.

Not having a moment to waste, he closed his eyes once more, concentrating his heavenly energy to restore the cow. After a few minutes, she mooed, pushing her face into Max's stomach before ambling to her feet and wandering to her feed.

"What is it?" Sam asked.

"A Leecher. A feeding parasite that's placed inside a host to consume blood directly from the heart."

"Why would a Vein insert a part of themselves to feed off a pure-soul? Why not just feed from them as we've seen?"

"Because when they leave this part of themselves, a Leecher, inside a pure-soul, overtime, the blood ferments and becomes an exceedingly pure dose of raw energy."

Sam frowned. "If its left inside a pure-soul, how does a Vein feed off it?"

"He'd do what I just did, plunge in a vein and feed off the Leecher."

"Not remove it?" She sounded horrified.

"No, he'd feed from it, then leave it behind until the next hit was required."

"Hit?"

"Yes, extracting blood this way, is similar to that of a pure-soul having a hit of drugs."

Sam shook her head. "You learn something new every day," she muttered.

He blew out a long breath as he stood, reaching for Sam's hand and pulled her to her feet.

She placed her hand on his arm. "You feeling okay?"

He nodded, tiredly.

"Do you need me to restore your energy?"

"I'm fine."

"No, you're not."

He sighed, "I just need to find out who did this."

"Yes, you do." Sam dropped the dead parasite onto his open palm, her eyes flashing in anger. "Then I can kick their arse, but first, you need your energy restored."

He couldn't help the grin that broke across his face. She sounded like Bowie. One thing about the Storm siblings; they had the purest of hearts and were loyal to a fault.

She raised an eyebrow.

He shook his head, looking at the vein in his hand. "Part of me doesn't want to find out who this belongs to."

She titled her head. "You're disappointed?"

He shrugged. "I shouldn't be. They're new to all of this."

Sam nodded as splashes, screams and laughter reached them. She forced a smile. "Well, I'm here to help and someone is having too much fun for my liking after performing that vile act."

He closed his hand around the vein as he followed her out of the barn. After a final check, he pulled the hefty doors shut, securing them. He turned to see Sam marching around the back yard and jogged to catch up to her, grasping her arm before she could start accusing or abusing anyone.

She frowned up at him.

"Look," he said, "I know this act seems really repulsive, but..." He trailed off as she glared at him.

"Seems?" The word wounded like a hiss while she attempted to tug her arm out of his grip.

He held her tighter, bringing her flush up against him, bending his dark head closer to her face.

"Sam." He dropped his voice low, watching her eyes flare with anger. Hints of golden honey swirled and as she blinked, he could have sworn he saw a flame flicker in her glorious eyes. Never a good sign. He shook his head. "You're not thinking of zapping me are you, Samantha?"

He raised an eyebrow when she didn't answer and continued. "Like I was saying. Yes, it is inexcusable what one of them has done, but that is why they are here. So I can help them resist their inner, darkest urges. I've a way of managing this sort of thing and I need you to trust me. Can you do that?"

Sam screwed up her nose. "I'm not going to let this slide."

He sighed. "I don't want you to, but I do need you to let me take the lead, okay?" His thumb stroked the soft flannel shirt that clung to her upper arm.

She sighed. "How do you want to do this?"

"You go wash up."

She nodded. "Don't start any arse kicking without me. Then, herbs, restoring etcetera."

He nodded as he watched her turn and run up the stairs of the deck and disappear through the back door. He looked at the limp parasite in his hand and frowned. To pull a Leecher out of an animal shouldn't have depleted his energy this much. It didn't feel like it belonged to any ordinary Vein. He sighed and looked out across at the pond. Despite the chill in the afternoon air, Gemma, Daniel, and Rick were running and jumping off the small pier, laughing as they bombed one another. Nadine was sitting on the swing and waved when he caught her eye.

He held up a hand. "Everyone inside, showered and downstairs within the hour," he said.

"*Bene*," she replied.

He turned, heading inside. After running up the stairs, he paused outside Sam's room for a moment, hearing the shower running. He turned up the small twist of stairs towards his room, trying not to think of her naked body, glistening under the spray of warm water and how good he knew she looked wet.

CHAPTER SIX
SAMANTHA

S am was itching to get downstairs, desperate not to miss any action and was intrigued to see how Max would handle this situation. Once that jet of hot water hit her sore muscles however, she turned into a greedy lush wanting more. She remained under the rejuvenating spray for as long as possible. She was proud of Max and loved seeing him in the role of protector and teacher. Sam saw the way they all looked up to him, respected him as if he were a High Lord himself. No doubt they were grateful to him for the chance he'd given them. Which was why it infuriated her that one of them would betray his kindness this way.

After drying her hair and lathering herself top to toe in Angel's homemade herbal moisturiser, scented with honeysuckle and musk, she pulled on jeans, shoved her feet into white sneakers and grabbed a white tee shirt with giant sequined red lips biting into a cherry.

A final check in the mirror confirmed she looked as fresh and fabulous as she felt. She jerked open her door and ran straight into a solid chest. Sam swallowed a moan as his scent wrapped around her and looking into his dark green eyes, was satisfied to see a flash of desire mirrored in his gaze as he steadied her. He looked mouth-watering; hair still damp from his shower.

By the Angels, he looks good enough to eat. She shielded her thought from him.

"I was just coming to get you." He let her go and shifted back.

She rubbed her hands together, grinning evilly. "Let's get this show on the road, shall we?" She went to head downstairs.

"Hang on, Sam."

She turned, waiting.

"I need you to come with me for a moment." He pointed up to the small stairs behind him.

"Okay." She was intrigued and followed him up the stairs, admiring the way his jeans fit snuggly to his firm thighs, trying not to ogle his backside.

They reached a small landing. He pushed open the heavy carved door and stepped aside, allowing her to enter before him.

"Very nice." She looked about, marvelling at the sheer size of the bed sitting right in the middle of the spacious room, the décor and the vines dripping from the ceiling rose, twined around the impressive black chandelier. "You know," she looked at him mischievously. "If you wanted to be the perfect host, you'd swap rooms with me, even for a night."

He stood looking at her as she looked about his room, a small smile upon his lips. "I've got something to show you. Come." He held out his hand and when she placed hers into his large, warm palm, her heartbeat raced.

Calm down fool. She internally rolled her eyes at herself as Max led her across to the long wall, lined with the most eye-catching photographs of animals, plants and places, including her homestead at the college and its healing garden.

"Who took these?" she asked.

"I did."

"They're great."

"Thanks. Don't let go of my hand, okay?" Max reached towards the photograph of the homesteads healing garden, his fingers brushing against the glass.

"Okay, what are we?"

Sam didn't have time to scream as she felt every molecule in her body evaporate and get sucked into the photograph in a vortex of energy that twisted and pulled at her insides. It was as unpleasant as it was thrilling and didn't last long enough for her to decide if one feeling could win over the other. Her breath whooshed out as seconds later, she collapsed against Max, right on top of the chamomile bed in the healing garden.

Max's hands were around her waist, his breathing ragged. She stared down at him, wide-eyed. "A bit of warning next time would be nice," she said breathlessly.

"Yeah, sorry." He smiled, not looking sorry whatsoever.

"Which Soul Keeper elder created that portal in your room?"

Max shrugged, averting his eyes. She sighed, pushing off his chest, but his grip was firm, his body beneath hers, warm and solid. Secretly, she could have happily stayed there all night. Surely one little kiss wouldn't hurt? She leaned down towards him. Would he stop her? She delighted in seeing his eyes darken, his lips part. His hand snaked around her waist, slid up her back to then cradle her head. Gazes glued to each other, as their lips drew closer, Sam's insides melted as knowing anticipation stole her breath. Before she could draw her next one, Max had spun her about and reversed their positions.

She was stunned for a moment at the speed in which he'd flipped her on her back. She stared at him, wide-eyed and was shocked when he brushed his lips across her cheek and whispered against her ear, "You've got a job to do, so I can get on with mine."

He sat up, looking down at her, waiting.

She forced herself not to pout as she glared at him. "Fine," she snapped. "Lie down." She took a steadying breath and watched as he lay amongst the cheerful flowers. She pushed both her irritation and longing for him away and knew she had to get herself in a positive, loving frame of mind to restore his energy. His eyes remained on her face as she placed a hand against the earth, drawing its sweet energy into her before placing her other hand on Max's warm, solid chest.

After a few minutes of calm, she felt her elemental energy flow through her, to soak into Max's heavenly heart. She felt it, the moment he was fully restored as harmonious energy pulsed between them, a sweet hum in the air flowed around them.

He smiled as he sat up, taking her hand to squeeze it. "Thank you."

She pulled her hand free as she stood. "You're welcome."

When he stood, he surprised her when he gathered her in his arms and held her close. She forced the delightful shiver down as he pushed his face into her neck.

"Your mixed signals aren't helping me, Maxwell," she said stonily, not returning his embrace.

He loosened his hold to look upon her face. "I'm sorry. It's just being back here when we… were…"

"Yeah… when we *were*. But we *aren't* any longer, are we?"

He sighed. "I wish things could be different, Sam."

She scoffed. "Wished they could be? You're with Nadine. Why would you be with her if you wished things could be different between us?"

"Nadine?" Max frowned, looking confused. "What gave you any idea that I'm with Nadine?"

"Um, because, *honey*, she's all over you like a rash?"

Max laughed dryly. "Samantha, Nadine and I are *just* friends. And she's not all over me in any way," he said.

She raised an eyebrow as a sensual flutter spread in the pit of her belly, his arms still holding her. "So, Nadine and you are *just* friends and you and I are *just* friends?"

He was silent for a moment and she thought he wasn't going to reply until he said, "What we once shared Sam, made me the happiest soul in the world, but we can't go back."

"Just like that?"

He didn't respond. She sighed, shaking her head in frustration as she stepped out of his arms.

"It's for the best."

"You have to give me more than that, Maxwell Black!" She folded her arms, trying not to feel angry or dejected.

"It's Maxwell Obsidian now and anything I give you won't be good enough Sam!" he cried in frustration.

"Bloody well try me, *Maxwell Obsidian*! And don't give me any crap about you holding me at arm's length for my 'own safety,' 'coz that will just piss me right off."

"Sam, we don't have time for this now!" He shoved his fingers through his hair, shifting it out of his eyes that gleamed down at her.

She glared back, knowing her eyes must be fireballs of fury.

They were. Max stepped back, holding a hand up, saying, "Sam, I promise. After we deal with the situation back at the mansion, you and I will talk."

She frowned as a sharp pain niggled behind her eyes. She didn't normally get headaches. But then again, she didn't normally want to hurt the man she loved with every inch of her fibre, either. Arguing with Max, seeing him frustrated and upset, was draining her. She had to stop this.

"Okay, look." She sighed in resignation. "I'm sorry, it's just…" She shrugged, dropping her gaze to his feet.

Max hooked a finger beneath her chin and raised her face to his. "You never have to apologise to me."

She stared into his eyes; could lose herself in his gaze forever but blinked herself from under his spell before whispering, "I'm starving."

He chuckled, reaching for her hand. "Well, we'll have to do something about that, won't we?"

"Please do," she replied. He waved his hand as she'd seen the Soul Keeper elders do to create a portal before once again, feeling her spleen and other body parts, split into a million pieces before being sucked into the vortex and fly through the photograph, landing back in Max's room.

She wanted to laugh, but her head throbbed.

"You okay?" Max frowned.

"Sure." She rubbed the back of her neck where she thought she'd felt a disturbing ripple under her flesh. *What was that?* Probably the aftereffects of the portal and spaghettification.

"Come on." He took her hand and led her downstairs. "Food first," he said, directing her to sit by the roaring fire where Rick placed another log onto it.

"There you both are," Gemma said in her singsong voice as she passed them a champagne.

"Thanks Gemma." Max said.

"You really should have joined us for a swim."

"Next time," he said a Gemma headed towards the kitchen. Taking a mouthful, he noticed Sam wasn't touching hers, and took the glass off her. "Coffee?"

She shook her head. "Just water, please."

She stared into the flames as Max went to get her a glass of water.

"Food's ready." Nadine called.

"Yes," Daniel said with a cheer.

"Agreed." Rick got up off the couch. "Farm work builds up the appetite, that's for sure."

"Farm work?" Max chuckled returning with Sam's water. "You ain't seen nothing yet, boy," he joked while passing the glass to Sam.

As the others headed towards the dining room, he frowned and knelt in front of her. "You don't look so good."

She raised an eyebrow. "Charming."

He shook his head, smiling a little. "No, you always look good, Sam. I'm saying, you look like you're in pain."

"Yeah, a little. I think I'll take my food up to my room if that's okay?"

"Of course it is."

"Damn, I'm going to miss out on your interrogation." She winced, standing.

"You'd only be disappointed in me not drawing blood." He grinned.

She wanted to smile at him but couldn't.

"Go upstairs, I'll bring your plate up."

She nodded, disappointed they wouldn't be able to have their 'talk.'

"Eat, then sleep. We've got plenty of time to talk." He ran his hand down her hair. He'd read her thought she'd been unable to block because of the pain.

"Okay," she whispered and headed out of the room and towards the stairs. The clan's vibrant dinner conversation followed her up before she stumbled into her room, collapsing onto the bed. She pulled the donna over her body as she shivered in pain, curling into the foetal position as the throbbing in her temples pushed her hunger pangs at bay.

MAXWELL

Max waited until everyone had had their fill and the kitchen was clean before drinks were carried out to the fire. He'd taken a plate up to Sam earlier, but when she didn't answer, he left a note to say her plate was in the fridge if she woke.

"So, are we doing some training tonight?" Rick asked, sitting on the raised hearth nursing a cold beer.

"We are," Max said, waiting till everyone took a seat to begin.

"Fantastic." Daniel grinned at Gemma before saying to Max, "Can I try to heal something? Are we leaving the property?"

Max shook his head. "Not leaving the property, but yes, you will get the chance to heal."

Daniel grinned as Nadine sat beside Max. "Earth or flesh?" she asked before taking a dainty sip from her glass.

He looked at her and felt the usual stir within him when she was close. Not the same longing he felt for Sam, but something else he couldn't put his finger on. There was no denying the chemical attraction between them. Warranted or not, it was there.

"Flesh."

"Yes!" Daniel rubbed his hands together.

"Why so pleased?" Nadine raised an eyebrow.

"I guess for me, it's more satisfying being able to feel and see the pain leave a living soul." Daniel shrugged. "And knowing I did that can relieve some of the guilt for all the wrong I've done. The pain I've caused…" He trailed off.

Max nodded. "That, I completely understand. And it's why you are all here."

Rick nodded as Trent held up his red wine, saluting them all.

"Before we get started, there's something we need to clear up." Max reached into his back pocket and pulled out a zip-lock bag. Opening it, he leaned forward and tossed the parasite onto the table.

Gemma gasped in horror, ".Is that a..."

"Leecher," Rick finished for her.

"Yes." Max met each of their eyes before continuing. "I removed it from a cow this afternoon."

"This isn't good." Nadine shook her head, standing. "Come on guys, we are here to make a difference. Not be puppet-junkies to the damn dominating forces of evil!"

"Nadine, it's okay." Max stood and rubbed her arm.

"No! It's *not* okay," Her furious glare met his. "Why aren't you angrier?"

Max nodded, turning to the others. "I'm more disappointed than angry." He noticed Trent flinch before averting his eyes.

He continued. "I'm trying to appreciate the degree of difficulty it must be taking each of you, to fight against your natural instincts. But you've entrusted me to help you become more than the *parasites* the royal-souls have labelled us. We *can* make a difference. One Vein deciding to make the change at a time. But let's face it, planting a Leecher in a host victim isn't showing restraint. It isn't showing you truly want to change. It's an act of defiance and that you're willing to commit that crime again."

"Okay, fess up." Rick stood, looking around the small group. "Trent, It's got to be you, man."

Trent scoffed angrily. "Piss off, *stronzo*!"

"Righto." Max turned to the arguing pair. "I don't want us pointing fingers at one another. I want the person responsible to own it. There's no judgement here, despite the gravity of the act, but moving forward, I need to know I can trust every one of you before more join us."

No one moved. No one spoke.

Max sighed, disappointed once more before reaching for the

Leecher and before anyone could stop him, flung it toward the fire. As the amber tongues licked at the parasite, Trent screamed, clutching at his forearm.

"Thought so." Rick snickered.

Trent raised his face to glare at him. Tears of pain filled his eyes, but he blinked them away before turning to Max.

"I can explain."

"Please do." Max folded his arms.

"You don't deserve the chance to explain yourself," Gemma cried. "That poor, sweet defenceless creature…" She folded shaking arms.

"You missed your chance thirty seconds ago, *vigliacco*!" Nadine hissed.

Trent stood, facing the furious red head, an angry-red line ran along the flesh of his lower arm where his vein had once been. "Coward? Really?"

"*Si, really*, you *disgust* me!"

"Nadine," Max began, but she cut him off, screaming.

"*No*, Max, we should *banish* him for what he's done!"

"Maybe a little extreme," Daniel muttered.

"Debatable," Rick whispered under his breath.

"Everyone, please." Max held up his hands. "Can we hear what Trent has to say?"

Nadine folded her arms, tossing her mane of hair. Max sighed internally and pushed his heavenly energy towards the room, hoping to influence them with calm. In a matter of seconds, everyone seemed more relaxed and willing to sit down and listen to Trent's explanation.

Trent stood and paced alongside the arched glass wall, rubbing a hand over the back of his neck. "It's simple really," he began. "Simple and selfish. I had a craving and my initial thought was to test myself, to see if I could fight the cravings. Then, if I couldn't resist them, I was going to come to you." He turned to Max. "I'm sorry I wasn't honest. This is all new territory for me." He dropped his head, shoulders stooping as he went to rub at the angry burn under his flesh.

Max nodded, feeling sorry for Trent. He'd done the wrong thing himself, not so long ago because of urges he couldn't control. He understood the cravings, although not as intently as Trent and the others, but he empathised all the same.

"Well, if we can all take something positive away from tonight, its honesty is always the best policy." He crossed over to Trent and placed his hand onto the burned flesh, meeting Trent's eyes. He placed his other palm against his chest and whispered a healing incantation, grateful Sam had gifted him with energy earlier. In a matter of seconds, Trent's flesh soothed and healed.

He gasped in surprise. "Sometimes, I forget what you are," he whispered.

Max shrugged. "Are we ready for tonight's training?"

"Finally." Rick stood, looking at Trent. "No hard feelings?"

Trent shook his head. "We're all good." He looked at Nadine. "Are we?"

Nadine tilted her head. "We'll see."

"All right, head off to the gate lodge. I'll meet you there shortly," Max said.

They nodded, then exited out the front door, leaving Max alone for a moment. He ran a hand through his hair, taking a deep breath before turning to the kitchen to pull out a plate of food. After heating the underside of the plate with his palm, he headed towards the cellar door. He whispered an incantation to unlock the heavy door, and it swung open. He took a deep breath and headed down the stairs, hearing the door lock behind him as he went to feed the person he held within.

"It's about time," a smooth European accent greeted him.

"Sorry, I've been busy." Max frowned into a face that was a mirror image of his own before sliding the plate of food onto a sill that sat between gaps in the bars.

Kyle Black ignored the food, curling long fingers around the bars, leaning closer to Max. "And I've been bored, *fratello*."

Max nodded, looking about the cell, which had been fitted within the large cellar. It had been a forethought in case he needed to secure one of his clan in it if they couldn't control themselves. The ironic fact it now housed a blood-sibling of his wasn't lost on him. The small shower, sink and toilet was sectioned off, and a cot sat in the far corner beside a desk piled with books. Max wasn't heartless enough to lock him down here with nothing to do.

"When are you letting me out?"

"When I feel I can trust you."

Kyle snorted. "Seriously, you kidnap *me* and you talk about trust?"

"Technically, stealing someone from a prison cell isn't kidnapping."

"What the hell is it then?"

Max met his brother's steady gaze. "Call it healthy curiosity, plus a strong dislike for the Light Accords' ways of doing things."

"You do know why they locked me up, don't you?"

Max folded his arms. "You were captured after being found absorbing the essence from a heavenly soul. Pretty straight forward."

"So, you know I'm one of the 'bad-guys'," Kyle made air quotes before snatching up the fork and stabbing a roast potato.

"My interpretation of what passes for a 'bad-guy' has altered the past several months."

"Whatever. When are you going to answer my questions? Why did you save me? Better yet, how the hell did you create a portal?" He shoved the potato in his mouth and chewed.

"I don't have time for this conversation."

Kyle swallowed, pointing his fork between the bars towards Max. "Too bad, I want answers. How the hell do you have powers unlike any other Vein I've ever seen?"

"How the hell did I not know you existed until only days ago?" Max shot back.

Kyle shrugged. "That, I can't answer that. We always knew about you, the *special son*, away at boarding school. When the decision was made that it was time for you to come home, we were shipped off to Italy to live with Brendan."

"We?"

"Yeah, our other sibling."

"What's his name?"

"You want to know? Let me out."

Max shook his head. "Why did our father never tell me about you? Why did they separate us?"

"Brendan said, in part, it was because of your blood. Said we would be drawn to your essence, that we wouldn't be able to resist the temptation of sucking you dry."

"It doesn't make sense that our mother gave birth to three of us, yet I was the only one who inherited her royal blood?"

"A lot of things don't make sense. Like your abilities."

Max remained quiet.

"Listen, you did me a big favour getting me away from those bastard royal scum."

Max frowned at Kyle's term for the royal-souls, feeling he was betraying them just hearing his brother curse them.

"If you need me to do anything, I'm your guy. You can trust me, hell... we're brothers after all."

"Just, give me a bit of time."

"Sure, a bit of time." Kyle shook his head, spearing a carrot before

71

continuing.

"Hey, I felt a spark of energy early yesterday morning. I've never felt anything like it. Who was your visitor?"

Max forced a calm he did not feel. How could Kyle have felt Sam's presence from down here in the cellar? It was something he'd feared since the council had told him they were sending her his way; having her around a group of Veins. He shrugged. "I was performing a few healing spells yesterday morning."

Kyle titled his head, green eyes narrowing in suspicion. "It wasn't you; I can feel your energy signature a mile away."

"Whatever." Max blew out a breath. "Do you need anything else before I go?"

"Yeah, I want to know what your plan is?"

"I'm working on it." Max headed past the cell and towards the far wall, pushing another door open, he called, "Eat, I'll see you in the morning."

"Is that all I'm getting?" Kyle yelled.

"For now." Max closed the door on Kyle's muffled reply, feeling a little guilty about caging his own flesh and blood. For now, it had to be done until he figured out if he could trust Kyle and if so, what he was going to do with him.

When the Light Accords had informed him about his and his sibling's birth, he'd been overwhelmed. On top of his father absorbing his mother's essence to the point of her death, it was all most too much for him to wrap his head around. Then they'd dropped the bombshell that one of his siblings was right there in their custody and when he'd asked them if he could see him, they said, no. *Typical.*

That same night, while he'd been in the cellar, musing all he'd heard, he'd imagined meeting the imprisoned sibling and before he knew it, he'd created a portal that led him straight to his triplet. He'd grabbed

Kyle before rational thinking came into play and had returned to the mansion in the blink of an eye, securing Kyle in the cell.

He hadn't thought much more about the next move. Hell, he'd been in shock he had the ability to snatch Kyle so easily and he was still trying to figure out what he was supposed to do about it. Not to mention the fact he'd committed a criminal act, stealing a Light Accords prisoner.

He headed along the twisting tunnel that would take him close to an exit near the gate lodge and shook his head to clear it of decisions he wasn't ready to make.

He took a deep breath as he prepared for a healing class, followed by a demonstration that would cause one of his clan severe pain, with the hopes of seeing if the others could absorb the illness and heal the volunteer. He was sure, after what had gone down today, Trent would suck it up, literally and volunteer for the role of diseased host.

CHAPTER SEVEN
SAMANTHA

Sam sat on the swing under the weeping willow. It hadn't gone past six am, but after an early night and a deep sleep, she'd woken just after five and was relieved that the headache was gone. She'd had a decent run up the mountain, a quick shower and was taking a mindful moment with a latte.

She loved this time of morning, when the rest of the world was deciding whether to wake or sleep some more. Was Max still sleeping? She turned to look up towards the large attic windows and saw a flicker of movement. She hoped he'd join her before the others did. Sam was curious to hear what had gone down last night after she'd crashed.

Meanwhile, she marvelled at the sprawling gardens awash with decadent bursts of colour from the native wattles to the lavender, roses and winter bulbs sprouting from between rocky crevices and tree roots. It truly was a magnificent property under Max's nurturing hands. The clucks of the chickens exploring under the sun as it poked its head around the south side of the mountain filled her a joy.

"Good morning," Gemma called as she approached, walking onto the small dock nursing a hot drink, a bright coloured hoodie covering her head.

Sam smiled, there was something so sweet about this girl. She often had to remind herself she was a 'Vein.'

"Morning, how was training last night?"

Gemma flinched before meeting Sam's eyes. "Tough."

She nodded. "It will get easier. You wanting to do the right thing will ease the difficulties in your transition."

"I sure hope so, because last night wasn't pleasant."

Sam sipped her latte before saying, "Can I ask you something?"

"Yes."

"Why were you all referring to me as, *la stella*, 'the star' the other day?"

"You don't know?"

When Sam continued looking at Gemma, Gemma flushed and dropped her gaze towards the water, then back at Sam. "Max told us you were one of the main reasons Brendan Black was destroyed. Because of you, I was freed from years of brutality. When I turned thirteen, my elder brother took me away from our parents and he moved me into the city and said my 'real' education had to begin." Gemma paused, hugging her hot drink, looking out towards the ponds still-waters, her eyes losing focus.

"It's okay, you don't have to continue if it upsets you," Sam soothed.

Gemma shook her head, drawing in a deep breath before blowing on her drink, steam swirling in her eyes before meeting Sam's gaze. "For five years, I was not allowed to return to my home in the country or speak to my parents. My brother's so called 'education' consisted of being tortured if I refused to torture the innocent."

"Oh no!" Sam cried. "That's deplorable."

Gemma shook her head. "That word doesn't even begin to cover it, but, yes, it was beyond deplorable. I had no idea what I could even do, that I could make my veins exit my flesh."

"That would have been so difficult." Sam sympathised.

Gemma flushed, looking embarrassed for a moment before she continued with a soft confession. "I had no idea how delicious the taste of an innocent soul would be and the moment I absorbed their blood, destroying their soul, I had never imagined anything could taste so sweet." She shook her head. "But, in the end, no matter how good it felt, I always, always hated myself for what I'd done afterwards." She sat on the pier, legs dangling above the water as she continued. "I felt so guilty for the pleasure I felt after every evil deed, that I began self-harming with the intention of killing myself. I wanted it all to end. When my brother found out what I was doing, he imprisoned me in the tower to be beaten and starved... amongst other things."

"Gemma, I'm so sorry you had such a horrific time at the hands of someone who should've protected you." Sam felt like crying.

Gemma shook her head and smiled. "For the first year, I felt happy about it. It was like karma prevailed. I deserved the punishment, and it felt better than self-harming. When others were imprisoned with me, their suffering was worse than any punishment they could have inflicted upon me. It was hell for years. But then, Brendan Black was killed and when he died, so to, did many that he'd created, including those who held us captive."

"How did you come to find Max?"

"He found me." Gemma got to her feet, beaming. "All the guards at the tower had disappeared, or died, leaving us locked in our cells. We would have starved to death if Max hadn't come. At first, we were terrified of him because we recognised him as Brendan's cousin. We learned to trust him once he told us about his dearest friends, and how they killed Brendan. How *you* killed him. So, that is why we called you, *la stella*. Your actions were the beginning of a new future."

Sam laughed. "If you think I'm a star, wait until you meet my Angel. Your minds will be blown."

"Will we really get to meet her?" Gemma sounded excited.

Sam chuckled, knowing how embarrassed Angel would be knowing Max's 'clan' idolised her. "Yes, you will."

"Her name is Angel Cloud?"

"Yes."

"Max said she's your brother's soul-partner, like, married in the human world?"

"Yes, well, we call the humans, pure-souls. And yes, our version of marriage, is a soul-essence ceremony, where we are matched with our soul-partner."

"Weird." Gemma whispered, making Sam laugh.

"I suppose it is, for those looking in from the outside."

"If she's with your brother, why isn't she Angel Storm?"

"Because she is *that* special and as a team, they are that unique."

"I… see." Clearly, she didn't. "Can I ask you something else?" Gemma asked.

"Of course."

"What is it exactly that you do? I mean, I know you're an elemental, born of the royal-souls, which makes you a bit of a legend."

Sam scoffed before Gemma continued. "So, can you tell me what it is you do?"

Sam nodded. "I'm connected to the elements and Mother Earth. Once, my role was solely to protect Angel, but after she and my brother became soul-partners, I was no longer needed for that role."

"Do you have a soul-partner?"

She shook her head, replying, "I did once, but Brendan killed him not long after our ceremony."

"Oh, I'm so sorry." Gemma's face fell, and she looked into the water.

Sam didn't want to see the kind girl sad again, so whispered to the wind, waving her fingers across the water, creating a small funnel of air to stroke the water, before creating a mini cyclone. Swirling and spinning the pond's water around, she collected it into a vortex. With a flick of her fingers, she shot the spinning water sky-high, its tip reaching the height of the mansion.

Gemma's laughter was soon joined by the others, who had stepped out onto the deck with hot drinks in hand.

Sam grinned, catching Max's gaze before she whispered to the air once more and flung her pointed fingers towards the crowd on the back deck, waving in a fluent, elegant gesture. The water flew into a sphere, sparkling and twisting as it flowed past Gemma and approached the onlookers. Nadine gasped, covering her hair, certain she was about to get soaked, but the water weaved around each of them, not dropping a drip as it flowed like an entity, greeting them all. Its tip drew close to Max, who remained still, drinking his tea, as it brushed his cheek, leaving a cold droplet.

His eyes flashed to Sam, who grinned before waving her fingers back to herself. The water flew towards her, returning to the pond in a circular motion, then dropping back down. Not a wave was made as it settled into its basin.

The onlookers applauded and Sam slipped off the swing to take a bow.

Gemma clapped loudly. "Wow," she sang. "Just wow."

Sam laughed, waving her hand. "That's just play." She smiled.

"Well, I can't wait to see you in action, seriously."

"And you will," Max said from behind Gemma. "Good morning, Sam."

She noticed he looked a little tired, smouldering tired. How she wished she could turn him around, tuck him back into bed and join him.

"Good morning," she replied, keeping her thoughts under lock and key.

"I guess after that little performance, you are feeling better this morning?"

She drained her latte. "I am, thanks. Hungry though."

"Well, it's Daniel's turn for breakfast, he's dishing up."

"Great."

"I'll help him." Gemma smiled at Max before heading inside.

Sam walked around the pond and met him at the dock before they turned to walk back to the house together.

"How was last night?"

He nodded, watching as the others followed Gemma inside. "Trent was the one who placed the Leecher in the cow."

"Bastard." She hissed.

"Hey." He stopped walking to turn to her. "I get it, but imagine being on crack your entire life and then, only with sheer will power and determination, you decide to get off it."

She tilted her head as she considered her reply. "Right, fair point. But still…"

"He was punished. Don't worry about that."

"What did you do?"

"He was made ill by my unsavoury side and the others' took turns in attempting to draw the sickness out."

"Did they?"

"Eventually, with some help."

"Baby steps." Sam said. "Are you doing case notes for each test to present to the council?"

"Supposedly. Are you?" He asked.

"Supposedly."

He grinned as they continued to the house. "You never did like the rules much, did you?"

"Well, you should know, I broke them half the time to keep you safe."

"Yeah, funny too."

"I know." She winked before sauntering ahead of him and through the backdoor. Her stomach backflipped as the breakfast aromas assaulted her.

"Daniel," she groaned. "If you're not married by the time this band camp is over, you're mine!" she exclaimed.

He grinned, turning red. "You're on," he said, clearing his throat as it came out croaky.

Sam smiled and joined Rick and Nadine at the table as Gemma dished out bacon, eggs, muffins and baked beans. "Thank you." Sam grabbed her cutlery and the seasoning as Nadine poured teas and coffees.

"So," Sam asked Max as she scooped up a spoonful of BBQ Baked Beans. "What's on for the day?"

Max buttered a muffin and spread vegemite on the top. "Resistance training."

Sam chewed on the juicy warm beans, grateful when they hit her stomach, which demanded more. "Oh?" *That sounds intriguing.*

He nodded and continued eating.

A man of many words as usual, our Max is. She sighed internally and decided to fill her belly first, ask questions later.

Everyone else joined them at the table as cheese, tomato sauce, salt and pepper was passed around and conversations were mumbled around mouthfuls of food.

Just like a normal family. A sudden pang of missing her tribe hit her. What were they all getting up to right now? Probably wanting to discuss council business, or what Max was getting up to here, whilst no doubt, steering Mrs McGoldrick out to go into town so they could talk freely. She almost smiled at the thought and looked across at Max.

He reached for his tea, taking a sip as he watched her from over the rim. "You okay?"

"Remember all those mornings Tom, or Jess would send Mrs McGoldrick off on an errand so we could talk Soul Keeper stuff?"

He grinned, nodding. "What a woman."

Sam nodded, thinking of Red too.

"You miss them all already?"

She shrugged. "Yeah, kinda."

"Your family?" Nadine asked.

"Yes."

"Well, why don't they come and visit us, they're just down the road aren't they?" Nadine asked.

Sam nodded, scooping up some eggs. "No offence, but I don't think you're ready for a house full of heavenly souls."

"Oh." Nadine flushed, dropping her eyes to her plate. "True."

"We might see if Bowie will pop in for a visit though." Max nodded to her.

She beamed at him, thrilled to have the opportunity to see her brother so soon.

"Yes, let's do that."

"Why don't you give him a call after breakfast?"

Sam nodded, digging into her food more heartedly. The thought of seeing Bowie soothed her soul and no doubt, whatever this resistance training that Max had in mind, Bowie would love to participate in.

"*That's* your brother?" Rick's eyes sparkled while his gaze ran up and down every inch of Bowie as he got off his dirt bike. Bowie placed his helmet on the handlebars before unzipping his jacket, revealing a firm torso.

Sam beamed with pride as if she hadn't seen him in a year. "Yup, that's my brother."

"Why am I not surprised?" Rick whispered in awe.

Sam chuckled as the small group stood looking out of the front window as Max met Bowie in the driveway to discuss ideas about training for the morning.

The men shook hands before Bowie pulled Max into a manly embrace and slapped him affectionately on the back.

"So, where's my sister?" Sam heard Bowie ask as Max opened the front door.

"Right here," she said as she ran across to hug him.

Bowie swooped her up, hugging her hard as he laughed. "I swear it feels like a lifetime that I haven't seen you, not a few days!" He dropped a noisy kiss on her cheek before lowering her to the ground.

"I know." She reached up to ruffle his dark blond hair. "How's Angel?"

"You saw her yesterday," he chuckled.

Sam shrugged, grinning.

"She's good, sends her love, can't wait to visit, all of that." Bowie turned to the small group. "*Ciao*," he flashed an irresistible smile as he said 'hello' in Italian.

Sam wanted to roll her eyes at Rick, and Nadine who shook in appreciation of Bowie's beauty. She heard Nadine whisper, "*Bellissimo.*"

She caught Max's eye, noting he wore the same grin and couldn't help the laugh that burst from her. It felt like old times.

"Everyone," Max stepped forward, "this is Bowie Storm, Sam's brother who is going to assist us with training today and any other day he chooses to help us. You'd be wise to listen when he gives an order." He smiled to soften the command.

"Oh, I will do anything you need me to do." Rick stepped forward and offered his hand. "I'm Rick."

Bowie shook his hand, grinning knowingly. "Hello Rick."

Max pointed to the group making the introductions as Bowie shook all their hands in turn.

"Nadine, Trent, Daniel and Gemma."

"Hope you're all settling in okay." Bowie smiled, turning to Max. "You've done a superb job creating a calm, harmonious environment here, Max."

Max agreed, looking around.

"Ah, now that's more like it," Bowie strolled across to the pool table, running his hand along the glistening black wood. "What, no piano, Romeo?" He grinned over his shoulder towards Max.

"I thought I'd settle for something everyone could participate in." Max shrugged.

"So, Max-like of you," Bowie said under his breath, but Sam caught it.

"Would you like a coffee, Bowie?" Rick asked.

"No thanks." He slung his arm around Sam's shoulder, pulling her close. "I'm in the mood for some training though. How about you, little sister?"

"Always."

"Come on everyone, let's get started." Max opened the front door.

The group headed out, chatting excitedly. "I can't believe we're getting the chance to work with Max again and *two* royal-souls," Daniel whispered to Gemma.

Sam caught Bowie's eye as they'd overheard the excitement in Daniel's voice and he grinned before turning his attention to the group where Max had led them.

"First up, I'd really like to see what you are all capable of, without killing my sister, or myself, of course." Bowie grinned. "You see, although we've been attacked plenty of times by your... brethren."

"Ex-brethren, thank you," Rick interrupted.

Bowie bowed in apology. "Ex-brethren. This is our chance to see up close and personal how you use your body as a weapon."

"What do you want to see?" Trent asked.

"Everything. How do you fashion a lasso from your veins? Make projectile spears, or a swarm of tiny flesh-eating arrows?" He grimaced as he said the last example.

Sam recalled when Brendan Black had sent an arsenal of the lethal weapons into Bowie's chest years ago, causing him severe agony, almost killing him. It was the same night Max's father had been killed. She looked across at Max to find his watchful eyes on her, as if recalling the incident, too.

He broke eye contact and asked the clan, "Who would like to oblige Bowie?"

"Oh definitely me." Rick grinned, rolling his sleeves up and rolling his shoulders, taking a deep breath. Sam watched as his forearms split open and a wriggling mass of black veins broke through the surface.

"I know what weapon I want to fashion before I release my veins," he said to Bowie. "For example." He faced a large tree, opening his arms wide. "Flesh-eating veins, formed into arrows." He released too many veins to count and Sam watched, mesmerised as they flew through the air before piercing the trunk of the tree and borrowing inside.

"Nice, in a disturbing way." Bowie rubbed his chest, a slight grimace on his face.

Nadine stepped forward. "This won't hurt," she assured Bowie and opening the flesh along her wrist, released a long, thick vein. "Lasso, minus the toxic barbs," she said as she flung her wrist out like one would if they were roping cattle. "This weapon is deployed for one reason and that is to cut the victim in half." Her lasso-vein swirled around Bowie's throat, restricting any movement, tightening with each breath.

"That's great and enough," he choked out and Nadine snapped her wrist, calling her vein back to disappear inside her flesh.

"If you were fighting an enemy and couldn't retract your vein back into your body, what happens?" Sam asked.

"I would cut it off and leave it." Nadine shrugged. "It would be painful and I would need to recoup my energy. Usually that would entail consuming a Heavenly soul's essence or kill a pure-soul." She shrugged again.

"I see." Sam shuddered and Trent laughed.

"Is it really so disgusting to you?" he asked, when she turned to him, eyebrow raised.

"Consuming a Heavenly Soul's essence is on par with rape in my world."

"Well, not in ours," he returned.

"It is now," Max said to Trent, a dark glint in his eyes.

"Of course, sure." Trent said apologetically. "I was just trying to say, we have all been raised with a different outlook, that's all."

"True enough," Bowie agreed.

Max watched Trent for another moment before asking Bowie, "Do you want to see more?"

"No, that's been great for a start." He placed his hands on Max's shoulders and turned him, placing him in the centre of the group. "I'd like you," he pointed to everyone else, "to place yourselves in a circle around him." He waited for everyone to take their places and quieten down before he began. As he spoke, he ambled around the outer circle. "I understand you all know what Max is?" He wiggled a finger towards Sam before pointing to a tree on the outside of the circle.

She didn't ask, but wandered towards the tree and stood by it, folding her arms.

"Yeah," Trent replied. "Half heavenly soul, half Vein."

"Half. Heavenly. Soul." Bowie said each word with impact as he circled the group once more. "Heavenly. Soul," he repeated before joining Max in the centre.

"And we've just witnessed what you are." He looked at each of them.

Nadine raised an eyebrow, folding her arms in a defensive gesture.

Bowie held a hand up to Nadine. "I'm not trying to offend you, but to make a point."

"Which is?" Trent frowned, mirroring Nadine's stance.

"How strong are you? How ready are you to fight the change?" In a flash before Sam could blink, Bowie pulled his pocket knife out from his back pocket and drew the sharp tip along Max's forearm.

Bowie! Sam screamed her alarm against his mind only.

Relax, he returned. *Max and I have this under control, little sister. You know I can heal him.* His eyes met hers briefly before returning to the group.

She ran her hands over her face before focusing on Max. She hated seeing him in any pain. His precious blood flowed, making a red stain on the green lawn near his feet.

Max? She pushed her concern towards him.

86

I'm all right, Sam. Like Bowie had done a moment ago, his dark eyes met hers briefly before focusing on the task at hand.

Bowie turned to each of them. "Can you feel that? The heavenly power? Can you smell it?"

Sam noticed that everyone in the group's eyes had turned black and soulless. She shivered, remembering seeing Max's eyes like that too many times when he'd absorbed Angel's blood-essence. She was frustrated that Bowie and Max hadn't warned her what they'd planned to do. Now she felt useless and had no clue to their end game. Surely, Bowie didn't want any of them to attach their veins to Max?

"My god! I can't help myself!" Trent screamed as his forearms split and long, black veins burst from his flesh to shoot towards Max like spears. And his weren't the only ones.

Gemma cried as her veins slid from her pale flesh to join Trent's. Daniel's and Rick's were seconds behind. Sam swore she heard a 'sorry' mingled in Gemma's lustful cry of dismay.

Max was surrounded by several veins, millimetres from penetrating his wound. And that wasn't the worst part, a black rimmed, transparent force field had burst around Bowie and Max, immobilizing them in a prison of pain. If Max and Bowie had a plan, Sam was sure that wasn't a part of it.

Rick's and Daniel's veins licked along Bowie's flesh as Trent's and Gemma's brushed over Max's wound, seeking entrance into the cut. Sam's heart raced, and she froze for a second.

Just as Trent's razor-sharp, tiny mouths were about to slide into Max's flesh, Sam flicked her fingers towards them and struck them with a small zap of lightening. Trent screamed, falling to his knees as he extracted his veins, pulling them back to him. Sam whispered for ice and stung the tips of every extended vein with burning frost bite, forcing them to return to their host.

The force field dissolved, releasing Max and Bowie from its prison. Bowie met Sam's eyes, nodding his thanks before he turned to Max, taking his arm. He ran long fingers over the bleeding wound as he whispered a healing incantation.

Sam was relieved once the blood had stopped flowing, and the wound sealed shut and only then turned her eyes towards the clan, who were all on their knees, moaning in pain. All except one. Nadine stood, arms folded, an angry glare on her face as she stared at Bowie.

Sam looked forward to those fireworks. *Bet she doesn't think he's so beautiful now?*

Max cleared his throat and was about to speak before Nadine burst out.

"*What* the *sanguinante inferno* was that? Do you call that fair? It's like throwing a bloodied carcass into the ocean and asking the sharks not to touch it." She stared furiously at Max; hands planted on her hips.

Max turned to her. "Nadine, it may seem brutal and unfair, but you'll be placed in situations that you won't be prepared for. Sometimes, unexpected things happen and you all need to build up a tolerance to resist feeding."

Gemma pushed herself to her feet, looking worn and wretched. Sam felt sorry for her and walking over, asked. "Are you alright?"

Gemma shook her head. "I'm furious." She looked at Max. "I didn't want to hurt you, but I couldn't resist. Nadine's right. That *wasn't* fair." She turned on her heel and fled towards the front entrance.

"I'll check on her." Daniel looked at Max, who nodded before he ran after Gemma.

"Listen." Max pushed hair out of his eyes before placing his hands on his hips. "I know that was rough, but if you can't build up a resistance to wanting my blood, then we're going to find ourselves in a world of trouble."

"It's not called resistance training for nothing. You have to greatly desire the thing placed before you, to be build up a tolerance and learn to resist it," Bowie reiterated.

"I couldn't resist him for a million dollars if he was placed before me," Sam heard Rick whisper to Trent and rolled her eyes, catching Bowie's grin. Yeah, Rick didn't whisper that quiet enough.

"If I knew training was going to be this barbaric, I would have opted out." Nadine tossed her hair over a shoulder.

"Don't be naïve." Sam sighed, folding her arms.

"I beg your pardon?" Nadine spun to glare at Sam.

"She said, don't be naïve. And I agree." Trent snapped, rubbing his arm where his veins had slid back into his flesh.

Sam felt guilty, knowing she must have hurt him like hell with her strike of lightening and frost burn. "Sorry about that." She nodded to his arm, feeling a pleasant tingle creep along her flesh the closer she stood to him. *Weird.*

"No." Trent shook his head. "It's fine."

"Explain why I'm naïve?" Nadine was shooting Sam a death stare.

"I don't mean to judge, really, but let's face facts. When you consider your past is equivalent to a Stephen King novel of murder and brutality, well, compared to that, this was a nursery rhyme training session. It wasn't unfair, or brutal. It was just what it needed to be."

Nadine scoffed, dropping her eyes as she kicked at the grass.

Sam continued. "Congratulations for being the only one to exhibit such willpower and restraint."

Nadine raised her eyes and smiled at Sam. "I did, didn't I?"

The tension between them seemed to have passed.

"Anyone else have something to say about training?" Max asked.

Trent shook his head. "We all knew what we signed up for. You're not making us kill but reinforcing our desire to do good." He shot a look at Nadine before returning his gaze to Max. "I, for one, am grateful. You won't hear me complain about anything you or your Soul Keepers make us do."

Max nodded. "I appreciate that. After all, it's for your own protection in the end."

Sam enjoyed watching her brother and Max interact as a team. It made her heart beat pleasantly. "What's next?" she asked.

"Can we grab a quick break with refreshments?" Rick asked.

"Sure," Max said.

"I, for one, am looking forward to some training that entails a bit more complexity." Rick's eyes shone as he looked at Bowie.

Bowie chuckled. "I hope you feel the same way once we're done?"

"Oh I've no doubt." Rick's enthusiasm wasn't lost on any of them.

Nadine turned and headed inside, followed by Trent, then Rick.

"I'll give you two a moment," Bowie said. "I'll make myself at home, shall I?"

"Please do." Max answered as he stepped closer to Sam.

Once they were alone, Sam reached for his arm, running her fingers along his flesh, tinged with dry blood. "Did you know he was going to do that?" She looked up at him.

He shrugged. "Kind of. We had a plan and then, Bowie did what Bowie does best."

She shook her head, reaching up to push his silky hair out of his forest-green eyes. "Bloody Bowie," she whispered.

He caught her wrist and held it between them. "At least he placed you out of harm's way before he started the show."

"Big brother has always been protective, even when he doesn't need to be."

"Well, in this case, you rescued us, so it was perfect hindsight."

"Yeah, it was." She smiled up at him. "Max?"

"Mmhmm." He caught a stray blonde hair that stuck to her lip gloss, pulling it free from her mouth.

She waited until his eyes met hers and felt herself grow warm under his intense gaze.

"Yes?" He repeated when she didn't continue.

"We are going to have that talk later, aren't we?"

"We will."

She nodded. "Good. Now, let's get a tea for you and a nice large coffee for me."

"Sounds like a plan." He didn't pull away when she looped her arm through his as they went to join the others for a ten-minute break.

CHAPTER EIGHT
SAMANTHA

Training continued throughout the day and Sam was thrilled to have the opportunity to witness Max demonstrating the removal of an oil spill from the pond he'd created.

Bowie stood beside her and was just as wide-eyed and fascinated as she was. Max had closed his eyes and spread his arms wide. The flesh of his forearms split, allowing his obsidian veins to slither towards the pond's surface, performing an eerie, yet elegant dance across the top of the slick, shiny patterns the oil had made on the water's surface. Max's tiny, mouthed veins opened wide into large, hollow tubes, revealing glistening razor-sharp teeth before sinking beneath the water's oily surface.

Sam bit her lip as she watched Max focus on the task of absorbing a decent amount of the slick matter. Minutes later, he opened his eyes, which flashed pure black before returning to his beautiful bright green. Sam forced a swallow as he retracted his veins, snapping them back into his arms in an instant as his gaze met hers. She noticed how pale he looked and a light sheen of sweat dotted his forehead.

"Do you feel sick after absorbing that?" Rick asked.

Max pulled his eyes away from Sam. "A little, but it will pass. Right, who's ready to give it a go?"

No one budged. "Nadine?" he asked.

She shook her head.

Bowie sighed and went to take a step forward, when Sam grabbed his hand, holding him in place. He looked down at her, an eyebrow raised in question.

Max has got this, they're his people, give him a moment. She knew her brother was used to taking charge and didn't have much patience when it came to getting tasks done. Max had a different approach and watching him deal with things his way filled her with a sense of peace and pride.

Okay, sure thing. Sam heard the grin in Bowie's reply.

Max looked at the group, shoving his hands into his pockets as he dropped his gaze to the pond's surface, remaining quiet and thoughtful.

"I'll give it a go," Daniel said, after another minute of silence, moving forward.

"Me too." Gemma stepped beside Daniel.

"Well, we can't have the quiet achievers steal all the thunder. Come on Trent, Nadine." Rick moved towards the other side of the pond as he rolled up the sleeves of his jumper. "After all, what the hell are we here for if we aren't prepared to roll up our sleeves and get dirty?" He met Bowie's eyes and grinned mischievously.

Someone's got a crush. Sam's comment to Bowie was filled with laughter.

Who can blame the poor guy? Bowie responded.

Cocky much? Sam snickered.

Always, Bowie replied good naturedly.

Sam elbowed Bowie in the stomach before they wrestled each other to the ground laughing. The group stopped, entertained as they watched the two beautiful royal-souls wrestle close to the pond's oily surface before Max cleared his throat.

When a still laughing Sam lifted her gaze to his, she could see his twinkling in amusement. "Sorry," she said, jumping up and reached a hand to pull her brother up beside her.

Max shook his head. "No need to apologise."

He's always been so irresistibly sweet... She sighed to Bowie, who slung his arm around her, pulling her close and under the dripping arms of the weeping willow.

She sat on the swing, as Bowie stood behind her, holding the ropes as they waited, respective and quiet now, so Max could continue the lesson.

"I know that the energy will feel wrong and your instinct will be to reject it. But remember, for as ill as you may feel, it won't last. We were essentially created for this."

Essentially created? Sam pushed towards him. Max looked her way but shook his head slightly as he continued.

"Afterwards, Bowie, or I can give you a boost of energy if need be. Okay?" He met each of their concerned eyes.

"Okay," Rick nodded to the others. "Let's snack on some oil, shall we?"

Nadine took a deep breath and like Gemma, released her veins from her flesh.

"There's a kind of beauty to them, isn't there?" she whispered to Bowie when as Trent, Rick and Daniel, released their veins, too. Max walked around the pond, instructing and encouraging each of them.

"You're right. When they are not behaving like parasitic aliens, absorbing innocent life, yeah, there is a kinda beauty to them," Bowie said.

It took an hour for them to absorb the remaining oil from the water's surface and any that coated the pond's plant life. Afterwards, Sam pushed her hands into the water. Any remaining miniscule of oil was zapped with a hit of fire, vaporising it before Bowie cast a healing spell towards all the biodiversity in and around the pond that may have been affected.

"All good," he said when he had finished.

"Thanks, Bowie." Max said.

"No worries." Bowie grinned at Max. "What's next?"

"Follow me." He led them all towards the back gate of the property and out onto the mountain. Several large trees were diseased and smaller bushes and shrubs were blackened and dead, much to Bowie's and Sam's surprise, as the entire area had been healed well over a year ago.

"I'd like to see if we can work as a team and draw as much poison from the earth that we can," Max said as the flesh on his forearms split open once again. Several long veins flowed towards the earth before plunging into the soil.

Sam watched as the clan mirrored Max's movements, sinking their veins deep within the poisoned soil killing the plant life on the mountain. After twenty minutes, she was concerned to see them all swaying with fatigue before Bowie called, "That should do it for now, Max."

Max opened his eyes, nodding to everyone and they withdrew their veins from the mountain's soil.

"That wasn't fun, at all." Nadine moaned, looking pale.

"I'm going to agree with you on that." Daniel nodded. "That tasted…"

"Disgustingly evil," Rick finished for him.

"Yeah." Daniel nodded.

Max sighed, rolling his sleeves down as his flesh sealed shut.

"What is it?" Sam asked.

He met her concerned gaze, pushing his hair out of his eyes. "Whatever it is, it's saturated deep in the soil."

"I'll organiser for the Soul Keepers to check the soil around the district, see if we can find out where the source of the poison is stemming from," Bowie suggested, sinking to his knees and placing his palms onto the grass.

"Thanks Bowie." Max nodded before Bowie poured healing energy into the earth.

Once he was finished, Sam called for a light rain to replenish the depleted soils. "All done here, for now. What's next?"

"I know it's mundane, but we have a few maintenance chores to attend to," Max said to the group as they all headed towards the back gate.

"Wonderful." Nadine muttered inspecting her nails.

"Why don't you and Daniel get lunch organised then?" Max offered.

Nadine brightened and linked her arm through Daniel's as they headed towards the mansion.

After a late lunch, Max decided weapons and combat training were a good idea, as both Sam and Bowie excelled in that area and it would benefit his clan.

After kicking Bowie's butt in one out of three rounds, Sam called it quits and let starry-eyed Rick have a go with her brother. She took the opportunity to check in on Gemma, who had been quiet during the day's training activities, after Max's and Bowie's morning session which had tempted them all, bar Nadine. Sam found her bottle feeding a couple of the orphaned lambs, snuggled in a warm stall in the barn.

"They're so sweet." She sighed, reaching for one of the prepared bottles and tipped it up to a hungry little creature, who sank on its front knees, bum in the air and tail wiggling like mad as it suckled on the warm milk.

"Yeah." Gemma's reply was barely a whisper.

"You shouldn't feel guilty for what you did earlier. It's in your nature."

"Exactly. It's in my nature. But it's not *who* I am." Gemma shook her head. "Not anymore."

"Training is meant to suck at times, trust me on that. It's meant to test us. Push us to our limits until we either break or excel." Sam stroked the lamb's woolly little head as it drained the bottle and releasing the teat, ran off with a spring in its step. She turned to watch as Gemma finished feeding her lamb.

Gemma stood, brushing some loose hay off her knees and reached for Sam's empty bottle. "I'll wash these."

"Gemma?"

"I'm okay, I understand what you're saying, I've heard it all before from Max."

"He's right, you know."

Gemma headed towards the deep sink and ran water into it, adding a splash of detergent before plunging all the used milk bottles into the soapy water as bubbles filled the sink.

"Of course he's right. He's Max." Gemma grinned over her shoulder at Sam.

Sam released a relieved breath, happy to see Gemma's spirits lift.

Gemma continued. "Sometimes, Max being right doesn't make any of this any easier. There's a lot to process and a lot of pressure."

"I understand that. I do. Just be kind to yourself while you're processing it all, okay?"

Gemma nodded. "You know, Sam. I can understand why Max is in love with you. You really are some-kind-of-perfect."

"What," Sam snorted, waving her hand in the air. "Trust me, Max is *not* in love with me. We just have a really complex history and are nothing more than friends."

"Really?" Gemma tilted her head, grinning playfully. "I wish my *friends* would look at me the way I catch Max looking at you."

"Pfft." Sam scoffed, feeling her cheeks warm.

"Sam," Bowie called. "I'm leaving."

"Gotta go." She headed out to Bowie, relieved he'd interrupted any further conversation about hers and Max's complicated whatever it was. She felt a little sad Bowie was leaving. She'd loved hanging out with him today and watched as he shrugged into his leather jacket before reaching for his gloves.

"Don't look sad, little sister." His voice swam with concern at her expression as she reached him.

She forced a smile. "I'm not sad," she lied. "It's just… I miss you already."

"Don't worry, I'll be back soon enough to drive you crazy."

"Promise?" she asked as he reached out to pull her under his chin for a quick hug.

"I do." He kissed the top of her head as she grabbed his helmet, passing it to him as Max walked out the front door.

"All set?" Max asked.

"Yep. Thanks for today. It's nice to mix things up a bit. By the way, now that we're alone, those trees are a worry."

"Yeah, I agree. They've been tainted by something deep within the soil."

"How can that be?" Sam frowned. "Nothing and no one has been on that part of the property since Angel healed it."

Max shook his head. "It has definitely been tainted by Vein activity.

"Do you think another Vein has moved into the area? Maybe before you arrived?" Sam frowned worriedly.

Max shrugged. "I have no idea, but I will see if I can track them."

"Can you do that?" Bowie asked, surprised.

"I can try."

"How?" Sam was intrigued. Max seemed to have developed some interesting skills since they had last been an item, including creating portals.

He can create portals too, you know. She pushed towards Bowie, shielding from Max.

What? How is that possible? Only elders like Red or Fletch can create portals?

Are you two having a private conversation? Max joined in.

"Sorry, that was rude and yes we were." Bowie grinned. "But I'll leave that for Sam to discuss with you. I've got to fly. Max, take care of Sam, Sam, try to behave."

"Funny," Sam muttered as Max nodded. She stood back beside him as Bowie flicked the engine on and revved the bike.

"See you soon," he yelled over the engine's roar before flying down the driveway and towards Glenormiston road.

"It's always interesting when the Storm siblings get together," Max said grinning at her.

She turned to face him, keeping it light. "Oh, I'm sorry, would you like us to dull it down a bit for you next time?"

He laughed, shaking his head. "No way."

She loved watching his eyes sparkle brightly. "Are we going to be able to have our talk, Max?"

His smile vanished as he looked down the driveway where Bowie's dust trial was disappearing in the late afternoon breeze. "I guess we can't really put it off, can we?"

"Not really."

"Tea is ready," Rick called.

They looked at each other. "Well, at least until after tea." Max smiled.

"After dessert?"

"Even better."

They headed inside to join the others.

Sam watched Nadine laughing in the kitchen as she helped Max put the dishes away, noticing she took every opportunity to touch Max. On the arm when she laughed, patting him on the back as he moved by her in agreement to something he said. Even slapping him on the backside with a hand-towel when he teased her.

I'm not jealous, I am absolutely not jealous, I am as equally fabulous as Nadine.

"Sam, you want a coffee?" Daniel interrupted her silent, shielded pep talk.

"No thanks." She blinked away from watching the 'just friends' playing during tidy up, noticing Gemma and Trent rubbing their arms. She cursed herself and whispered the chill in the air away.

Max turned in that moment, a dark eyebrow raised over a penetrating green stare. She flushed pink and looked away. She felt the familiar uncomfortable throb in her temple that seemed to be hitting her at this time of night.

"A game of pool?" Rick offered.

"Maybe tomorrow, I'm pretty beat. I'm going to head up to my room. I'll see you all in the morning," she said, forcing a bright tone in her voice. "Goodnight."

"Goodnight," Gemma said. "Thanks for today."

"You're welcome." She chanced a quick look in Max's direction as she waved to everyone and headed out towards the stairs with sounds of Billiard balls being racked up and Daniel crying out, "Game on," as he took Rick up on the offer.

She hoped she'd have enough time for a quick shower before her Q and A with Max began. She needed to wash the impending headache away.

MAXWELL

Max slotted the plate of food on the bench and levelled a fresh towel between the bars. "How are you going?"

Kyle ignored him, laying on the cot, arms behind his head, staring up at the cellar roof lined with intricate patterned cobwebs.

"Look, I'm sorry. I don't like locking you down here, any more than you like being down here."

"I doubt that. I can guarantee you; I don't like it a whole lot more than you do."

Max sighed, his guilt enormous. "Yeah, fair play."

"I may be a Vein, but I also deserve fresh air and exercise in nature. You should have left me with those Soul Keepers, I would have at least had some sort of entertainment. Torture? Something!" He sat up to glare at Max.

Max thought for a moment before nodding. "Eat. I've got an errand to run, but I'll be back in a few hours and I'll take you outside to exercise."

"You will?" Kyle's tone lightened immediately.

"Yes."

"Thank you." He sprang up from the cot with enthusiasm, and reached for his meal.

Max nodded. "See you later."

Kyle grinned. "I'll be here."

Max felt lighter himself, not liking locking anyone up; even if it meant he had an unpredictable situation to deal with. *One thing at a time.* He headed up to his room to prepare for Samantha Storm.

SAMANTHA

Sam considered slipping into a sexy little number after her shower, to torment Max, but decided not to be a tease and opted for a pair of black leggings and a black tee shirt with a logo, '*There is no planet B,*' wrapped around a vibrant looking Mother Earth. She tucked her long, damp hair up in a messy bun and headed upstairs to Max's door. After taking a deep breath, she knocked and waited.

"Come in, Sam," he said.

She cursed herself for the butterflies that scattered in her stomach upon with hearing her name roll off his tongue. "Pull yourself together," she whispered before opening the door.

The second she stepped into the room, his seductive scent wrapped around her. He'd taken time for a quick shower too; damp hair curled above the collar of his tee shirt. Casual jeans hugged firm thighs and his feet were bare.

After shutting the door behind her, she stayed where she was. Maybe this wasn't such a good idea?

"I'm not going to bite, Sam, come in."

Damn shame. She kept that thought shielded as she stepped further into the room. "You didn't think to put any more furniture in this room, other than your bed?" She crossed to one of the small window seats that overlooked the pond and sat, tucking her legs underneath her.

Max shrugged, walking over to where she sat and leaned against the wall, folding his arms. "Didn't give it much thought, no."

She looked up at him. "Today went well."

"It did." He returned her steady gaze.

She didn't mind that, at times, conversing with Max was like pulling teeth. She enjoyed the challenge of getting him to open up. "I have questions."

Max nodded.

"You took those photos." She nodded to the photographs lining the opposite wall.

"I did."

"And that photo of the homestead's healing garden is a portal?"

"It is."

"And you created it?"

"I did."

"How?" She prayed he would give her more than a two-word answer.

He dropped his gaze to the floor, as if wondering where to start.

He was quiet for a few moments before lifting his gaze to hers and began. "You remember when I absorbed Angel's soul-essence after her ceremony to Bowie?"

"I'm pretty sure I'm too young to have dementia, Maxwell."

He waited a moment before she answered without sarcasm. "Yes, I remember."

"And then, when my ruby absorbed all of your combined soul-essences, when Brendan tried to kill you?"

She nodded solemnly, not liking the memory that surfaced when Max had abducted Angel to trap Brendan. When his ruby had been activated by a command from Brendan, it had absorbed their soul-essences before Bowie and Angel had obliviated Brendan before the ruby somehow gave him the power to rise from blood and bone in the form of Bowie.

"Not one of my favourite memories," she whispered.

"Nor mine," he said. They stared at each other before he continued. "Then you hit the ruby with a bolt of lightning."

Sam shook her head. "I was so frightened I was going to burn you to a crisp, but you didn't even get a scratch, which was strange."

He nodded. "Yes, it kind of was."

Sam tilted her head. "What aren't you telling me?"

Max sighed and pushed off the wall, strolling into the middle of the room near his bed before turning to face her, pushing his hands deep into his pockets.

"After that night, I felt something, unusual, stir within me. Something I had never felt before."

Sam frowned. "What was it?"

Max pulled his hands out of his pockets and sank onto his bed, dropping his elbows onto his knees as he leaned forward. Sam wanted to go over and sit beside him, put her arm around him and kiss the worried expression off his face.

"Please tell me Max, the suspense feels like it's going to kill me."

A corner of his lip turned up as he looked her dead in the eye. "We wouldn't want that."

"Ha." She grinned back at him.

"I wish Red were here. She can tell this story much better than I."

"Well, can't you weave a little magic and take us to Red's then?"

Max smiled and pushed himself to his feet. "I can. Come." He held out his hand.

Sam uncurled her legs before her bare feet hit the cool floorboards and crossed over to him, watching his eyes darken with every step that brought her closer to him.

As she reached out to take his hand, he closed the distance in a lightning-fast move. As soon as their palms connected, his fingers wrapped tight around hers. She saw him wave his other hand, and he whispered something she couldn't make out. She gasped before being sucked into a vortex of emerald light and squeezed her eyes shut as she slammed against him. Just when she didn't think she could take it for another second, her feet hit cool grass and the world stilled around her.

His arms loosened around her as she leaned back to look up at him, shaking her head. "I've never become used to portal travel and now, you've taken it up a whole other level."

He ran his hand down her back before releasing her. "Come on," he said, turning towards Red's back door.

She took a steady breath chanting silently, *Just friends, just friends* as she followed his broad back. A little creature darted out from under a rose bush and stealthily slipped towards Max.

"Hey Alana." Max bent to pat the fox's silky head as it blinked up at him.

"Hello gorgeous girl." Sam smiled down at the sweet little fox, who had lived with Red for as long as Sam could remember. Alana pushed her nose into Max's hand before moving forward to poke her nose into Sam's leg and then darted off into Red's potting shed where she liked to sleep.

They crossed under the porch as the back door slid open and the homeliest, sweetest little face peered out. Corn flower blue eyes glistened behind gold-framed glasses that sat on perfectly pert nose and her short mop of auburn hair shone under the back porch light.

Red beamed at Max as she stepped back, allowing him to pass. "I've been waiting for you, my dear boy."

"Hello Red." He dropped a kiss on her cheek as he walked by.

She turned to Sam and Sam's throat caught as she reached out and wrapped her arms around the gatekeeper, who had always been like an aunt to her and Angel.

"It's so good to see you, Red."

"Oh no, it's good to see *you* dearest. Come in, come in. We've lots to discuss."

Sam walked into Red's little back room and followed Max through the door leading to Red's bright, open kitchen with green splash back that always made Sam hungry for a juicy Granny Smith apple. She was surprised when instead, she stood in an old fortress where damp, crumbling stoned walls, revealed a black night sky, with one lone silver star twinkling above.

Sam raised an eyebrow in confusion and turned in a circle, finding herself totally alone.

"What the… Max? Red?" Her heart started an uncomfortable gallop. How had she followed Max into Red's back room and ended up in the Light Accords fortress? The last time these stones had been beneath her feet, the High Council had assigned her to pour lightening into Angel's body, punishing them both for disobeying their laws when she had kept Max and his crime of absorbing Angel's soul-essence a secret from the council.

"What am I doing here?" she whispered before demanding, "What do you want with me?" She glanced up at the night sky. Where was the Man in the Moon? He was always a great comfort to her in the dark. That was when she noticed the lone star in the sky moving, shifting, then falling and heading straight towards her with lightning speed. Sam halted the scream that wanted to rip out of her throat as she threw her hands up and spun a protective, transparent shield around herself, just as the star collided against it. It sent a waterfall of silver flames to lick against every inch of the barrier. Her breath exploded out of her as the star pulsed outside her protective dome and although she didn't want to take her eyes off it, she had to turn her face away before its glare blinded her.

"What's happening?" she whispered, frustrated she didn't have the strength to yell as holding her shield against the powerful star was taxing her energy. She struggled to maintain it and cried in despair when she felt the shield slipping before a smooth voice whispered.

"Do not be afraid, elemental princess, we do not want to harm you."

"I'm no princess and if you didn't want to harm me, why drop on me like a firebomb?" she snapped.

"If you lower your shield, all will be revealed to you."

Sam squinted at the ridiculously bright star and sighed as its light diminished. It surprised her to see the most exquisite looking man standing before her, wearing an impeccable grey suit. His luxurious silver hair was tied back to drip down well past his shoulders. He stared at her with the most unusual silver, pupilless eyes. Shivers of fear and pleasure rippled along every inch of her flesh.

He smiled knowingly, revealing the whitest teeth she'd ever seen aside from the Colgate commercials. He held a hand towards her and she narrowed her eyes, contemplating what to do, when her instincts of trust kicked in and she waved her fingers, removing her wanning shield, taking a step back just to be safe. Yet, with a single blink, he was right in front of her, a hair's breadth between them.

Sam's pulse raced, and she wished Max was with her.

"He is." The too-beautiful-star-thingy smiled down at her.

Sam frowned, looking over her shoulder, confused as she was alone with the 'star.'

"Who are you?"

"My name is Methuselah Obsidian."

Sam tilted her head. "Methuselah *Obsidian?* Methuselah... Obsidian."

He tilted his head, watching her repeat his name once more.

"You're not actually *the* Methuselah Star?"

"I am."

"Impossible." She gasped.

"Not really."

"But that means you're older than the universe itself," she whispered.

"That's correct."

"You're over fourteen billion years old?"

"I am."

Is he related to Max, with these two-word answers?

I am, he replied in the way royal-souls could communicate without speaking.

Sam's gaze widened, and she hastily took another step back, holding her hand out in front of her to keep him at a distance, heart racing.

What the actual hell? She wasn't sure what frightened her the most, that this 'thing' was related to Max, or that he could read her thoughts.

You've nothing to be afraid of, Princess. We would never harm you.

"Please, stop calling me princess and who is, 'we'? I only see you."

Methuselah held out his hand, just like Max had done earlier, waiting for her to take it.

"Please, little Soul Keeper, allow me to show you."

Sam looked up into his silver pools, which reflected her worried face. "Show me what?"

"The past, present and future."

She felt a prickle of fear. "I want Max," she whispered.

"Soon." He stood, hand outstretched, waiting.

Sam swallowed before taking a hesitant step forward, placing her hand in his, marvelling at the silkiness of his, *flesh?*

As soon as her hand was in his, they spun in a silver vortex, but one that didn't make her feel as if her spleen was being ripped out. Although they were moving at the speed of light, it was a smooth ride and not without entertainment. Sam looked about her in wonder as she was taken to a vibrant green paradise, filled with rainbow-coloured birds, that sang so sweetly it brought tears to her eyes. A crystal-clear waterfall flowed over the lip of earth that smelled rich in fertile soil and glistened brightly as the sun reflected the prisms of billions of gems scattered throughout the land. Vegetation unlike any she'd ever seen and trees, taller than she thought possible, stood proudly, filled with bird life.

A small figure walked out from beneath the waterfall yet remained dry; silky red hair flowed behind her, brushing her waist as she walked across the smooth surface of rocks before stepping onto the grass. Once the figure stopped walking, the vortex Sam and Methuselah were in stopped spinning, giving Sam the opportunity to take in the entire scene. It was a serene land where only harmony reigned.

Sam gasped as a man appeared from between the trees, almost identical to Max and walked towards the beautiful lady, who in turn, ran laughing towards him and into his waiting embrace.

As the pair kissed passionately, Sam and Methuselah were once again spun into a silver vortex before halting to a scene where the man was wiping the brow of his labouring beauty before he delivered their baby girl; whose glistening red hair dripped in silver blood.

Like Max's birth.

The next image showed years had passed by and every year on the child's birthday, the lovers got to see each other. On the child's fifth birthday, the Max-look-alike embraced the sobbing red-haired lady imparting some devastating news and in the next scene, the child was removed and re-homed at a pure-soul's home in Terang.

Sam felt tears lodge in her throat for the sweet lady's despair, who seemed to cry every day for the following twelve months before the man returned, holding a small wriggling red pelt. Sam's tears did fall then when the little fox poked its nose out of the man's arms and she saw him mouth the word, 'Alana,' as he handed the little creature to his lover. As she took the fox from him, she held out her hand, offering him a ring that shone as black as the fox's shiny nose.

Max's ring? Sam was confused but continued watching. The lovers kissed and Sam knew without them having to speak a single word that they were kissing each other goodbye.

As the man stood back, he nodded once to his lover before placing the ring on his finger and in a flash of light, he shot towards the black night sky where Sam had seen Methuselah earlier.

She was about to speak, when the vortex spun them about and Sam stood in the Black's mansion, witnessing Max's birth. The scene didn't last long before they were outside the mansion surrounded by a horde of Veins, the lawn no longer green, but crimson, drenched in blood as familiar and unfamiliar faces were being slaughtered. Sam could feel pure hatred fill the air as it washed over her and inside her, with every shallow breath she pulled into her lungs. The scene before her was barbaric.

Her eyes fell on a figure, lying broken amidst the chaos and in that moment, she felt as if she would die. *No!* She felt the scream lodge in her throat. Max's forest-green eyes stared sightlessly up at the darkening sky. She swallowed a sob, stumbling forward before meeting the glare of an exceptionally large Vein heading straight towards her, its face unrecognisable.

Its inhuman scream filled her with dread as it shot its wicked veins towards her. She cried in dismay, knowing she wouldn't be fast enough to block or avoid its blow. Indescribable pain ripped through her as its multiple razor-sharp teeth pierced her flesh before ripping into her stomach, driving hundreds of miniscule veins into her blood stream. In that moment, she could barely remember her own name as a foreign

OBSIDIAN SOULS

wave of dizziness consumed her. She closed her eyes as her world tipped on its side.

CHAPTER NINE
SAMANTHA

S am woke to quiet voices and for the first time in a long time, felt the urge to cry her heart out. She had a feeling the beautiful lady in the vortex-vision had been Red, which explained why she'd refused her own soul-essence ceremony back in her day. She'd been in love, had a child in secret and had hidden that child, who appeared to be Max's... *mother?* She squeezed her eyes shut tighter, covering her face with her hands. Everything felt upside down. She couldn't take it all in.

"You're awake," a calm voice stated. She opened her eyes to find herself sitting on Red's bed, propped against a mountain of pillows. Her gaze widened as Red's lover in the vision looked at her, waiting to see if she was all right.

She looked past him and cried in relief to see Max, leaning against the door and leapt past the concerned man, running towards Max. He opened his arms and wrapped them around her as she pushed her face into his chest.

"It's okay, Sam, we'll explain everything." He dropped his cheek against the top of her silky, messy bun, made all the messier by her trip through the vortex.

"He looks like you. It doesn't make sense," she whispered into his chest, grateful his strong arms were around her. She was struggling to stay warm with the shock of it all and shivered against him.

"Samantha, dear, let's get you a nice hot cup of tea." Red patted her on the back.

Sam turned and pulled Red into her arms, holding her warm little body close. "You've suffered so much Red and you never told me. Why?" There was a hint of betrayal in Sam's tone.

"Tea first, dear, come on." Red took Sam's hand and led her out of her room and down the small corridor into the cosy kitchen and patted one of the bar stools that sat under the kitchen bench that separated the kitchen and open lounge area.

Sam resignedly sat, glancing at the man who joined Red in her kitchen as she filled teacups.

Max sat beside Sam. "You okay?" he asked.

She glanced up at him. "Do you want an honest answer to that?"

"I only ever want honesty from you Samantha."

I wouldn't bet on that. Sam shielded her thought.

"And honesty is what she shall have," the man replied, pushing a cup of herbal tea towards them both before sitting opposite them.

Sam would have preferred a latte, but said, "Thank you..." She waited, not knowing his name.

"Have you not worked that out yet?" He tilted his head.

She stared at him before raising the cup towards her lips, blowing carefully, then taking a small sip, hoping her silence would answer his question.

Max shifted beside her, his scent, as always, overpowered her senses, but she ignored him. She couldn't get distracted by his proximity just now.

Sam watched Red pat the man's arm lovingly as she said, "Just reveal yourself love; I think Samantha has had enough guessing games tonight."

"You're right, my love, I apologise." He smiled lovingly into Red's shining eyes before stroking her cheek.

As he turned his face back towards Sam, she had to shut her eyes as a blinding silver light filled the room before dying down just as soon as it had flared.

She opened her eyes and gasped as Methuselah sat opposite her where the Max-look-alike had sat. "What does this mean?"

Red smiled. "Let me help you, dear one. I am not the age the council believe and I refused my soul-essence ceremony many, many years ago because my heart and soul already belonged to another."

"You *were* the woman in the other world?"

"I was, although, it was this world before it truly began."

"Are you really a royal-soul?"

"Of course my dear. One of the first."

"And you?" Sam asked, shifting in her seat while Methuselah's silver, pupilless eyes seemed to hang on every thought she tried to keep to herself.

"I am many things, Princess."

Sam shook her head before turning to Max. "He keeps addressing me as 'princess'." She made air quotes.

"Well, you are royalty, Sam. There's nothing unusual about that." Max responded as if it weren't odd whatsoever.

She narrowed her eyes to stop them from rolling as she turned back to Red, who was smiling warmly, patiently waiting.

"I'm sorry." Sam apologised.

Red nodded. "I know it's all a bit overwhelming. I fell in love with Methuselah, which was forbidden. Interspecies relationships were against our laws. A royal soul to be with one of *his* kind was unheard of and punishable by death."

"His kind?" Sam interrupted again and was surprised when she felt Max's large, warm hand slip over her knee and squeeze, silencing her so that Red could continue. She froze, hoping Max would not remove his hand as it was sending a calming, pleasant flow through her. She met Methuselah's gaze and knew instinctively that he knew where Max's hand rested under the opposite side of the bench and that she liked it.

Her narrowed eyes shifted back to Red, who continued. "As I was saying, it was forbidden, but our love was one of the greatest that this universe had ever felt and with it came a healing energy that the entire universe benefited from."

Sam smiled, loving the fact that Red, whom they all thought had never known a great love, seemed to have one of the greatest of all. She had a million questions but bit her tongue.

"Unfortunately, we were only ever able to see each other once a year, as Methuselah's obligations to the world and universe were many, but we made the most of our time."

Red turned to smile up at the handsome man and reached to tuck a silky, silver strand behind his ear. He caught her wrist and lovingly kissed her pulse point.

Sam felt Max's hand tighten around her knee and she wished they could leave to give Red and her eternal love some private time.

"We don't require it, Princess, thank you for your thought though," Methuselah said.

"I shielded that thought," she said, surprised.

He smiled a breathtaking smile and replied, "Nothing in this world can be shielded from me, little one."

"So you already know all the questions I have?"

"I do." He smiled, which she returned as she had just been thinking, *Back to the two worded answers.*

Red continued with her story. "We had a beautiful daughter, who we were blessed to spend fifty-five peaceful years with. It was easy to keep her hidden as I lived far from any other soul, but the time came when she needed to be introduced to the pure-soul world and I had to let her go." Red smiled sadly, which broke Sam's heart.

She reached across the table and grasped Red's soft, wrinkled hand in her own.

"Why Red? Why did you have to keep her hidden? Why give her away?"

"The law would have seen us both put to death."

"Stupid laws." Sam muttered before asking, "You say your daughter was fifty-five when you gifted her with a new life, but she looked to be five?"

Red nodded. "You know we age differently from pure-souls."

"Of course." Sam nodded. "I knew that." She smiled sheepishly, dying to know exactly what Methuselah was and hoped they'd put her out of her misery soon. She was grateful when Methuselah stood, brushing a sweet kiss across Red's hair and tilted his head towards the back door. "Come Princess, Maxwell."

Sam looked at Red, who nodded and felt a small thrill run through her when Max's hand moved from her knee to grasp her hand. They slipped from their stools and followed Methuselah outside. She avoided his knowing glance.

Alana ran from the potting shed and headed straight towards Methuselah who bent to run his fingers through her pelt. "Hello sweet one."

"You gifted her to Red?"

116

"I did." He turned towards them as Red stepped out under the porch and Alana ran towards hers.

"Then that makes her…"

"The oldest fox ever," Max finished.

"And, that ring…" She glanced down at Max's hand, seeing the Obsidian stone wink at her, sitting on Max's finger.

"Yes, a gift from Mother Earth and Red."

"And, once you gifted these things to each other, you never saw each other again?"

"I always saw Red. I see everything, always and forever. And although Red never saw me, she knew I was always watching over her."

Sam nodded, trying to process this information. She had too many questions.

"Red…"

"You want to know what I am." Methuselah interrupted her next question.

"Yes, sorry."

Methuselah's silver eyes glowed so brightly that Sam had to shield hers. Before she could blink, he burst towards the night sky, leaving a trial of silver fire before suddenly stopping to rest amongst the Milky Way.

"A star? That I kind of knew already." Sam looked up at Max, who was stroking his thumb back and forth absently over her knuckles.

"Just wait," he whispered.

You know already?

Yes, this is not the first time I have met Methuselah.

She forced herself not to feel angry that Max had kept her in the dark before, once again, Methuselah began his bright, silent decent back towards them, furiously fast, blinding them with his silver light. He was in front of them in a flash, standing impeccably still in his grey suit.

"So, you're *just* a star?" Sam asked.

"That is where I sit in the universe to watch all that occurs. I appear as a star to the eyes of those below. But up there is a whole other world."

"Heaven?"

"No."

She nodded before asking, "What are you and why were you calling yourself, 'we' earlier."

"Because I am many things, little one." He stepped back and opened his arms wide.

An uncomfortable tingle travelled down Sam's spine and she squeezed Max's hand, fearful of what was about to happen. He squeezed her hand back, reassuringly. An explosion of silver veins shot out of Methuselah; but not from where Sam was expecting them to. Instead of the flesh of his forearms splitting open to release his silver mass of hungry mouths; they exploded out of his shoulder blades and formed massive wings, like that of an angel.

Sam stumbled back as the thousands of lustrous silver veins moved as one, like a silken mass and Methuselah rose ten feet in the air above them.

"What *is* this?" She gasped in wonder at the beautiful, yet eerie vision before her.

Methuselah hovered for a few moments before lowering to the ground; his vein-wings fluttering.

Sam frowned, letting go of Max's hand as she stepped towards the silver wings and reached out to run her fingers along them. They were silky soft to touch, slimy but, not unpleasantly so, which was weird. She looked up at Methuselah as she ran her fingers down the length of wing she could reach.

"Not *nasty* veins?" she tilted her head.

To answer her question, one, lone vein broke away from the others and slid towards her, its tiny mouth opening and she stepped back as she spotted rows of razor-sharp teeth.

"He would never hurt you, Samantha dear," Red called as she joined them on the lawn and ran her hand along Methuselah's large wing before it wrapped around her, bringing her tiny body up against his tall frame.

Sam remained still as Methuselah's vein inched closer before it brushed against her cheek, almost lovingly before returning to the mass.

Sam grinned, looking over her shoulder at Max, who stood silently, arms folded. She thought he had a lot of explaining to do and she still didn't really have answers.

"Samantha." Methuselah demanded she look at him, which she did at his commanding tone.

He held his hand out towards her, which she reached for as Max stepped beside her and clasped her free hand. In a flash, they were whisked in Max's signature green vortex and back in his bedroom before she could draw breath.

Methuselah released her hand and wandered over to Max's photography wall, hands clasped behind his back, vein-wings nowhere to be seen and no Red.

Sam missed her already.

"I am an original. I am both Angel and Vein."

"So, your mum and dad…" Sam tried to work out which one was Vein and which was Angel.

Methuselah turned to her, smiling as he shook his head. "I have no parents, little one. I exist."

Sam blew out a breath as she paced the length of Max's large bed, pulling the band out of her bun. She ran her fingers through her hair and snapped the hair tie onto her wrist, placing her hands on her hips as she continued pacing.

"Okay, I get that you and Red were… lovers, and that you had a daughter together, Rebecca."

"Correct."

She stopped pacing to look into his silver eyes. "That makes you Max's… grandfather?" She looked across at Max who was sitting on a window seat watching her every move. The usual pleasant current of energy passed between them, but she forced her eyes back to Methuselah as he answered her.

"In human terms, although, I am connected to Max in many ways."

Sam nodded, although she was confused with that statement.

"I am, in fact, the creator of all Veins. In the other worlds throughout the Universe, it has been my role to absorb all foreign matter that polluted and destroyed, that did not belong, or add any benefit to that world. Over the billions of years, those worlds, like Mother Earth, became infected, with disease spreading and destroying all in its path. I created the Veins to assist me in the cleansings. That proved successful in the first few millenniums, as we were able to cleanse and cure the worlds. But, in time, the toxicity we absorbed, weakened us and we needed healing energy from Mother Earth. She could only provide so much and I would not risk harming her and so, it was then that I created the Angels to aid in the healing of the Veins. They would feed on the Angel's pure powers to restore their energy. Sadly, overtime, my Veins developed an insatiable hunger for only the good energy they absorbed from the Angels and refused to absorb any more toxicity in the worlds."

"Typical." she interrupted, shrugging when Max shook his head.

Methuselah continued. "It was then that the Angels created the first of the Heavenly and Elemental Royal Soul Keepers to assist me. And not long after that, was when I found and fell in love with Red."

Sam hung onto every word that slipped through Methuselah's

perfect lips and sat on the end of Max's bed to listen, grateful he was getting down to the nitty-gritty details, but one thing didn't make sense to her.

"If you created the Angels, and they created the royal-souls, why was it forbidden for Red to be with you? After all, you seem to be the 'boss' of all things?"

He smiled sadly and shook his head. "Like most great loves throughout time, ours was forbidden by ridiculous notions by the Light Accords, who made the rules for all Soul Keepers."

"Like Romeo and Juliet?" Sam suggested, waiting.

Methuselah inclined his head before continuing. "As the creator of Angels and in turn, the Angels' creator of Royal Soul's, I was considered their creator and them, my children."

"So, not their boss, but their father? They viewed your relationship as incest then. How *ridiculous*." Sam scoffed.

"As it was and as Red said, interspecies relationships were forbidden." Methuselah was silent as if reflecting on that time before continuing.

"After a time, the Veins decided to only add to the toxicity of this world, realising they could grow more powerful when inflicting pain on Mother Earth and her subjects. I begged the Angels for their assistance, to stop the Veins in their destructive behaviours, but they fled, leaving me to deal with the species I'd created and said they would not return until I'd cleaned up the mess I'd made."

Sam felt a pinch of sorrow for him. He'd created the Veins to do good, to heal not just their planet, Mother Earth, but so many other worlds she had no idea had even existed. And then, the Angels he'd created had abandoned him, She frowned. She always knew Angels were fickle creatures... not that she'd ever really met one, but if some of the Light Accords members actions were anything to go by, that spoke volumes.

Methuselah was watching her carefully, as if waiting for her thought flow to stop before he continued. "I did everything in my power to appeal to the Veins. I begged them to see the good in why they were created. I would have forgiven them their crimes if they would have only listened to my appeal. Yet they refused my wishes and so I began to destroy them, one by one, one city at a time."

"That must have been difficult, having to destroy what you created."

Methuselah tilted his head, his pupilless eyes looked towards Max. "We do what we must."

His smooth, cryptic reply sent shivers to dance across her flesh. Sam looked at Max, but he uncharacteristically avoided her eye. She opened her mouth to ask what that was supposed to mean when Methuselah interrupted her.

"When I entered the sinking city, I met a Vein who had power unlike any I'd ever encountered during my process of elimination. He led me to believe he would help me exterminate his brethren, but, alas, he betrayed me and used my own essence to destroy me."

"Brendan?" Samantha spat in disgust.

"Yes, you saw the vision when my beautiful Rebecca gave birth to Maxwell and his siblings. Brendan absorbed the remainder of my essence, which had surrounded Max before his birth."

"Max, not the others?" Sam looked at Max, who had grown tired of sitting and was standing by the far wall, looking out towards the mountain.

"Correct."

"Is that why Brendan was so strong? Because of your blood-essence?"

"Partly and because he was the first one I created."

"Oh." Sam frowned, thinking of everything she'd been told in the past few hours. "Earlier, you said you were showing me the past, present and future. That battle, all those Veins here, slaughtering us..."

122

She looked at Max, wondering if Methuselah had shown him the same vision.

"Will be the future if Maxwell continues on his quest of convincing Veins to change their ways from evil to good."

"I'm not changing my mind." Max spoke for the first time in what seemed like forever.

"I know and for that, I respect you more than I thought possible." Methuselah smiled fondly at Max.

Her anger rose with the familiar, almost loving exchange between the two men. Fury on behalf of Max for all the years he'd been abandoned and alone, lost and fighting his way through confusion and unknown rules. And now, here stood a relative with ultimate power who could have saved Max from all the suffering he'd endured, the loneliness and longing for true family connections.

A ripple of energy ran along her flesh as she addressed Methuselah.

"Where were *you* when Max's dad and his evil cousin tormented him with a rotten childhood? Where were *you*, when he was lost, alone and had no idea what was happening when his dark-essence was activated and he absorbed *my* sister's soul-essence? And where were *you* when the council hunted him down and made him out to be a *criminal*, a *parasite*. Where were *you*...?" She could feel her blood boiling within her.

"*Samantha*!" Max said, his tone abrupt, a trace of fear lingering in his tone.

She turned blazing eyes towards him and saw him flinch and was horrified to see pinpoint blue flames licking along the floorboards and circling him, waist-high. She gasped and called the flames away, flushing guiltily.

Her protective thoughts towards Max had circled him, but her fury had turned them to the hottest of flames.

123

"I'm sorry," she crossed to him, placing her hand on his arm. "Did I hurt you?"

He shook his head, placing his hand on top of hers. "Never."

They both knew that was a lie. She had hurt him, although it was unintentionally done, through her soul-partner ceremony to Peter. She didn't want to take her eyes off Max, but Methuselah continued.

"To answer your questions, Princess. Brendan had imprisoned me, using an impenetrable force field that not even I could escape. He had weakened me considerably and had all but consumed the last drop of my essence and I could feel myself fading. Luckily, the Arch Angel Azazel, took pity on my plight and returned to Mother Earth to rescue me."

"Azazel?" Sam frowned. Of all the Angel's, she wouldn't have thought *he'd* be the one to lend anyone in need, a hand.

"Yes." Methuselah continued. "He was furious that the Angel's had turned their backs on me; their creator." He smiled at the memory. "There was only one place I could go, if I ever hoped to recover and that was my other world… but, I could not leave without saying fare-well to my beloved Red. And so Azazel granted me that final wish." He strolled towards them and stopped just short of crowding their personal space.

"Once I ascended, I could do nothing but watch on as the army I had created to do good continued to destroy. It was when Maxwell made the ultimate decision to lead willing Veins on a different path that I found myself by his side in an instant. His determination to help those who wanted change and who wanted to work as one, towards a brighter future for all souls and Mother Earth, is ultimately what restored my essence."

"So, you're here for good? You'll fight with us when the time comes?" Sam was hopeful that the vision of Max, dead, could be avoided with Methuselah's help. That hope faded as she watched Methuselah shake his head once. She frowned, folding her arms, but bit her tongue and tried not to think a negative thought about Methuselah right at that moment.

He heard it regardless. "This is not my journey, Princess, but Maxwell's."

"Sam, Methuselah and I spent many months together while I was in Europe. I'm prepared for what's coming."

"Are you?" she asked. "Do you actually know what's coming? Because I've seen your lawn turned from green to red as a bloodbath was shed and it wasn't looking good for any of us."

She returned her gaze to Methuselah, only to find him in her personal space. She was about to take a step back when he grasped her upper arm and drew her against him. His silver vein-wings exploded out from his shoulder blades. She swallowed, not sure what the 'creator of many' planned to do but being so close to his 'silveriness' made her nervous, despite the fact she knew he would not harm her.

In a flash, his wings enveloped her and everything in the room disappeared from view except for iridescent silver. She forced herself not to panic as his veins stroked her flesh, moved in her hair and along her body as if searching for an entry point, dropping thousands of tiny little kisses over her, causing involuntary shivers. She gasped as she felt a tiny bite on her neck and immediately, the headache that had been coming and going, flared angrily once more.

"You were created for one specific reason, Samantha Storm," he murmured against her ear.

"Yeah, I know, to be soul-sibling and protector to Angel Cloud before her essence connected her to her soul-partner," she whispered.

He smiled his ethereal smile down at her, as he shook his head once. "Don't believe everything the Light Accords tell you, Princess. You were created for what yet has not come to pass."

"Could you possibly be any more cryptic?" She frowned, feeling more confused as this conversation continued. She tugged her arm from his grasp and stepped back, colliding with Max's chest, which she didn't mind so much and stayed right where she was.

"I think that's enough for one night, Methuselah." Max said, placing a large hand on her shoulder.

Sam bit her lip, thinking she had only about a hundred more questions.

"And they shall be answered, Princess, when you wake up."

"Wake up?" she frowned.

He smiled, tilting his head. "Of course, you just have to wake up, Samantha. Wake up."

CHAPTER TEN
SAMANTHA

"Wake up Sam. Wake up!"

She bolted upright, startled as repetitive banging outside her door broke her free from the uncomfortable dream. If it weren't for the throbbing in her neck where Methuselah's vein bit-kissed her, she would've been convinced last night had been just that. One big, confusing, complicated dream. Her headache niggled in a nasty manner.

"What?" She groaned, rubbing her palms against her eyes, feeling disoriented.

"Open up, Sam."

She slid off the bed with a sigh, crying out as the sheet entangled around her legs. She lost her balance and fell in a heap to the floor. Then she groaned when the doona slipped off the bed to cover her completely. She went to push it off, but feeling utterly exhausted, gave up and lay back amongst the pile, not bothering to move. The banging stopped as the door opened and footsteps crossed towards her. The intruder of her sleep pulled the doona back to peer down at her.

She frowned up at Max, who was offering a hand to pull her up. She slapped it away before folding her arms, noticing he looked fresh and handsome in his usual calm, pleasant state.

He grinned, tilting his head, silky hair falling into bright eyes as he studied her for a moment before squatting down. "You okay?"

She refused to answer.

"Samantha, are you alright?" He reached across and brushed soft waves of hair from her furious amber eyes as she lay glaring up at him.

She knew it was silly, but her exhaustion, the pesky headache and confusion with whatever the hell had happened last night was triggering tears.

"Hey," he said, his grin fading as he reached for her. "Come here."

"No." She avoided his reach and rolled away. She scrambled to her feet and headed across to the bathroom, wiping tears away, angry they were there in the first place.

She turned the tap on and splashed cold water onto her tired face, hoping it would give her time to calm the storm she felt brewing within her. Drying her face, she winced feeling her neck sting where she was bitten.

"Do you want to talk about it?"

She spun around and stalked back towards him and she could see by the look on his face, her storm of emotions hadn't calmed.

"Did what I think happened last night actually happen? Was it real?"

"Yes, it was."

"Where did Methuselah go? And how did I end up in bed?"

As Max was about to answer, Daniel knocked against the doorframe. "Excuse me Max, I…" He didn't get a chance to finish as Sam whispered to the air and flicked her hand towards the door, slamming it in Daniel's face, her eyes not leaving Max's.

"I guess I'll see you downstairs, Daniel called, a hint of concern in his voice.

"I'll be down soon," Max replied as he frowned at Sam, displeased with her. He folded his arms. "Was that really necessary?"

Sam shrugged, feeling volatile. "I want some answers. *Now.*"

"When Methuselah disappeared in a trial of stardust, you passed out and I carried you to bed." He shrugged.

"He told me I was created for something that had yet come to pass. What does that even mean?"

It was Max's turn to look confused. "I didn't hear him say anything like that, Sam."

"It was when he put his vein-wings around me! Surely, they're not soundproof?"

Max raised an eyebrow, confused.

After running her hands through her hair in frustration, she let out a deep sigh, shaking her head. "So, you're related to a pretty-big-deal, huh?" She raised an eyebrow.

"Apparently."

"I'd like to hear what the council have to say about that after everything they've put you through." She folded her arms.

"Me too, which, is why I was banging on your door. We've been summoned before the Light Accords."

"Why?"

Max shrugged. "I guess we'll find out. I'll wait downstairs for you. Take your time, you look like you need it."

She narrowed her eyes dangerously. "Thanks a lot."

He sighed. "Are you okay?"

She shrugged. "I feel a bit washed out, but, if you make me a toasted sandwich when I'm done here, I'm sure I'll feel more like my old self."

"Done. Sandwich and a latte will be waiting for you."

"Thanks." She headed to the bathroom and closed the door. When the water ran hot, she stripped off and stepped under the reviving spray, wondering when she would have a conversation with Max, regarding their 'just friends' status.

MAXWELL

Max ran downstairs, hoping the shower would help Sam feel better. He'd never seen her look so depleted. He paused for a moment, outside the cellar door and closed his eyes, sensing that Kyle was still sleeping. After he'd tucked Sam into bed last night, he'd returned to Kyle and had taken him outside via the tunnel entrance. They'd walked up the mountain, talking for a few hours, sharing a bit of their past with each other. He'd learned that although Kyle had led a life of destruction and death, it wasn't one of his choosing, which pulled at his heartstrings.

He felt comfortable enough to share his plans with Kyle, to return the Veins to their old ways, in which they'd originally been created for. To do good. To absorb evil. When Kyle heard about Methuselah and Red, he'd begged Max to allow him to join his quest. He said it was only fair that he too, had the chance to meet his family and be a part of something greater than what he'd been subjected to his entire life.

He'd agreed and was giving Kyle the chance to prove himself and had left the tunnel unlocked, so Kyle could discreetly come and go and remain hidden for a short time. He did not want the Light Accords knowing he'd helped his triplet escape. Kyle was happy with this current arrangement, knowing he could walk the property and mountain freely whilst the others were sleeping and still be shielded from the High Council. Max knew he'd have to tell Sam, but now wasn't the time. She'd already been bombarded with an overwhelming amount of information in the past twenty-four-hours. He didn't want to overdo it.

Heading into the kitchen, Daniel all but pounced on him. "Max, I'm sorry, I didn't mean to interrupt anything up there." He pointed above their heads.

Max shook his head as he clapped Daniel on the back before grabbing ingredients to make Sam a gourmet toasted sandwich. "Don't apologise. Sam just had a rough night and needs a bit of TLC."

Daniel nodded. "I just wanted to let you know that Nadine and Trent went for a horse ride. They left the property an hour ago."

Max paused before he continued popping filling in between two thick slices of bread, then sliding it into the focaccia maker. He reached for a mug to make Sam's latte and said, "That should be fine."

"You said no one was supposed to leave the property?"

"I advised you all, for your own safety and that of the pure-souls, that it would be best if you *didn't* leave the property, until you felt more in control of your urges. I'm sure they'll be fine." He felt an unfamiliar flare of anger they'd left without telling him themselves. He didn't expect them to ask, he wasn't a dictator like Brendan had been. Still, he'd suggested rules for the protection of all.

The back door opened and Gemma and Rick strolled in looking like they'd had a busy morning already attending to the chores.

"Morning," Gemma smiled brightly when she saw him.

He returned her smile. "Good morning." He turned as footsteps ran downstairs and he was pleased to see Sam looking more like her usual sunny self. In fact, she looked mouth-watering. Golden strands framed her face with waves falling down her back, eyes sparkled like amber jewels and an easy smile flitted across her pretty lips. Her tee shirt had a large horse eye staring at him soulfully and her jeans clung to strong thighs; her high tops affording her a bit more height.

Sam's eyes met his before she addressed Daniel. "Morning." She smiled sheepishly. "Sorry about before."

Daniel shook his head. "All good."

She rubbed Gemma's back before sitting up on a bar stool. "Hello Rick."

"Hello sunshine." He leaned close to Sam before asking in a husky voice. "Do you think Bowie will return for more training soon?"

Sam's eyes glinted before she met Max's as he pushed her sandwich and latte across the marble bench towards her. "I'm sure we can arrange that, can't we, Max?"

He reached for his tea, taking a mouthful before answering. "Of course."

"Sweet!" Rick exclaimed as he headed out of the room.

Gemma grabbed a glass and filled it with water. "Have I got time for a shower before training?"

"You do. Sam and I have to go out for a bit, so take some time out."

"Oh that sounds great. Can I borrow a book and sit at your pond?"

He smiled at the always pleasant girl, who seemed content with the simplest of things. "Your pond, Gemma. This is your home now." He watched her flush as she looked at Sam before meeting his eyes, then ducking her head.

"Thanks." She nodded before heading out of the room.

He watched her until she disappeared before returning his gaze to Sam, who was chewing and watching him thoughtfully.

"What?" he asked after she continued staring, a knowing glint in her gorgeous eyes.

She shook her head. "If you don't know, Maxwell, then I'm more concerned for you than I thought."

He raised an eyebrow as he took another mouthful of tea, watching as she picked up her mug. "Glad to see you're back in fine 'Samantha

Storm' form."

"Are you? What you mean is, you're glad to see I'm looking calmer and not ready to rip more answers from that precious mouth of yours?" She smiled beautifully at him before finishing her latte.

He chuckled, bravely, considering he could see fire flicker behind her eyes.

"You are so related to Bowie." He shook his head, reaching for her empty plate and mug to put in the sink with his. "Come on, let's go, don't want to keep the council waiting."

"Angels forbid if we did that." Sam slid off the stool. "How are we getting there?"

He smiled and tilted his head towards the front of the house. "I'll show you."

He headed towards the fireplace and stood up on the raised hearth, holding a hand down to her.

"Oh goody, another portal." Her smile was saccharine-sweet when she looked up at him.

"Come on, you know you love it." By the narrowing of her eyes, he knew she was about to say something sarcastic, but he closed the distance between them, grabbing her hand and pulling her up beside him. He couldn't help the small shiver of satisfaction as her eyes widened when he slipped his arm about her waist.

He placed his hand on the photograph with the five elms that stood grandly in Quick's paddock. In an instant, they were sucked through an electric blue wild wind before being transported to the crumbling fortress where Sam had met Methuselah the night before. Ancient cobble-stones met their feet and damp scented the air. Max kept his arm around Sam's waist until she got her balance.

As he removed his arm, she whispered. "You're lucky my breakfast stayed down."

He grinned. "I'm grateful it did."

"Hm." She murmured, looking around them.

He forced his gaze off her lovely face before turning, intrigued to see only Fletch, Tom Liam and Michael Cloud.

Sam squealed when she saw the men and ran towards Michael, throwing her arms around him and kissing him noisily on the cheek before doing the same to Tom.

"Well, this is all a bit formal for just us." She grinned at them before clearing her throat, turning to Fletch. "Hello."

"Hello Samantha, Maxwell." Fletch addressed them solemnly. "And, unfortunately, this situation calls for more than *just us*." Fletch waved his hand and twenty Light Accord Council members surrounded them. They looked official in their amethyst capes, which fluttered about them in the breeze.

Max felt a familiar prickle of unease whenever those amethyst capes surrounded him and folded his arms, hoping it didn't look like a defensive gesture. "What situation?" he asked.

Sam turned towards him before looking over her shoulder at Fletch, then returned to Max's side, standing close, hands on hips. He felt her intention to defend him and pushed a calming vibe towards her.

It's going to be fine Sam; I've done nothing wrong. He shielded his thought from everyone but her.

That hasn't stopped them in the past though, has it? Her eyes met his before they both turned their attention towards Fletch, waiting.

"Maxwell Black, you assured us that when you brought Veins to Noorat, no harm would befall any pure-soul."

"That's right. I did," he replied, wondering where this was going.

"Last night, a group of campers were slaughtered. Sucked dry by what can only be described as feral leeches. We've never seen anything like it."

Max shook his head, frustrated that the council would typically blame Veins.

"And you assume it was my clan?"

"Your clan?"

"Yes, my Obsidian Souls."

"Nice," Michael said.

"From a Soul Keeper, to an Obsidian Soul. I like it." Tom agreed with Michael before Fletch raised a hand to silence them.

"Obsidian Souls?" Fletch raised an eyebrow.

Max shook his head, not elaborating.

Fletch answered. "We do assume it was your, Obsidian Souls."

Max scoffed. "I assure you; my clan were tucked up last night safe and sound and in no way caused any harm to a pure-soul."

"You can guarantee this?"

"I can."

"Regardless, this was Veins and we haven't had any activity of the sort until you returned."

Max shrugged, running his hand through his hair in frustration. He didn't know what to say. "I can only tell you it wasn't us."

"If that's the case, then we have a problem."

"I agree." Max nodded.

"Well, that's a council problem though, isn't it, not Max's?" Sam asked. "And this could have as easily been addressed by sending Michael or Tom to the mansion."

"We're not finished, Samantha." Fletch clipped out each word. "If this wasn't your *Souls*, Maxwell, then other Veins have swarmed the area. This was not a single attack and until you came back, all has been quiet since Angel and Samantha destroyed your cousin."

"What would you like me to do about it?" Max said.

"You must have had some idea that there would be a rebellion of some kind, with your attempt to turn parasites into something decent!"

Max's spine stiffened and his fury, simmering to a boil, burst to the surface of his calm resolve. Before he could even think to defend his clan and what he was doing, Sam bristled beside him.

"I. *Beg*. Your. Pardon." She spat each word out in a quiet tone as she stepped forward, eyes blazing.

Static swept over Max's flesh, charged with Sam's fury. He met Michael's look of alarm.

Keep her calm, for both your sakes. Michael pushed towards him. He nodded once to let Michael know he'd heard him.

Max could feel the energy of resentment spark off Sam and reached out to clasp her hand in his, startling as a static shock passed between them. He pulled her back beside him and shook his head once as she looked up at him. *Calm down, love.*

He watched her pretty lips part and her cheeks fill with a becoming pink before she averted her eyes, shielding her thoughts from him.

He took a steadying breath and addressed the council. "I understand your concern for the pure-souls. It's why I'm doing what I can to encourage and support my kind who wish to walk a different path from the one they've been ordered to."

"That may be so, but until we feel we can trust your Obsidian Souls, I am sending Red out to place a boundary spell around your property to ensure none of your Veins leave without our permission, or an escort of some sort."

"I'd like to see you try that," Max said in a much too calm voice.

"Would you? Perhaps a stint in a prison cell would help you rethink your stance on our decision?"

Max laughed. "I'd *really* like to see you try that."

Max, what are you doing? Michael pushed towards his three family members.

He is about to kick arse, Sam brushed back. *And I am about to help.*

Sam, Max, deep breaths, please. Tom joined in their chat.

Deep breaths? Tom, are you hearing this conversation at all? Sam scoffed.

Before Tom could reply, Max squeezed Sam's hand as he felt her anger spark between their joined palms again. *Sam, It's okay.*

It is so not okay, I am disgusted and not for the first time, with how the council treat you. Don't they know if it wasn't for your grandfather creating the Angels, they wouldn't even exist? Actually, neither would I. Should I start calling you my Prince, or bowing to you or something? She shielded the last part of their conversation so only Max could hear.

Max couldn't help himself and chuckled as he met Sam's gaze, happy to see her return his smile. The fire in her amber eyes banked for the moment.

"What is this?" A council member stepped forward, a furious look on his face. "Do you think this is some kind of joke? Do you think Veins slaughtering a group of pure-souls is funny? Where is your *compassion?*" he cried.

Max, Samantha, what are you two up to? Michael demanded.

Sorry mate, no disrespect to you, or Tom. Max pushed towards Michael and Tom before he addressed Fletch and the others.

"No, I don't think that deplorable act is funny whatsoever. What I'm struggling with, despite everything, is your total lack of faith in me. You've never let me forget that I was never completely one of you. That I couldn't be trusted, regardless of the fact that I am *half* royal-soul. For the longest time that bothered me. As a young boy when I found out about my despicable family, I struggled, riddled with guilt by my innocent association with them. I tried to do everything to fit into your world, even though your world was also mine. If it weren't for the Soul Keepers of Glenormiston South, I could've easily fallen and given into my dark side. There was a brief time when I thought it would have suited me better."

He felt Sam cringe as images of her and Peter after their soul-essence ceremony filtered through his mind towards hers. He'd been in such despair, feeling lost, hurt and alone. To turn towards the darkness would have filled that empty void of losing Sam. He tightened his grip on her hand in apology before continuing.

"Yet, despite your treatment towards me, I've always remained loyal to the Soul Keepers ways, protecting the pure-souls and Mother Earth and I shall continue doing so moving forward. But on my terms, not yours."

"I beg your pardon?" Fletch's eyes widened in disbelief as the other council members muttered their discord at his statement.

"I am no longer yours to rule, or command. Red is always welcome, but not to cast a boundary spell around my property."

"What are you saying Maxwell Black? That you are no longer with us?"

Max shook his head. "I'm known now as Maxwell Obsidian and I will always be faithful to the Soul Keepers ways in defending the innocent. But I will no longer be taking orders from you or receiving any punishments that you dictate, nor will any Vein under my protection. If that's all, I have to be getting back."

Fletch took a step forward, concern etched in his ever-serious face. "You cannot do this, Maxwell."

"It's already done." Max waved his hand and an emerald portal opened up.

The fortress filled with disbelieving gasps that one so young and a half royal-soul at that, had conjured a portal so easily.

"Samantha Storm, you will remain with us," a commanding voice called from amongst the amethyst capes.

Max looked down at Sam, releasing her hand. "It's up to you whether you come with me."

The portal whipped a wild wind around them and Sam's golden locks flew around her like a silken cape as she looked up at him.

It's okay, Samantha, go with Max. Max heard Michael push towards them.

Sam stepped towards Max and wrapped her arms around his waist, pushing her face into his chest. He stepped into the portal, taking her with him.

CHAPTER ELEVEN
SAMANTHA

Sam remained still, her face pressed against Max's chest when the world stopped spinning. She could hear his heart beating, feel his arms firmly around her, his chin resting against the top of her head. She pulled in a slow breath, breathing as much of him in and making the most of every second being in his arms; his scent of orange and sandalwood wrapping around her in a comforting way.

"What just happened?" she whispered.

"I believe I've just banished myself from the Light Accords council."

"That's what I thought."

"Are you sure you've made the right decision coming back with me?" he asked, releasing her from the pleasant nest of his chest as she looked up at him.

"Of course." She thought about Michael's gentle persuasion and wished her family were here also, so Max could tell them about Methuselah and Red.

"What thoughts are swirling around in that beautiful brain of yours, Samantha Storm?" he asked, running his hand over her hair before cupping her chin and staring into her eyes.

She swallowed as a flutter of butterflies kicked off on the runway of her stomach and launched around her insides when his thumb brushed against her bottom lip. Then they exploded into a swarm of bliss as his dark eyes drank her in, his lips parting slightly.

He was so *damn* beautiful, and she was falling. Again. Hard. She needed one taste. Just one.

"If you stop me," she whispered, closing any distance between them. "I'm going to zap you."

She thrilled as his head lowered, eyes darkening as he replied in a husky whisper,

"I wouldn't dream of stopping you, Samantha," his lips a breath away from hers.

She sighed, smiling seductively before his mouth claimed hers. She could have wept in that moment and stretched on her toes to wrap her arms around his neck, pressing herself as close to him as possible. Every inch of her body that came into contact with his hummed in pleasure and she felt an urgency from him she'd been longing to feel in what seemed like forever.

In an instant, he moulded her against him like a second skin, his large hand splayed across the small of her back as he reached with his other to cradle the back of her head, angling it to deepen their kiss.

She moaned as he slid his tongue on a silken trespass into her mouth, twirling hungrily against hers before his lips assaulted hers repeatedly.

She slid her fingers into his silken locks, drawing him closer, wanting to eat him right up as she sucked on his tongue, rubbing against him like a cat in heat. She gasped when he lifted her hips, wrapping her legs tightly around him as he cupped her bottom, nestling her closer as if that were even possible.

In three strides he was at the bed and after another mind-blowing kiss that had her head reeling, he reached for the hem of her tee shirt and ripped it over her head before placing her on his bed, which felt like a cloud beneath her.

She tried to catch her breath, watching him as he tugged his shirt over his head, revealing a muscular six pack and narrow waist. Her mouth watered as her gaze followed the fine line of dark hair that trailed under his waistband. She bit her lip when he popped the top button of his jeans and he grinned. Giddy with excitement and desire, she wriggled out of her own jeans and underwear.

"Finally,," she whispered as she reached behind her and unclipped her bra.

He laughed when she lay back like a content kitten, waiting for her bowl of cream. He crept towards her, forest-green eyes pinning her in place before he positioned his body an inch above hers. An electric pulse hummed in the surrounding air, filling them with a pleasant heat, increasing every second they looked at each other.

This is going to be fast, I'm sorry to say, she brushed against his mind.

Don't be sorry, sweetheart, he replied, sweeping his hand up along her thigh, across her hip, over her stomach before cupping her breast, flicking his thumb across her plump nipple, making her see stars. He lowered his lips to hers; the anticipation was killing her. His scent beckoned her like the call a siren; mesmerizing and blocking the world itself out. His lips slid across hers, opening hers wider, the tip of his tongue gliding over her bottom lip, sucking it into his mouth. Molten lava pooled between her thighs and a pulse beat flared as he kissed her like she was the most beautiful creature on earth.

You are.

She moaned as he swept the hair from the side of her neck before pushing his face against her warm skin, trailing his nose along her flesh, taking a deep breath like he was inhaling her essence. Sam shivered in anticipation as he stroked his hand along her soft belly before his fingers dipped lower to cup her moist core. She could have wept with sheer delight as his fingers played her like a familiar instrument, hitting every cord correctly. His lips ascended along the trail his nose had taken and she shivered, goosebumps forming under his lips as they slid along her flesh. He sucked on her earlobe before kissing her cheek, then collecting her lips once more as he stirred a pulsing fire between her legs.

She wantonly moved against his hand as she returned his passionate kisses, feeling a pool of emotions flood to the surface that she'd kept at bay for months. Sam forced any regret and pain away, focusing on the here and now, running her hands along the smooth, firm flesh of his back, then up into his hair, returning his feverish kisses with every bit of love and hunger she'd ever felt for him.

He was driving her crazy with his skilful, knowing strokes against her core and knew if she didn't stop him right at that moment, she would melt then and there. She refused to have their first time back together be her exploding in ecstasy, separate from him, and pushed against his shoulders, forcing him away for a split second.

When she saw confusion dance in his beautiful eyes, she grinned sexily.

"Sorry, I can't wait one second longer." She flipped him on his back and grabbed the length of his pulsing member, feeling a flash of satisfaction as his eyes closed in ecstasy.

"Open up, Maxwell… I want you to see what you do to me when I take you inside."

His eyelids drifted open, and he pinned her in place with a stare filled with desire. She bit her lip shaking her head as his hands swept up her sides, holding her hips as his thumbs made slow, hypnotic circles over her flesh.

He raised an eyebrow, and she laughed before leaning down, pausing to rub her nose against his as she whispered, "I've never wanted you more than right at this moment, Maxwell Obsidian." He pulled in a deep breath as her hand rhythmically pumped his pulsing shaft before her lips collected his in a mouth-watering dance of passion.

She positioned his tip near her moist entrance, then slid down upon him, watching his eyes cloud over as she stilled, taking all of him in, embracing the moment. Sam ran a finger along his cheekbone and began to move, taking him deep inside her before moving up, his tip almost leaving her warmth before sliding back down.

Sighs were matched as he trailed his fingers along her flesh, damp with passion before holding his palms up to her. She smiled as she rocked against him and slid her palms to fit against his as his fingers wrapped around hers. He thrust his hips to penetrate her, hitting her core and sending sparks of pleasure within her. As she rocked, Max sat up and placed their entwined hands behind her back, holding her tenderly.

Sam lost herself to the sensations building as each thrust, slide and glide made her lose her grip on reality. She dropped her head back, sighing and closing her eyes, absorbing every sensation Max's lips delivered as he trailed sweet kisses along her jaw and neck, igniting a wildfire within her. She wrestled her hands out of his, sliding them up his chest before slipping them around his neck, dropping hot kisses along his flesh before her lips met his.

As they pumped and rocked, the fiery passion building against each other, a glorious fire danced within her, creating a beat of lust that had her pulse points sparking towards an all-consuming inferno. Their gazes locked, and they drank from each other as if their thirst would never be quenched. An intense orgasm burst within her, stealing her breath away. As it peaked and swelled, Max pumped into and against her. She almost sobbed in delight as her body continued to throb in pleasure. He tightened his arms around her, dropping his face into the crook of her neck as he shuddered inside of her, breathing heavily against her skin.

They were silent for what felt like forever. Sam shielded her thoughts from him as her mind raced. Where would this leave them?

"Sam? Why are you shielding your thoughts?" He began a gentle massage on her back, stirring instant longing deep within her again.

She sighed and leaned back in his arms to meet his steady gaze, thrilled when, with his eyes locked on hers, he brought her flush up against him to kiss her solidly.

When he released her, she smiled and said, "I'm shielding my thoughts, so you won't be able to see my mind doing cartwheels. Don't want you getting an ego." She smirked, causing him to laugh.

"Me, an ego?"

She ran her fingers through his hair, smiling. "I know, as if, right?"

He collected a handful of her hair and tilted her head back to trail another lingering kiss across her lips.

She could sense a wave of regret seeping from him and stilled in his arms.

"What the *hell* was that? Regret?"

"No, not regret. It's just that I'd planned on keeping you at a safe distance, so I could…"

"Don't you dare say it, Maxwell." She glared at him.

"Okay," he whispered, fingers running back down the flesh of her back to collect her hips before flipping her onto her back with lightning speed. Her breath whooshed out as he slid back inside her in the swiftest stroke, penetrating her and making her eyes cloud over in sheer bliss. "I won't say it," he said in a husky whisper as he thrust inside her repeatedly, sending them both out of their minds. The morning passed in a blur of passion as they made up for all the lost months they'd been forced apart.

Memories surfaced, surrounding them with those first moments of young love, to discovering Max was half royal-soul. Then the time when they had made love for the first time and all the moments in between before the heart break of when Sam had to attend her soul-essence ceremony, connecting to Peter and being forced apart from Max. Followed by Peter being slaughtered by Brendan. The horrifying moments where the council declared Max their enemy before hunting him and worse, when Max absorbed essence that he shouldn't have, including Angel's. Hundreds of shared memories swam between them as they worshiped each other and every touch, kiss and stroke filled the other with a deeper love and contentment they'd both not felt for months on end.

MAXWELL

Max grinned as he rubbed the towel through his hair, watching Sam get dressed after they'd shared a lengthy shower together.

With a raised eyebrow, she straightened after pulling her boots on. "Enjoying the view?"

"You know I am."

She returned his grin. "I know something else, too."

"Do tell."

"I know how happy you are right in this moment because I am too." She crossed over to him, standing an inch away.

He smiled.

"And I guess that makes our conversation regarding, 'just friends,' void?"

He sighed, shaking his head as he bent and brushed his lips across hers, enjoying the taste of her sweetness. "Honeysuckle," he whispered before deepening the kiss, which she seemed more than happy to return before a desperate energy hit him. He pulled back, frowning.

"What is it?" she asked, concerned.

"We're about to find out." He threw the towel towards the hook and crossed towards the door before pounding shattered his concern. He pulled it open to reveal Gemma, hand raised in mid-knock, stark white, with tears in her eyes.

"What's wrong?" He placed a hand on her shoulder, feeling her tremble beneath his touch.

Gemma looked past him at Sam before replying shakily, "It's Nadine and Trent. They were attacked."

"Are they injured?" he asked, heading down the stairs.

"Yes," she said, following him, Sam five steps behind them.

He kept the dialogue of curse words shielded as he hit the bottom step, then headed down the corridor towards the open lounge, cringing when he saw Nadine laying on the couch, covered in blood. Trent stood beside her, not looking much better.

"What happened?" He touched Trent's shoulder before kneeling down to run a hand over Nadine's face.

"I'll get some water and clothes." Sam said before disappearing.

"We were ambushed," Nadine replied angrily, despite the fact she looked like she had no energy.

"Not just ambushed," Trent cut in.

Max turned to look up at him as Sam returned with a bowl of water that swam with healing herbs. He made room so she could deal with Nadine.

Hands on hips, he waited for Trent to continue.

"Here." Sam passed Trent a wet cloth before turning back to Nadine, wiping blood from her face.

"Thanks." Trent ran the cloth over his face as he continued. "We weren't just ambushed; we were leeched off by other Veins," he spat out disgustedly.

Sam's head whipped up. "What?" Passing the cloth to Gemma, she stood.

"Yeah and they gave us a message. That they will suck every one of us dry if we continue on our treacherous path, betraying the Veins' ways."

"Treacherous? What garbage," Gemma muttered, cleaning Nadine's face and neck.

"Oh, I wished I'd been with you," Rick cracked his knuckles, a gleam of murder in his eyes.

"It wouldn't have mattered," Nadine said, pushing herself up into a sitting position, taking the cloth from Gemma. "There were over twenty of them and one of them wasn't human?"

"Well, technically, are any of us?" Daniel raised an eyebrow.

Gemma rolled her eyes. "Seriously?"

"Debatable, if you look at our past," Rick joined in.

Max held a hand up, cutting off their banter. "Repeat that?"

Nadine sighed, "One of them wasn't human. He couldn't have been, he was… a *mostro*."

"But he was Vein?" Max asked.

"Unlike any we've ever seen, but yes," Trent said.

He watched Sam rub her arms, as if chilled and frowned as he felt her shield her next thought. Their eyes met he ran his hand through his hair.

"A modified, monster-Vein?" Sam whispered.

Max glared at Nadine, then Trent. "This was one of the reasons why I didn't want you leaving the property. Not just for the sake of any pure-soul, but for any resistance within the surviving circles of Veins that may be hunting us."

"Sorry." Trent dropped his gaze.

"What are we going to do, Max?" Nadine stood, pushing her silken mass of red locks, drenched with blood, off her shoulders.

"First things first, you both need to go shower, then meet me out in the carriage house. We'll revive you with some healing herbs."

Nadine nodded. "I don't think I've ever felt so dirty having all those tiny mouths feeding off me, sliding inside me." She shuddered.

Sam rubbed her arm. "You'll feel better after a shower and I'll help Max with the healing."

Nadine met her gaze and placed her hand on top of Sam's. "Thank you."

"Sam, while they shower, will you help me out with a protective boundary spell?"

"Of course." She nodded. "Shall I ask Red to assist us?"

He shook his head, seeing tears slip from Nadine's eyes. He placed a finger beneath her chin, lifting her face. "I'm sorry this happened to you."

"They *know* where we live. They were waiting for us," she cried, lifting her chin out of his hand before pushing past him on shaky legs.

"Come on." Gemma followed, slipping her arm around Nadine's waist. "Let's get you in the shower, then restored."

"Thanks, Gemma," Max said. "Trent, go on, you'll feel better after you wash that blood off."

Trent nodded, handing him the bloody cloth before heading upstairs to his bathroom.

"What a shemozzle." Rick shook his head as Max headed out the back door.

"What can I do?" Daniel asked.

"Can you make lunch? I know it's late, but food always helps," Sam said as she followed Max outside.

"Yep, on it." Daniel replied.

"I'll make coffee," Rick offered.

"Thanks," Max said before Sam joined him and together they headed towards the pond.

"So," Sam said as she stood by his side looking out across the water, "you can create protective barriers now?"

"I can."

"What else can you do?"

"Oh, you know, this and that." He sounded tired, even to his own ears. He had so much hope not just for his clan, but for others who may join them. He expected resistance, but for his new family to be attacked whilst under his protection. It didn't sit well with him whatsoever.

Sam tilted her head as she turned to face him fully. "I'm sorry they were hurt." She reached up to trace a finger across his cheekbone.

He took hold of her hand, bringing it up to his lips to drop an absent kiss against her wrist. "Whoever they were, they will suffer," he said and watched her eyes widen.

"That's unlike you, Maxwell," she whispered. "Wanting them to suffer."

He shook his head. "Not really. They obviously know what I'm attempting to do here and instead of joining us, they've marked themselves our enemy. They deserve what's coming to them. But first, protective barrier."

"How can I help?"

He reached for her hand, smiling a little. "Be my spark," he said before turning his gaze towards the mountain.

SAMANTHA

She watched Max close his eyes, feeling a stir in the surrounding air as he raised his free hand and began whispering in a language she did not understand. It was intricate, ancient and beautiful as the words flowed from his lips; like poetry that was felt, but not understood.

Our Maxwell speaks another language, creates portals, barriers and no doubt possesses other magical powers I have no idea about. The wind increased and her hair stirred about her shoulders. Max raised his voice and drew a circle in the air with his hand and as he continued to chant, she also heard him say, "Sam, spark the energy, please."

She followed where he'd indicated and saw the black outline of a ring enlarge before them, forming a circle of energy. She raised her hand and called on her elemental gift before thrusting an amber spark towards Max's ring and gasped as it flared into a roaring inferno. Max held her hand tight before pushing his palm straight up towards the sky and flicked his wrist like a racket slamming a tennis ball for a grand slam.

The energy-ring-of-fire flew up towards the sky and stretched out before falling down around the boundary of the property.

Energy hummed in the air, as the wind whipped around them and she whispered it away. They stood silently for a moment before she glanced up at Max. A concerned crease sat between his eyes.

"Hey," she said, waiting for him to look at her. When he turned towards her, she smiled. "Cheer up, we have some serious arse kicking to look forward to. That's got to be some sort of consolation?"

He cupped her chin, bending to brush his lips across hers. "It is," he said in a quiet tone.

She returned his kiss before pulling back and whispered, "Come on, let's get those herbs ready.

"You mean to tell me, there are cannibal Veins lurking around town?" Bowie sounded incredulous, leaning against the deck railing holding a cup of coffee that Rick had eagerly made for him the following morning.

"Something like that," Trent answered.

Sam watched her brother as she sipped her latte, hoping Max would return soon from the drive with Nadine. They'd left Noorat at first light to revisit the location where the Veins had jumped them the day before, hoping to pick up a trace or a trail of their whereabouts.

"There's something weird here Sam, an odd energy. Have you felt it?"

"I have, but considering we've never been in the company of so many Veins, I just assumed that the 'odd' was normal?" She cringed, hoping that didn't sound rude and followed through with, "No offence, Trent."

"Oh please." He smiled at her in a charming manner. "None taken whatsoever."

Bowie snorted as Rick joined them on the deck, followed by Gemma and Daniel, who were both holding warm bottles of milk.

"We're going to feed the lambs." Gemma smiled brightly.

"I would not have guessed that." Trent cried with false glee, palm on chest. "Gee, thanks for clearing that up," he smirked.

"Funny guy." Daniel shot him a dark look. "Why don't you roll your sleeves up and help out by mucking the stalls?"

"All in good time, my young friend. Max has enlisted me with an important task this day and it doesn't involve manure." Trent grinned before heading inside.

"Come on." Gemma nudged Daniel with her elbow before heading past Bowie and Rick.

"I'll be there soon to do the stalls, so you won't be on your own,"

Sam reassured them.

"Thanks." Daniel nodded as he followed Gemma towards the barn.

Bowie raised an eyebrow as he caught Sam's gaze. "I see all the kids are getting along."

Rick laughed. "Usually." He shook his head. "I think we're all a bit rattled after the attack."

"Understandably so." Bowie nodded.

Sam heard Max's car roll up the driveway as she was finishing her latte. A tingle of excited anticipation ran down her spine at being able to see him again. It had only been an hour or so since he'd left, but she realised that was one hour, too long. In a matter of minutes, he stepped through the back door; his silky hair resembling a Raven's wing as it glistened under the morning sun. His eyes met hers and butterflies scattered in every which direction around her stomach as she spied a hungry glint of lust in his gaze. Then, she was startled speechless as an image of him worshipping her the night before flashed before her.

She could see herself clearly as if she were watching them on a screen. She was laying beneath him, looking golden and temptress-like; amber eyes half closed in wanton pleasure as his hands swept over every inch of her soft flesh. Lips parted, moist in anticipation as he pulled her towards him to claim kisses that consumed them both. Kisses that left them breathless as each touch triggered pleasure that was close to torture in their all-consuming passion. She pulled in a quiet breath, feeling unsteady as the image had every nerve ending in her body pulsing in pleasure.

She blinked in confusion. Sure, Soul Keepers could share their thoughts with those they chose to, but images? Memories? Feelings? Deep, complicated and elated feelings, like those they'd shared the day before, washed over every inch of her flesh. How was it possible?

Another new tick in the box of what Maxwell Bl... Obsidian can now

153

do. Anything else you'd like to share with me? She pushed towards him, feeling uncomfortable with Bowie five steps away, as desire danced in her veins and the air crackled between them.

I wanted you to know what distracted me as I hunted for Veins, he replied.

She shook her head and attempted a glare. *That's not fair!* She recognised the satisfied glint of knowing in his expression before he turned to Bowie.

"I'm glad you're here, we've got a bit to catch up on," Max said.

"So I've been told." Bowie drained his coffee and followed Max back inside.

Sam was about to join them when a blood-curdling scream erupted from the barn. She spun around and ran down the steps and across the lawn towards the sound of poor Gemma, screaming hysterically; her heart beating to an anxious drum of, *What now, what now?*

"What the hell now?" She heard Bowie exclaim as he ran behind her and instinctively knew Max would be with him.

Sam raced into the barn and clutched her chest in horror; a strangled cry escaped her lips. Bowie and Max arrived five steps behind her.

"Holy shit," Bowie whispered, stepping around her where she stood, frozen in shock for the second time in as little as five minutes. Max placed a comforting hand against her back as they tried to absorb the horrific scene before them.

Daniel had his arms around Gemma, who had quietened down with their arrival, her face pushed into his neck, avoiding the grotesque scene. The glass bottles lay shattered at their feet and the spilt milk was turning a pretty shade of pink as it swirled amongst thick puddles of dark red blood. A pile of animal carcasses were stacked high like a macabre game of Jenga, the top carcass touching the highest beam of the barn roof.

Sam swallowed bile and leaned forward, resting her hands on her knees, taking a deep breath to steady herself at the devastating sight. The deep breath was a mistake as the stench of death crept into her mouth and danced across her taste buds. She slapped a hand over her mouth, raced outside and pitched forward, hurling her latte and pitiful meowing sounds over an Agapanthus bush.

"You alright, Sam?" Bowie called.

She waited until she was, and breathed in a lungful of crisp, clean air before replying. "Yep."

Feeling more prepared for the barbaric scene, she turned and headed back into the barn as Daniel walked by her, leading Gemma towards the house. He nodded solemnly as they passed.

Bowie stood, arms folded across his chest, head hung slightly, seeming devasted at the innocent loss of life. He met Sam's eyes as she joined him. She shook her head, not knowing what to say about the situation in front of them before glancing across at Max, who was standing beside the mountain of carcasses.

They stood silent before Max lifted his head to look across at them and Sam held her breath at the look of cold fury dancing behind his emerald gaze. She didn't know what to say and was grateful when Bowie broke the silence.

"Sam told me about your protection barrier. Looks like that didn't work."

"If anyone passing through that barrier intended harm, I should have felt it and they should have been vaporised." Max kicked the dirt in frustration, planting his hands on his hips.

"Who could have eluded it and survived?" Bowie asked.

Max shrugged before running his hands over his face, turning back to the pile.

"I have no idea, but I can tell you this, only an inhuman entity could have eluded that magic."

"One of us? Or one of you?"

"Neither. We were born, albeit of magic, we still have 'human' qualities. This did not have a soul."

"That doesn't make sense?" Bowie frowned.

Max looked at Bowie. "Tell me about it."

Sam listened as she looked at the innocent creatures, who only yesterday had enjoyed a frolic in the afternoon sun before being placed back inside their warm pens for the night.

"I hope they didn't suffer," she whispered.

"Whoever did this, will." Bowie spat, putting his arm around her shoulder.

"It has to be those Veins who attacked Nadine and Trent. There's no one else."

Sam patted Bowie's arm before heading towards Max to place a hand on his back. "Do you think Methuselah can find out where they are?"

Max shook his head. "He doesn't work that way, Sam. He made that clear from the moment we met. This quest to make the change is mine alone."

"But you're not alone, not now and surely he wouldn't want those who inflicted this kind of act to go unpunished?"

"That's just it, Sam. Methuselah is entrusting me to deal with anything that comes my way. Just as he once did."

"Can someone please fill me in on who *Methuselah* is?" Bowie folded his arms

"Max's... grandfather."

Bowie raised an eyebrow. "You have more family the council don't know about?"

"Yeah, I do and as of yesterday, the council aren't my problem, nor am I theirs."

"I can't wait to hear this one."

"It's good." Sam wanted to grin at Bowie, but the situation before them stopped her.

"Is your, Methuselah, full Vein like Brendan?" Bowie asked Max.

Sam cut in. "He is more than full Vein, Bowie, he is *the* maker."

"The maker?" Bowie looked confused.

Max shook his head. "It's hard to explain and I will. First, we have to do something about this." He waved his hand towards the pile.

Sam could see the grief etched in his expression, hardened by anger. She shouldn't be feeling the pull of lust that hit her when he turned his angry eyes towards her, surrounded by death. But she did. By the way his eyes darkened, he'd felt it too.

"Okay," Bowie clapped his hands together, breaking the spell. "I'll ring the knackery."

Sam gasped. "You will not."

"I know it's a horrid thought, little sister, but they're dead. Their spirits have gone to a peaceful place and their bodies will feed others."

Sam shook her head. "No, I won't have it. Their deaths were too cruel. They will benefit Mother Earth more."

Bowie raised an eyebrow towards Max. "Talk to my sister, would you Maxwell?"

Max shook his head. "Sam's right, we'll turn them into Mother Earth's arms. They can nurture each other that way."

Sam grinned at Bowie; pleased Max had her back.

"Righto. Well, I'll ask Jess to bring the truck over, we'll winch them on and take them out to the mountain."

Max nodded. "I'll get the dozer. Send the truck to the east side. Sam, can you send Trent and Daniel out to give us a hand?" He ran a hand over her hair.

She nodded, taking hold of his hand and bringing it to her lips. She kissed the pulse point of his wrist, her eyes not leaving his.

"When did this happen?" Bowie, once again, interrupted their moment, waving a finger between the two of them.

"About a decade ago." Max answered.

Sam laughed at his quick reply and reached on tiptoes to brush her lips across his. "I'll make everyone some healing tea too."

He dropped another kiss against her lips, "Good idea, love."

She beamed at him before she turned and this time grinned at Bowie as she headed out of the barn and away from the sad stench of innocent death.

CHAPTER TWELVE
MAXWELL

"I don't know what to say." Bowie paced the length of the room.

"I know, it's a lot." Max waited, watching Bowie process all the information concerning Methuselah, Red, his discussion with the council, along with details of the Vein attack on Trent and Nadine. They'd spent most of the day burying the animals in a crevice in the mountain, then cleaned the barn, followed by a house meeting.

Bowie came to a stop in front of the fireplace. "You need to come to the homestead. Tom, Jess, Michael and Angel need to hear about all of this, directly from you."

Max sat back, crossing an ankle over his knee and balanced his mug of tea on his calf muscle before shaking his head at Bowie's statement. "They're welcome to come here, I'll make sure they're safe, but I'm not stepping one foot onto Soul Keepers grounds."

"*Maxwell*," Sam cried. "How can you say that? That's your home, too."

He sighed, hearing the hurt in her voice. "It *was* my home, Samantha, for the longest time. But not anymore and after what I said to Fletch the other day, there is no way the council wouldn't have put an order out for my arrest. I'm safe here."

"Bullshit." Bowie rubbed his jaw before reaching for his mug. "They wouldn't dare."

Max shrugged, taking a mouthful of tea, watching Sam over the rim. She was frowning, and he reached forward to run a finger between her eyebrows, smoothing out her worry line. "Don't worry about it, love. I'm not."

"I can see that." She folded her arms.

He smiled, leaning closer and whispered, "Would you rather me be stressed and worried about what the council may or may not do?"

She sighed, lifting her gaze to his. "I guess not."

He kissed her softly. "Why don't you have a shower? Rinse the day away."

"Yeah, good idea." Bowie nodded. "That will give me time to round up the gang and see if Red can join us. It will be good for everyone to hear her side of the story."

The front door opened at that exact moment and Red walked in right on cue, followed by Michael and Angel.

"And so they already have, dear boy."

Sam beamed. "Angel!" Max watched as she ran across the large room towards the arched entrance to throw her arms around her soul-sister.

"I've missed you too." Angel laughed, returning her hug.

Sam kissed her before reaching for Red, then Michael.

"Where's Tom and Jess?" Bowie asked.

"They have just had a visit with Methuselah." Red's eyes glistened as they met Max's.

Angel shook her head as she walked across to Max. "Max, your grandfather is an impressive… man."

He smiled as he stood, hugging her tightly. "Yeah, he is."

She beamed up at him as Michael dropped a kiss on Sam's head before reaching out to shake Max's hand.

"What a story, hey?" Michael looked across at Red, who clapped her hands once.

"Let's have a drop of wine, shall we? Maxwell, is your cellar stocked?"

"It is. I'll grab something," He smiled warmly at her.

"Oh my!" Rick called in delight as he entered the room. "This must be the famous Angel and Michael Cloud?" His pupils dilated.

Bowie grinned as Nadine, Gemma, Daniel and Trent burst in behind him to fill their eyes with the vision of the Cloud siblings they'd all heard so much about. Angel returned their smiles, but Michael remained cautious as he returned their curious gazes.

Max was ready to step in between the enthusiastic Veins and his adopted-siblings, keeping a close watch on their eyes. So far, so good; No shark-eyes appearing.

"What an honour!" Rick squealed in delight. "And you are?" He reached a hand politely towards Red.

"My grandmother," Max said.

"Let's go with 'Nana' shall we?" She smiled.

"My nana," Max said with pride and all eyes turned towards him. He knew the Storm and Cloud siblings were in as much awe with that statement as he was. It was still sinking in for him. *Red* was *his*, and he belonged to her. He *belonged*. It was almost too inconceivable.

Rick shook Red's hand enthusiastically, as did the others while Max made the introductions around the room.

Michael turned to Max. "So, you and Jane, cousins, huh?"

"Seems so."

"Does she know?" Sam asked Red.

"Not as yet. Jane has been on an assignment the past several months and we've had no contact with her."

Max smiled as he slipped an arm around Red's tiny shoulders. "It will be lovely to see her once she returns home."

Red nodded up at him, eyes shining with happiness.

"I love what you've done to the place Max." Angel looked around as Bowie walked behind her and pulled her into his arms.

She tipped her head back, smiling up at him and Max smiled back, realizing how much he'd missed having them all together. Sam met his gaze at that moment. From the look on her face, she'd felt it to. The joy of them all being together again.

"Well, we know about your family history and have heard a bit about your... skill set." Michael raised an eyebrow. "But I think we need to talk about the incident you had to deal with today regarding the animals."

"Speaking of." Sam headed over to Angel and took her hand. "I'm desperate to wash the day off me before dinner and I want to show Angel my room."

"You've got plenty of time." Red smiled. "I'm cooking tonight." She turned to the group of silent Veins as they stood staring, watching the Soul Keepers as if they were a completely different species.

Max guessed, in a way, they were to them and felt a flash of pity for his Obsidian Souls. For most of their lives, they were regarded as parasites. The disease that needed to be vaccinated against. Extinguished. A stirring of anger rippled beneath his flesh for all the injustice they'd had to endure and even now they looked as if they felt 'less' than the Soul Keepers who stood under his roof.

"Max?" Sam called.

He met her concerned gaze and realised he'd made the room stifling hot with his anger. He watched a bead of sweat slide down her smooth forehead; and it wasn't because of the fire.

"Cool," she whispered and swept her fingers towards him and then around the room.

"Thanks for that." Daniel sighed gratefully, using his sleeve to mop his forehead.

"No worries," Sam whispered, her eyes not leaving Max's.

"Sorry," he said to her before meeting Bowie's, then Michael's intrigued expressions.

"It's nice to actually see your skill set in action," Bowie said, dropping a kiss against Angel's hair before nodding to Max.

"Speaking of skilled," Max said, changing the subject and wanting all the eyes in the room off him. "Nana, you've got some pretty skilled cooks here to give you a hand." He nodded towards Nadine and Daniel.

"*Si.*" Nadine grinned, rubbing her hands together. "The pantry is fully stocked. What have you got in mind?"

"We'll explore our options, shall we?" Red crossed over and smiled up at Max as she patted his cheek affectionately. "Cooking is always nicer with a glass of something, dear," she reminded him.

"I'll get it before my shower," Sam said as she headed towards the cellar door with Angel.

"*No*, you won't," Max said more forcefully than he'd intended.

She turned around; eyebrow raised.

"It's okay." He forced a smile and shielded every thought of what else was tucked below in the cellar. "Go show Angel upstairs and have a relaxing shower. It's been a big day; I've got something special in mind for Nana."

He waited, hoping she'd just go upstairs and was relieved when Angel tugged on her arm, pulling her towards the staircase.

"Right." He smiled at Red. "Nadine will show you the kitchen and I'll get your wine. Trent, do you want to grab some beers for the others?"

"Champagne, please," Nadine sang out.

Trent grinned. "Sure, why don't we get the deck set up?"

"Sounds good." Bowie followed Red and Nadine into the kitchen before heading towards the back door. "I'll get the fire on. Michael, where's Beth?"

"My darling wife and her sister went into Warrnambool with a group of their friends for a Hen's weekend."

Max heard Bowie chuckle and mention something about trouble and hangovers in the morning before their voices trailed off as he headed towards the cellar. He glanced over his shoulder, then placed his hand against the door and whispered an incantation to remove the invisible lock. The door swung open, and he headed down the stairs, to grab Red's favourite wine and to see how his brother was fairing.

SAMANTHA

"I can't believe there are a handful of Veins downstairs and you seem as chill as the breeze." Angel sat on the window seat as Sam stepped under the steaming shower, eager to wash off the day's combination of dried blood, sweat, dirt and death.

Sam shrugged. "Despite the ghastly events that have recently occurred, which I do feel extremely upset about, they are a good group of people."

"I'm glad and happy for Max. He seems... actually, I can't put my finger on it. Anyway, there's something different about you too?" Angel waited for Sam to explain.

"Yeah, about that." Sam grinned. "Something has happened." She was thrilled to have Angel here to talk to. It had felt like forever since she'd had her soul-sister with her.

"I can see that."

Sam lathered herself from head to toe. "Is it that obvious?"

"Yeah, you're glowing. I haven't seen you this happy for close to a year, Sam. And from the way Max was looking at you, like he was a dehydrated man, who could only be hydrated by you, I'd say you've got some juicy beans to spill."

Sam chuckled before plunging her head under the water, rinsing conditioner from her hair. She turned the shower off, stepped out and wrapped herself in a fluffy towel. "I wouldn't know where to start, honestly, considering everything he said when he first came home, about us being *just* friends." She shook her head. "Let's just say that we knocked that statement right out of the ballpark."

She dried herself before pumping out a fistful of lotion and applying it all over. Sam sighed. "Max has always had such a gentle, yet alluring force about him, at least to me. But now, it's almost as if he's… untouchable?"

Angel grinned slyly. "Not *that* untouchable, obviously."

Sam met her gaze. "Good one." She shook her head. "I can't put my finger on it. It's like he's the most unintimidating, intimidating soul I know. Does that even make sense?"

Angel laughed. "Yeah, it does."

"And I don't mean that he seems more untouchable because of all these powers he now has, or his connection to Red, or Methuselah, he just seems… superior somehow?" She shrugged, running a brush through her glistening locks.

Angel laughed. "Our humble, kind Max, superior? Never."

"Yeah, you're right, it does sound ridiculous when I say it out loud." She shook her head and headed into the bedroom where she threw on underwear and pulled on jeans and a sexy black top. "He's just got this edge about him." She shrugged, pushing her feet into tall wedges. "I don't know. There's more going on than what I can see."

Angel smiled and crossed over to her, placing her hands on her shoulders.

"Sam, you've been separated for almost a year. He's been through a great deal from what you and Bowie have told me. And protecting and training these Veins, after everything the council have done? That would change anyone. Including everything that has happened in the last forty-eight hours."

Sam nodded, "I know, it's just…" she shrugged. "So much had passed between us."

"Yeah, it has. Your hearts were torn apart and broken with your soul-essence ceremony to Peter and then you had to deal with his death. Now our Maxwell has come back, slightly changed and head over heels in love with you. And he isn't just 'our' Max anymore. He's a leader, who apparently doesn't just have the Light Accords council to deal with, but an enemy right on our doorstep. It's a lot to compartmentalise, for anyone."

"He's not telling me something, I can feel it."

"I'm sure there's a lot he hasn't had time to tell you, Sam and knowing Max, if he hasn't told you something, it's because he's trying to keep you safe."

Sam sighed. "I don't need him to keep me safe."

"Sam, he loves you, just let him."

Sam looked into Angel's gorgeous aquamarine eyes and knew how much her soul-sister wanted everyone to be as happy as she and Bowie were.

She wrapped her arms around Angel. "I'm still trying to get my head around everything. His gifts, his lineage."

"I know, it's amazing. I always knew there was something phenomenal about our Max."

Sam grinned at Angel as she headed towards the door. "And that has never changed."

"No, it hasn't. But something has." Angel said softly.

Sam spun towards her. "*See*, you feel it too?"

Angel shook her head. "I can't put my finger on it either. But as soon as I do, I'll let you know."

Sam nodded. "Do that."

"It's nothing bad, I'm sure of it."

"I hope you're right." Sam said, slightly relieved, as she trusted Angel's instincts. "Now, are you ready to be eyeballed all night?"

Angel laughed as she headed to the door. "Well, I don't know about that. But as long as I have the night with some of my favourite people, I'm ready."

The atmosphere after dinner, was a festive one. Soul Keepers and Veins alike, getting to know one another as they shared likes and dislikes. Growing up in Australia versus Italy and then, of course, after the laughter and banter, as they sat around the fire nursing a drink, stories of their upbringings induced curious questions and sympathetic glances from both sides.

"It must have been unbearable, having all those amazing gifts, yet being unable to use them?" Daniel said to Angel after she had shared a story of when she'd been twelve and healed a pure-soul when she hadn't learned to cloak her energy signature.

"It was, I hated it." Angel smiled.

"And we heard about the time you and Sam were punished for trying to save Max from the council after he consumed your essence," Gemma said.

Angel shifted uncomfortably as she exchanged a look with Max.

"I'll never forgive myself for that, or what followed," he said, taking a deep swallow of beer as if to wash down the regret he'd felt after consuming Angel's blood.

They knew the first time Max had attacked Angel, he'd no control over his actions. No awareness. The second time, he'd done it to convince Brendan he was loyal, in order to help the Soul Keepers trap and kill Brendan.

"It was another lifetime ago." Angel reached across and rubbed his arm. "And we'd do anything to protect you, no matter what."

"You're amazing." Trent stared at Angel. "Like, a *real* Angel."

Sam chuckled, knowing Angel did not like being praised for anything she considered her duty.

Bowie grinned. "You are right, of course." He agreed with Trent as he brushed a kiss across Angel's cheek. "She is that."

Angel melted under Bowie's attention, flashing him a gorgeous smile.

"When you have family, you protect them. At any cost." Sam said, reaching for a glass of Brown Brothers Zibibbo.

"That is true, dear Samantha." Red smiled at her affectionately. "You do what you must, exclusive of judgement, or opinion." She looked meaningfully at Max.

He nodded, flushing slightly as he met her eyes.

Interesting. Sam pushed privately to Angel, who had noticed the exchange too, as she nodded her head slightly, so as not to give their private conversation away.

I wonder what that's all about? Angel returned, sipping her champagne.

I want to know, that's for sure. This is Red and Max, after all, it will be something worth knowing.

Agreed. Oh, there is so much happening here! Angel responded.

Sam grinned.

"So," Michael cut in on their private conversation. "I know we covered most of it before dinner, but the Vein attack and then the animals being slaughtered…"

"Oh *Cara*, this conversation is going to completely ruin dessert." Nadine cut in, standing abruptly, knocking over her glass.

Sam's reflexes were quick, but before she moved to rescue the glass from smashing into pieces on the glossy deck, an obsidian vein shot out and curled around the stem, snatching it up before fluently placing it back on the table.

All eyes followed the veins retreat from the glass, across the scorching fire pit, appearing unaffected by the searing flames before disappearing into Max's forearm.

"Right." Bowie said after several heartbeats of silence. "That just happened."

"You didn't burn?" Michael raised an eyebrow.

Max shrugged. "No."

"I guess we shouldn't be surprised, you have the lineage of a… *star*, so to speak." Sam stood. "I'll help with dessert."

Nadine looked relieved and nodded. "Thanks."

"Well, I'm a little tired. Max, walk me to the door. Goodnight, everyone. Lovely to meet you." Red smiled at the Veins before dropping a kiss on Angel's, Michael's and Bowie's cheek.

"Goodnight," they chorused.

Sam went into the kitchen to pull out plates as Nadine bent to grab the fruit pie out of the oven.

"Samantha?"

Sam turned as Red placed a hand on her arm. She smiled into Red's small, dear face that she had loved since she was a baby. "Yes?"

Red patted her cheek. "You'll take care of Maxwell for me, won't you, dear?"

Sam pulled Red into her arms and hugged her. "You know I will, you never have to ask me that."

Red sighed, squeezing Sam tightly before dropping a kiss on her cheek.

"Thank you."

"It sounds like you're getting ready to say goodbye?" Concern laced Sam's voice.

"Oh, *no* dear, not yet!" She beamed.

Sam smiled, relieved.

"Goodnight." Red waved to Nadine before joining Max at the front door.

Once they were alone, Nadine raised an eyebrow towards Sam. "Your family sure are touchy-feely." She ran the sharp blade through the pie, cutting it into slices for everyone.

Sam opened the fridge to pull out the whipped cream. "Do you have a problem with that?"

"No, not at all." Nadine flipped a cascade of auburn hair over her shoulder before scooping up some cutlery as Sam grabbed the plates.

"Glad to hear it." Sam headed back outside towards the conversation and laughter.

CHAPTER THIRTEEN
MAXWELL

"Max, are you doing the right thing, keeping Kyle a secret?" Red asked, zipping up her vest.

"You knew?"

"Of course dear. Methuselah sees all."

"Of course." Max whispered to himself.

"Why not tell Samantha? And why didn't you feel you could tell me?"

He dropped his eyes, kicking at a stone as he considered his answer. Meeting her steady gaze, he answered. "At the beginning, it was to protect Kyle. No matter what he's done, he's still my brother. I wanted to give 'us' a chance without the council's interference. After everything that has transpired with the council, I didn't tell you or Sam because I didn't want you to be punished for keeping my secret if they found out. They can't be trusted R... Nana."

Red sighed. "Yes, they can, dear." She raised a hand to silence him as he opened his mouth to object. "I know many of the things that they've done, is unforgiveable and they have made your life unbearable at times. For that, I am sorry and disappointed in their actions more than I can say. But the Light Accords *are* good at the core of it all, Maxwell."

"We will have to agree to disagree on that score. You do know they wanted to throw me in a cell because I refused to have you place a barrier around my property, preventing my clan from leaving?"

"Yes, I didn't agree with that at all."

"You see?"

Red chuckled. "Yes, I do. And if I can see one side of the story, can you see the other?"

He shrugged, stuffing his hands in his jeans pockets.

She smiled. "You beautiful boy, come here." She opened her arms wide, and he stepped into her embrace, returning it.

"I'm so proud of you."

"Thank you."

"*My* Maxwell Obsidian," she whispered.

My Maxwell Obsidian. It sure did have a nice ring to it. He swallowed the lump of love that crept into his throat. Hands down, he'd felt loved over the years, with the Soul Keepers of Glenormiston South, but he'd always been reminded that he was half of something else. Something… unsavoury.

"I love you, Nana."

She beamed at him. "And I love you, dear boy." She offered him her cheek.

Max bent and brushed his lips across her soft, wrinkled cheek as he spun a finger to the side of them.

Red chuckled, shaking her head as she spotted her lounge room within a silver cloud, rimmed in forest green, Alana peering out at

172

them both. "I'm still amazed at what you can do. You'll be truly magnificent one day."

"One day?" He raised an eyebrow, grinning.

She laughed. "Even more so when you're older. You're all just babies in the grand scheme of things."

"I'll take that." He smiled as she stepped towards the portal.

"Tell Samantha, Maxwell," she called over her shoulder.

"I will, tonight. I promise." He nodded as she stepped into the portal and in a flash, was gone.

He stood there for a few moments before hearing the laughter of his family reach him, feeling like the luckiest man alive. Then, Samantha's laugh washed over him like a silken kiss and his gut clenched, desperate to be alone with her.

Get ready to say goodnight, Samantha Storm. I'm coming for you.

I've only been waiting all night, she replied.

He smiled, sensing her heartrate accelerate as he headed around the side of the house and towards the back of the property. Lustful anticipation sped through his veins, thinking about all the things he wanted to do to, and with, Samantha Storm.

"Hello Maxwell," a familiar voice chortled from behind him.

He paused before spinning around, gasping at the figure before him. It couldn't be? Before he could throw a weapon, call a warning, or take his next breath, the world around him vanished in a void of black mist, stealing everything from him in an instant.

SAMANTHA

Sam's spoonful of fruit pie was halfway to her mouth when the hairs on the back of her neck snapped to attention.

"What is it?" Bowie stood at the same time she did. "Michael, get Angel out of here! Get up to Max's room," he ordered, watching his soul-sibling grab Angel's hand and tug her inside without question.

Daniel, Rick and Trent shot to their feet as Nadine put her arm around Gemma's shoulder. They turned to face a mob of Veins walking towards them from out of the darkness of the yard. At least fifteen of them.

Max? Sam pushed out, waiting. "Bowie?" She whispered, hating the fear in her voice.

"Yeah, we're outnumbered. Don't let that frighten you." He sounded confident, as always.

"I'm not." She assured him.

"Let's kick some arse, shall we?" Trent cracked his knuckles.

"Yeah." Rick leered, catching Bowie's eye, who grinned back at him.

"We've got this." He nodded to Sam.

Taking a deep breath, she flexed her fingers, forcing a calm throughout her body, preparing to inflict pain.

The Veins stopped ten feet away; silent. Waiting.

What are they waiting for? Sam pushed towards Bowie.

We're about to find out. "Have you come here to apologise for being cannibals to your own kind?" he demanded.

"We've come on behalf of a thousand others."

"For what?" Trent snapped.

"No one wants the change your leader is attempting to bring," A skinny woman with oily, black hair snarled.

"Well too bad, we don't give a toss about what you all want," Nadine hissed.

"We will give you one chance to change your minds about that," A tall, broad man said, almost sympathetically.

Sam laughed dryly. "*You'll* give us a chance? How about you hightail it right now and we won't fry you to a crisp." Lightning danced along her fingertips.

The man turned cold eyes towards Sam. "We weren't talking to you, *little* Soul Keeper. You will die here tonight. It's *our* kind we offer a final chance to."

Bowie stepped forward beside Sam, amber eyes ablaze with fury.

"You think you can threaten *my* sister? You've just signed your own death warrant." He spat vehemently as he flung a sizzling bolt straight towards the arrogant man's chest. Before the lightning could strike a hole in the Vein's chest, an impossibly large python-vein shot out of the dark, taking Bowie's bolt in its mouth; snuffing it out as if it were no more than a candle flame.

"Not possible," Sam whispered.

A dry laugh seeped from the shadows. "It certainly is. And that was no threat." A familiar voice followed. "But a promise."

"It *can't* be," Bowie whispered, matching Sam's identical expression of disbelief.

She was momentarily shocked frozen as the dark figure loomed towards them.

The assembly of Veins parted and something that resembled Brendan Black stepped forward. A thick, pulsing vein, responsible for destroying Bowie's lightening, hung around his neck like a monstrous snake.

I guess there's the answer to the inhuman entity that got through Max's barrier, Bowie pushed to Sam.

How can this be? she asked him.

I have no clue.

Sam kept her eyes on Brendan, as hard as it was to look at him. He'd been blown to a hundred glass shards by herself and Angel over a year ago, then buried in sacred ground around the world by the Soul Keepers, for 'safekeeping.' Somehow, those pieces had been located, dug up and by the looks of things, thawed out and sewn back together, and poorly at that, with no thought to those who had to look upon him. Gangrenous looking pus leaked between thick folds of scar tissue and the scent of septic rot drifted towards them.

I may well disgrace myself and throw up any minute now. She could sense Bowie wanted to laugh at her statement.

"Well, well, well…" Brendan's voice grated. "If it isn't the *Royal Soul Keepers of Glenormiston South*, come to fraternise with the enemy." He shook his enormous head, red eyes blazing.

"The only enemy here is you," Rick said bravely, stepping forward. "And you'd better leave, if you don't want to die a horrific, painful death."

"Been there, done that." Brendan narrowed his eyes towards Sam.

She held up a hand. "Before we destroy you all, what the hell do you want?"

"I already have what I want. Killing the rest of you will be a bonus." Brendan's lips curved, creating a grotesque smile.

Gemma gasped behind Sam. Brendan's teeth were shards of black glass.

"It's ok," Daniel whispered to her.

"Is it though?" Gemma's voice quivered.

We should have asked Michael to take Gemma inside! Sam said.

Should have, Bowie said.

He must have Max! She cried.

I gathered, he'll be okay, Sam. Bowie assured her.

Her fingers twitched, as her body vibrated with the longing to shoot a jolt of electrifying power right through Brendan, wanting to blow him to pieces once again.

Brendan looked around at their group. "Where's your little friend? She needs to be punished too."

"The only one being punished here tonight is you," Sam threw back at him, her hair whipping about as she called on her elemental powers. Lightening licked along her skin, sparking at her fingertips as the wind circled her.

Brendan laughed. "Oh, this will be fun."

"That's one thing you've got right," Bowie grinned, unperturbed as amber flames, tinged with blue, dripped off his fingertips, ready and waiting. Energy rolled off him in waves and slid over Sam's flesh, sparking an eager desire to perform her royal duty, to destroy evil and protect all. She waited impatiently for her brother's order.

Brendan rolled his massive shoulders, opening meaty arms, revealing several emerging veins that dripped from his flesh, engorged and dangerous, covered in barbs that leaked toxins.

Now Sam! Bowie pushed towards her and in an instant, they threw a blaze of lightening flames straight towards Brendan.

With their combined raging inferno, Sam was satisfied to hear Brendan roar in pain as the stench of his already putrid flesh, burned. But only briefly before his laughter ensued as their flames were extinguished.

Bowie swore in frustration as Trent and Rick raced past them, heading down towards the Veins who were waiting to challenge them. Trent threw a solid punch in one Vein's face, injecting minuscule flesh-eating spears as Rick avoided a barbed-vein. He dropped low and aimed a round house kick towards his opponent's legs, swiping him off his feet. As the Vein fell to the ground with a grunt, Rick dove onto his chest, pinning the furious man's arms beneath his knees and released a wrist full of vein-arrows into the man's torso, to burrow deep, ripping him apart from the inside out.

Daniel leapt over the deck rail and threw his wrists forward, shooting several vein-arrows towards a Vein, who wore a murderous expression as she headed towards Sam, shooting bullets at her head, which Sam sent a blazing inferno to engulf them.

Daniel's attack caught the enemy by surprise, as he drove his weapons into her stomach, causing her to scream blue murder as she fell to her knees, writhing in pain. She clutched desperately at her abdomen as if trying to remove Daniel's wriggling mass as they devoured her insides before she fell dead, in a bloody heap.

The greasy haired woman tossed a barbed-lasso around Gemma and Sam watched, horrified as it tightened dangerously, blood flowing as the wicked barbs sawed into Gemma's flesh. Sam called over the battle cries, "Gemma, close your eyes, don't move!"

Gemma nodded, tears falling down her face as she gasped for air. Sam sent a thin line of fire to burn through the putrid, parasitic rope. It dropped and Gemma stomped on it before kicking it off the decking as the greasy haired woman screamed in pain.

Sam nodded towards Gemma before throwing a strike of lightning to her left, smouldering her target that was inching towards Daniel. Nadine ran by her to attack the greasy haired woman who was moaning in pain.

Trent pummelled at his enemy with fists of fury before he was struck from behind by a vein-spear. He fell to his knees, gasping as it punctured his lung.

Sam spun around, hearing Trent's cry and called for water from the pond. As the stream of water flew towards her, she waved her fingers and whispered a chant, turning the water to ice and fashioned a sword. She leapt into the air to catch it and as she fell to her feet, sliced the head off the Vein, jerking its weapon out of Trent's chest.

Bowie dropped on one knee, placing his hand over Trent's gaping hole and placing his other hand onto the soil and whispered to Mother Earth for her healing energy to assist him and within moments Trent was healed.

"Thanks," he said to them both, getting to his feet and turning to his next opponent.

Sam surveyed the area, relieved their being outnumbered wasn't impacting them too severely. Blood flowed with every strike and blow as each side fought with the determination to destroy the other. A scream burst from Nadine and Sam spun towards the petrified sound, startled to see Brendan's python-like vein wrapped around Nadine's waist, lifting her ten feet in the air and thrashing her about like a rag-doll.

CHAPTER FOURTEEN
SAMANTHA

"You don't see that every day," Bowie muttered to Sam.

Sam was terrified Nadine's head was going to snap off with the intensity in which she was being shaken about. "We have to destroy him, Bowie, now."

"Yeah, I'm working on something."

Sam gasped as another enormous vein whipped towards Daniel, punching him before he could avoid the attack, sending him twenty feet to disappear into the darkness of the yard.

"Work on it faster!" she cried.

"Sure thing." He smirked briefly before slamming his hands together, sending an ear shattering clap of thunder to vibrate around them. A roaring wave of energy rolled through the surrounding air, sending their hair and clothing to whip madly about.

The Veins looked startled as the earth shifted beneath their feet and Sam caught Rick shooting Bowie a worried look. Her eyes flew to her brother and saw him cast a quick wink at Rick before clapping his hands together once more and the gale of wind slammed into him without budging him an inch.

Pointing long steady fingers, oozing with power, Bowie sent an amplified blast of energy to punch Brendan in the chest, sending him hurtling in the air. Nadine dropped to the ground and Trent ran to help her up, tucking her beneath his shoulder before taking her to safety.

The earth shook as Brendan's massive body fell beneath the impact of Bowie's attack and Sam sighed in relief as Bowie sent a continuous volt of electricity into Brendan's motionless form, stopping only after smoke rose in the air. Brendan's loyal Veins cried in protest before being silenced under the hands of the Obsidian Souls.

Bowie blew out a long breath as he turned to Sam, placing his hands on his hips. "I think we're done here. Now, time to find Max."

Sam nodded, feeling a flicker of relief. The deep breath she took jammed in her throat as Brendan's laughter reached them.

"Not possible," Bowie whispered, turning back to Brendan.

"Can't he just die already?" She groaned as Brendan stood on shaky legs and sent a wicked smile in their direction.

"You'll die soon enough, now," said a Vein, earning a whack in the side of the head from Rick.

"Who's first?" Brendan called, walking towards them.

"You." A quiet voice spat from behind them.

Sam spun around to see Angel step through the back door with Michael a step behind her. "Angel?" She gasped in concern.

Angel shook her head to both Sam and Bowie as she stepped beside them.

We can do this, together. She pushed towards them.

Okay... Sam replied.

I'd prefer you safe. Bowie sounded worried.

Trust me? Angel implored Bowie, as she reached into his back pocket to pull his pocketknife out.

Always, Baby… but? He raised an eyebrow.

Angel shook her head once, eyes on Brendan.

"Ah, at last." Brendan crowed. His massive vein-python snapped towards Angel.

She stood, unfazed as the thick cord of sinew reached her, pulsing in anticipation. Angel drew the knife along her wrist, releasing sweet, intoxicating blood to all the Veins.

Brendan swooned, mesmerised by both the sweet scent of the Heavenly Soul's blood in the air and the sight of it inches from him. As his python-vein inched closed, Angel ran her fingers along the cut, then tossed a splatter of blood in Brendan's direction, covering the tip of his vein.

He moaned in ecstasy, focused entirely on the blood lust in that moment. He'd brought the tip of his python-vein towards his mouth to taste Angel's blood orally, closing his eyes.

Now. Angel implored Sam and Bowie. *Let's send him from this world.*

Sam nodded, as they called to the wind.

"Wind of day, wind of night, come together, end this blight,
Send it away from earth so green, away from here to worlds unseen."

With each word that fell from Sam's and Bowie's lips, a tornado of wind sprung instantly to encircle Brendan, whose lips were smeared in Angel's blood. It whipped viciously and with purpose, as it effortlessly scooped up the monstrous form and with a burst of light, shot him towards the night sky, vanishing in seconds. Silence filled the air.

"What *have* you done?" A Vein, laying under Trent's boot screamed before Trent kicked him silent.

Sam looked about their group as Daniel hobbled in from the dark yard. Although none of the clan had escaped injury, at least they were all alive. Out of the fifteen Veins who had arrived to kill them, only six remained breathing. If this was the vision she had with Methuselah, she was at least grateful that Max was not here and laying dead on the grass. She shuddered at the thought. Where was he?

"We need to put this lot somewhere." Rick pointed to the injured enemy as he wiped blood from his neck.

Michael nodded. "Tom and Jess will be here any minute to collect them. We called them the minute we went upstairs."

"Great." Bowie clapped him on the back as he put his arm around Angel, hugging her tight against his chest. Michael placed his hand over her cut and whispered a healing incantation.

"Thank you." Angel nodded to her brother before turning to the clan. "Please, allow me to heal you."

Sam patted Gemma on the arm and nodded towards Angel before turning towards their enemy. "Okay, you lot, time to go." She waved her hand over them, creating an energy field that enveloped them all before collectively scooping them up in an amber-like-bubble and with a flick of her wrist and a whisper to the air, they glided around the side of the mansion, towards the front of the driveway. Happy to see them vanish from sight, as Michael followed behind them to greet Tom and Jess who would take them to the Light Accords prison.

"Is he really gone?" Gemma asked, staring up at the blackened sky as Angel ran her hands over her, removing any toxins before closing her wounds.

"He is," Bowie answered.

"For good?" she whispered.

"Let's hope," Daniel said.

Sam left them and hurried inside the mansion, searching the rooms before heading out the front door, seeing Tom and Jess loading up their enemy in a cattle truck.

"Hey Sam," Jess called, raising a hand in greeting. "We'll sort this lot out."

"Thanks Jess. Tom, pump them for information, Max is missing," she said, feeling oddly calm considering the love of her life seemed to have vanished from the face of the earth. She forced a niggle of hysteria aside. Now wasn't the time. She had to put her energy into finding Max and the one place she'd yet to explore: the cellar.

Waving the cattle truck off, she turned and headed inside. Angel and Michael were finishing healing the clans wounds and Bowie and Rick were handing out hot drinks.

"I've a question for you, *Bella*." Nadine was looking at Angel.

"Yes?" Angel waited as she stroked her hand along Daniel's chest, closing a deep gash.

"If you are so 'mighty,' why did your brother take you upstairs? You could have stayed and done that thing you did, sooner."

Sam detected judgement in Nadine's tone and tensed, waiting to defend her sister.

Angel sensed Sam's protectiveness and smiled in her direction. "It's okay, Sam."

Sam nodded before Angel continued.

"Yes, I am destined to become mighty, but as yet, my abilities are still young." She shrugged. "It was my blood, more than my abilities tonight, that defeated Brendan."

"In saying that," Bowie cut in, placing the hot beverages on the table, glowering at Nadine. "She is spectacular."

"Keep your shirt on, handsome." Nadine raised an eyebrow taking a coffee. "It was just a question."

"Please, take it off." Sam heard Rick mutter under his breath as Michael healed his wounds.

"What's our first step in trying to find Max?" Trent asked no one in particular.

Everyone turned towards Sam, who opened her mouth to answer before the atmosphere outside shook the mansion. Timber and stone groaned before the floor beneath their feet shifted, as if the earth were moving like a wave, rolling along the ocean as an unnerving sound penetrated the air like a cry of doom.

"What the actual…?" Rick cried, as the front door smashed open and a foul gust of wind flew in.

Sam's warning cry to shield came too late, as a twisting black funnel shot towards them, breaking every glass panelled wall as it flew around them. Spiteful laughter filled the air. Sam spun a protective shield around those who stood closest to her and was grateful to see her Soul Keeper family do the same to the others, but not before the flying pieces of glass had cut them all. The black mass tapped at their shields, seeking an entrance point, yet finding none. It swirled furiously in the centre of the room before taking the form of Brendan Black.

"Bullshit." Bowie hissed.

Brendan laughed. "Oh the joys of being reconstructed via a powerful being."

"There shouldn't be a Vein powerful enough to put the likes of what we did to you back together." Sam frowned, keeping her shield solidly over Gemma and Trent.

"Oh, you'd be right about that." Brendan leered. "But who said it was a Vein?"

"Who else would there be?" Michael frowned, protecting Nadine.

Brendan turned dead eyes towards Michael. "Who else indeed? You Soul Keepers have a traitor in your midst. One who was more than willing to travel the globe and dig up every shattered piece of my flesh and soul." He laughed, clapping meaty hands together.

Angel scoffed. "You never had a soul."

Brendan turned towards her, staring for several moments before replying in a hushed tone that sent chills down Sam's spine. "I'll take yours before we are done."

"I'd like to see you try!" Sam said.

"Would you?" He turned cavernous eyes towards Sam. "And so you shall." He opened his arms, releasing odd shaped veins from his mutilated flesh.

Gemma groaned in terror as the massive tendrils of flesh slid towards each of them, stroking against the Soul Keepers shields, once again, seeking entrance.

"It's okay," Sam whispered to her.

"You're wasting your time." Bowie said in a bored tone. "You might have been glued back together, but you're no match for us."

"I think I just proved otherwise, *boy*." Brendan grinned.

Sam forced herself not to flinch as one of Brendan's revolting, slug-like veins smeared a slimy residue over her transparent shield as it sought entrance.

Sam, two counts. Let's fry his insides. Bowie pushed towards her.

Okay. Angel, Michael, keep your shields in place. Sam pushed towards them and within the two counts, matching Bowie's force, Sam threw her most destructible blast of heat into Brendan. She wasn't expecting it to have too much of an effect after what had happened earlier, but was pleasantly surprised when Brendan roared in agony, his veins retracting in stiff, jerky movements as he tried to move away from their onslaught.

She felt exhilarated, her palm pulsing as her heat blast shot out, sending an amber glow with blue flames dancing along its edges to burn a gaping hole in Brendan's chest. Bowie stepped forward, thrusting both palms forward and Brendan fell to his knees, the floor shaking beneath the impact.

Sam frowned, disgusted as Brendan curled into a foetal position, then was alarmed to see his putrid flesh rolling and folding in on itself until he resembled nothing more than a blob with eyes, which was shrinking.

What now? she asked Bowie, who remained silent as they continued blasting Brendan with their full force.

Suddenly, the blob exploded into ash before lifting into the air, forming into a black cloud before shooting out the front door, leaving a burnt pile of ash on the floor. Sam and Bowie dropped their blasts, and the group stared at each other, dumbfounded.

"Why the *hell* can't we kill him?" Bowie frowned as Angel rushed to his side, running her hand along his back.

"That's the question of the century and one that needs answering right now. Let's call a council meeting." Michael addressed the Veins. "Are you alright here by yourselves?"

"Of course." Daniel nodded.

"They won't be by themselves. I'm not coming."

"Sam?" Angel turned to her sister.

Sam shook her head. "I need to find Max."

"*We,* need to find Max." Nadine placed a hand on her hip. Sam nodded.

"Alright little sister, send us a message if you need us."

Bowie kissed the top of Angel's head before crossing over to pull Sam in his arms. She hugged him back before saying goodbye to Angel and Michael, then turned to the clan as the front door closed.

"What can we do?" Rick asked.

"Clean up this place, to start," Sam said before waving her fingers to the pile of Brendan's ashes and lifted them in a tidy swirl, depositing the black matter into the hearth. Then, she waved both hands and every piece of glass lifted from the floorboards and rugs and made their way towards the front door, which Trent opened and Sam sent them out towards the recycle bin.

"How do we find Max?" Rick folded his arms.

"I don't know," Sam said before marching towards the cellar door. "Why don't you all get cleaned up. We can regroup when you're done." She sighed when no one argued and as they left to shower upstairs, she placed her hands on the carved door, fingers scrolling over the intricate patterns, wondering how she was going to find Maxwell Obsidian.

CHAPTER FIFTEEN
MAXWELL

Max groaned as his head pounded. Opening his eyes to darkness, he pulled in a deep breath, frowning at the damp and mould that scented the air. He pushed himself off the dirt floor and stood, brushing palms over his thighs.

"Light," he whispered.

As the room lit up, he looked about the small cell with green-tinged walls and black mould growing in the corner of the ceiling. Bars, not dissimilar to the ones he had in his cellar, blocked his exit. In the cell opposite him, a small figure was hunched on the ground, arms wrapped around drawn knees and a curtain of dishevelled auburn hair hung limply.

"Hey," Max called. "You okay?"

The figure jolted before lifting tired, red-rimmed eyes towards him and he froze when he recognised who it was. "*Jane?*"

"Max!" She crawled towards the bars, pressing her face close to peer towards him. "Thank the Angels you're alive."

He frowned when he saw that her hands were as black as night. "What's on your hands?"

"Tar," she replied sadly. "They tarred my hands to stop me from using my gifts." Her gaze dropped to her hands, turning them this way and that as if she could hardly believe what they'd done to her. "Bastards," she whispered.

He grinned internally. He'd always loved Jane's spunk but seeing her in such a poor physical condition angered him beyond belief. He looked around, waving his fingers hoping to portal across to her and get them out of here. Nothing happened. Not one spark or swirl of power could be drawn from within the cell. He cursed inwardly before asking. "How long have you been here?"

"I hardly know."

"How did they get their hands on you? What do they want with you?"

Jane looked him dead in the eye; a lone tear fell, leaving a clean trail along her dirty cheek as it descended. She shook her head, dropping her voice to a whisper.

"Oh Max, I can't tell you. You'll hate me forever. So will with Red, Angel and Sam. I've done the most vile, unforgivable act."

"Jane, stop it. None of us could ever hate you. Just tell me."

Silence ensued before Jane began. "I've betrayed the Soul Keepers." She whispered before covering her face, sobbing.

He swallowed his fury, seeing her blackened hands, hearing her quiet cries. *His* cousin.

"Hey," he soothed. "Jane... it's going to be okay."

"No, no it's *not* Max. You don't understand."

"Well, help me to, then."

She shook her head. "I'm afraid." She fidgeted with the bars. "Max, what they're planning, there's no stopping them now. We'll all be dead within the month."

"That's not going to happen."

Jane bit her lip, shaking her head once before saying. "You don't know what I've done."

"Tell me then, Jane. Please."

"Brendan Black is alive."

He nodded. "Yes, I know. But how is that possible? He was scattered around the globe, buried on sacred Soul Keeper ground. Only a few knew of the locations."

She pushed herself away from her cell door and began pacing, wrapping her arms around her thin frame.

He frowned again, hating seeing her so thin and distraught. "Jane?"

She stilled, turning to face him. "I am the one who showed the Veins where Brendan's body parts were buried. I helped put him back together and now he's alive and indestructible because of me! I am a *traitor* to our people," she cried remorsefully.

He processed the information, trying to block out the mayhem he'd left behind back at the mansion. What could Brendan and his Veins have done to his Obsidian Souls and his beloved Soul Keepers after he was knocked out. He dreaded to think, yet could feel deep within his soul that Sam was okay.

"*See*. You are upset."

"No, that's not it." He shook his head. "I was just thinking. When Brendan startled me, I was having drinks with Sam and some... others." He didn't think now was the time to go into details about him training Veins to become the 'good guys.' "I'm hoping they aren't too worried about me."

"Oh stars above," she whispered. "You don't think Brendan would have..."

"Killed them?" He finished for her. "No, I can feel that he didn't, that they're all right."

"How can you know?"

He shrugged, knowing now wasn't the time to dive into everything he knew and how. "You said you made Brendan indestructible. How?"

It was Jane's turn to shrug, as she sat down tiredly, facing him. "Shortly after you left for Italy, I met someone when I was on assignment. He was fascinating, educated. Not to mention *entirely* too good-looking to be human."

"Ha." Max smiled.

"Yeah, should have been a dead giveaway, right? Anyway, he had a lot of information regarding the Vein culture, interesting things I'd never known." She sighed. "After Angel and Sam obliviated Brendan, I hoped any further information I could gather would assist in the demise of our enemy. I was completely consumed with everything that came out of his perfect mouth. Long story short, I fell in love and I fell hard." She swallowed, looking away.

He didn't like seeing the look of regret that swept over her features.

"It's okay Jane, go on." He encouraged her, curious to see where this would lead.

Jane ran a hand over the back of her neck. "He wasn't who he said he was and when he learned that I had knowledge of where Brendan's remains were buried, he handed me over to a group of Veins and I never saw him again. I was their prisoner for close to a year."

He frowned, riddled with guilt that his own cousin had suffered so. "What did they do to you?" He wasn't sure if he wanted to hear the answer.

"I was interrogated for information regarding the whereabouts of Brendan's remains. I refused. They brought innocent pure-souls before me and I was forced to watch several of them being tortured in the cruellest of ways. Then I was given the option to save the others only if I divulged the locations. Months later, I was forced to assist in the reassembling, reviving and recharging of Brendan, using every one of my elemental gifts, along with a Vein, who had powers I had no idea they possessed." She sighed, leaning her forehead against the grimy bar, peeking at Max through her fringe. She tilted her head. "This Vein was so bloody strong, it's a wonder they needed me at all. She was… different."

"Different how?"

She shook her head. "I can't explain. Her face was covered, and she didn't utter one word in the week that it took us to bring him back. Foul job." She shuddered. "After I did what they needed me to do, I didn't see her again. They tarred my hands before locking me in a crate and I've been down here for I don't even know how long, or where I am."

"You're back home Jane."

"Home?" she whispered.

"I'm going to get you out of here."

"How?"

"I'm working on that." He walked around his small prison, running his hands along the dank walls, peering up at the mouldy ceiling. "You said we'd all be dead in a month. Do you know how?"

"No. Brendan just said he had a way of destroying every Soul Keeper that ever was through another Soul Keeper."

"Right," he whispered before extending a hand towards the ceiling and allowing one of his veins to slip from the flesh of his wrist to reach towards the black mould.

"What are you doing?" She sounded slightly horrified.

"Just seeing what's above us, to get an idea of where we are." He pushed at the plaster, twelve feet above him, seeking for a vulnerable break and slammed his vein into the dampest part. Plaster fell, revealing wet concrete. He retracted his vein before meeting Jane's curious gaze. He shrugged.

"There's no way out, Max."

"There's always a way out and we'll find it when the time's right."

"Well, I'm happy for that time to be right now, if you don't mind."

He was happy to hear her usual spunk return after enduring months of pure hell.

A grating sound filled the air as a metal door scraped along concrete before footsteps approached. "Just a little longer. I need answers first," Max said to her in a hushed tone before two men approached them.

"You." The taller of the two said pointing to Max. "Don't try anything funny, or we'll slice her through." He jerked a thumb towards Jane.

The other man released several wicked veins, hungry for blood, towards Jane, who'd scurried to her feet and moved against the furthest wall.

"Hey." Max snapped, turning cold eyes towards them. "I'll come peacefully, there's no need to hurt her."

The shorter one laughed, revealing teeth sharpened to points. "Where's the fun in that?" He pushed his veins closer to Jane, causing her to scream as one bit her face.

Max balled his fists by his side.

"Come on, knock it off." The taller one grunted to his side-kick. "Brendan's waiting."

Now we're getting somewhere. Hold tight Jane, I'll be back for you. Max pushed towards his cousin, who nodded once as his cell door was unlocked and he was dragged out, hands cuffed behind his back and led towards another cousin of his who he could not wait to see dead. Again.

SAMANTHA

Sam tried everything to get the cellar door to open. Her strongest blast of wind sent her back several feet. Her lightning bolts only ricocheted sparks back at her when she tried to melt the hinges. She kicked it hard before turning around and falling against it. Sliding to the floor, she wrapped her arms about her knees, dropping her head against the wood, she closed her eyes whispering, "Where the bloody hell are you Maxwell?"

"Here."

She opened her eyes to see Trent standing above her, holding a glass of water.

"You look like you need this." He passed it to her.

"Thanks." She took it, taking a long swallow before rolling the glass between her hands, watching the water swirl about.

He squatted in front of her, nodding towards the door. "What's the point of opening that?"

Sam shrugged. "It's one room I haven't been in. Maybe it has a clue where Max could be?"

"Doubt it. Brendan's maggots have Max, there wouldn't be a clue in this house where they could be hiding out."

Sam raised an eyebrow as she lifted the remainder of the water to her lips.

"You're probably right."

"I thought you'd be falling to pieces with worry."

"I'm stronger than I look."

"I can see that you are. I wonder how strong Max is? I wonder what they'll do to him? Are you worried about that?"

"Are you?"

He shrugged. "I mean, it's Brendan Black."

Sam sighed. "Max has unpredictable gifts and powers I don't even know the half of. I have faith that he can take care of himself."

"And who's going to take care of you whilst he's gone?" he asked, a glint of interest sparkled in his chocolate-brown eyes.

"Oh Trent, surely by now you've noticed I don't need anyone to take care of me."

"Yes, *Bella*." He nodded, standing. "I've noticed."

Sam pushed herself to her feet. "Good."

"Sam," Gemma called from the front of the house. "Protection barrier is up."

Sam headed out to Gemma. "Whose?"

"Mine, my dear." A warm voice sang out.

Sam sighed and reached out to hug Red. "Thank you. Max will be able to cross when he returns?"

"Of course." Red nodded, looking behind her. "Bowie asked me to come and place the barrier around the property. It's only around the first two acres, so no one must cross that."

Sam nodded before asking, "If Brendan was able to cross Max's barrier, would something like him be able to break this one?"

"No, even Brendan Black himself would be unable to pass this one." Red winked at Sam. "I had help." She jerked her thumb towards the dark sky, where the stars twinkled merrily.

Sam looked upward to where Methuselah sat. "Nice one," she whispered.

Red smiled, waving a portal open. "I'm off." She cupped Sam's cheek. "Don't you worry. Maxwell will be fine. I've no doubt of it."

Sam sighed, feeling better hearing it from Red. "Sure."

"Get some rest, I feel we have some big days approaching."

"You too. Goodnight Red." She watched as Red stepped into the portal and vanished in a mist of electric blue.

"Neat," Nadine said behind her.

Sam nodded, turning to go inside the house. "Yes, she is."

"Call it a night? Everyone's settled in, there's nothing more to be done about Max."

"Yeah." Sam headed upstairs. "You're right, goodnight."

"Night," Nadine called as Sam bypassed her room to go and shower in Max's. Afterwards, she pulled on his long-sleeved black skivvy and snuggled in his bed, pulling the covers up to her chin before attempting to reach out to him.

Goodnight Max. Please, come back to me.

To which she thought she heard a faint reply.

Soon, my love. Soon.

CHAPTER SIXTEEN
MAXWELL

Max was dragged down a dimly lit corridor where damp concrete walls were soon replaced with rough plywood as he was ushered up a narrow staircase and into the expanse of old church. Massive beams dripped in silver cobwebs. Stained glass windows that would have held such beauty with the sunlight filtering in, had been painted over, giving the church an oppressive feeling of doom. Sam's sweet voice in his head allowed him a sense of calm before facing Brendan.

"Well, well." Brendan clapped ham-like fists together. "A family reunion! Your father would be pleased."

The hundred Veins that filled the cavernous church pinned Max with hateful glares as he was shoved forward until he fell to his knees in front of Brendan. Dust mites scattered in the beam cast from a spotlight. He pulled in a calming breath, knowing he had a role to play to get answers from Brendan regarding the 'downfall' of the Soul Keepers. He dropped his eyes hoping to look the 'nervous-prisoner' as his cousin boomed with laughter.

"Ah, young Maxwell Black. You are such a disappointment to our brethren. You chose wrong, boy. And now you will die alongside your precious Soul Keepers and the traitor Veins you've tried to turn against us. What have you got to say for yourself?"

Max lifted dark eyes towards the filth that was Brendan and could barely maintain eye contact, he was that grotesque. He shrugged. "I've nothing to say that would make any sense to you."

"Indulge me."

"You had a chance to make this world a better place. A place where you could have maintained power, dignity, respect. For our kind to live in peace. *You* chose wrong. You chose to make our people viewed as *less*. As parasites. A disease that needed to be vaccinated against because of your greed, your *weakness*." Max shook his head. "We could have been so much more. But you and those like you dictated what the rest of us should be. Dictated what path we should lead, no matter the cost to any of us. Our mental health, the beginning of our downfall before we ever had a choice." He shook his head in anger. "You did this to what should have been an entirely powerful species. You *destroyed* that!"

"Ha!" Brendan cried as he stormed to his feet, kicking the wooden pew behind him, sending it smashing into the wall, splintering into a pile that resembled match sticks.

"You're right about one thing, boy! I made us who we are and what we are. We may have once been no match for the filthy Soul Keepers, but that is all about to change. But you and what you've done is far fouler than anything I've done. You're a *traitor*!" He roared in fury. His supporters noisily agreed as they cheered him on.

Max laughed grimly. "*Bullshit*. I and those I've rescued from your vile clutches, disagree. I'm offering them a better way to live. A chance to choose, to become something greater than what you've told them they *had* to be." He stared into Brendan's red pits where his eyes once were and got to his feet, testing the cuffs behind his back.

Brendan took a step towards Max, leering unpleasantly. "Shall I tell you, how you're going to die, along with all your little pet Soul Keepers? Shall I give you hope, in order to make killing you all the sweeter?" He took another step forward, filling Max's view with all the revoltingness that was now Brendan Black.

"Do what the hell you want, but I can guarantee you one thing, you'll not be killing a single one of us."

Brendan threw his massive head back, roaring in amusement, spraying spittle as his monstrous head shook upon his thick neck before turning blazing eyes back towards Max. "Ah, there's that Black optimism." He took four steps, closing the distance between them.

Max forced himself not to cringe as the stench of Brendan's decaying body assaulted his nostrils. "It's not Black optimism," Max said, looking up at the grotesque being. "It's *Obsidian*."

Brendan's grin faltered and Max assumed he was frowning as the misshapen flesh that hung between his eyes moved.

"What do you know of anything to do with *Obsidian*, boy?"

Max tilted his head. "Enough. All."

"Really? There's only one way you could ever know it all and that's if you've exceeded your father's wildest hopes."

Max shrugged. "Want to see?"

Brendan's answer was barely heard as he replied, "I do," before throwing a thick vein towards Max, wrapping it tightly about his waist, squeezing as he lifted him off his feet.

Max willed the cuffs that bit into his wrists to disintegrate before Brendan could expel the air from his lungs. He struggled as he was jerked from side to side and sucked in a lungful of air before it was snuffed from his lungs. Brendan thrashed him about like a plaything before thankfully, he was held still and could focus on Brendan below, hoping the room would stop spinning enough for him to get his bearings. Just when he thought it was over, he gasped in pain as hundreds of sharp barbs broke through his flesh, cutting deep. An odd, sickly heat leaked into his body as Brendan injected toxic fluid, making him dizzy. He groaned as severe pain unlike any he'd experienced, rendered him paralysed. He tried in desperation to force the filth out of his pores, using his Heavenly abilities to no avail. Surely this wasn't the end?

"How do you like *that*, boy?" Brendan leered before releasing Max, dropping him from ten feet in the air.

The crowd of Veins cheered as Max fell with a sickening thud to the dust covered floor. He lay there, winded, unable to pull air into his lungs, unable to cringe as he felt the toxins piercing vital organs, liquefying his insides.

Holy shit. This wasn't part of the plan. *Sam!* He cried before the toxic, worm-like-barbs made their way up towards his brain, blinding him with what felt like a hundred aneurysms repeatedly exploding. Hot blood leaked from his nose, ears and other uncomfortable places. His instincts were to gag on the foul matter, which crept up his throat and into his mouth; but, having no way to purge it in his paralytic state, choked over and over again.

He could feel every organ inside, shut down individually, his heart thudded once before intense pressure pushed behind his eyes.

Sam, I love you, was his final thought before his eyeballs exploded out of their eye sockets and the world as he knew it, vanished.

SAMANTHA

Sam woke with a start, bolting up in bed, whisking the covers off before she raced towards the door, thinking she'd heard Max call to her from downstairs.

201

"Max?" she cried.

His tone had held such a sad urgency. "Max?" She raced downstairs. *Please be here, for Angels' sakes, please be here!* she begged as she ran into the open lounge, then heading towards the empty kitchen and pushing the back door open, stepped out into the chilled morning air. Sam stood, feeling an overwhelming urge to sob as she looked up at the sky that was greeting dawn. She could only describe the feeling churning throughout her as hot, sickly and toxic. The cry of a corella calling out to his feathered flock shattered the quietness as many answered his song.

Sam wrapped her arms about herself and pulled in a lungful of cool air, scented with eucalyptus and lavender. "I am not going to lose my shit," she whispered sternly. "I am *not* going to cry." She sobbed the last word and allowed a tear to fall.

"Funny how that always happens." A calm voice commented from behind her.

She jumped out of her skin, startled. She turned, frowning at the sight of Methuselah. He stood in his usual attire of pristine suit, not one hair out of place, silver eyes pinning her like a moth stuck to honey.

She wiped her tears away and returned his silent stare. What was he on about?

"Usually, when people are trying not to cry, yet they speak the word *cry*, or talk about being emotional, it sparks that emotion or reaction," he replied calmly, reading her thoughts.

She wanted to know what that had to do with anything and as he opened his mouth to answer her thought, she snapped out. "Do you know where Max is?"

"I do."

"Can't you find him or portal me to him then?"

"I could."

She tilted her head. "But you won't?"

He shook his head slightly. "I came here for one reason, Samantha. To prepare you and Max. That is all."

"Prepare me for what?" She placed shaking hands on her hips, not liking this conversation's direction.

Methuselah looked skyward, as if he had all the time in the world before replying.

"For change."

"What sort of change?"

His silver eyes met hers. "You do love him with every inch of your being."

It wasn't a question. "Of course."

"He'll need that. Your absolute unconditional love and strength for what's about to transpire. Because if you can't, chaos will ensue."

Riddles, always riddles with this bloke. She ran her hands over her sleep-crumpled hair. "Can you please just give me a straight answer?" she asked.

He smiled, stepping closer as he ran a hand over the back of her neck. Her pulse points tingled, as he bent his head close and whispered against her ear. "Where's the fun, or lesson in that?"

"I don't need a lesson, Methuselah and this is no time for fun! I need answers. Where is Max?"

"Soon," he whispered. "In the meantime, the cellar is unlocked."

"How is the cellar..." She broke off as the backdoor opened and Methuselah shot up into the sky, leaving a trial of silver stardust in his wake.

"What was that?" Trent asked, as Nadine joined them.

"That was, as always, a complicated puzzle," she said, not clearing anything up as she headed towards the cellar door.

"Coffee?" Nadine called.

"Yes please." Sam waited a beat, placing her hand on the carvings before turning the knob. Nothing happened.

"Really, Methuselah, it's open?" She whispered in frustration before a click sounded and the door opened a crack.

"What magic spell did you use to get that open?" Trent asked from behind her.

"It's hard to say," she replied.

"Can I come?"

"I think I'd like to explore this one on my own. Max was pretty firm on wanting to keep this area private. When he returns, I'd rather he be just peeved at me, not you too."

"Considerate of you. Thanks." Trent smirked as he walked backwards towards the kitchen.

Sam slipped into the cellar, firmly locking the door behind her as she cast an amber glow to light up the bottom of the stairs. Taking a quiet breath, she headed down whispering, "Sorry, Max, number one rule, broken."

"Oh, he'll forgive you, if your scent is anything to go on," she heard before stepping into the open cellar.

She gasped when her eyes landed on the face of the handsome individual who was lounging back, leg swinging lazily over the arm of the chair, an open book sitting in his lap. He raised an eyebrow, snapping the book shut as he stood, taking a step towards her.

She hastily stepped back before getting a grip and stood her ground as the 'Max-look-alike' stepped closer.

"Weren't expecting me then, huh?" Kyle tossed the book on a ledge that wrapped around the cellars wall, lined with books, shaded plants, scented candles and old homestead paraphernalia. His gaze swept up and down her body.

"Can't say that I was." She offered her hand, wishing she didn't look so sleep-crumpled. "I'm Samantha Storm."

"Kyle Black." He grinned, reaching for her hand. "The better-look-ing brother." His grin faded the instant his palm met hers, roaring in pain as she sent a swift lightening zap into his hand.

"Holy shit!" He yelled, yanking his hand free, shaking it as if to remove the pain.

"Nice to meet you, Kyle and no, not the better-looking one, sorry." She returned his earlier grin, folding her arms.

"Well, shit," he repeated. "Is this how you greet all of my brother's guests?" He rubbed his palm over his chest.

Sam looked past him towards the large cell. "Guest, is it?"

"Well, lady, I'm not sitting in the cage, am I?"

"But you were, weren't you?"

"So? Now I'm not. Where's Max?" He mirrored her stance.

Sam wasn't sure how much to tell him. Wasn't sure why the hell Kyle Black was here in Max's home. Obviously, Max was the one who had helped Kyle escape the Light Accords prison. But why? And why hadn't he told her? She pushed her irritation aside.

"Want to share? I can hear your thoughts ticking over."

Sam walked past Kyle, keeping the corner of her eye on him as she surveyed the area. "Max obviously extracted you from your previous cell. Why?"

"Why? Isn't it obvious. I'm the brother he never knew he had. I'm family and I agree with his cause."

"The Light Accords took you after you'd been caught consuming a Heavenly Soul's essence. When did you decided *his* cause was right for you?"

Kyle shrugged. "After he explained what he was all about. I didn't think you royal-souls were supposed to be all judgy?"

She raised an eyebrow, hoping she wasn't coming across like the arrogant council members who had once made Max feel like an unwanted parasite. Before she could apologise, he explained.

"Look." He sighed, turning to watch her walk around the space. "When you are raised knowing only one path, then offered another, with a brother you never thought you'd meet, it kinda helps change your ways."

"Yes, I can see that it would. But why are you down *here*?"

Kyle offered her a tiny smile, raking a hand through his hair, not dissimilar to the way Max did. Her heart lurched, thinking of Max and hoping she would see him soon.

"Even long-lost brothers need time to be convinced that all can be well after ghastly deeds are performed." He shrugged. "I'm proving that he can trust me by staying hidden from the likes of you, I suppose."

Sam snorted. "Max never has to hide anything from me. Why don't you come upstairs, meet the others?"

"I don't know if that's a good idea."

"Why? The Veins upstairs are as desperate to change their ways and support Max's vision as you are. They've battled a monster to prove it."

"Monster?"

"Brendan Black."

"Brendan's *alive*?"

"If you can call what he is 'alive' then sure. They've taken Max god knows where."

"Shit," Kyle said

"Shit, indeed," Sam replied before facing Kyle squarely. "Listen, we're going to get Max back, I can feel it. So, come upstairs and be on your best behaviour and remember, I can fry you in a second if you decide to sample things you shouldn't. Got me?"

"Sure." He mock saluted.

She rolled her eyes and headed up the stairs, hoping she was doing the right thing.

CHAPTER SEVENTEEN
SAMANTHA

"I don't like this." Trent scowled at Kyle after the introductions had been made over coffee and egg muffins.

Sam took a mouthful of the bitter coffee, enjoying the burn as it took away the pain her heart had held onto every second since Max had been taken.

"You don't have to like it Trent, it's not your decision," she said, watching Daniel slide another serving of breakfast across to Rick.

"Well, why should it be yours? If Max put him in a cell underground, I'm sure he had a really good reason for it." Trent turned on Sam. "You're not one of us. You shouldn't have any say in such matters."

"Oh, really? Please, enlighten me, *Trent*." Sam put her coffee down, glaring at him, feeling a spark of anger run along her flesh.

"Hey, hey, listen." Rick stood between the pair who were looking to get into a heated argument. "I think we've got more important things to talk about, like how we're going to find Max?"

Sam blinked, breaking the trance of her fury and walked away from Trent, noticing Gemma looking at Kyle in total awe. She couldn't blame her. He was an extremely attractive guy. *Obviously*. She caught Nadine turning away, busying herself at the sink. She'd barely said a 'hello' to Kyle, noticing an awkward exchange between them, after she'd introduced him. She probably couldn't believe there was another Black son roaming the earth. She got it. She was still processing the information they'd received after learning Max was a triplet and now, she had one of them under his roof. But where was Max?

"Yes, Max." Sam ran her hands over her face. "I'm going up to get changed, then I have an idea I'd like to try."

Gemma looked hopeful. "If there's anything I can do, let me know."

"Keep your eye on him." She nodded to Kyle, who was enjoying an egg muffin and offered Gemma a charming smile as her eyes met his.

"Sure," Gemma replied quietly.

"Thanks." She met Kyle's stare briefly. "I'm going to need you all to stay here, to be safe. If you stay close to the house, you'll be protected."

"Where are you going?" Nadine asked.

"I'm going home to the Soul Keepers healing garden. It will give me insight to locate Max. I'm hoping." She shrugged, remembering a time it had helped Angel locate Bowie after Brendan had taken him.

"Can I come?" Rick asked eagerly.

Sam smiled at him, knowing he'd jump at any opportunity to see Bowie again.

"I'm sorry, no. It's safer for you here."

He sighed. "Okay."

She could feel Trent's eyes boring into her back as she left the room. He'd have to simmer the hell down too, or she might have to zap a bit of arrogance out of him. She took a deep breath and pushed her frustration away, knowing it was time to cleanse her body and soul to hunt for Max, hoping a quick shower would also wash away the headache and sick feeling growing within her.

"Just lay back, take a deep breath, we've got you." Angel smiled as Sam lay on the bed of chamomile in the healing garden, surrounded by every healing herb and plant known to mankind and many that were not.

She smiled up at Angel. "Just like old times, huh?"

"Not quite," Michael knelt on the other side of her. "There's something going on inside of you Sam. Something I've not felt before." He looked too worried for Sam's liking.

"Oh, yeah?"

"Yeah." He nodded, his eyes dark.

"What is it?" Angel looked at her brother.

He shook his head, placing his hands either side of Sam's face. "I'm not sure," he whispered, frowning as he ran fingertips over her flesh, rubbing behind her neck.

Sam winced.

"Sorry." Michael looked down at her.

"No, it's been irritating me on and off all week." She shook her head. "Must have slept on it funny."

"Mm."

"Plus, I've been feeling unwell since Max woke me this morning."

"Max woke you? How?" Angel rested her palms on the herbs surrounding her as she leaned closer to Sam.

"I heard him, he... called to me?" Sam watched as Angel's eyes widened.

"What?" She raised an eyebrow as Michael ran a hand down her arm before sitting back on his heels.

"I think that's probably a good sign, that's all. If Max can communicate with you, then he *must* be all right. When Brendan took Bowie, he couldn't communicate with me at all, remember?"

"Yeah." Sam nodded. "But his essence did though, didn't it?"

"Yes, it did," Michael answered. "Let's begin, Sam."

"Okay." She settled into the garden bed, feeling the soft petals stroke the bare skin of her arms as Angel and Michael sat either side of her. They placed a hand above their hearts, the other against her chest. Michael smiled.

"All you have to do is feel him. Let your love reach out to him. His essence will do the rest."

She nodded, watching as they closed their eyes and began chanting, whispering to the Angels above and Mother Earth below. Her heart swelled with love for the two Heavenly Souls who poured cleansing, healing energy into her, offering their assistance in locating Max.

"No matter where you are Max... I will find you," she whispered. She closed her eyes and drew in a deep breath, releasing her heart's hope that the breeze which caressed her face would lead her to her love. She relaxed fully in that moment before an eery ice-cold finger ran along her spine raising goosebumps over every inch of her flesh. The calm vanished instantly and she was suddenly sucked through a blinding vortex of pain.

Eyes watering, she screamed in agony as every nerve ending in her body burned. Sam sobbed in fright, her insides literally tearing themselves to shreds before painfully stitching themselves back together again. She was horrified to see her limbs stretching abnormally long. Spaghettification was a nightmare. She didn't think she could stand it for one second longer without losing her mind when the unexpected journey of torture to who knew where ended as soon as it had begun.

Her breath was knocked out of her as she fell hard on solid ground.

She gasped and rolled onto her side, clutching frantically at her midriff, waiting until her lungs allowed her to suck in a lungful of air. When she was confident she could stand without falling flat on her face, she did so on shaky legs as she rubbed her hands up and down her arms, grateful they were back to their normal size and that she appeared intact.

She looked about the dim area and released a cry of relief when she saw someone she knew and loved dearly. Jane, sitting upon the dirt floor, huddled in a corner crying softly.

"*Jane.*" She cried, racing across to her friend.

"Oh, Sam!" Jane sobbed, pushing to her feet and opening her arms to hug her hard.

"Are you all right?" Sam held her at arm's length to take a good look at her.

"No, don't answer that, stupid question. What's happened to your hands? What are you doing here? Where *is* here? She rushed in one breath before shaking her head. "Sorry," she whispered, hugging Jane, rubbing her back as she looked about the darkened space.

Sam raised her hand and flicked an amber glow to float out and shine light around them. She became aware of the hairs on the back of her neck standing when she discovered they were in a tomb.

"This is just great," she whispered, then gasped at the object in the middle of the room.

There, on a raised sarcophagus, was a torn, broken body. A thick black substance leaked from every orifice. Sam swallowed a sob of fear and squeezed Jane softly before hesitantly heading towards the body of who could only be Max. His obsidian ring glistened, the only clean thing visible without a trace of gore, or grime.

She pushed his hair away from his forehead, slick with the thick, wet matter, his face unrecognisable and swollen.

"I don't understand," she whispered. "This *cannot* be, he *called* to me."

Jane shuffled in the dirt behind her before standing on the other side of Max.

"He hasn't moved since they dumped him here hours ago," Jane said. "He was bleeding red earlier, but then that black stuff started coming out. It stinks."

It did. There was so much of it. A foul odour permeated the air around Max.

"So strange." Sam whispered, leaning forward to wipe the 'stuff' from under his eyes. It was sticky to touch, thick and hot. She wiped more from his lips and chin before wiping her fingers across her jeans. Leaning down, she brushed her lips across his.

"Max? Can you hear me?" She rested her forehead against his and closed her eyes. *Please Max, feel me, hear me. Come back to me.* She begged, brushing against his mind alone, hoping for a response. Silence greeted her. There was nothing. No air in his lungs. No heartbeat. Nothing. The black ooze began seeping from his eyes and lips once more, dripping down to join the pile on the dirt floor that was growing larger with every second that passed.

She bit her lip, leaning back. "Ok, buddy. If you're still… bleeding, then you're not dead just yet."

"That's what I was hoping too," Jane agreed, taking Max's hand.

Sam took his other, threading her fingers through his as she absently rubbed her thumb over his obsidian stone. "Max?" she whispered, running her other hand over his chest, then his stomach before hooking her fingers into the material of his jumper to pull it up. She wiped her hand across his stomach, removing the thick matter, revealing swollen, bruised flesh which was covered in too many wicked cuts to count. The black filth oozed once more.

"Do you know what happened, Jane?"

"No, I've been in a cell for months, then, they brought Max in and he was taken away in the early hours this morning. I was thrown in here and a few hours later, Max was dumped in here too. I thought I'd have to sit here and watch him die, alone." Her pale face filled with sadness.

Sam shook her head in anger. "Well, you're not alone now and I want to know how the Light Accords didn't realise you were missing sooner! Surely you were doing monthly check ins, Jane?"

Jane flushed, averting her eyes.

"What is it?"

"I was on assignment and yes, I was checking in with someone… only, they weren't the someone I was *supposed* to be checking in with." She shrugged.

"Oh, yeah?"

"Yeah."

Sam sighed. "We've so much to talk about." She dropped her eyes back to Max. "But first, how do I get you both out of here?"

"My question is, how did *you* get here in the first place?"

"With a little help from our friends," Sam smiled. "Michael and Angel."

"Yes, but Sam, how did you portal *here*, if you didn't know where *here* was?"

Sam shook her head. "I really have no idea; I just assumed my essence would float out and seek him."

"But you are here in the flesh?"

"It seems I am."

"Interesting."

"It's something." She agreed and frowned as she felt Max's finger's tighten around hers momentarily. "Did you feel that?"

"Feel what?"

"He squeezed my hand," she whispered, returning his squeeze. "Max?" Her eyes met Jane's with hope before Jane returned her gaze to Max.

"What the hell is that?" Jane's voice was filled with both curiosity and horror.

Sam followed her gaze, startled to see a shimmering silver fluid pushing the black ooze out of Max's body.

"What *is* that Sam?" Jane repeated.

"I'm not sure." Sam reached a finger towards the iridescent fluid, but it slid away from her touch. "What the…" She was cut off as Jane scrambled away from Max.

"It's changing." She gasped, pointing to the black mass rolling about on the dirt floor.

Sam watched as the black ooze began twisting and turning in on itself, growing larger in the blink of an eye. She dropped Max's hand and hurried backwards before it could reach her feet.

"Don't let it touch you!" she called.

"You don't have to tell me twice." Jane said, moving around the mass to reach Sam's side.

Sam threw a bolt of fire towards it, crying out in frustration when her flame fizzled out. "What the *bloody* hell is this?" The uneasy feeling in the pit of her stomach grew as the filth rose higher and formed into the shape of an enormous man towering eight feet over Max's body.

"Why don't your powers have any effect on it? That would have knocked twenty Veins on their arses!" Jane sounded worried.

Sam shook her head. "I have no idea. There's only one thing that hasn't been affected by my powers of late and that was Brendan," she whispered, eyes not leaving the 'thing,' as it lurched over Max. Her heart raced as it raised ill-formed, blackened hands towards Max's face before pushing putty-like fingers into Max's eye sockets.

"What the actual…" Jane whispered in fright as Sam gasped in surprise.

The silver liquid continued streaming out of Max's body, when suddenly it formed arms, with large hands and elongated fingers. As the black entity lurched forward, trying to insert itself back inside Max, the silver liquid grabbed it forcefully, wrestling it out and away from Max's body.

The two entities fought in an eerie silent combat and as the silver liquid fought its way out of Max's body, growing larger with every frantic heartbeat, Sam was alarmed to see his swollen flesh stretch beyond its capabilities.

Come on Max, please, please wake up! she implored him silently. She had to do something before the 'things' could do further damage to his poor, battered body. Sam stepped forward and took a deep breath as she raised her hands towards the foul-smelling ooze and the silver entity.

Prepare to be vaporised! Her fingertips sparked. Before she could send her blast forward, a silver arm shot towards her, wrapping around her waist and moving her against the furthest wall. Despite the speed and efficiency in which it moved, it almost seemed as if it were being careful with her, as it placed her down. Its protective manner seemed familiar.

Sam froze in shock. Every inch the silver entity had touched, tingled in sheer delight. It ran a 'finger' along her cheek bone, then returned to the fight in a snap. It wrapped a silver arm around the black mass's neck, then plunged what looked like several knives into the black mass's body, cutting and slicing. This only temporarily weakened it before it fought back with a vengeance. Both entities continued to grow at an alarming rate.

"We need to get out of here." Jane took her hand.

"Yeah, but how?" Sam whispered, unable to tear her eyes away from the entities as they tried to tear one another apart. It was a disturbing, voiceless battle, with only moist sounds filling the air as each blow was delivered. She could feel Jane trembling beside; hand clammy in hers.

Michael, Angel… I need to come home. Now!

She didn't expect them to whiz them out of trouble, but she didn't see any harm in trying. Her body developed the most uncomfortable pins and needles and she cried in horror as the black ooze shot a massive arm forward, sending a dozen arrows straight towards them.

Jane screamed, covering her face.

Shield, Sam threw her hand out, hoping to protect them from the piercing arrows and was relieved when they disintegrated against the outline of her shield.

"Oh no, *Sam!*" Jane cried.

To Sam's horror, the black filth split in two and one half marched towards them, as the other continued wrestling with the silver entity, which was growing rapidly. It exploded out of Max in its entirety and with such force, that it ripped Max's body to pieces.

Sam made a chocking sound, horrified at the scene before her.

"Max! *Max!*" She screamed, gripping her hair in anguish, hardly believing her eyes as Max's mutilated body fell to pieces on the dirt floor. Her shield dropped in that moment, utter devastation consumed her as her hearing faded in and out. Jane sobbed beside her.

The black filth reached them and without the protection of her shield, struck them with its massive arm, smashing them against the wall before returning to and melding back with its other half. Sam blinked to chase the fog away, almost numb to the throbbing pain in her head as she stared in disbelief at Max's crumpled body. She was in shock as she watched the silver entity burst forward, diving into the black mass before burrowing itself completely into its black folds, then disappearing entirely inside it in seconds.

Jane... Sam fought back tears.

It's okay, Sam. Jane soothed, steadying her tears as she grabbed Sam's hand.

Watching the violent tumble as the black entity seemed to inflate, then shrink before expanding as if it were about to explode, was a horrific sight. When she glanced at Max's remains, Sam groaned; hysteria building uncomfortably as the pins and needles consumed her from the inside out. Suddenly, her body dissolved into nothingness. She had no time to scream and no mouth in which to release it as every cell spun before being sucked through a vortex of utter agony, taking the heartbreaking image of Max's destroyed body with her.

CHAPTER EIGHTEEN
SAMANTHA

Sam rolled onto her side, wrapping her arms around herself as the ache burrowed deeper inside her chest. She squeezed her eyes shut, curling into the foetal position, not daring to breathe, knowing if she sucked in oxygen, she'd explode. The residue pain lingering within her was building to a dangerous degree and on top of the image of Max's mangled body, it was too much to bear.

She flung herself onto her back, slamming her fists onto the ground beside her and allowed the pain to slip from her lips as an almighty scream of rage, sorrow and grief burst from her lungs, piercing eardrums and hearts alike. Thunder clapped as the wind howled, knocking Angel, Michael and Jane ten feet back as the earth beneath Sam's fists, cracked and split, forming twenty feet deep lines in both directions, heading towards Terang and Mortlake.

Bowie burst out of the homestead, taking in the scene before counteracting the damage to the earth as he called the wind quiet. The rumbling stilled and as he sank to his knees, placing his hands upon Mother Earth, he chanted a healing incantation that sealed her wounds shut.

Sam's focus was glued to Bowie. She was grateful he was there to heal the wound her broken heart had created, yet a part of her was furious no one else seemed to be suffering as she was.

Bowie's eyes met hers, full of concern as he helped Angel to her feet, running his hand lovingly over her golden locks before striding towards Sam. He bent, scooping her up without a word and turning, headed towards the homestead. Sam took a careful, slow breath, assessing her resolve, knowing if she allowed herself one tear, the rain would be torrential and would not stop for months.

Bowie placed her down on the couch in front of the blazing fire before turning to Michael. "Can you call Red?"

Michael nodded, leaving the room.

Bowie turned as Angel asked Jane, "Where have you been? What happened to your hands? How did Sam bring you back?"

Jane shook her head, trying to take a deep breath, clearly trying to stop the waterfall of silent tears that fell as she wrapped shaking arms about herself.

"Hey, baby," Bowie placed an arm around Jane's shoulder as he smiled tenderly at Angel. "Questions can wait for Red, but in the meantime…" He didn't get to finish before Mrs McGoldrick breezed into the room carrying a tray of steaming mugs.

"Hot lemon and honied tea," she sang, placing the tray on the coffee table before dropping a kiss on both Sam's, then Jane's heads before exiting the room with an "I'm off now Bowie, Angel. See you in the morning." No questions asked as she vanished out of the room.

"Thanks Mrs McGoldrick," Angel called before sitting beside Sam, rubbing her back as she reached for a cup to push into Sam's trembling hands.

"Sam?" she whispered.

Sam shook her head once, hoping her soul-sibling would not ask again.

Angel nodded, looking across as Bowie steered Jane towards a chair. He placed a cup into her hands before pacing in front of the fireplace as they waited for Red and Michael.

Sam watched her brother through the steam of tea, holding the mug near her lips to appease both him and Angel. The pressure of pain, anger, disbelief, grief and heartbreak was churning and brewing to the point of explosion. She wasn't sure how much longer she could sit here and hold her emotions in, for not only the sakes of those she loved with every inch of her fibre, but Mother Earth and all she was born to protect. Relief flooded her when Red and Michael walked in the room.

Finally. Her thought was tinged with impatience.

Michael raised an eyebrow.

Sam didn't blink or avert her eyes in apology.

Red pointed to Bowie. "Whiskey in that tea should help," she said as she reached Jane's side. "My dear, what have they done to your poor hands?" She clasped Jane's hands before raising them to her lips, kissing the black tar. "We'll have this off in no time," she reassured her niece before turning her full attention to Sam. "What has happened?"

Sam shook her head, one tear clinging to her eyelash. There was no way she could say the words. Bowie dropped a dollop of whiskey in her cup, then did the same to Jane's, who gratefully obliged him by taking a large mouthful.

Red crossed over to Sam and knelt as if she were years younger.

"Close your eyes, dear," she whispered, placing her hands either side of Sam's face.

Sam blew out a soft breath, lowering her mug before closing her eyes.

"Keep them closed until I tell you to open them," Red advised.

Sam nodded, sitting as still as a statue, hardly daring to breathe, when she heard Michael exclaim softly, "Angels above, what the *hell* is that?"

"I've no idea," Bowie replied as Angel cried her despair.

"I've never seen anything like it. What's happening Red?"

"Silence," Red commanded uncharacteristically.

The room fell silent and Sam was itching for whatever was going on to be over. She needed to run. To scream. To do something more than sit, as her soul dissolved into the universe.

"Just breathe," Red soothed.

Sam released a long breath before Angel's anguished sob was met with Bowie's and Michael's gasp of disbelief, which almost had Sam opening her eyes. Red's fingers cupped her face, stroking her flesh until the room fell silent and after several more moments, Red's hands fell away leaving her feeling as if she were all alone in the world.

"You may open your eyes, dear," Red whispered.

Sam met Red's tired, cornflour blue eyes, which were filled with anguished tears. It broke her heart, seeing Red distressed, and she swallowed her tears down that threatened to fall.

Their elder rose on shaky legs.

Jane reached for her. "Please Aunty, sit down," she begged.

"Thank you, dear," Red said, wiping tears away as Michael swooped up a box of Kleenex, handing it to Jane.

Sam blew out a long breath, hoping to keep her emotions under control as she met Bowie's, Angel's and Michael's looks of utter despair. "What did you see?" she whispered.

"Everything," Bowie said when Angel and Michael clearly could not.

"Come here." He strode towards her and before she could stand, swooped down and gathered her in his arms, holding her close as he dropped his face into her neck. "I'm so bloody sorry, Samantha." His voice, filled with grief, caught as he uttered her name.

Sam wrapped her arms about Bowie's waist, his muffled sob snapping her out of her own pain as she realised she was not alone in the loving and grieving of Maxwell Obsidian.

"This cannot be," Angel cried in anger. "*How* can this be, Red?"

"That, I do not know dear." Red's reply was filled with agony and disbelief.

"Why don't we get you and Jane home, Red. I'll call the council members to assist with Jane's hands, then Jane can give a report of all that's happened?" Michael suggested, holding a hand out to the clearly shaken lady whom they all loved.

Red nodded, taking Michael's hand and one of Jane's tarred hands as she allowed Michael to pull her to her feet.

"Samantha, I will be along in the morning."

"Oh, no Red, you don't need to do that. I'll be all right, you just… rest," she finished lamely.

"I will be along in the morning dear," Red said, sounding more like her usual, strong self.

Sam nodded before adding, "I'll be at the mansion. There's something else I haven't had the chance to tell you."

"What?" Bowie wiped the back of his hand under his nose.

She met her brother's clearing eyes. "Max's triplet, Kyle is at the mansion."

"Really?" Michael frowned. "What else has Max been keeping from us?"

"Max has a *triplet*?" Jane exclaimed.

Everyone turned to Jane. She was still unaware she and Max were cousins.

Red saw the look everyone cast in Jane's direction and said, "We have much to discuss Jane, but first, home, healing and a report is owed to the council."

Red turned to Sam. "I'll be along in the morning. Go and do what Max cannot. Watch his Obsidian Souls." She ran a hand along Sam's hair.

Sam nodded before hugging Red, then kissed her cheek. "Of course."

"Alright then, Jane. Let's go home."

Sam watched as they left the room before turning to meet three pairs of sympathetic eyes.

"Don't." she whispered. "Please, don't look at me like that. I'm only just keeping it together."

"That's just the thing, you don't have to keep it together, Sam." Angel reached for her soul-sister.

"Yes, she does, baby." Bowie injected, eyes not leaving Sam's.

She would have smirked at him if she'd had the strength; her brother knew her too well. If she gave in to even the tiniest amount of pain she was feeling, there would literally be hell to pay. A storm of fire would be unleashed from within her and she wouldn't have the strength to stop the destruction welling in her heart. Nor the desire.

"Okay then, distraction-question-time." Michael sat on the coffee table, looking at Sam until she too sat.

"How did you portal yourself out of the healing garden and into wherever?"

Sam shook her head. "I have no idea."

Michael rubbed the dark stubble that ran along his jaw line. "Okay, how did you bring Jane back with you?"

"Again, I have no idea." Sam shook her head.

"It's unheard of, one as young as yourself doing these kind of transportation spells, Sam," Michael frowned, rubbing a hand along his jaw.

"Tell me about it," Sam agreed. "I've no idea how *any* of this has happened. You said, 'All you have to do is feel him, let your love reach out to him, his essence will do the rest.' So that's exactly what I did. I felt for him and then, bam! I'm in a tomb and well… you saw the rest." Sam dropped her elbows onto her knees as she leaned forward.

"Those entities seemed to be fighting over Max as if he were a prize needing to be claimed? Yet the silver one protected you and Jane from the black one, so, was he a good-guy?"

"Hardly," Angel said, running her hand over Bowie's shoulder.

He looked down at his wife, one eyebrow raised.

"Well, he was the one who killed Max in the end, so…" she shrugged, wiping a tear away.

Bowie pulled her into his arms, dropping his chin against the top of her head.

"I need to go," Sam whispered, standing abruptly.

"I'll drive you back," Michael offered.

"No." She shook her head before adding, "Thanks. I need to run all of this off before I face the others."

"You don't have to do this alone, Sam. Let me come with you. You know I have sway over a couple of them," Bowie reasoned.

"No, it's all right."

"How do you think they'll react?" Angel sounded worried.

"I'm not sure." Sam ran her hands over her face before holding them up. "Furious, devastated?" She dropped her hands by her side before adding "I'm just hoping I can keep them contained."

"You'll have to." Michael shook his head. "If even one of them step out of line, the council will be on them without mercy."

Sam released a humourless laugh. "Let them try," she spat.

"Samantha." Bowie cautioned her, his tone wary. "Let's just deal with one thing at a time. We don't need you holding a grudge with the council right now, no matter their past crimes."

Sam scoffed. "They think they can just get away with their actions, their judgements of others, especially the way they treated Max! Now, he's *dead* and I will *not* allow them to hurt any of his clan, even if they do seek retribution in their grief!"

"Hey, hey." Bowie held his hands up as if soothing a wild animal caught in a trap. "All right, look. Just go for your run, get back to the mansion and wait till the morning to tell the others anything. That way, Red and I can be there to help you support them."

"That's a great idea," Angel nodded. "You can focus on you. Take this time to grieve Max, solely for yourself…" She ended on a quiet sob before turning her face into Bowie's chest.

Sam crossed over to Angel, putting her arms around hers and Bowie's waists as she leaned her cheek against Angel's back, feeling Michael's hand on her own. Instant calm swept over her and she bit her tongue, shielding the ungrateful comment that would hurt Michael as he attempted to soothe her pain.

She would save her savage anger for those who deserved it.

She turned, cupping Michael's chin and forced a soft smile. "Thank you, for trying," she whispered, brushing a kiss across his cheek. She left the room, heading out of the homestead for a run she hoped would hurt the pain away for several minutes at least.

CHAPTER NINETEEN
SAMANTHA

S am sat at the window seat in Max's room, watching as the moon
cast shadows over the yard throughout the night. She stayed there
as the sun chased those shadows away hours later. His scent lingered,
only just calming the tide of fury and sadness from which she wanted
to claw at her insides and escape. Murderous thoughts kept her company as she fumed at both Brendan Black and the council, who had
served Max with such injustice in the past. She wanted them to suffer.
For everyone in this world who had caused harm and hurt to others,
to suffer. For justice to be done and for her to be the one wielding the
sword and scales of that justice.

The room glowed with her growing rage and the contrast of the
morning chill outside and the heat in the room cracked the window
with thermal stress.

"*Stop it,*" she whispered, calming down and returning the room
to a normal temperature. "Max wouldn't want me destroying the one

place he created as a sanctuary." She dropped her forehead against the shattered glass before a sharp knock at the door had her jolting.

"What?" she snapped, not turning around.

The door opened behind her, followed by. "Have you not slept? Showered? Eaten?" Bowie's tone was both annoyed and concerned.

She turned towards him and knew her eyes were blazing pools of amber flames by the look on his face and the hesitant step back he took.

"Why the *hell* should I do any of those things, Bowie, when my heart is literally *dying*!" she screamed, thumping a fist to her chest.

"Sam…"

"Don't!" she cried, trying to squash the sob wanting to escape. "*Don't* tell me everything's going to be all right! And *don't* tell me that I'm going to be fine and that everything happens for a reason! *Don't* tell me we've got to keep it together. That we have to make Max's vision a reality! And don't you *dare* tell me anything that is going to make this rage go away, Bowie… because if I'm not feeling *this*, I'm *terrified* of what I'll do." She wrapped shaky arms around herself, sucking in the sob that almost slipped past her lips.

He took four purposeful strides towards her and gathered her in his arms. She tried to push him away, but he held her firmly and hissed against her ear. "*Stop it*, Samantha!"

She frowned against his chest, feeling more conflicted than ever. She wanted to rage and cry. To scream until it rained blood. She wanted to be strong and resilient at the same time, but the tidal wave of grief and numbness was playing havoc with her elemental soul.

"You know how dangerous you can be if you don't control this rage, Sam." Bowie soothed, tightening his hold again when she tried to push against him. "Listen," he tried patiently.

"I can't," she whispered, forcing her eyes shut as she pushed her face harder against his chest, feeling every emotion battling within her. And it was torture.

"I can't do this Bowie… I can't breathe without it hurting, without my heart feeling as if it is literally breaking in two. As if my soul is growing thorns of steel inside of me and slicing me apart with every memory I've ever had of Max. I only just got him back Bowie. It's not fair," she cried. "It's not *fair*!" she shouted as the room roared into an inferno around them and the house shook beneath their feet.

Bowie cast a cloud, heavy with moisture to quell the roaring inferno, keeping his other arm tight around her.

She didn't recognise the animalistic sound that escaped her. Her moan ended as deep, guttural sobbing escaped from deep within. Her legs buckled beneath her before Bowie swooped her up and headed into the bathroom. She sat on the side of the bath and watched as he waved a hand over the tub, filling it. She clung to him for several minutes, sobbing against his chest as if the world was about to end.

It hasn't though, sweetheart. No matter the depth of your hurt and despair, we need you to want to go on. We need you, Sam. Bowie tried to sooth her.

And I need him. I need him Bowie. She sobbed. Painfully. Heartbrokenly until she was depleted of an ounce of energy.

Bowie's silence calmed her somewhat and her sobs ebbed to mild hiccups.

"You can get undressed pet, or I'm going to plonk you in there as you are."

Bowie's use of Tom's and Jess's pet name for her and Angel since they were children jolted her momentarily and fresh sobs followed.

Bowie ran a hand over her hair, as a knock sounded at the door. "Come in," he called.

Footsteps headed in their direction before Red stepped into the bathroom.

"Ah, good dear, you've allowed the pain to seep out. That's the only way forward," she said in her 'matter-of-fact' tone.

Sam looked up at Red and was saddened to see her elder's eyes were swollen from crying, too. It immediately made her want to comfort and not be comforted. She slid off Bowie's lap and reached for Red.

"Why don't you have a bath, Red?"

Red hugged her. "I'm okay. I just need to see you doing well."

Sam nodded before turning to the bath and seeing Bowie remove his hand. Steam rose, and she was grateful he'd warmed it for her. "Thanks," she said

Bowie kissed the top of her head. "You're welcome."

"Breakfast is just about ready; everyone is assembled in the kitchen. They know something has happened, but not what." Red sounded tired.

"I'll just have a quick soak, then I'll join you," Sam said, shrugging out of her jacket.

"No, you will relax and heal, as much as this time will allow you to." Red pulled a small jar out of her jacket pocket and unscrewed the lid, tipping the contents into the bath.

Sam watched the oily contents slip across the surface of the water as the sweetest scent carried by the steam wrapped around her, soothing her anguish, numbing her grief a little. Her eyes met Red's, who smiled knowingly.

"Secret family recipe… I'll give it to you, but for now, in, soak, heal." Red popped her arm through Bowie's.

"Come on, dear. There's a young man downstairs waiting to not only drool over the delightful brunch young Daniel has slaved over, but you, too!" She winked at Sam before leading Bowie out of the bathroom, closing the door behind them.

Sam almost smiled, but stopped herself short, shaking her head as she got undressed and slipped into the calming water. How could she even think about smiling at a time like this? She took a deep breath, closed her eyes and slid under the water, staying under longer than humanly possible, feeling the pressure of the surrounding water soothing as it caressed her skin. She remembered the last time she and Max had been together. Every sigh of pleasure induced by the other. Every kiss. Touch. Shared laughter and conversations. Every exchange from the age of eleven till now. She pictured his beautiful, forest-green eyes, larger than life, staring at her with his ever-serious gaze, as if contemplating the weight of the world.

Tears mingled with the water as every inch of her fibre ached with missing him. She released a small bubble of air, followed by another, till each sweet breath, escaped her body. As her lungs emptied of air, an unusual, pleasant pain, replaced the unbearable, grieving pain.

What if...? she thought hopefully.

She opened her eyes, watching the beams above her, waver through the watery-view, then opened her mouth and sucked in a lungful of water. Sam gripped the sides of the bath. She held on tight as the seconds ticked over to minutes. She squeezed her eyes shut and concentrated on the pain that stabbed behind her lungs, eyeballs and ears as she held herself under the water. Sam embraced the utter agony within her tortured lungs and body and fought the natural reflex to gasp for air as she choked on the warm water.

Samantha! Stop this at once! Max's eyes, filled with fury, flashed before her.

She gasped, choking on more water as the image jerked her out of her self-induced punishment. She bolted upright, vomiting and gagging, desperately trying to purge the liquid as her lungs screamed for oxygen. Sam gripped the side of the bath. Water sloshed over the edge, falling on the marble floor as she gratefully sucked in a lungful of air.

What was that? Was her mind playing a cruel joke on her? She ran a shaky hand through her hair, looking about the bathroom. No sign of Max. Of *course* her mind was playing tricks on her, after everything she'd endured the past day. She sighed, shook her head, wringing her hair before Bowie cut into her thoughts.

If you're done with hurting yourself, Sam, can you get down here now, please?

Bowie sounded calm, yet she detected the frustration in his tone, as only a sister could.

On my way. And I wasn't trying to hurt myself, I… just fell asleep. Yeah, that sounded reasonable.

Hurry up, Trent's getting antsy and if you don't get down here, I might decide to zap him and his arsehole attitude.

Sam almost felt like laughing. Almost. She got out of the bath, opening the window to send the water out to fall onto the garden below.

Don't you dare do any of the fun stuff without me, she said to him.

Like I said, hurry up.

On my way, big brother.

"*Maledetto inferno*, just tell us what is going on!" Trent yelled as Sam walked into the kitchen, looking fresher than she felt.

"*Finalmente*, so nice of you to join us, *Bella*!" he snarled.

Sam didn't break her stride as she changed direction from the breakfast layout to Trent and stepping up against him, wrapped her fingers around his wrist. "I've missed you too." She smiled prettily before sending a searing jolt of electricity into his pulse point, dropping him to the floor in an instant, knocking him out.

"*Sam!*" Bowie called sternly as Nadine rushed to Trent's side.

"What did you do that for?" Nadine cried, slapping at Trent's cheek.

Sam shrugged, catching Rick's gaze filled with awe before crossing to the kitchen bench to select a piece of French toast and rock-melon. She bit into the fruit and sat on a stool, turning to watch Nadine try to wake Trent and ignored Bowie shaking his head.

"So, this is the family I've heard my brother talking so fondly about." Kyle chuckled as he strolled into the room.

Sam noted Red's shoulders stiffen before relaxing once more, her eyes not leaving Kyle.

"That's right." Bowie walked towards him; hand outstretched in greeting. "Bowie Storm."

"Of course you are." Kyle smiled as he looked from Bowie to Sam. "As pretty as each other I see."

Gemma snorted, flushing when Kyle looked towards her. "Although, not as pretty as some." He grinned cheekily as he crossed over to Gemma, taking her hand and kissing the back of it. "Good morning, *zucchero*."

"Morning." Gemma flushed.

Cute. Sam knew Gemma was 'in love' with the look and idea of Max. And now, here his brother stood, alive and available. Poor Daniel.

"Now, can someone please tell me where on earth Maxwell is?" Kyle turned to Sam. "That is to say, you disappeared yesterday to find answers and so far, we've been given none. I think we've been patient long enough, don't you?"

Trent groaned and everyone turned to watch Nadine help him get to his feet.

"Fast healer, I see," Sam stated, licking melon juice off her fingers before biting into her French toast.

Trent took two menacing steps towards her. "Why you…"

"Don't even think about it." Bowie clicked his fingers and an amber spark sizzled at his fingers tips.

Trent turned towards Bowie. "You think she can just get away with electrifying me?"

"I do, actually."

"So, it's free for all then?"

Bowie shrugged, fingers blazing, a dark, smouldering look crossed his features. Sam stopped chewing when concern at the unpredictable situation hit her. It didn't bode well. Bowie's underlying grief for Max, that he'd been keeping at bay for her had clearly risen to the surface.

"Well, if that's the case," Trent leered, snapping his arms open, releasing a thick vein to strike towards Bowie.

Bowie's searing amber flame turned frost white, freezing the vein before its gapping mouth struck him.

Trent shrieked in agony as his burnt flesh froze solid. He gave Bowie a furious death stare before releasing several veins as he lunged forward in retaliation.

Bowie sent a blast of wind towards Trent before he could reach him. The frozen vein snapping off instantly, falling to the floor with a disturbing clunk. Trent fell to his knees, his outraged scream filled the otherwise, deadly silence.

Disbelieving, wide eyes filled with uncertainty flashed at each other.

"Are you *pazzo*?" Kyle asked, grinning at Bowie.

Bowie raised an eyebrow. "Depends on who you ask."

Kyle roared with laughter. "Oh, I am liking your brother very much, Samantha." He shook his head, clapping Bowie on the back before walking around to reach for the coffee pot.

"Well, that's all that matters," Sam muttered sarcastically, finishing off her toast.

Kyle turned with a steaming mug in hand as he faced Sam. "Now, I'd like to know where mine is?"

He blew on the steam, watching Sam over the rim of the mug, making her shift uncomfortably. He looked *too* much like Max for her liking.

She shared a brief look of concern with Red and Bowie before confessing. "I don't think I can, Red."

"Then we will show them, dear." Red looked around the room. "Prepare yourselves. Be strong. Be ready for the worst kind of news."

Everyone shifted, looking anxious as they met Red's steady gaze, nodding, clearly confused and unsure.

"It's going to be okay," Sam whispered, looking at Gemma, then Kyle.

"Show us." Kyle tilted his head.

Sam swallowed as she met Red's gaze when her elder reached to cup her face, whispering, "Close your eyes, dear."

Sam did and during the next several minutes, she heard murmurs of disbelief, cries of anguish, screams of outrage, then sobs of despair.

Red's hands fell away from her face and she opened her eyes to see looks of anguish and fury.

"How is anything about *that,* okay? Nadine hissed, tears falling down her beautiful face.

Sam shook her head, slipping off the stool to go towards the distraught beauty, who held up her hand, stopping her.

Sam nodded. *Okay…*

It will be Sam… just give them time to process. Bowie soothed.

She met his amber eyes and nodded, noticing an odd look pass between Trent and Nadine.

"Who was the girl with the black hands?" Rick asked.

"A Soul Keeper and a dear friend," Bowie answered.

"My niece," Red explained.

"This can't be…" Kyle's desolate tone had Sam turning towards him and was startled to see his eyes filling with tears. He'd only known Max for such a short time and had been a prisoner for most of that time. Was their connection as triplets that strong?

"Come, dear," Red said, placing a hand on the clearly shaken younger man and led him to a chair.

"A drop of whiskey might help." Red nodded to Daniel over her shoulder, as she sat next to Kyle.

"On it," Daniel said in a hushed voice.

Trent leaned against the door frame, holding his arm where Bowie had seared his vein as the others sat around the kitchen table. Sam perched back on the kitchen stool as Gemma sobbed. Bowie steered Gemma to a seat as Rick began pacing. He was the only one who didn't appear distressed.

Interesting. Bowie pushed towards Sam, who nodded once to let him know she thought so too.

"This cannot be happening," Rick said, after his seventh turn of pacing up and down the island bench.

"Well, wise up, because it is happening. It's happened," Trent spat unkindly, earning a greasy look from everyone in the room. He snorted, shaking his head and looking down at the floor.

Sam wanted to zap him again.

I'd let you... Bowie smirked.

She smiled, shaking her head before turning her attention back to Rick.

"I just don't get it. Why would Brendan come all this way just to kill Max?"

"He didn't kill Max, those 'things' did." Gemma wiped her nose on a tissue after Red pushed a box of Kleenex towards her.

"Yeah, but, you know what I mean. Brendan was resurrected, had the opportunity to go anywhere with his new 'powers,' but came here to kill Max? Why?"

"Simple," Bowie answered. "Revenge."

"If he wanted revenge, he would have killed *her*." Nadine stood, placing her hands on hips as she stared hatefully at Sam.

Sam was almost certain she saw flames dancing in the red-haired beauty's eyes.

"Ease up, Nadine," Rick snapped. "You know she was one of the most important people in Max's life. You disrespect *her*, you disrespect *him*."

Sam returned Nadine's glare, itching to unleash her grief she was only just containing. "If you want to go a round, I'm happy to oblige." she whispered calmly, although feeling anything but.

"Oh yeah, bring it on…" Nadine stepped forward.

"Enough." Bowie snapped. "*You*." He pointed a finger under Nadine's nose. "Watch your tone, or you'll be dealing with me." He then looked pointedly at Sam, not having to say a single word for her to understand his frustration.

"What do we do?" Daniel placed a small glass of whiskey in front of Kyle before facing Sam. "Do we have any idea where Brendan is? Can we retaliate?

"Sure, we could." Sam shrugged. "We will. But we can't do anything until we are stronger."

"How do we do that? Become stronger?" Rick asked.

"Training." Bowie replied. "A lot of training."

Sam shook her head. "I poured everything I had into that black 'thing,' and nothing affected it. It's like my energy only strengthened it."

"Then how are we supposed to take Brendan down, if you can't even take down one of his minions?" Gemma sniffed.

"With difficulty." Sam sighed.

"We don't possess any of the skills that you do... what hope do we have?"

Daniel sounded as worried as Sam felt.

"None," Trent said.

Sam frowned at him but remained quiet.

"Not true." Bowie looked thoughtful before adding. "We'll need more numbers and you'll need a lot of training and maybe... a little magic." Bowie tilted his head towards Red.

"It is completely forbidden for us to share any of our powers with our... enemy." Red flushed guiltily as she looked around at the Veins before meeting Bowie's gaze. "I'm sorry, but the council will deem you an enemy too, if you inject any of your powers with any Vein."

"Seriously, Red? Can't they see once and for all, that these Veins and others like them are not our enemy?" Sam cried in frustration. "We are on the same side, all of us wanting to protect the innocent souls and Mother Earth and put a stop to Brendan Black!"

"I know it's frustrating, dear. I understand all too well, as you know. But our laws are our laws."

"Well, they're not my laws anymore." She slid off the stool.

"Sam," Bowie warned.

She shook her head before asking Kyle, "You've got connections, no doubt. Prove your loyalty to Max and recruit every Vein you know who wants to convert to Max's way of life."

Kyle nodded. "I can do that."

"We can too." Daniel nodded towards Rick and Gemma. "We know others who were waiting for Max to call on them once we were established here. Now is as good as time as any."

"Will they come if they know Max is..." Sam couldn't say it.

Everyone was silent for a few moments before Daniel nodded. "I believe so."

"Great." Bowie nodded to Sam. "It's a start. I'll get Tom and Jess to give us a hand converting the barn to a bunk house."

"There's a lot of work to do. How long can we expect these Veins to arrive once you contact them?" Sam asked Daniel.

"Possibly a week."

"Then, we've got less than that to set up." Sam nodded to Bowie.

"Yeah, we do and it's going to take all of us working together, peacefully." Bowie looked at Trent. "If you can't do that, there's no place for you here."

"Who put *you* in charge?" Nadine folded her arms.

Bowie turned towards her and Sam thought Nadine was possibly the stupidest person alive, facing her brother with a haughty attitude, after what just went down with Trent.

"No one," he answered calmly. "I'm really just trying to help out in what can only be described as an unbearably sad, unpredictable, sorry shit-show."

Nadine held his questioning gaze before dropping her arms, saying, "Fine, I'm sure we're grateful for any help you Soul Keepers can give us. Aren't we, Trent?" She looked over her shoulder towards Trent, who was still leaning against the wall.

"We are," he answered, looking first at Bowie, then Sam.

"Good." Red clapped her hands. "I'm going to check the barrier. I believe it is still holding strong, but I urge you all to stay close to the mansion, just for safekeeping."

"Too easy," Rick agreed.

Bowie reached for Sam and, slipping his arm around her shoulder, led her from the room. "Do you want me to stay?"

"No, I've got this."

His eyes narrowed in concern and before he could open his mouth, she smiled.

"Bowie, go home to Angel. Honestly, I've got this."

"If you need me…"

"Yes, I'll call. I love you, now go."

He smiled tenderly down at her. "I'll be back tomorrow with Jess and Tom and everything we need to set up the barn." He dropped a kiss on her forehead before heading out the front door.

"Bye," she whispered as he disappeared. She took a deep breath and wrapped her arms around herself, closing her eyes briefly. Max's forest-green eyes flashed behind her lids.

Samantha? he called from behind her.

Sam gasped, spinning around, but found no one there. "I'm going insane," she whispered, knowing grief could make you see and hear things. "Keep it together, Sam. For Max and those he was trying to protect."

Overwhelmed and exhausted thanks to a long stint without sleep, she headed upstairs, pausing on the stairway leading to Max's room, but turned and went into the room he'd appointed her. There was something peaceful about being in a room she knew he'd designed with her in mind.

Sam closed the door and flung herself face first onto the bed. She allowed gentle tears to flow before sleep consumed her.

CHAPTER TWENTY
SAMANTHA

The rain pelted against the barns tin roof as the wind blew a gale.

"So, your friend Jane helped put Brendan back together again?" Gemma asked, smoothing a sheet across a mattress.

Sam nodded. Nine days after she'd seen Max's body disintegrate, she remained depleted, no matter how much healing energy Michael and Angel attempted to pour into her.

"So, she thought she was dating a good-guy, who ended up betraying her? Typical." Rick snickered, earning a dark chuckle from Bowie.

"Trust issues?" Bowie flung the last of the bedding down as it was all hands on deck making up the thirty-eight beds expecting bodies by that night.

Rick turned to Bowie. "I'm this good-looking and single. What do you think?" He flashed a charming smile.

"I think you shouldn't be. There's someone out there for everyone." Bowie shrugged.

Sam cringed, shoving a pillow into its case before tossing it up towards Daniel on a top bunk.

"Maybe so." Rick snatched up a doona, sheet and pillow and headed to the last six bunks that needed making up. "Shame you weren't a twin." He joked.

"I know, imagine the world with two of me?" Bowie grinned.

Sam rolled her eyes as she bent to grab the last doona as a pillow hit her in the head. She turned to Bowie. "Funny."

"What did Mum and Dad teach you about rolling your eyes?" He smirked.

Sam tilted her head, feeling a pinch around her heart at the mention of their parents. They'd shared a conversation via Zoom after they'd been informed of Max's death, but they couldn't come home because of an alarming rate of increased tsunamis and global earthquakes. They all knew it was contributed to Brendan's growing forces. Suicides had not been as high in the last five days as they had been before Sam and Angel had destroyed Brendan over a year ago.

Sam glanced around the room. She could feel the dark energy of the clan as they made up the bunks and filled the mini fridges and make-shift pantry with enough supplies for a fortnight. They were trying to remain positive in their grief, but Sam could feel the heaviness of missing Max wrap around every one of them. Well, almost everyone. She watched as Trent shoved loaves of bread into the pantry without much consideration of how one would make a sandwich with a mangled piece of bread.

Nadine was huffing and puffing as she wrestled with her doona and cover and Kyle was walking around with a clip board ticking off the to-do list. They were, for the most part, soldiering on and had been for the past week. In fact, they hadn't stopped, apart from getting a few hours' sleep at night.

Max would be proud of them. She whispered against Bowie's mind, trying not to choke on Max's name.

He'd be proud of you.

She smiled at his kindness. *They need some fun before the others arrive.*

What do you have in mind?

Something the council wouldn't like. She grinned.

I'm in.

"It looks like you two have something on your minds?" Kyle stood between Sam and Bowie, tapping the pen against his clipboard.

"We do. Who wants a swim?" Sam asked the group.

"Out there? No thanks, it's too cold." Nadine gave up stuffing the doona into the cover and tossed it onto a bottom bunk.

"How about in here?" Sam smiled before raising her hands towards the doors, whispering to the rain and wind. The doors burst open and a torrential stream of rain poured in and gasps filled the barn. Not a drop fell on anyone, nor the floor, as Sam wiggled her fingers, creating a floating pool of water. She whispered to the air and warmed the water before dropping her hands.

"There you go!" She smiled.

Everyone stared at the large, floating pool of water.

"Seriously?" Gemma asked with delight before shrugging out of her jumper and unzipping her jeans.

"Give it ago," Bowie too, stripped off everything but his boxer shorts, climbed up on a top bunk and dove into the water, sending splashes into the water itself, but once again, not a drop was spilt.

"This is slightly insane and I'm loving it." Rick stripped off, eyes not leaving Bowie's golden frame as he swam in the water.

Before Sam could blink, everyone had stripped off to their underwear and had climbed up onto the top bunks to allow them access into the floating pool.

She smiled, heart full at giving them all a little a happiness, a little respite from the heaviness of missing the one who had brought them here.

Max, how I miss you, my love.

Sis, get in here, now.

She hadn't shielded from Bowie and sighed away her grief as she shrugged out of her jacket, dropped her jeans and climbed on a bunk to join the others, who were laughing and enjoying the water. Before she dove in, she caught Kyle's eyes flash admiringly over her body, clad in a matching pink bra and underwear set, wishing now she'd owned some ugly cotton ones.

Bowie laughed, and she caught his eyes as she surfaced. *I really need to shield my thoughts around you, don't I?* She chuckled aloud.

"Yep," he said, sending a spray of water over her head.

After several minutes of swimming and treading water, Sam called, "Okay everyone, I've got a treat for you."

"Like this isn't a treat enough?" Daniel smiled.

"Another one then. Close your eyes, lean back and relax."

"Treading water isn't relaxing." Nadine scoffed.

"Yee of little faith." Rick flopped onto his back and before he sank into the water, Sam whispered to the air and waved her fingers. Millions of little air bubbles massaged his body, allowing him to float as if he were laying back on a lounge.

"Ah, you truly are a *stella*," Rick moaned in pleasure and Sam waved her fingers, whispering a floating incantation towards the others as they all flopped back as one.

Bowie grinned at her. "Nice one."

Her heart swelled momentarily, feeling good she'd given Max's clan something to enjoy. After half an hour, Daniel said, "I'm starving. How do we get out of here?"

"Good question." Kyle looked pointedly at Sam.

"Like this." Sam nodded to Bowie, who had waved towards the open door and the water lowered until each person could place their feet upon the ground and then, the water slipped away from each individual, streaming back out of the barn's door as smoothly and as silently as it had entered before re-joining the rain.

Gemma laughed, snatching up her clothing. "That was incredible! Thank you."

"Yeah, thanks so much." Daniel reached towards Sam and noticing she was practically naked, flushed red, stepped back and grabbed his pile of discarded clothes.

"It was my pleasure. I think you've all been amazing, supporting one another during this time. Let's make Max proud by really welcoming the others when they arrive and help them settle in."

Bowie nodded, zipping up his jeans and running his hand through his wet locks.

"Training will start in the morning. I'll be bringing Jane and Michael with me."

"You're actually going to bring a *Heavenly Soul* here on the first day with untrained Veins?" Trent asked, looking slightly flushed. "Are you *plazzo?*"

If one more person insinuates that I'm mad.... Bowie trailed off as Sam interrupted his thought.

"Listen, we don't have time for this and the new Veins don't either. We have limited helping hands and have to accept it from those who are willing to give it. So don't start." She stared Trent down.

"Well, it's their funeral if things go wrong." He shrugged.

Bowie laughed, shaking his head. "Oh boy… you really don't know who you're dealing with, do you? But you will and so will they."

Trent looked like he was about to say something smarmy, but Kyle cut him off.

"Well, let's finish up in here, then clean up and get ready. Tonight's going to be a big night. Sam, are you leaving with Bowie?"

"Why would I?"

"You are a Soul Keeper; Max isn't here to protect you? Wouldn't it be smart if you too, would be absent until we've had a conversation with them all?"

Sam paused, thinking it did make sense and wondered what Max would want her to do. "I can protect myself as Bowie demonstrated earlier this week." She nodded to Trent. "No offence, Trent."

He raised a cool eyebrow as water droplets fell from his hair and ran down his face, not bothering to reply.

He is handsome, in a disturbing way. She mused.

Pfft, came Bowie's reply. "I'll see all you delightful people in the morning. Seven AM sharp." He saluted before turning to head out.

Nadine groaned. "Seven. Seriously?"

Bowie stopped mid stride and turned towards her. "Do you think Brendan's army are sleeping in?"

"I don't care what Brendan's army are doing. I need my sleep and Max wouldn't want me, of all people, not feeling energised before training." She stormed past Bowie and out into the rain towards the mansion.

"I'll finish up then, shall I?" Gemma muttered as she turned to finish the bunk Nadine had been working on before the swim.

"No, go on. Everyone out, freshen up, have dinner, relax before the others arrive." Sam reached for the doona as an eery sound carried by the wind, trembled in the surrounding air. It increased in volume as the ground shook and vibrated beneath their feet before rolling away, as if a giant mole was searching for an exit.

Gemma clung to Kyle as Rick rushed to Bowie's side, who held a hand to steady him as the ground heaved and lurched.

"What is this?" Nadine screamed as the wind whipped her hair about her face, causing the strands to slice into her flesh. She screamed, throwing her hands over her face, protecting it from the lashing before the wind did the same to Gemma and Sam. Bowie threw a shield around them all, preventing the elements from harming them.

The ground stilled as the wind vanished, leaving them all gasping in shock.

Sam looked at Bowie. "What the hell was that?"

"It felt elemental?"

"It couldn't have been. None of us would injure our own."

"But *we* are not *yours*," Rick said solemnly.

Sam bit her lip, wiping a stream of blood from her face. "Is this some sort of lesson? Is this the Light Accords?" she asked Bowie, who had healed Gemma, then Nadine before crossing towards her.

He cupped her face and whispered away her cuts before pulling her into his arms.

"I have no idea, but I think you should come home with me."

"No," she whispered before kissing his cheek. "I am home."

He looked into her eyes before sighing. "Of course you are. I'll go talk to Tom. Maybe he can reach out to Fletch to see what's happening?"

She nodded as the others left the barn to go into the house. "It's worse than before, isn't it? Before Angel and I killed Brendan the first time?"

"Yeah, it feels different."

"We have to end him Bowie. Somehow, we have to."

"We will." He hugged her again before turning to leave the barn. "I'll be in touch. Stay safe."

"You too," she said before making the bed and checking everything was in its place for their visitors. When she left the barn, she looked up into the darkening sky and saw a lone star, twinkling too brightly, after what had just happened.

"Why aren't you helping?" she whispered, waiting, yet not really expecting a reply. She sighed and headed along the path towards the house, kneeling here and there to lay her hand over deep cracks in the earth the unknown entity had created. She whispered healing incantations, sealing the wounds of Mother Earth, knowing Bowie and the other elemental souls would be doing the same.

After showering, Sam waited in her room for Kyle, who'd suggested she allow time for the Veins to settle in before making an entrance. They'd been informed they were under the same roof as an Elemental Soul, a Royal Soul Keeper, who'd be assisting them in their training, along with other Soul Keepers. Kyle thought it best they process this information with the encouragement of their own kind.

Sam agreed giving them time to wrap their heads around her being here was a good idea, considering it hadn't been all that long ago, that many of them had consumed and destroyed Soul Keepers. She leaned her ear against the door, curious about their conversations and their reaction to her. She was pleased to hear occasional laughter which filtered up to her through the white noise of the forty-odd Veins downstairs. A knock where her ear rested sounded against the door.

"Sam, are you ready? Kyle asked.

Startled, she held a hand to her chest, shaking her head at her own jumpiness.

"Get a grip," she whispered before answering. "I'll be right there."

She checked her reflection in the mirror, pausing to run a hand over her sleek high ponytail that brushed against her bare shoulder blades, pleased she'd taken the time to straighten her curls. It gave her a slightly more sophisticated look. She needed to feel confident facing the large group of what used to be and not all that long ago, the enemy. Bold eyeliner emphasised sparkling amber eyes, which smouldered with grief. Red lipstick gave her a pouty look she wasn't used to. The black, halter dress hugged every inch of toned flesh and sat just above her knees. It was a bold look. She almost didn't recognise herself.

Beautiful... she thought she heard whispered through the open window as the night breeze caressed her cheek. With a shake of her head, she spun on black, heeled boots and headed downstairs.

Kyle was waiting for her at the bottom step. Him watching her descend with hungry eyes, the colour of Max's, had her seeing red. She stopped on the step above him and tilted her head.

"If you don't start looking at me like anything other than the love of your dead brother's life, I'm going to microwave your insides, then, make you suck them up through a straw before I kick your arse."

He grinned mischievously. "That almost sounds like fun."

"Ugh!" Sam groaned, going to walk by him, when he stepped in front of her. She raised an eyebrow, making sure her eyes held a glow of flame as she stared down at him.

"Hey," he said. "I'm sorry. I didn't mean any disrespect. You're a beautiful woman, on top of being a royal soul and the fact that you were my brother's love intrigues me." He shrugged. "I promise that from now on out, I'll look at you like you're my own sister."

Sam sighed, looking past him towards the loud conversations.

"Thank you."

"Nervous?"

She met his eyes, allowing her shoulders to relax. "Yeah, a little."

"Don't be. The ones who kicked up a fuss were soon sorted out by Rick and Gemma." He smiled. "Max and you sure have some loyal followers."

"Not followers," Sam said, looking past him again. "Family."

Kyle's smile was genuine. "Yeah, I can see that they are…"

She met his gaze once more and saw his eyes filled with admiration. "What?"

"It still amazes me that right before me stands a Soul Keeper of Glenormiston South, who considers a handful of once 'villainous, diseased Veins,' to be family." He offered her his arm, stepping aside. "I think world peace could in fact be achievable." His eyes twinkled.

She couldn't help the light laugh that slipped from her lips as she wound her arm through his. "Anything is possible, if you believe in it enough and have the right people to help make it so."

He looked down at her, suddenly serious. "Will you ever be happy again?"

"No," she whispered without hesitation.

"You're that sure?"

"I am," she answered without a hint of self-pity. "How can one ever truly be happy when an actual piece of their soul is missing and they can physically feel as if their heart is torn and broken?"

"Well, when you put it like that…" he said, patting the top of her hand before leading her into the open lounge where the fire roared cheerfully.

The word, 'diversity' was the first thing that popped into her mind as her gaze swept around the room, captivated by their alluring skin tones. Accents from around the globe greeted her: African, South American, Irish, Polynesian, Canadian, New Zealand, and some which were foreign to her.

She was overwhelmed by the magnitude of what this could mean. If these Veins could convince their communities, that by collaborating with the Soul Keepers, they would remain - if not become, more powerful in their own right. Sam took a deep breath. Then this group would not only be the vessel to assist in the take down of Brendan's army, but also in the healing and caring of Mother Earth and protection of the pure-souls moving forward. Maybe it wasn't so naïve to think that world peace could be achieved?

She was so deep in thought, she hadn't noticed the room had fallen silent, or that all eyes were on her.

"If you think she's gorgeous, wait till you see her brother, Bowie Storm. Mm, to die for." Rick said to a group of well-groomed men, snapping her to the present conversation.

"Bewitching…" a dark-skinned beauty muttered.

"Tasty too, no doubt." Another quiet voice reached her.

Kyle yelped, drawing his arm away from Sam as a current of blue energy sparked along her flesh, dripping off her fingertips, and falling to the polished floorboards. She couldn't help it. It was her body's way of protecting herself, with so many hungry-eyed Veins looking at her as if they were starving. Never had her body reacted like this before, like her own personal security system switched to high, without her calling it forward.

Interesting… she thought. *And handy.* It made sense though; she'd never been surrounded by so many Veins in her lifetime.

"As dangerous as our elders say," a woman whispered.

"Out of control animals, the lot of them," came another's retort.

"I wouldn't have come if I'd known *it* was here."

"Oh, I certainly would have, even though *it's* not Heavenly. Can it be dessert?" A dark chuckle followed.

"I wouldn't want to taste it, *diseased* garbage, no matter how good *it* looks," another spat.

Sam whispered to the warm air in the room and sent a searing blast of heat towards the obnoxious twit who mentioned she was an 'it,' and was delighted when the individual screamed in horror. Her silken locks turned to a frizzy brown, singed mess.

Samantha...

She frowned, thinking the familiar reprimand sounded like Max.

"Samantha!" That explained the familiarity as Kyle stepped in front of her, breaking her out of her trance-like state. She removed the heat blast immediately with a snap of her fingers.

"Looks like we're off to a great start," she whispered, looking around at the mistrusting eyes.

"Well, you burning them isn't helping," he said, equally as quiet for their ears only.

"Well, them looking at me like I'm something to eat isn't helping either!" She hissed, wishing Bowie were here.

Do you need me, Sam? Bowie's powers were gaining every day since his ceremony with Angel.

No, I'm all right, I've got this. Go away, she said, almost playfully.

Goodnight little sister. Don't kill anyone till I get there in the morning.

She snorted aloud before realising she had and cleared her throat.

"Hold up, everyone." Rick called, holding his hands out and looking pointedly at Sam. "We are all here for the same goal. In-house bickering, isn't going to help us."

Daniel joined in. "You don't realise how lucky we are, to have Samantha Storm on our side in this war. She's your ally."

"Doesn't seem like much of an ally," a woman spat, comforting the singed-haired woman. "If Maxwell Black were here, *it* wouldn't be able to do this and get away with it."

"If only he *were* here, we wouldn't be needing *it,* at all," a high-pitched voice said, almost snarling.

"I so wanted to meet him. If his brother is anything to go by, he must have been divine," a nasal tone interjected.

"No doubt." Another joined in.

"I still don't see why *it* needs to be here at all, let alone the other *things* coming in the morning!" All these throw about comments were wearing Sam down.

She sighed internally, feeling tears threaten as they spoke of her love, as if they knew him. As if he were *theirs*. She felt both exhausted and spent. *Oh Max... if only you were here.*

She took a deep breath and reached behind her, pulling a glossy green leaf off the potted Peace Lily and walked through the crowd, towards the one she'd singed. Bodies parted and she grit her teeth hard as whispered comments of lust and hate reached her.

She wondered if the Soul Keepers in general were ever as hateful towards the Veins as these Veins were being towards her right now?

She was disappointed with the knowledge that they had. Two powerful species, with so much potential, at war with each other. It was ironic now, that standing in a room full of *them*, she wanted nothing more but for them to accept her. To be her friend and ally, as Max would have wanted.

She ignored the pain in her heart and tried, uselessly, to push Max from her thoughts as she tilted her head back. She felt the silky brush of her hair tickle her lower back as she met the cold stare of the unusually tall, furious looking woman with the singed mop-top. Sam reached towards the woman, who shrieked, stepping back as if Sam were a diseased animal.

"Don't you *dare* touch me," she all but hissed.

"I'm trying to help you." Sam assured her.

"She sounds like an angel." She heard another whisper.

Sam sighed, looking past that individual, meeting Nadine's eyes. "A little help?"

Nadine's smirk was unusually cold and Sam frowned, not liking how taciturn the red-haired seemed to be amongst her 'people.'

"Enough!" Gemma snapped, stepping forward, facing the others. "Sam is trying to help *you*." She spat.

The outraged woman pointed to her hair. "Helping?"

"You deserved that and yeah… *helping*. Sam's here to help us all. You've seen the disturbances in your own regions, the global disasters, animals dying, old diseases spreading again. It's because of *him*, Brendan Black." Gemma's fists were balled at her sides and Sam felt a great deal of pride in her as she watched her face the others.

"Well, we heard it was a *filthy* Soul Keeper who helped dig him up and put him back together."

"And they call *us* evil!"

"Angels above!" Sam cried, unable to stay silent a minute longer. "The Soul Keeper who did that refused to give any information on Brendan's whereabouts even when she was tortured. It was only when *your* people decided to torture innocent souls, that she gave *any* information!"

She could feel heat radiate from her flesh and from the way those around her backed away. Sam knew flames were dancing along her flesh and took a calming breath to cool down.

"She had no choice, *none whatsoever*, but to assist with the restoration of Brendan Black," she said, her tone calmer. "Now." She turned to the woman whom she would now privately refer to as 'mop-top.' "Please accept my sincere apology and allow me to fix my mistake."

The woman frowned.

"You'll only get this offer once," Gemma said.

Sam hid her grin as the woman stepped forward. She held the leaf to her chest and grasped the woman's wrist before whispering a repair incantation, her eyes not leaving the woman's. As the leaf wilted in her hand, she heard impressed murmurs and shocked gasps around the room as the woman's hair returned to its natural glossy beauty.

The woman reached up to touch her hair, then raised an eyebrow before whispering, "I too, apologise for my inappropriate comments."

Sam bowed her head before looking around the room, catching another odd exchange between Nadine and Trent. Before she could think on it, Daniel approached her, passing her a glass of champagne.

"Well, this has been entertaining." He attempted cheer.

Sam shook her head, giving him a small smile, hoping to ease some of the tension that clearly lingered in the air, wishing she had Angel's ability to manipulate moods.

I can be there in a flash… Angel brushed against her mind.

Sam felt happier than she had in days, hearing her soul-sister's voice and a tear automatically spilled from her eye. She wiped it away, raised her glass, took a small mouthful, and answering Angel. *I love you, but I'm okay. You and Bowie relax, go do… couple things.*

She heard Angel's laugh brush warmly against her mind before fading, leaving Sam feeling desperately alone and wondering how she was supposed to do any of this, whilst feeling less than half herself.

"Samantha Storm?"

She turned to look into the sweet face of a boy with intense brown eyes in his late teens. "Sam," she replied. "Just Sam."

He smiled, flushing, offering his hand. "Jarrah. Just, Jarrah."

"Hello, 'just-Jarrah'," She grinned, shaking his hand. "It's nice to meet you.

He bobbed his head, eyes taking all of her in like a star-struck teenager. "I'm so sorry some of them were… rude." He shrugged. "Our people have been through a lot, because of your kind."

Sam sighed, biting her tongue on what 'his-lot' had done to the world in general, but knew it wasn't fair to group them all as one, so said instead, "Yeah, I'm really sorry about that too."

He nodded, taking a mouthful of Sprite.

"So, are you here with your parents?" she asked.

He looked down at the floor before meeting her eyes, his filled with sorrow before shaking his head. "Nah, my parents are dead."

"Oh, I'm sorry to hear that." She felt bad for the handsome boy. *How had he come to be with this lot of Veins?* "So, what made you want to fight against the old ways?"

"Max." He smiled sadly. "And my cousin Rick." He nodded across to the Vein Sam had always liked.

She grinned. "I'm glad you have each other."

"Yeah," Jarrah grinned. "I'm lucky."

"Did you meet Max?"

"I wish. He's kinda a legend amongst our kind."

"Is he?" She mused, swallowing her love and admiration that rose on a wave of grief.

"He gave us the first sign of hope in hundreds of years that things could be different. He showed us that we could survive and be strong by absorbing all that is wrong in the world and not have to destroy, poison and pollute. That we didn't have to be the bad guys." He waved his arm around the room, tipping his drink on the floor.

"Shit, sorry." He flushed, embarrassed.

"Don't be." She smiled kindly and waved her fingers towards the liquid, hearing his delight as it rose in a fluid stream off the floor. She sent it flying over the heads of the Veins and towards the kitchen sink.

"Cool…" Jarrah nodded looking impressed.

She shook her head. "It's nothing. Will you excuse me?"

"Oh, yeah, sure." He nodded.

"It was really nice meeting you."

"You too, can't wait for training tomorrow."

She smiled and turned, hoping to escape the stares and whispers, desperately needing to be alone. If she was going to allow her pent-up tears to flow, she wanted it to be in private before another day that was sure to be filled with tension began.

She wasn't that lucky as Rick, Daniel and Gemma stopped her escape, wanting to introduce her to some of the friendlier crowd. Ten minutes felt like five hours as she smiled and exchanged small talk with their guests. It was a relief when she could slip out the back door to peace and quiet and into the chill of the night air's arms.

The whispers about Max was tearing at her torn heart. Most of the Veins had no idea of the relationship she'd shared with him. She was just one of the 'Evil Soul Keepers' their idol had grown up with. She ran her hands over her face before going back inside and slipping around the crowd, headed up to her room.

"Hey, Sam?" Kyle called as she was halfway up the stairs.

She turned, waiting.

"Would it be okay if you grabbed some of Max's clothes for me? A jumper and jeans. Maybe something to train in tomorrow." He looked away before meeting her eyes, his filled with regret.

"You don't want to help yourself?"

"I wouldn't feel right about it, you know, going through his things."

She nodded, totally understanding where he was coming from. She didn't really want to go up there and be surround by his scent. See his empty bed where they had, not all that long ago, celebrated each other's bodies and souls, for endless, blissful moments after too long apart.

"Are you sure you wouldn't like to grab something?"

He nodded solemnly. "I'd only just started getting to know him, you know?"

She felt sympathy for the brother who had been separated from his, for too many years without a say so. She had the urge to go and put her arms around Kyle, offer him some sort of comfort; but the thought of being in his arms? The image of Max alone hurt too much. "I'll leave them outside my door for you to collect when you're ready."

"That would be great, thanks, I'll grab them later, after I've helped settle our guests in the barn."

"Thanks Kyle."

"No problemo."

She watched him walk off for a moment before turning to head up to Max's room. Sam paused to blink back tears. She knew his scent would overwhelm her and blew out a long breath before pushing the door open.

CHAPTER TWENTY-ONE
SAMANTHA

When she stepped into Max's room, Sam sensed she wasn't alone. How *dare* one of the guests think they could roam around Max's private quarters!

"This room's out of bounds." She gritted her teeth angrily, tears vanishing as she marched into the centre of the room, standing beside the bed. She narrowed her eyes as a figure near the window moved slightly, his broad back to her as he peered out into the night, no indication he'd heard her whatsoever.

She huffed out a breath, folding her arms to prevent herself from frying his intruder-arse as she tapped her foot.

"Excuse me, do you have a hearing problem?" she asked, sarcasm dripping off her honied tone.

He turned his head then before turning to face her fully.

Sam gasped, unwillingly taking a step forward before freezing, not believing her eyes. What was this?

"Kyle?" She already knew the answer, but if it wasn't Kyle and she *knew* it wasn't Max… then who? The other triplet?

The imposter slowly shook his head, dark eyes sweeping her from head to toe, then back again before taking a measured step forward, then stopping as if waiting for her permission to move closer.

She shook her head once, stepping back as the electricity and tension building in the air was making it painful to breathe. She felt an unfamiliar dizzy wave hit her before sucking in a lungful of air, forcing herself to stay alert, to focus on the imposter before her.

Yes, Kyle and Max were as identical as siblings could be and both undeniably striking in their individual ways, but this man before her was beyond deliciously perfect to be real. She blinked twice to make sure he was in fact real before narrowing her eyes, tilting her head, thinking that would remove any glamour. If this was some sort of ruse, she'd unveil it.

He mirrored the tilt of her head, as if patiently waiting for her to make her next move. His five o'clock shadow accentuated his jaw line, gifting his chiselled features a sultry look that was incredibly appealing. His lips were the most kissable she'd ever seen on a man; the tip of her tongue slid between her lips automatically at the thought of walking forward to ravish his.

When his gaze traced the movement of her tongue, she felt heat warm her cheeks and she shook her head, ashamed she'd even thought about locking lips with this too-perfect mirror image of her beloved, now gone from this earth. Despite her guilt, he was overwhelming all her senses.

She watched as he drew his large hands up to slip long fingers into the pockets of his black jeans that hugged strong thighs like a second skin. She caught the glint of an obsidian ring and frowned.

"Are you one of the Black triplets?" She hated hearing the fear in her voice.

"I certainly look the part, don't I?" His voice, velvety and low, had her gut clenching and pulse racing erratically. The longer he stared at her with such intensity, quivering butterflies scattered recklessly about her stomach.

Do not fall under his spell, she begged herself, swallowing before replying.

"That's not really an answer, is it?" She snapped her fingers, casting an electrifying bolt to dance brightly along her fingertips.

His eyes filled with amusement and something else she couldn't decipher, dropped to her glowing fingertips before returning his eyes to hers. "Do you truly not recognise me, Samantha?"

Sam wanted to cry at the cruelty that surely had to be Brendan Black and his mischievous, heartless ways.

"*Brendan*." She swore, shaking her head, clicking the fingers on her other hand, sending an amber glow to burst around her, creating static energy that danced at a high voltage.

He raised a perfect dark eyebrow. "Sam." The imposter warned. "Please don't. Just listen to me."

"Not gonna happen, *buddy*," She said, eyes blazing. She hated that Brendan had the ability to sound like Max. Just as he had sounded like Bowie over a year ago when he'd taken his body and had used his essence to imitate her brother. What she hated more, was that she'd wanted to throw herself into this creature's arms and pretend it was Max, just for a moment, so she could feel his arms around her. Feel those lips against hers, kiss her pain and emptiness away.

He folded his arms and Max's obsidian ring reflected her amber sparks, which thankfully snapped her out of the daze of ever thinking about wanting the deceiver. She blinked away the callous image of Brendan pulling the ring from the pile of Max's remains as if Max himself were nothing but a pile of garbage to be used and disposed of.

Fury coursed through her veins and burst out of her palms, shooting twin, amber-hot lightning bolts towards him as she released an ear shattering scream.

His gaze did not leave hers as he waved a hand swiftly in front of him, creating a transparent shield that had her sparks raining along the sides, protecting him.

She frowned, watching her lightning bolts fizzle to nothing. What would have turned any other enemy to ash, did nothing to him whatsoever. She groaned in frustration, slapping her palms against her thighs and saw the corner of his lip twitch as if trying to hide a smile. The arrogance of this monster.

"*Bastard*," she said with a hiss.

"Samantha, can you please just look at me, really look at me?" He stepped forward once more.

She bit her lip and scurried backwards to get away from him. Every step she took, he unhurriedly took another forward, closing the distance between them unnervingly fast. Her back pressed against the wall and she threw her shield around her, hoping it would prevent him from touching her.

He was in front of her with her next heartbeat.

"Sam." His voice held a note of remorse as he shook his head. "You don't have to be afraid of me."

She scoffed, proud that she sounded disgusted and not terrified. "*Please*, I would burn out your eyes if you had a soul. I'm *not* afraid of the likes of you!" She lied.

He nodded as his eyes raked along her amber shield.

She glared at him. "I don't know what you hoped to achieve, stealing Max's identity, although I can't blame you, your last attempt was an abomination. At least now you look like an angel."

"Do I?" He sounded pleased and raised a finger to trace along her shield.

Her breath caught in her throat, heart thumping nervously. If her lightening had no effect on him, would her shield hold?

As his fingertips traced the shield, she heard a satisfying zap and smirked as he pulled his hand back to examine his fingertips, which she hoped were stinging. *Thank the Angels, at least the shield held steady.*

"I give you my word, I'm not here to harm you."

"Your word means *nothing* to me," she spat vehemently.

He sighed. "Sam, I'm trying to explain myself. Please, we don't have time for this." He shook his head.

"Actually, *you've* got zero time. The only thing I'd ever want to hear from you is how I can destroy you. Honestly, did you think any of us would fall for this trick again? You, pretending to be one of us? How stupid do you think we are?"

He tilted his head, causing raven strands to fall into forest-green eyes that didn't seem to miss a single movement she made. She watched them drop to her chest before holding her breath, stopping her chest from rising and falling rapidly in fear. He watched her flick her pony-tail behind her when it fell forward in a glossy wave to brush against her breast. Watched the trace of her tongue, the narrowing of her eyes.

"Have you finished?" She snarled, hating that Brendan, the vilest of all, was eying her off as if she were his, through Max's beautiful eyes. Why hadn't he tried to kill her yet? Perhaps, after being slaughtered, buried in hundreds of shattered pieces in sacred ground, then dug up and was 'Humpty-Dumptied' back together, along with what she and Bowie had done to him, he wasn't of sound mind? Then again, had he ever been?

His calm eyes met hers and her breath caught. Angel's above… he was too *damn* beautiful. *Bastard!*

He raised palms forward, facing her, whispering, "Don't be afraid," then placed them against her protective shield. Amber sparks licked along the back of his hands, yet he showed no signs of it harming him.

What the actual... her heartbeat accelerated at an alarming rate as fear clawed up her throat. If he got through, what defence did she have? He seemed immune to everything she threw at him.

Bowie, Angel, I love you! she screamed to her brother and soul-sister, desperate to send them love before she died. Her eyes widened as his palms absorbed the entirety of her shield. It hissed and fizzled against his flesh before disappearing in a flash.

He reached for her then, and she closed her eyes, not wanting to give him any satisfaction of struggling. Why fight a lost cause? She barely drew breath, willing herself still and couldn't help the small gasp of fright that escaped her when his fingers eased around her throat.

This is it, she thought. *Max, I'll be with you soon, baby.*

Samantha, I'm with you now, my love.

Her eyes flew open as *his* voice brushed against her mind as his fingers wrapped around her throat and swept almost lovingly, along her flesh before cupping her face. She stared into the depth of his eyes, feeling an all too familiar pull.

Not possible. Is it?

He stroked his thumb along her cheek as he raised a perfect dark eyebrow.

"You catching on now, love?"

She couldn't catch her breath as *his* scent wrapped around her, invading her lungs, preventing her to draw breath. This *wasn't* real. *He* wasn't real. She'd seen his body destroyed by the silver entity until there was nothing left of him. Nothing but a slushy pile of bloody pulp. She considered herself to be a highly intelligent individual, but this situation, right here, right now, was proving difficult for her to comprehend. Especially when her emotions were at an airport with no flight control to steady or direct her.

Sam grabbed hold of his wrists, trying to remove them from her face, but it was useless against his effortless strength. His eyes darkened, then narrow as he tilted his head, huffing in frustration as if rapidly losing his patience.

She bit her lip as she watched his eyes change to an intense shade of... was that silver? No way... it *couldn't* be?

Can't it?

My angels... he sounds just like...

Methuselah. Yeah, sorry. I've spent the past week in his company.

"A week!" she cried in disbelief just before the bedroom door slammed open, revealing a frantic looking Bowie and Kyle as they barged in.

"What the *hell* is this?" Bowie didn't stop in the doorway, but continued marching towards them, lightning-charged balls of fire in both palms.

Yes Bowie, zap him! she cried, grateful to have some back up, not missing the glint in 'Max's' eyes.

Without shifting his gaze from hers, 'Max' held up a hand and Bowie seemed to run into an invisible wall, preventing him from taking another step forward.

Bowie cursed, then flung the blazing inferno balls towards the man who had his hands on his sister, then cursed again as they fizzled to nothing against the wall.

"Great party trick." Kyle muttered as he slowed to a stop beside Bowie, poking his finger into the invisible wall.

Bowie, I'm trying to explain to your sister that all is well.

Sam clearly heard 'Max' who hadn't shield his thought from her as he spoke to her brother.

Bowie frowned at Sam. *Brendan couldn't hear any of us the time he impersonated me?*

Yeah, but he isn't what he used to be. Clearly he's evolved and using some kind of trick.

I'm not, Sam.

She pulled her gaze away from Bowie and met *its* eyes, his breath sweet across her face as he closed the gap between them, making her breath hitch.

"It's not a trick," he implored. "And I know after what you witnessed it would be incredibly hard for you to believe that I'm anyone other than Brendan, but Sam, if you can believe anything, then believe this."

He bent his head towards hers, his body pinning her against the wall, his strength stunning her. She whimpered as his lips drew closer and with no way of escaping, squeezed her eyes shut, hearing Bowie's frustrated curse.

The kiss itself would forever be unforgettable; but what came with that kiss made her weak at the knees and brought tears to her eyes. Everything in her world ebbed and flowed on a ride of confusion and hope, the moment his lips collected hers.

Behind her closed eyelids, she could see twelve-year-old Max kicking a goal in the school yard during recess at Noorat primary school. She saw him collecting tadpoles on a school excursion and handing her a bouquet of dried flowers. Saw their old teacher, Mr Kemp, console him at his father's funeral. Saw him absorbing Angel's essence and then witnessed him punishing himself with remorse for weeks on end. Their shared moments and ones she'd never been a part of. Those when Brendan had been killed and when Max left for Italy to escape heartache and start afresh. To when they had reconnected as a couple, to Brendan abducting him and then, the silver entity destroying his body before she watched the silver entity form into and become the love of her life, Maxwell Obsidian.

She gasped against his lips, breathless and dizzy as tears poured down her face. She stared wide-eyed up into his eyes, which blazed with both desire and relief.

"*What is it?*" Bowie roared in frustration the longer Sam stared with a stunned expression at the man in front of her.

"Sam?" Kyle's voice held a note of concern, snapping her out of her daze.

"Why didn't you just *say so?*" Sam screamed at Max as her adrenalin of relief, expelled her fear, worry and anger. "Why didn't you just *start* with that?" she cried, folding her arms to stop herself from striking his gorgeous face.

Max sighed as he stepped back, giving her room to escape his proximity, which she did so, by stepping as far away from him as the wall behind her allowed, still feeling trapped as his questioning gaze held her prisoner.

"*What* is going *on?*" Bowie yelled, eyes blazing.

Max turned to Bowie. "Bowie, it *is* me, Max. No tricks, I'm not Brendan in disguise as me. It's really just me."

"How the hell can that be? We saw what happened to you. You were totally destroyed." Bowie's glare would have made a lesser man nervous.

Max waved his hand, the air stirring as the invisible barrier dissipated. "Let me show you." Max curled his fingers towards himself, indicating Bowie move closer.

Kyle joined Bowie and as he approached Max, asked Sam, "You all right?"

She nodded, arms wrapped around her waist, not really knowing if that were true, but she didn't have time to analyse her feelings. Max reached for Bowie, offering his other hand to Kyle.

"Hello, brother." Kyle raised an eyebrow.

"I see you've joined the house?" Max looked at Sam before returning his gaze to Kyle.

"I'm glad that your eyes still work after they exploded out of your head," Kyle returned simply, placing his hand in Max's.

It was Max's turn to raise his eyebrow as Bowie took his other hand.

Sam watched as both men shut their eyes before their bodies jerked as if they were on a roller coaster.

She took the chance to eyeball Max, who also had his eyes shut and shook her head. She was utterly spent from the last ten minutes, which had felt like hours. Was this really happening? Could she be so lucky to have Max back? She tilted her head, squinting her eyes as she examined him.

Yes, he looked exactly like 'her' Max, although… he was also different in his perfection. His beauty. His strength. His power. His… everything? That much was clear. But was he still *hers*? The kiss sure indicated he was, or was it something else? Him perhaps trying to convince her of who he was?

Bloody hell! She rubbed her palms over her face. It had been a long, draining night as it was, but on top of all of this commotion, she didn't know which way was up or down. One thing was for certain, there was going to be several happy Veins tomorrow at training.

Bowie and Kyle were wearing similar expressions of disbelief as Max shared his journey of abduction, death and evolution of the man who now stood before them.

Bowie gasped, opening his eyes as he pulled his hand from Max's.

"Well, you've had one hell of a week my friend." He clapped his hand on Max's shoulder, grinning with relief.

As simple as that.

"You could say that." Max returned Bowie's grin.

"Well, brother," Kyle shook his head. "I still don't understand how you became," he waved his hand up and down in front of Max, "this? But I'm sure glad you're back."

Max nodded. "It's a lot to take in, I know, but essentially, I'm still just me. I was born with this… *potential*, for lack of a better word." He turned to Sam then and she felt the heat of his gaze and *his* seemed to hold a question of whether she was going to accept him.

She tried not to squirm as his unwavering gaze locked on hers.

It's just Max. Nothing to be intimidated about, despite his total Angel-like appearance. She reassured herself, keeping the thought firmly shielded. Yet, did his lips turn up ever-so slightly?

"Despite your lack of love for them, I need to inform the council about your transformation," Bowie said.

Max nodded. "Do what you have to. Their opinion in this matter means nothing to me."

Bowie cringed but didn't respond.

"I think Red and Jane would like to hear from you that you're alive," Sam said quietly.

"Will you come with me?"

Sam swallowed, arms still gripping her waist. She looked between Bowie and the man she loved with every inch of her fibre, yet was somewhat terrified of all she'd seen and felt overwhelmed at the week that was.

"Sam?" He all but whispered, taking a step closer.

Her shoulders hunched, halting him instantly.

"I'll come with you," Kyle said. "I'd like to meet Jane myself and Sam's had an exhausting week." He defended.

Max nodded, a fleetingly look of hurt flashed across his stunning features, eyes pinning her in place. She dropped her gaze to escape the pain his hurt look caused her.

"Righto, let's call it a night." Bowie interrupted the tense moment. "Max, Kyle, why don't you spend the night at Red's? I think you going downstairs right now would cause too much excitement at this hour."

"Agreed." Kyle angled his head. "So, how are we going to slip out of here?"

Max held his hand out to Kyle as Sam felt his eyes burning into her, but still refused to meet his gaze.

As Kyle placed his hand into his brother's, Sam heard Max whisper against her mind. *We will have a discussion soon, Samantha.*

She lifted her head then, just as the room was flooded with a bright, blinding sliver light, which had her squeezing her eyes shut. When she opened them again, she was alone in the room with Bowie, who was shaking his head.

"What?" she whispered, bone tired.

"Our young Max has always been able to surprise us, since the day we brought him home."

"Hmm," was all she had in her.

"I thought you'd be thrilled. You okay?"

"I am. I'm just..." A tear fell from her lashes.

Bowie crossed to her, engulfing her in his arms, resting the top of his chin on her head. "Overwhelmed, confused, exhausted and totally in awe?"

She laughed at the last comment. "Yes, all the above." She sighed against his chest. "I know it's Max and I will never have the words to describe how ecstatic my soul is that he is still with us, but I'm also..." She shrugged. "I don't know. Afraid? He's something more than he was. I saw his body get ripped to pieces by the silver entity, which was always within him and now, apparently, it is him?"

"I know, I know." He squeezed her before releasing her. "What you need is sleep. Come on, let's get you to bed." He started toward the door and she followed him to her room.

"How did you get in here without the Veins noticing?" Sam asked.

He grinned. "I used a distraction spell and Kyle whisked me up here."

"Nice," she whispered.

"Bed, sleep." Bowie pointed towards her bed.

"Yes sir." She saluted, causing him to grin. "Goodnight Bowie, thanks for coming." She felt such love for her brother in that moment.

"Always. I'll see you in the morning for training. Let's show them, what we're made of."

She nodded before he closed the door behind him and was grateful to allow her overwhelmed tears to flow, in private, with a plan to shower and have a long, rejuvenating sleep. She hoped to present herself with her usual strength and Soul Keeper vitality the following morning. She'd need to be in her best form to face Maxwell Obsidian once more and keep her surge of emotions in check.

CHAPTER TWENTY-TWO
MAXWELL

Max stood, hands behind his back, as he looked down at the crowd of Veins who'd assembled on the back lawn the following morning. He felt hope, seeing the numbers who'd arrived. They'd need them after what he had witnessed at Brendan's hideout.

"Is there enough?" Bowie asked, standing beside him as they watched Sam, Kyle and Nadine, explain the training schedule for the day ahead.

"There's enough," Max said with confidence, his gaze following every movement Sam made. Her glossy hair was tied up in a high ponytail, revealing her slender neck that he missed kissing. A black crop top revealed her soft curves and toned stomach. Three quarter leggings, which would allow her to stretch, kick and roll smoothly, left nothing to the imagination of what lay beneath, but he knew how smooth and soft her flesh beneath that fabric was.

"Max?" Bowie had obviously been trying to get his attention.

"Sorry."

"Distracted much?"

"Yeah, too much actually." He shook his head.

"You and Sam definitely need to sort things out, but now isn't the time."

Max chuckled.

"What?"

He shook his head. "Just you, Bowie. Promise me that you will never change how you treat me."

It was Bowie's turn to laugh. "I can promise you, that is never gonna happen, mate."

"Good." He grinned. "I need some things to remain the same."

"Despite all your extra talents," Bowie waved his hand at Max, "you're still just Max to me."

Max sighed. "I wish your sister felt the same way."

Bowie looked at him for a moment before suggesting, "Just give her a bit of time to process everything that's happened."

"Yeah." Max nodded, returning his gaze to the scene below.

"When do you plan on making your grand entrance?" Bowie nodded to the group below.

"Soon. I want to see how they respond to your instruction first, see how willing they are to work with those they would never have otherwise."

"Fair enough. How much time do you think we have till Brendan takes a stand?"

"It won't be long and it will be diabolical for us all if we don't work together."

"Soul Keepers and Veins. Who would have thought?"

Max nodded, thinking there was one who knew all along and who had hoped this day would come. He glanced towards the sky where he knew Methuselah watched all below, whilst maintaining balance on other planets.

"How did it go with Red and Jane last night?"

"Great actually. Jane cried a lot. Red opened a good bottle of wine and I don't think they could have bestowed their welcome on a more grateful relative than Kyle." He grinned at Bowie.

"Yeah, your brother is something else. Any news on the other triplet?"

Max opened his mouth to answer as raised voices caught their attention below. Max felt his gut clench in a protective way. Sam stood nose to nose with a tall Vein who wore an expression of disgust, as he looked down at Sam.

Sam looked glorious as she stood firm, hands on hips, eyes blazing wickedly bright at the man who continued to scream in her face. Unlike himself, the man had no idea when Sam's eyes twinkled with that enticing amber blaze; pain was sure to follow.

"Maybe I shouldn't wait?" Max sighed, unfolding his arms.

"No, you should, this'll be entertaining. I want to see what my sister does," Bowie said as Sam's raised voice reached them.

"Doesn't it make sense? You exposing your weakness will help us defeat the others."

"Why would we expose our vulnerabilities to you? We don't need *your* help!"

"You do, actually."

Max could hear the annoyance creep into Sam's reply as someone in the crowd yelled. "And why is that?"

"The more we know about your vulnerabilities, the more we'll know about our enemies' weaknesses. That gives us an edge over them." She answered as if it were common sense. She rolled her eyes towards Jane.

"The fact is." Jane stepped beside her, placing a hand briefly on her shoulder, as if to calm her. "We are a team now; we have to work as one."

"As if that can ever happen. Do you think we can trust the likes of *you*?" Someone else yelled with a vicious snarl.

"I thought we cleared this up last night?" Sam shook her head.

"I don't think we should be showing *you* a damn thing!" The man in front of Sam sneered, shoving a hand against Sam's chest, sending her back two paces.

"Silly move," Max whispered.

"Oh it's going to be on." Bowie grinned.

"That's what I'm afraid of." Max frowned.

Sam snapped her fingers and an amber ball glowed brightly in her palm, which she held chest height, holding it out to the furious man. "Want to try that again?"

"Well, if this working together, bring it on." The man leered, snapping his hand out, sprouting a web of tiny veins from his wrist to shoot towards Sam, who in turn tossed her amber ball towards the onslaught, sizzling them to ash.

The man screamed in fury, retaliating by throwing another set of viciously sharp veins towards Sam while other Veins cheered him on.

Jane sent a gale towards the menacing veins, sending them sky-high, obliviating them in a ball of ice.

"I'm going down," Bowie said.

"I don't think I'll be too far behind." Max murmured; eyes pinned on Sam as Bowie slapped his back affectionately before leaving the room.

Things were about to get interesting.

SAMANTHA

The conflicted crowd surged forward as Sam and Jane stepped away from those whose intention was to harm them. Gemma and Rick were yelling at the disgruntled newcomers, trying to get them to calm down as Kyle stepped in front of her and Jane.

"You don't need to defend us Kyle. We've got this." Sam assured him.

"Where's the fun in that?" Kyle grinned at her before throwing his arms out, sending long, obsidian veins flying, whipping and slashing at anyone who came close enough to cause harm.

Looks like someone's been cooped up too long. Jane chuckled to Sam.

Looks like. Sam was too worried by the surging crowd to return the laughter and was relieved when she spotted Bowie striding towards them.

The front line of Veins argued with Daniel, Gemma, Rick and Nadine, who were desperately trying to get them to see reason and calm down. Sam was glad Trent hadn't joined them this morning, accompanied with his sarcasm and unhelpful jabs of late. One less person to zap.

Just as the argumentative Veins broke through the line of defence, sending Gemma to the ground, Sam stepped forward, a flood of anger shooting sparks to her waiting palms, ready to send a protective shield around the clan. Then every new arrival was swept fifteen feet in the air, their screams of protest blissfully contained as their fists of fury pounded at their invisible prison, struggling to escape.

Sam raised an eyebrow towards Bowie as he walked beneath the infuriated crowd. He joined her and Jane, and held a hand towards Gemma, pulling her to her feet.

"Thanks," she whispered, flushing.

He nodded, meeting Sam's relieved eyes before turning towards the crowd who were floating above their heads.

Sam leaned into her brother as he placed an arm around her

shoulders, hugging her once before releasing her.

"Nice one." Rick grinned at Bowie, eyes gleaming in awe.

"That wasn't me." Bowie placed his hands behind his back.

"No?" Rick raised an eyebrow.

Bowie shook his head once, looking up towards the mansion.

Sam followed Bowie's gaze and a tingling sensation swept over her flesh as her eyes connected with Max's. He was studying her with such an intense expression, that she wanted to look away, but for the life of her, could not.

She swallowed the conflicting emotions that made her want to run as far from him as possible, yet, straight into his arms to melt against every inch of his fibre so she could feel whole once more. He'd been heart-stopping sexy before this… transformation, but now the quiet darkness that swirled around him, within him in an intense, defined, delicious way; only heightened her attraction to him. What the hell was she supposed to do with this confusion, along with trying to sort out this antagonistic mob?

It's going to be okay, Sam, Max brushed against her mind.

Is it though? She shielded her thought, but saw him nod, frowning as he whispered.

It is, I promise you.

What the hell? Are you hearing my shielded thoughts?

Sorry. Should I not be? I didn't think we had any secrets from one another.

We didn't when you were… She didn't know how to finish that thought.

She felt him sigh. Felt his hurt. How could she *feel* his hurt?

I'm sorry. She was. She didn't want to hurt him. *I just need a little time.*

Then you shall have it. He nodded, stepping back from her view.

She sighed and shook her head.

Kyle asked Bowie, "What now?"

"Now, we wait."

"For what?"

"I'm sure we're all about to find out." Bowie angled his head towards the back door and they all turned to see Max stroll towards them, hands casually tucked in his jeans pockets as if he were taking nothing more than a morning stroll.

By the Angels. Sam thought. *Could he be any more mouth-watering if he tried?*

She cringed as soon as her shielded thought slipped from her mind as his eyes met hers. A knowing smile flashed across his beautiful mouth before his expression turned serious once more. His eyes scanned the Veins above, all staring with gaping mouths and stunned expressions.

Gemma's cry snapped Sam out of her ogling, followed by Nadine's cry of glee, as both women ran towards Max, launching themselves like missiles into his arms. She was surprised he didn't topple over.

"How is this possible?" Gemma asked, wiping her tears as she stepped back. "I don't understand how…"

"Is it really you?" Nadine cut Gemma off, reaching to stroke Max's face.

He caught her hand before she could touch him, the questioning glint in his eyes confused Sam. As he looked away, she wondered what that was about and caught a glimmer of hurt cross Nadine's features. Max placed his hand on Gemma's back, nodding to them both.

"It is and I will explain everything to you all, just give me a moment."

"Of course. I'm just so happy you're alive." Gemma beamed.

"Whatever you say." Nadine sounded sulky, but stepped back as Max moved forward, clapping Rick and Daniel on the back before standing between Bowie and Jane.

"Where's Trent?" He asked.

"He wasn't feeling well," Daniel answered.

Max nodded, looking around at the Veins before his eyes returned to those who stood with him.

Sam forced her eyes off his face that was only distracting her, as she stood between Bowie and Kyle, wondering what the newcomers were thinking about this recent turn of events.

"What now?" Jane asked.

Max didn't answer, but raised a hand before snapping his fingers together, releasing a crack of thunder which rumbled in the sky above them. Unnervingly, the sky turned pitch black. Birds sang out in confusion as their morning was taken away from them, then silence, as the image of Max being abducted by Brendan, illuminated the area, projected against the darkness.

The image of Max being imprisoned with Jane followed, then his abominable torture. Gasps rang out as all witnessed his death, brought about by Brendan's toxic hands. Next came the war between the black and silver entities that ripped his body to pieces, followed by his astonishing rebirth on a planet none of them knew existed, beside a figure that was as imposing and impressive as Max himself.

Sam looked towards the sky, thinking, *Methuselah's home.*

Yes, it's impressive to say the least.

Max was looking forward when she glanced his way.

Total silence ensued before darkness vanished and they were once again standing under the morning sky. Bird song resumed as the wind stirred, gifting the air with scents of lavender and eucalyptus.

Max waved his hand before lowering it. The mass of Veins floated to the ground accompanied with silence, eyes wide and filled with disbelieving looks. Max was clearly allowing everyone time to digest what they'd just witnessed and Sam knew for many; it would be too much. She hoped now at least, they would be more co-operative and work respectfully with her and the other Soul Keepers.

"You've shown your willingness that you want to fight for change, by making the journey here," Max began, breaking the tense silence. "I appreciate it more than you'll know, but we've work to do and your arguing with our most powerful allies, will stop immediately."

"You're actually alive…"

"How is this possible…?"

"Where is your other triplet…?"

"If you're here, why do we need *them*…?" The questions fired as soon as Max finished before he held a hand up for silence.

"Know this. Our enemy, once your ruler, could arrive here at any moment to destroy everyone who opposes him. We don't have time for anything other than getting ourselves prepared." His eyes locked on those who had asked the questions and were returned with uneasy glances.

"I don't understand. Why do we need to fight if we have you?"

Sam recognised young Jarrah's question, filled with nothing more than curiosity.

Max turned to the young man, returning his hands to his jeans pockets, nodding.

"I've had one week to understand my new… gifts." His eyes met Bowie's, then Sam's before he returned his focus to the crowd. "I admit, I'm strong and have abilities that, to be honest, blow even my mind, but so does Brendan. Although we are all inhuman to some degree… he is inhuman in the worst possible way."

The crowd of Veins began talking amongst themselves as if deciding what to do when the ground rose and fell beneath their feet like a wave was rolling beneath them towards the shore.

Sam knelt, joined by Jane and Bowie and they lay their palms against the grass. The earth settled instantly as if soothed by their touch.

"It's contained to the property," Bowie said.

Sam nodded in agreement. "This time."

"Red said the surges have damaged Earth's crust around her globe and they've been consuming the majority of the Soul Keepers' time." Jane looked worriedly about. "Things don't look good if we can't get on top of this situation and soon."

"We're going to do what we always do," Bowie said calmly, standing. "We're going to heal her, then kick Brendan and his parasitic army's arse back to hell."

"You almost make it sound like fun." Sam grinned.

"I was about to say the same thing," Rick's eyes gleamed as he looked admiringly towards Bowie.

"We could actually use a bit of fun around here." Kyle agreed.

"Not your usual pace then, brother?" All eyes turned to Max, and it was clear everyone was doing the same as Sam was: eyeballing the similarities and stark differences between them.

Kye shrugged. "Yeah, you could say that."

"Well, this is great and all." Nadine snapped, clearly peeved about being snubbed earlier by Max. "But what are we doing about training?"

Max narrowed his eyes as he stared at Nadine for a moment and Sam wondered what she'd done to earn that unsettling look? Max's eyes locked on hers for a fleeting moment as heat flushed under her flesh before he turned to address the crowd.

"I know you have questions. Save them. I'm going to break you up into groups, trust that you are being placed with those who can help you the most with your skill set and strengths." He nodded to Bowie and the other Soul Keepers, along with his clan, as the group divided and organised for the next few hours of training.

CHAPTER TWENTY-THREE
SAMANTHA

S am squeezed her eyes shut, forcing her flood of thoughts away, not wanting to think about how his voice, filled with authority, made her breathless. How the way he stood, wearing respect and quietness like a cape, made her want to bow down to him. How that gentle hint of steel that shone in his beguiling forest-green eyes, made her wish everyone would disappear, so she could be alone with him. Yet did she really want to be alone with him…? *Don't think, don't think, don't think, Sam…* she begged herself.

Samantha, open your eyes.

His gentle, yet firm command had her eyes popping open, and she fought against the squeal that was about to escape her lips by biting her bottom lip. Max had bent, his eyes level with hers. He was too close, too magnificent for her to breathe properly. He immediately straightened, running his hand through his hair.

"I thought you could train with me. Bowie's going to join us after he prepares the others."

Sam looked over her shoulder, seeing Bowie, Kyle and Jane pair off with the other clan members, taking their groups to separate areas of the yard to discuss plans of self-defence and attack.

"I don't see the point of us doing any training together, *your highness*," she said, turning back to meet his ever-watchful gaze. "When you can read my every move before I make it." She forced her stance to look relaxed, although she was itching to fold her arms and place an extra barrier to protect herself from his all-seeing eyes.

"Sam," he all but whispered, "you don't have to be nervous around me."

"Do I look nervous?" She tilted her head, sending her silky hair to brush across her shoulder.

"No, you don't look nervous at all."

"There you go then," she said, feeling smug and grateful her lie went undetected.

"I *feel* that you are," he said in his deep, rich, intoxicating voice, shooting her false bravado down to the ground.

Her heart galloped. "Feel it?"

"Mmhmm."

"Great." She looked away before meeting his penetrating gaze. "Max, you just need to back off a bit."

"Back off?"

"Yeah, stop looking at me like I'm something you want to eat! Like I'm a puzzle you're trying to figure out! Like I'm the last breath you need to pull into your lungs, or you're going to die! AGAIN!" she yelled in frustration, throwing her arms out.

He tilted his head as he folded his arms, a warm laugh rumbled in his chest.

"Is that how you really feel?" he asked, infuriating her further as she had done exactly that. Thrown all her feelings back at him.

"Quoting our *'higher leader,'* we don't have time for this." She shook her head, turning her back to him and had taken three steps away, when a warm 'rope' slid around her waist. She looked down and gasped as a silver vein wrapped, almost lovingly, about her, stroking the bare flesh of her waist with its silken mouth before it tightened and in a flash she was whisked around and brought flush up against him. His arms, still folded, were the only thing keeping them apart.

Sam couldn't believe her eyes, at what she was seeing and from the surrounding gasps, nor could anyone else.

Behind Max, enormous, iridescent silver wings spanned three feet either side of his shoulders. Like Methuselah's wings, they were not formed of feathers. Like a rolling wave in the ocean, or a branch flowing in the breeze, hundreds of veins formed his wings and moved as one in a silken sea of silver.

The vein around her waist slid from her flesh, sending a river of goosebumps to follow its trial as it returned to its fold. Sam swallowed, not even attempting to hide the fact she was completely overwhelmed.

"Forgive me?" he asked in a hushed tone.

"For what?" she answered, mesmerised by his proximity.

"For this." He unfolded his arms and wrapped them about her waist.

Her breath caught, and she didn't have a moment to protest as his wings burst around them, sending them sky-high with such speed, the world blurred around her. She squeezed her eyes shut as tears streamed.

Blessedly, when her feet connected with solid ground, her morning coffee remained in her stomach.

He held her steady, his fingers splayed around her waist, stroking her flesh, as she swayed once, cursing and taking a deep breath. She would *not* appear weak.

"Weakness is not a flaw," he said.

She frowned up at him. *Is there even a point of me talking if you can read my every thought or feeling?*

He smiled, releasing her waist to tuck an escaped tendril of hair behind her ear.

"Of course, Sam. I love hearing your voice."

She ran her hands over her face, stepping away from him, yet not taking her eyes from him. "You're too *damn* beautiful for your own good," she said, matter-of-factly.

He didn't reply but gave her time to process.

"Where are we?"

"We're on a second Earth." He nodded behind her.

"Second Earth?" She reluctantly moved her gaze from him and turned to look about. The most vibrant plant life, which overlooked pastures of livestock grazing on the greenest grass that glistened like emeralds seemed to go on for endless miles. Towards the horizon, the sea rolled and swelled, the sky clear of pollution and the air the cleanest she'd ever smelled. "Paradise," she whispered.

"As intended. A sanctuary actually," Max replied.

She turned to him. "A second earth?"

Max nodded. "You know as well as anyone, the pure-souls aren't catching on enough, despite the influence the Soul Keepers continue gifting them with. Time is running out. This is Methuselah's way of protecting as many of the pure-souls as possible."

"But none, human?"

"That's right. They've had their chance."

Sam felt a wave of devastation at his declaration, but knew he was right. The human population outnumbered the Soul Keepers, fifty to one and despite the Soul Keepers constant effort, no matter how close they came to mending all, the humans continued making the wrong decisions. With the Veins influencing their destructive behaviour further over the decades, things had been dire.

Tears of regret welled in her throat. "How much time do they have?" She whispered as a lone tear fell from her eye.

"It depends." His hand moved in a blur as he caught her tear, bringing it towards his lips, blowing.

"Depends on what?" Her eyes widened as he cupped her hand, turning it over to drop the tiny tear in her palm. It felt heavy, despite its size and glancing down she was startled to see a diamond, filled with a rainbow prism.

"On you, Samantha," he replied.

Her eyes met his, and she shook her head in confusion. "That doesn't make sense, *Maxwell*." She raised an eyebrow.

He nodded. "I know, love."

She laughed without humour. "You really are related to Methuselah, aren't you?"

Instead of answering, she watched in disbelief as one of his veins slid towards her, to wrap around her neck before snapping a section off itself, then re-joining the mass of veins. She touched her neck and felt a cool, thin choker sitting surprisingly comfortable around her throat. "What is this?"

"Your protection when I can't be by your side." He took the diamond from her and tossed it in the air, his eyes never leaving hers. She gasped, thinking it would surely disappear if they allowed it to fall to the ground. She shouldn't have been surprised when he caught it without looking and glanced down to see the diamond had changed, glistening obsidian black under the gentle sunshine.

"Am I really so powerless?" she asked as he raised his hand, pressing the obsidian diamond into the choker.

"Never. But with *him*, I won't risk you." He cupped her chin, and they stared silently into each other's eyes.

"None of this makes sense," she whispered.

"It will."

She traced her finger along the chocker. It felt heavy, yet it was compliant beneath her fingertips. "It feels alive."

"It is. It's a part of me."

A part of Max, around her throat. She couldn't help the sigh that escaped her lips as she closed her eyes and leaned into his palm, wishing they could return to simpler days, when they'd been just, 'Max and Sam.' She felt him move closer and opened her eyes when his forehead leaned against hers.

His eyes, unblinking, remained on hers, allowing her to make the next move. What choice did she have? His scent wrapped around her. His body, so close, had hers throbbing with desire. He was *her* Max, and she felt powerless to do anything other than do what she'd been wanting to do since she'd laid eyes on him last night. She slid her arms around his waist and pulled him flush against her. She tilted her head and stood on tiptoes, pushing her lips against his.

Max returned her kiss gently at first. He appeared to take his time as he sampled her lips as though she were a decadent meal to be enjoyed, not devoured, before slipping his tongue hungrily over her bottom lip. As soon as she felt his tongue probe her lips, she parted them, allowing him access to her soul. His arms wrapped tightly around her, moulding her to every inch of him and she thought the word, 'electricity,' that sparked between them was an understatement.

Every single one of her molecules screamed for more and she thought she would evaporate if he didn't give her every inch of himself right now. She moaned as his tongue lapped at hers, as if he were the thirstiest man alive. His lips, the sweetest nectar she'd never tire of, could not get enough of, was sending her into a desperate frenzy for more as he ravished her mouth.

She reached for the zip on his jeans and as soon as their kisses had begun, it ended. He wrapped his fingers around her wrist, his lips lifted, breathing heavily as he looked down at her with eyes filled with silver; an obsidian pupil staring down at her.

She gasped, as breathless as he was.

"Don't be afraid, please Sam," he implored, close to begging.

Her heart throbbed. As if he would ever need to beg her. "I'm not afraid, just surprised." She ran her fingers along his stubble, thinking he was entirely too sexy for either of their own good.

"I'm sorry." She shook her head, looking away. There was so much to absorb.

He sighed, pinching her chin between his fingers, bringing her gaze back to his.

"You've had a lot to process."

"Understatement of the decade," she whispered.

"Perhaps. Although, I can think of another."

"Oh, yeah?"

"Mmhmm. The first day I told you I loved you." His thumb brushed her chin, tugging her bottom lip open ever so slightly. "Love isn't a big enough word to describe everything I've ever felt about you, Samantha Storm."

Her eyes widened as he dropped another lingering kiss against her lips before his wings burst behind him. He wrapped his arms around her once more. "We have to go. Prepare yourself. Brendan's mob have attacked."

She felt like she'd kissed all her opportunities, to get any real answers, away and before she could ask how he knew that, they were surrounded by a blinding silver light. As they leapt into the air, her eyes streamed with tears as they speed towards the Earth she knew.

She squeezed her eyes shut, grateful his arms were holding her close, giving her a moment's peace before they landed in what she could only describe as hell.

CHAPTER TWENTY-FOUR
MAXWELL

Even before their feet hit the earth, Max took stock of the number of enemies who'd infiltrated his property, already knowing Brendan was not amongst them. Although they flew towards Earth with enormous power, they caused no damage to her crust as they landed and Max placed Sam down. He was impressed as she launched into action, rolling away from a blast of black venom. She leapt to her feet, flying in the air as she sent a burst of smouldering lava to exterminate the culprit before landing with cat-like grace, preparing for her next move.

Bowie, who had just turned a Vein to ash and flung a blast towards another, locked gazes with Max.

Impressive. Max grinned at Bowie, who raised an eyebrow.

Yeah and what do you plan to do, your highness?

Max laughed. *Ah, you Storm siblings don't ever change.*

Yeah, we've covered that. Bowie's tone was filled with humour before he hissed, an arrow piercing the flesh of his upper arm.

Can you two focus? Sam sighed as she approached the Vein who had cut Bowie and placing her hands either side of his head, turned the enemy into a solid mass of ice. Jane threw a protective shield around young Jarrah before she spun and shattered Sam's victim to pieces with a screaming tornado of wind.

Pride swelled within Max as he watched Jane run past Sam, high-fiving her before they both spun to defend the other Veins who were struggling to protect themselves, let alone fight in the unexpected attack.

Blood flowed on both sides and Max cringed as another Vein fell to his death.

He counted five of theirs who'd fallen and, taking a calming breath, focused on the number of enemies still alive. *Thirteen.* When he sensed their whereabouts, he closed his eyes.

SAMANTHA

Sam cringed as an enemy Vein wrapped a thick vein-rope around the throat of the woman, who had given her nothing but trouble since she'd arrived. It would have been so easy to allow the enemy to take care of the pest for her, but that fleeting thought was just that. She sent a blast of fire to burn through the back of the enemy, whose screams of agony would stay with Sam for days.

When she heard Nadine gasp in pain, she turned, ready to offer her assistance. Then she froze in confusion, shocked to see everything around her moving as if someone had hit a slow-motion button and muted the volume.

Bowie was suspended five feet in the air, halfway through a side kick, his boot an inch from an unsuspecting Vein's head, who in turn, had his veins inside one of their newcomer's stomach, ripping out his insides.

Kyle looked like he was about to have his throat sliced open by a horrific looking female who had two arms fashioned into steel swords. Gemma was on the ground, covered in blood and Daniel beside her held the body of one of the newcomers. It was a bloodbath. And if this was them winning without Brendan here, it didn't feel like winning at all. She felt a heatwave wash over her before an eerie sound permeated the air as the earth groaned beneath their feet. She turned to call out to Max and saw him standing as still as night, eyes closed as if praying for help.

Help's not coming, she whispered to him.

He smiled then, his eyes opened, finding hers. *It's already here. Don't move.*

She pulled in a breath, waiting. With his eyes pinning her in place, he released thirteen vein-tips from his wings, shooting them out like arrows towards his prey. They sang as they pierced through the air before entering the hearts of their enemy, vaporising them in an instant.

Sam raised an eyebrow, startled as the world returned to normal speed, the screams of those who were wounded and in shock, penetrated her ears. She blinked twice as Bowie spun in the air, landing lightly, looking about in confusion, frowning as he spotted the dead Vein at his feet. Many of the others did the same, straightening as they took stock of the situation, confused, then relieved, cheering and slapping each other on the back, helping the wounded to their feet.

Those who had fallen for the last time were collected by the wind, lifted and carried towards the barn. Sam looked towards Max, knowing it was he who was transporting them there. He nodded once, confirming she was right. She shook her head, looking away, still getting used to him hearing her private, shielded thoughts.

You can hear mine, too, whenever you like. he whispered against her mind. She turned, watching Jane throw her arms around his waist. His vein-wings vanished in an instant as he returned her stare before smiling down at Jane, wiping a smudge of blood off her cheek.

Not sure if I can actually handle hearing any of your thoughts, just now, thanks, she thought before turning to her brother.

"Well." Bowie rubbed at his arm that gushed blood as he looked about the stained ground where the enemy had vanished to dust. "That was…"

"Liberating, exciting, wonderful to watch!" Rick gushed with enthusiasm.

"Clearly, you need to get out more." Kyle shook his head, reaching a hand down to pull Rick off the ground.

Sam reached out and offered her hand to a woman whose calf was torn open. The woman looked up as she took Sam's hand, gasping in surprise. "The pain has stopped!"

Sam smiled. "I can help with the pain, but Bowie or Max will help with the healing."

"Thank you." The woman sounded genuinely grateful.

At last, someone sees sense in working together. She pushed towards Bowie, Jane and Max as he answered.

It was only a matter of time. I need to speak with you all as soon as we clear this up. He nodded around them. *We need Angel here.*

"No way in hell," Bowie snapped aloud.

Max smiled, his teeth gleaming white under the sunshine, making him look wolfish. "Do you really think I'd let anything happen to her?"

Bowie's hands settled on his hips, eyes narrowing as he contemplated the danger of having Angel amongst this new lot of Veins. He sighed after a moment.

Sam could feel her brother was about to agree. "Bowie, no, it's not safe." She begged her brother.

"I promise you, love, Angel will be safe." Max assured her as he released Jane, meeting Bowie's gaze.

"Okay then." Bowie nodded in agreement and in a flash of silver, Max disappeared from sight, only to return seconds later with Angel in his arms, laughing in delight.

"I definitely want to do *that* again, real soon!" She smiled up at Max before stepping out of his embrace and running towards Bowie, throwing her arms around his neck. He swept her up, spinning her in a half circle, smiling down at her before kissing her soundly.

Sam grinned; their happiness was contagious. She met Max's eyes, which were, unsurprisingly, on her. She raised an eyebrow, shaking her head before she was almost knocked backwards as Angel launched herself at her.

Sam wrapped her arms around her sister. "I've missed you." She squeezed her tight, pushing her face onto her neck. *I've so much to tell you*. She brushed against Angel's mind, then groaned aloud.

"What?" Angel asked, frowning.

Sam turned to glare at Max. "This isn't going to work!" she yelled.

Angel ran her hand over Sam's back and she instantly felt calmer.

"One thing at a time, Samantha." Max turned to the Veins whose eyes were hungrily turning grey, to black. "This is Angel Cloud. Bowie Storm's wife. I know you've all heard about her. Trust me when I say, you do not want to know what I'll do to you if you so much as look at her with the wrong colour in your eyes."

The coldness in his voice was both chilling and sexy. Sam felt icy fingers sweep over her bare midriff and watched as the Veins wrapped their arms about themselves, looking around at each other. Max's warning was clear.

She felt an elbow in her ribs and met Angel's laughing eyes. Sam bit her lip, trying not to smile, because of the seriousness of their situation. She had *so* much to talk to Angel about. She glanced around at the crowd, pleased to see the Veins' eyes returning to a mix of brighter colours.

"Angel is here to heal and restore," Max continued in a friendlier tone. "We'll regroup in a couple of hours and have a ceremony for those who've departed this realm. Words cannot convey the depth of my sorrow for your loss." He turned and headed towards the mansion.

"Well, that was… interesting," Angel said to Sam.

"You haven't seen anything yet." Sam sighed.

"I'm intrigued." Angel rubbed her hands together.

"Hah." Sam chuckled humourlessly as Bowie walked over to them with Kyle and Jane.

"Let's get to work, baby." Bowie took Angel's hand.

She nodded. "Won't take long."

Sam looked about. "Do you want my help?"

"No, we've got this." Angel smiled.

"Daniel," Sam called, waving Daniel over.

Daniel lightly jogged over; Gemma two steps behind. "Yep." He swept his blood-speckled hair out of his face.

"How about after a quick clean up, we get some food prepared?" She touched his arm briefly, feeling his energy. It felt depleted, yet, as always with Daniel, he was eager to help others.

"That sounds good." He nodded. "Come on, Gem." He took her hand, leading her inside.

"You should clean up too." Jane pointed and, glancing down, Sam noticed her tee shirt was splattered with black blood.

"Yeah," she said, distracted as she watched Nadine march with purpose towards the mansion.

"Come on." Kyle linked his arm through hers. "Let's wash this death away."

"We'll meet up with you once we've finished here," Bowie said before turning with Angel to heal torn flesh, broken spirits and bones.

"Yeah, okay." She nodded as Kyle tugged her away from the grisly area, curious to see what the remainder of the day would bring, wishing Max could vaporise Brendan and his remaining cretins as effortlessly as he had the others.

MAXWELL

Max stood at his bedroom window, watching the healed head towards the barn. His door opened behind him, then clicked shut as the uninvited guest cleared their throat. After taking a deep breath, he turned to find Nadine wearing a furrowed brow and hoped he could remain calm. He'd been made aware of many things the past week that he'd spent with Methuselah, along with navigating his new skill set. Some things made his heart soar, others, plummet.

"So, you've risen from the dead?" she said.

"Apparently so."

"Have you got something on your mind, *Bello*?"

"Nothing I want to share with you just at this moment," he replied, his words like ice.

"Why not?"

"Because I don't trust myself not to hurt you," he said, uncharacteristically unfeeling.

Nadine paled before fury filled her eyes. "What the *hell* is your problem with me?"

"Problem?" Max folded his arms.

"Yes, your bloody problem!" Nadine's hands rested on ample hips.

"Mm, let's see, shall we? How about..." A knock sounded, interrupting his next words. "Come in." He sighed.

"Piss *off*," Nadine shrieked simultaneously.

"Nice." Sam smirked as she walked in the door.

Max noticed she'd taken a shower; her creamy skin looked fresh and dewy, hair rinsed of all traces of blood and hung in soft waves past her shoulders. Eyes sparkling dangerously, she placed hands on her hips, facing Nadine. A dark green camo tee shirt sat an inch above her midriff and faded jeans fitted snuggly to every inch of her toned legs. Knee-high, brown boots gave her those extra inches to meet Nadine's furious glare.

"I'm sensing some inappropriate attitude considering what just went down outside?" Sam raised a honey-blonde eyebrow.

"Are you? Good for you. How about you contemplate that in another room whilst you mind your business, *blondie,*" Nadine spat.

Sam chuckled, leaning back on her heel. "Wow. Did someone get out of the wrong side of bed this morning?"

"How about you go and f…" Nadine's rant was cut off as Max snapped impatiently.

"Ladies, *enough.*"

The door burst open once more and Kyle sauntered in. "I felt a commotion and hoped to be a part of it." He winked at Sam.

"I'm glad you did, because you are," Max said.

"Really? Spectacular, do share." Kyle grinned, earning a sharp look from Max and a chuckle from Sam.

"I'm not getting into any of it until we're all together."

"All together?" Kyle turned to his brother.

"Our clan, plus Bowie, Jane, Angel and Michael."

"Can we eat first though? I'm starving." Sam patted her stomach.

Max couldn't help but smile, despite the unsettling conversation that would soon take place. It was just like Sam to be thinking about food, no matter what had recently occurred. "Sure," he replied in a softer tone, causing Nadine's eyes to narrow once more.

"I want a word with you, in private." Nadine folded her arms.

Max shook his head. "It can wait, Nadine."

"It can't!"

"It *will*." He snapped, noticing Sam's eyebrow raise, giving her a sultry look, making him wish they were alone.

"Righto, this tension is making *me* hungry. Let's go." Kyle threw his arm around Max's shoulder and if Max were honest with himself, he was starving too, not remembering the last time he's eaten. Although he wasn't sure if he could swallow a bite, with what lay ahead as his gaze strayed to Nadine once more.

He felt it the instant Sam sensed his perturbed feelings and met her gaze.

It's going to be okay.

You keep saying that. She held his gaze.

I know, I'm sorry, I'm sure it's painful.

Only like pulling hairs with a tweezer.

He grinned and was about to reply when another knock sounded at the door before it was pushed open. Bowie, holding Angel's hand, walked in. Both scrubbed spotless.

"We used your shower, Sam, hope you don't mind." Bowie ran a hand through his damp hair.

"Not at all."

"Food's ready." Angel reached for Sam's hand. "Michael's downstairs."

"Great." Sam smiled.

"After we eat, we need to get to a council meeting." Bowie looked at Max. "There's a lot to discuss."

"For us all," Max agreed before leading everyone downstairs, feeling Sam's eyes on his back and daggers sent by Nadine. He walked towards the mouth-watering aromas and quiet conversations, hoping he could keep his emotions of disappointment and fury, contained until everyone had filled their stomachs. They deserved that much.

CHAPTER TWENTY-FIVE
SAMANTHA

"How did they get past Red's barrier?" Michael asked.

Jane licked the croissant crumbs from her fingers before saying, "They would have needed Max's blood, the owner of this property, or Red's, to diffuse that barrier. They didn't have Red's."

Everyone looked at Max, who shrugged. "I guess they could have taken mine when I was unconscious."

"You mean, *dead*, don't you?" Nadine remarked snidely before sipping her coffee.

Everyone in the room fell silent, looking between Nadine and Max as the uncomfortable silence grew. They'd filled their bellies with Daniel's selection of brunch items and had taken the opportunity to talk about the attack without startling the newcomers, who had taken their meal in the barn, and to mourn their fallen.

Sam frowned at Nadine, wondering about her change of attitude. She was usually falling over herself to please Max and make an impression, but now she was being downright snooty.

"What *is* your problem?" Gemma turned on Nadine with the unfriendliest look on her face Sam had ever seen.

"My problem is *this*." Nadine slammed her mug down, coffee sloshing over the rim and splashing onto the marble bench. "Maxwell, our *esteemed* leader, has come back to us, after we saw his death, complete with angel vein-wings, a superior attitude and no answers whatsoever how we can destroy Brendan. *That's* why I have a problem." Nadine glared at Max.

Sam sensed there was more to Nadine's outburst than what she was letting on. It was almost as if she were jealous that Max was no longer Max? Interesting and odd.

"Superior attitude? Bullshit." Rick sided up to Gemma, placing a hand on her back. "And so what if he's been... modified?" He looked across at Max. "Sorry, couldn't think of another word to describe you at the moment."

"No need to apologise." Max took a mouthful of tea, staring at Nadine with an unimpressed look. "But someone does have some apologising to do."

All eyes went from Max back to Nadine.

"If you're talking about me, you can forget it!"

"I've seen some things this past week I really wish I could forget." A silver ring swept around Max's forest-green eyes, filling them with a dangerous glint. Sam shivered with apprehension.

"Where is this going?" Nadine sounded exasperated.

"Start with an apology and you'll see," he said.

"What are you talking about?"

"As if you don't know." Max placed his mug down, eyes unblinking.

Sam had never heard Max speak so chillingly cold, not even when he'd been addressing the despised council members, who had treated him poorly over the years. She felt an uneasy, prickling sensation creep along her flesh, filling her with dread as she watched Max's handsome features morph into stone, giving him the look of an untouchable Angel. Sam placed a hand on her chest as her heart galloped out of control. Why was she feeling as if she were about to collapse?

What is it? Angel asked, sensing her sister's discomfort.

I'm not sure, but it isn't good.

It hadn't happened since the day she and Max had stood on his back deck, the day she'd arrived, but a vision was coming over her again and it was coming fast.

Everyone around her disappeared as an eerie white noise filled her ears. Now she stood in a grand white hall filled with marbled statues of horrific looking, mutated Veins. A small, dark-haired boy and a red-haired girl around five years of age were holding hands, wearing identical looks of terror. A beast stood above them with blackened eyes and a look of murder on his face. Robert Black.

Sam cried in dismay as he grabbed the children by their necks, separating them forcefully, their screams falling on deaf ears as he thrust the little girl towards Brendan before throwing the little boy with such violence towards the ground, it broke her heart. Another aggressive man snagged the boy by the elbow and dragged him towards the end of the great hall. The little girl's cries of grief and fright as her brother was dragged from her sight filled Sam with utter sadness. The devastation felt by both children had Sam falling to her knees. This separation was too cruel.

In a flash, she witnessed the girl's childhood, surrounded by cruelty, brainwashing and foul deeds performed in the never-ending quest for acceptance, approval and love. Sam felt it in an instant: the search for family. She sobbed once before taking a deep breath, trying to keep all the emotions that were swamping her at bay.

She lost complete sight of the young boy, only sensing he had been brought up with another clan of Veins, separate to his sister and like her, searching for a place to belong. Once they had both reached the age of twenty-one, an experiment was performed. Toxins injected into their blood stream, then days waiting, both close to death as their bodies fought against the black matter that wreaked havoc within their systems, until they regained their health. *There can be only one...* was the last thing Sam heard before the vision vanished.

Another sob caught in her throat when the room came back into view. The pain and sorrow that filled her heart suffocated her to the point of an unfamiliar panic attack. She couldn't breathe.

"Sam?" Max's tone was filled with concern.

"What's the matter, *stella?* Can't handle the pressure?" Nadine hissed.

Max's wings exploded out of his shoulder blades and one of his vein's shot towards Nadine, striking her backwards before wrapping around her throat.

"Max, no!" Sam cried, sucking in air, knowing he was about to strike his own sister... the second Black triplet.

His eyes shot towards hers as dark as she'd ever seen them. "You know?" he whispered.

She nodded, allowing Bowie to pull her to her feet. "Just now."

"Know what?" Bowie demanded.

"What he said," Kyle echoed.

Nadine gripped the pretty silver vein that was wrapped around her throat, sending Max the poutiest death stare if Sam had ever seen one.

"Looks like we're having this conversation now," Max said, eyes leaving Sam's before staring at Nadine.

"Can someone please fill me in?" Kyle snapped, sounding more like Max in that moment.

Sam wanted to chuckle, but the image of the destroyed little boy chased all feeling of laughter away.

"Do you really not know?" Max asked, a dangerous glint in his eyes.

Sam moved away from Bowie and stepped half in front of Kye as if to defend him, shaking her head as she answered. "He does not."

"Know what?" Kyle jammed his hands on his hips.

"How can you be so sure?" Max asked her, ignoring Kyle's question.

"Do you trust me?" she asked.

"With my life," he answered, deadpan.

"Then know this. He has had no part in any betrayal towards you, or the path you're on." She sighed as Max's eyes calmed, but noticed he remained furious with Nadine.

"You might want to reconsider killing her," she added for good measure, "before knowing the full story."

"I know enough," he said, his tone icy.

"I'm not sure that you do." Sam sighed, walking across to him to place her hand against his chest.

He looked down at her, his voice filled with disappointment. "She's a traitor."

"That may be so, but you have to see why first, Max."

His eyes dropped to her lips before meeting hers eyes once more and she felt his longing to be alone with her.

I know, she whispered against his mind. *But first, see this.*

She closed her eyes and concentrated on sending the scene she'd witnessed in the great white hall towards him. She hoped it would work and he would feel all she'd felt with the two young siblings being separated, tortured and manipulated throughout their childhood. Lost, alone and lonely, just as he had been before he came into the Soul Keepers lives. Into her life.

She watched, hopeful as his beautiful eyes filled with sorrow, heart-ache, then remorse as his vein slipped from Nadine's throat, returning to its silvery fold before his wings vanished. He put his arms around Sam, pulling her against him, breathing her in; she sensed, for comfort.

"Kyle doesn't know," she whispered, defending his brother.

"Kyle doesn't know what?" Kyle demanded.

"That your other triplet stands in this room." Sam answered, turning in Max's arms to look at Kyle, then Nadine.

"What?" Bowie placed a protective arm around Angel's shoulders.

Rick pointed at Kyle, then Max. "I don't see a third one of you two anywhere?"

"Because she's not a third, she's the second," Sam stated.

"No," Gemma whispered, staring in horror at Nadine.

"So, here stand the three Black triplets, together, in the home of their birth, after all this time," Angel said, her voice wistful.

Nadine raised an eyebrow at Angel before looking between Max and Kyle as she folded her arms. "This changes everything then, doesn't it?" She sounded confident, despite her precarious position.

"This changes nothing," Max said.

"I'm your sister!"

"And?" Max folded his arms.

"I need a bit more clarity to what's happening right now?" Bowie interrupted the siblings' exchange.

"You'll get it." Max nodded. "My sister is a traitor and is the reason Brendan was able to get to us so easily."

Bowie turned to glare at Nadine. "Is that so?"

"It is," Max answered.

"Hang on." Sam looked up at him. "You saw what I saw, right?"

"I did."

"Then you know she was as lonely and confused as you were as a child?"

"That maybe so, Sam, but she became an adult, with her own mind and common sense of what is right and wrong. She joined us with the intention of betraying us." Max glared across at Nadine. "Lives have been lost because of *you*."

"Lives will always be lost. It's a war in case you hadn't noticed." Nadine spat out the words.

"When is it ever going to end?" Sam heard sadness in Angel's question and placed a hand on her sister's arm.

Jane was staring at Nadine the entire time before exclaiming in dismay. "You're her, aren't you?"

Nadine didn't reply as she returned Jane's stare.

"She is." Max answered his cousin.

"Can someone please fill the rest of us in?" Michael sounded exasperated.

Jane looked at Max, tears filling her eyes as she answered Michael. "*She's* the one who used my power, my abilities, to bring Brendan back to life!"

Nadine scoffed.

Jane spun towards the red-haired beauty. "Don't you dare deny it!" she cried.

"I guess there's no point." Nadine shrugged.

"If I were you, I'd find some humility, quick smart," Sam said.

Nadine stepped towards her, eyes darkening. "Really?"

Sam dropped her hand from Angel's arm and stepped away from Max towards Nadine, flames dancing in her eyes; fingertips blazing.

"Yeah, really." She felt an anger towards Nadine override the pity she'd felt for the little girl earlier.

"I owe you nothing!"

"You owe Jane an apology." Sam took another step forward,

fingertips blazing as an electric current filled the air.

"Who do you think *you* are to threaten me?" Nadine smirked as a high voltage sound zapped on Sam's fingertips.

"Threaten you? I'm trying to help you out of a sticky situation that your pride is going to bury you in!"

"You have no idea what I've endured and I don't need the likes of *you*, helping me whatsoever, *Bella*!" Nadine hissed, opening her arms to reveal several thin, shiny obsidian veins that slid from her flesh, almost beautiful in their liquid grace.

"Do you really want to do that?" Sam whispered, hinting at the danger to come.

"Like you have no idea," Nadine said, responding in likeness, her veins drawing closer towards Sam.

"Stop!" Max snapped his fingers and Nadine screamed in pain as each vein reaching towards Sam became frostbitten.

Sam felt ripped off and by the slight lift to Max's lip, she knew he knew it.

"This isn't solving anything." Jane folded her arms, glaring at Nadine.

"What's to solve?" Nadine frowned, rubbing her aching arms, glaring at her brother.

"I think it's clear enough." Michael nodded towards Max.

"Clear as mud," Rick muttered. Gemma and Daniel nodded in agreement.

Nadine turned towards them. "I was raised by a man who could see a greater potential for *our* kind, instead of *your* lot." She sneered towards the Soul Keepers, "Claiming to be the rulers of us all."

"That's a claim that had nothing to do with anyone standing in this room," Michael pointed out.

"Yet, you follow the laws of your council, destroying *my* people at any cost."

"We've only ever destroyed those of you who kill the innocent, those of you who destroy Mother Earth and consume our Heavenly Soul's essence. Do you seriously think those acts should go unpunished?" Bowie shook his head.

"All I know is this, you Soul Keepers have had it far too good, for far too long."

"If you truly believe that, then you're deluded." Sam sighed, folding her arms.

"How so? Can you deny that your council view *you* as the superior race?" Nadine mirrored Sam's stance.

"Sure they do, but that doesn't mean that everyone who is under their rule see's themselves as such. Why do you think I'm here, that we're all here, standing beside Max, working together with your kind? Because we believe that together, we can save Mother Earth. That eventually, we can all live in peace and harmony."

"Only if the 'evil ones' die, right?"

"This is our chance now, to choose good over evil." Kyle stepped towards his sister. "Now is your chance to be more than a 'parasite' who follows orders to destroy all in your path for pleasure and power. Do you want that?" Kyle asked his sister.

Nadine dropped her gaze to the floor, not answering for a moment before giving a slow, one shoulder shrug.

Kyle closed the distance between Nadine and himself, his voice lowering. "I can only imagine the hell you've endured after we were separated as children and I'm sorry for that. Sorry I didn't recognise you till now, but you have to choose."

Nadine's head snapped up, meeting Kyle's stare.

"Choose?" she whispered.

"Them or us." Max answered for Kyle.

Nadine opened her mouth, but before she could make a sound, Max said, "Be honest. I'll know if you're not and I won't show you any mercy. Sister or not."

All eyes went to Max. *He can't mean that?* Sam brushed against Angel's mind.

I do, love. She had me fooled for far too long. His gaze met Sam's.

She swallowed before nodding once, looking back to see a pale-faced Nadine.

"It's not as simple as that." Nadine nervously met Max's eyes.

"Oh?" He folded his arms, sounding far too sexy for this serious situation.

Block your thoughts, block your thoughts… Sam chanted in her head, rolling her eyes as she saw Max's eyes light up knowingly.

Nadine's next comment snapped her out of her, *Max is too damn sexy for his own good*, thought.

"There's only one path forward for me if I want to live."

"If you choose us, I won't let Brendan get anywhere near you," Max said to assure her.

"It's not just Brendan. There are others interwoven in your circle of trust. If they know that I've been disloyal, they will kill me."

"The circle isn't that big," Max looked pointedly at Daniel, Gemma and Rick. "I'd know if it were any of them."

"Would you though? You didn't know a thing about me until the *father-of-all* took you to the stars, did you?" Nadine replied.

Sam groaned. "*Trent.*" She hissed before spinning around, running towards the stairs.

"Sam, wait!" Max called after her.

Hurried footsteps followed her up the stairs as she flung Trent's bedroom door open with a blast of wind.

CHAPTER TWENTY-SIX
SAMANTHA

Sam gasped in dismay at the gory sight before her. Trent's room was a bloodbath. Blood dripped from the ceiling and ran along the walls. Crimson splatters stained the rugs, bedspread and furniture. Severed body parts hung in mid-air around the room like macabre ceiling mobiles.

"It's not Trent." Max stated. "It's not his scent."

"I guess that answers the question of who the other traitor is." Bowie muttered.

"I *knew* there was something about him that I didn't like," Rick said.

"But it doesn't answer the question why you and Trent were here with us in the first place." Max turned to Nadine. "What did you hope to gain?"

"To pose as one of you, get close to you?" She answered honestly.

"You could have done that by stepping forward as my sister." Max shook his head. Disappointment laced his next words. "Things could have been so different if you'd just come to me and had a conversation."

Nadine flushed, averting her gaze. "You have to understand, Brendan has been the closest thing to family to me for my entire life. I couldn't disappoint him."

Rick scoffed as Sam asked. "Why Trent though? What was his mission?"

Nadine shook her head. "I think it was to plant something, but honestly, I'm not sure?"

Sam watched the red-haired closely, trying to decipher if she were being honest.

"Plant what?"

Nadine met Sam's gaze and shrugged.

"Listen," Michael stepped towards Max. "We've got to get to the Light Accords council meeting. There's a great deal to fill them in on. We'll leave you to sort this out."

"Sure." Max nodded.

"I think you should come with us." Bowie reached for his sister's hand.

"No, I'm good here."

"Sam," Bowie began.

"I promise, I'll be fine." Sam reached for Bowie's hand, squeezing it.

Bowie sighed before saying to Max. "Keep her safe"

Max ignored Sam's scoff and replied. "You know I will."

Angel hugged Sam, whispering. "Be careful."

"You too. Who knows where Brendan and his mob are?"

"Who do you think these belong too?" Daniel nodded around at the body parts.

"Pure-souls," Max said sadly.

"Magic, or elbow grease for the clean up?" Bowie asked.

"Out of respect for the pure-souls, elbow grease." Michaeal answered.

"Agreed." Sam sighed.

"Want us to give you a hand before we go? Angel asked.

Max shook his head. "No thanks, we've got this."

Angel nodded as Bowie reached for her hand.

"Here you go." Max waved his hand in a circle, opening a clean, white gateway in the otherwise bloodbath of a room.

"Thanks." Michael nodded before stepping inside, followed by Angel, and Bowie. As soon as they stepped inside, a bright light flooded the room before disappearing, leaving the others to stand in the gory atmosphere once more.

"I'll get a mop and garbage bags." Gemma sighed, heading downstairs.

"I'll help," Sam said, going to follow before warm, strong fingers wrapped around her upper arm, stopping her.

She looked down at those fingers, then up into Max's eyes, and raised an eyebrow. "Yes?"

"I need you to come with me." His tone indicated there wasn't another option.

"Okay."

"Kyle, can you take Nadine to your old room please?"

Kyle smiled a little wickedly before answering, "It will be my pleasure."

"You're locking me up in my own home?" Resentment laced her voice.

"Until we can talk more, yes." Max nodded before pulling Sam with him out of the room and upstairs to his.

Once the door closed behind them, he ran his fingers along the length of her bare arm before releasing her and wandered over to a window.

Sam released a long breath, running her fingers through her hair, then folding her arms, not sure what to do with herself and hated the fact she felt nervous; uneasy even.

"You don't have to be nervous or uneasy around me, love," he said, his back to her.

She felt heat spiral in her stomach when he said, 'love,' and pulled in a slow breath before replying. "We need to sort this thing out, where you can hear my every thought. It's putting me on edge."

"Is it?" He turned then, sitting on the window seat, placing his hands either side of his thighs as he looked at her. "I'm sorry. That was never my intention."

"Regardless, I need you to stop it." She tilted her head, waiting.

"Done." He agreed. "As of now, I can only hear what you are willing share with me."

"As easy as that?"

"Would I lie to you?"

"I'd hope not," she said, followed by a shielded thought to test his promise. *Because if you do, I will zap you, hard.* No reaction whatsoever. *Lucky*, she thought.

"So much has changed, but I don't want us to, Sam. I need you beside me, more now than ever."

She nodded, finding herself more entranced by him the longer she stood there looking at him, loving the way his jet-black hair fell across his smooth forehead, marred by worry. Her fingers itched to push those silken strands out of his eyes, which seemed to see all.

"How bad are things? What do you know that the rest of us seem to be in the dark about?" she asked.

"Do you recall the Tsar Bomb?"

"I vaguely remember studying it in high school. It was a hydrogen aerial bomb if I remember correctly?"

"Yes, one of the most powerful nuclear bombs ever created."

"Yes, but only one was ever created."

"So they said," Max said. "They lied."

"Who has control of these bombs?"

Max tilted his head. "The worst kind of men, controlled by Brendan."

The hairs on Sam's neck rose. "It can't get much worse."

"It can. Brendan's powers have increased the nuclear weapons. They will destroy everything in their path, leaving only Vein matter behind."

"How do you know this?"

Max didn't answer.

"Methuselah?"

He nodded, adding. "I've been gifted with seeing several impending disasters that will strike Mother Earth within in the coming weeks, if not sooner." He folded his arms. "Fact is, if we don't work together, with every Soul Keeper and decent Vein alike, we won't even have the chance to say goodbye to Mother Earth, let alone those we love."

"Just like that?" she whispered in dismay.

"Exactly like that." His eyes dropped to her lips as she nibbled on them nervously.

"Well, we need to get to that council meeting, A.S.A.P." Sam began pacing. "You need to show them everything you've seen, make them listen. Surely if they realise the seriousness of the current situation, they'll forget about their anal rules, bigoted opinions and work with you, with us, for the greater good?"

Max sighed. "If they don't, they will be the ones who will lose out in the end."

"What do you mean?" She stopped pacing, resting her hands on her hips.

"The other worlds that Methuselah has created, the second earth especially, is only for the purest of souls."

"The animals only?"

"Yes and any Soul Keeper, or Vein, who help destroy Brendan."

Sam raised an eyebrow. "Definitely no human pure-souls whatsoever?"

"They've had their time."

This again. "Yes, but they've been corrupted by Veins. Not all of them are evil... the children?"

Max shrugged. "The rules have been set."

"I never took you as someone who implemented such harsh rules."

"They are in place for a good reason."

"Are you serious?"

"I am."

Sam's hands slid off her hips, feeling as if she didn't know who this man was.

"You seriously *cannot* mean the children?"

"I do."

"*Maxwell.*"

"Who do you think they will grow up to be, Samantha?" Max's tone sent a shiver down her spine. He was deadly serious.

Could he really allow an entire species to be wiped out?

"You know they are not *all* bad, you *know* that."

"It's out of my hands." He sighed, pushing himself up from the window seat and casually strolled across to her, standing a foot away, shoving hands in his pockets as he looked down at her.

"They've had more than a fair chance and *you* know that deep down. Discrimination and segregation is ingrained in their DNA. Their behaviour and destruction is nothing more than an ongoing cycle."

Sam stared up into his eyes, wanting to disagree, but knowing he was right. They had. And Mother Earth suffered still and they couldn't blame all the evil in this world on the Veins.

"It just doesn't seem right."

"I know," he said. "But all is yet to be lost." He pulled a hand out of his pocket, and slid it across her hip before pressing against the small of her back, pushing her up against him.

She swallowed hard. Every inch of her that touched him tingled.

"So… if the Light Accords agree to collaborate with us and we can win the majority of Veins to our side, then there's still hope?" She was proud to get the words out clearly and couldn't take her eyes off his lips, which were curving ever so slightly, his scent overwhelming her.

"Mmhmm." He murmured absently as his eyes drank her in, his head tilted towards hers.

"Do we have time for this?" she asked breathlessly as his lips ever so lightly brushed across hers. Butterflies flew around her stomach in anticipation.

"Mmhmm." His breath was sweet, with a dark hint of honied whisky she hadn't seen him drink.

He slid his mouth across hers, deepening the kiss to a level that made her knees weak. He slid his hand along her jaw to cup the back of her neck, pulling her closer. Every nerve ending was on fire as he masterfully moved his body against hers, creating a pool of lust to slam into the pit of her stomach and trickle between her thighs. A pulse of sweet agony beat against her core, searching for a crescendo. Her jeans were too tight as she wiggled against them, seeking for that sweet release as the seam rubbed against her damp, throbbing sweet spot. It was just a kiss. Why was her body reacting like he'd already had his way with her?

Because somehow, she could see several images clearly; her body, naked, slick with sweat, every inch being licked, stroked and worshiped by his lips, hands and his magnificent body as if she were the most decadent desert on the planet.

She pulled her lips from his with great effort and stared into his eyes. They were both breathless. She would have grinned, seeing he seemed as equally affected by her as she was by him, but the seriousness of his gaze, filled with desire, stopped her.

"I'm giving you permission to read my mind," she whispered.

He grinned then, almost predatory like, as every desire, wish and fantasy she'd had in the week he'd been gone and the time he'd returned, flooded her thoughts and slammed into his.

It wasn't possible for his eyes to darken, yet they did.

"My pleasure," he said in a velvety tone. He tugged his shirt over his head in one movement, revealing a bronzed, six pack before swiftly popping the top button on his jeans. As they dropped around his ankles, he kicked them off, reaching for her tee shirt. He almost ripped it in half tugging it off her arms. He threw it towards his pile of discarded clothes before gripping her hips, lifting her up and settling her against his engorged manhood.

She ran her hands through his hair, wondering at the feel of those strands between her fingertips. They'd always been silky soft, but now? She'd never felt hair so incredible, like every strand was alive, almost moving individually, like those vein-wings of his.

Too much thinking, she thought before dropping her lips against his and having her way with his mouth. She swirled her tongue against his before sucking it, rubbing against him, not knowing if she could hold out much longer. He ran his fingers rhythmically up and down the flesh of her back before unclipping her bra. She moaned softly as she felt her nipples touch against his chest, tingling with pleasure and sighed in relief when he dropped her onto the bed, reaching for her jeans that felt damp between her thighs.

Sam watched him, wide-eyed as he pulled them down over her thighs, knees, then ankles before tossing them behind him. She sucked in a breath as he stood for a moment, gazing hungrily at her. She greedily thought of an act she desperately wanted him to perform when his eyes met hers instantly, gleaming.

Max reached for her ankles and drew her towards him with such speed, laughter burst from her lips. It vanished as she met his eyes, once again, startling serious as he knelt on the floor and settled between her thighs.

She swallowed again, suddenly thirsty, as nerves fluttered and her heartbeat accelerated. As soon as he brushed his lips across her thigh, trailing his tongue along her flesh, leaving goosebumps, with every open-mouthed kiss, her nerves faded. Sam arched her back in anticipation as his lips made a sensual dance up her thigh, closer to her throbbing centre. She clenched the sheets in tight fists, waiting for him to lap at her core, eyes widening when he bypassed her throbbing bud to trail along the soft flesh of her stomach and into her belly button before trailing across the other side and along the smooth flesh of her other thigh.

She sighed, thinking she could take his tongue bath all day, every day, when her body was slammed with other sensations; more intense than what she was already feeling.

She could sense with every trace of his lips upon her flesh, a sweet throbbing, which was bordering on pain. It danced faster to a beat she couldn't hear yet felt the tempo hypnotic. She sensed every urge, pleasure and desire Max feeling.

Her breathing increased as his lips circled back up to the top of her thigh and she moaned softly, pushing her face into the soft flesh of her bicep, closing her eyes as his warm breath hit her dripping mound. She arched her hips, bringing her throbbing bud to hit his open mouth and forced herself not to scream in delight. Sam rocked against him, wanting this deep, delicious, lustful feeling to last as his fingers gripped her bottom, lifting her higher. His shoulders spread her thighs further apart, gaining access to every inch of her pulsing centre. His tongue swirled over her bud, lapping at her as if devouring sweet drops of honey. He swept two fingers inside her, penetrating and hitting her aching core as his tongue circled her bud repeatedly, tonguing her passionately as the crescendo built towards a raging inferno which she could not escape.

Even if she were on fire at this moment, she would have gladly remained in his inferno till there was nothing left of her but golden ash. He kissed her dripping lips with such passion, such love before sucking her hot bud into his mouth and she screamed in pure ecstasy before falling over the edge of sheer bliss; the climax not only taking her breath away, but his, too. She reached for him, feeling every inch of her flesh turn to molten lava. Max reached for her waist, pulling her up onto the bed before positioning himself above her, eyes gleaming with lust.

"Thank you," she whispered, almost shyly.

He shook his head, running a finger along her cheek bone. "Samantha Storm, shy?"

She raised an eyebrow. "Don't worry, it won't last."

He grinned. "Good," he said before thrusting into her silken core, remaining still for a moment.

"Oh my stars." She groaned, rocking against him. "Please don't stop."

She felt the tip of his shaft tap against her still tingling core, stirring a longing deep within her only he could reach. He ran his fingers up along her sides, sweeping them over her breasts, tracing lightly across one nipple, then the other before moving back to cup her hip.

Max rocked against her, increasing the blissful sensations building. He moaned before dropping his lips against hers, which she hungrily drank from. He pumped faster, deeper, gliding with her on a ride towards absolute bliss. She was flooded with a pulsing desire, not just hers, but his before she climaxed once more and the feelings that swirled between them, didn't just steal her breath, but came close to knocking her out.

CHAPTER TWENTY-SEVEN
MAXWELL

Max pushed the cellar door open, focusing on the positive energy of the past four hours, with Sam. To breathe her in, hearing her laugh, and trying to answer her hundreds of questions to her satisfaction. It had been a relief when she had relaxed enough around him for them to reconnect. He smiled as he headed down the steps thinking he was the luckiest man on earth. His smile faded as he thought of Mother Earth and how close she was to becoming completely destroyed. How the lives of every human pure-soul, could be lost; void forever moving forward.

And his sister was part of the chaos that ensured the demise of all. *Sister.* He shook his head. He could hardly believe it when Methuselah took him to the Second Earth and allowed him to see everything clearly. That his other sibling and her traitorous ways were revealed to him.

He scowled, thinking it really shouldn't have surprised him. After all, they did come from 'Black' stock. He was confused as to why he'd seen nothing of Trent's wicked ways; why he'd been cloaked from him?

"You don't look so happy to see me *fratello*. Why the handsome frown?"

Nadine looked far too relaxed for his liking, almost as if she were exactly where she wanted to be.

"Knock it off, I don't need any sass from you." He stood opposite her as she lounged back on the cot, swinging her crossed leg back and forth as if she didn't have a care in the world.

She stood then, crossing towards him, resting her hands through the bars. "What do you need from me then, hmm?"

"Some honesty for a start."

"Go on then."

"Was it always your intention to follow through with Brendan's orders? To deceive me and put our clan in harm's way?"

"If you mean to follow the orders of the only parent I ever loved, lost and then had the joy of helping resurrect, then yes, it was."

Max shook his head. "As easy as that?"

"Why not? Haven't you followed the orders of those *arrogant* Soul Keepers most of your life?"

He folded his arms and shrugged. "For a time, sure, but then I discovered there was another way that didn't include following prejudice rules and orders that I didn't agree with."

"Well, haven't you had the *luxury* then, of being raised by multiple sets of rules your entire life," she said, her sarcasm evident.

"What do you mean?"

She sighed. "Think about it. Apart from the time you spent away at boarding school, you were raised by one man, trained by another and then handballed to the Soul Keepers."

Max slid his hands into his pockets and remembered the time Brendan came into his life when he was twelve-years-old. His father had announced Brendan would be training him in the family business. He'd no idea at the time what the 'family business' really was. He'd thought at the time it was cattle, but then he'd been introduced to the life-altering truth. The deplorable, earth-shattering moment when Brendan had forced him to watch a man jump to his death off a Ferris Wheel at the Noorat show. Not just watch, but to absorb the pleasure that the ultimate agony, confusion and grief Brendan's influence had caused the man before and after he had leaped to his death. All because Brendan had crept into his mind and manipulated his decision and action to jump to his death.

"They were monsters, both our father and Brendan."

"Do you call a spider a monster for trapping his prey and sucking the life out of it, for his own survival when that is all he has ever known?"

Max laughed without humour. "You compare the Veins way of life to a spider? What a cop-out."

"You think so?"

"I know so. And now, so do you. We have always had another option to not only survive, but thrive, as well as assisting the world to do the same. That is why we were created."

"*We* weren't created. We were *born* from one of the most powerful entities this world has ever seen." Nadine folded her arms.

"Yeah, we were."

"Fat lot of good it did us though. Look where we've ended up?"

"We ended up here because Brendan and those like him led our kind astray. Those are the reasons why the Soul Keepers have always looked at us as though we were nothing more than a disease on this world."

Nadine shook her head.

"You can't deny that? As you said, we were *born* for greatness." He

321

ran a hand through his hair.

Footsteps headed down the stairs and Max turned to see Kyle with his arm slung around Sam's shoulder.

"Hello siblings," Kyle sang out, grinning.

Sam's eyes connected with his and he swore the earth shifted beneath his feet. She patted Kyle's hand casually before slipping out from under his arm and crossing over to him. Max opened his arm for her to slip under and she wound her arms about his waist, resting her check against his chest.

He sighed, breathing her in before kissing the top of her head.

"So, what are we going to do with this one?" Kyle nodded to Nadine as he pushed his hands into his pockets.

Max chuckled. Kyle seemed to be enjoying the role reversal a little too much.

"That depends on her."

"Oh?" Kyle raised an eyebrow at Max.

"What do you want from me? A blood oath?" Nadine scoffed.

"What good would that do? You'd turn and run as soon as you had the chance," Max said, stroking his hand up and down Sam's arm, relishing the feel of her soft skin.

"Well, you can't keep her locked up here forever." Sam looked up at him.

He looked into her amber eyes, rimmed with golden hues of honey, which held a note of hope.

"What will you have me do?" he asked.

She shrugged, looking across at Nadine. "Give her a chance to have a real family."

He looked at his sister as he considered Sam's words.

Nadine laughed bitterly. "Who says I haven't already got a real family? Why don't you all piss off and leave me in peace? Brendan will come for me soon enough."

She pushed away from the bars and sauntered back towards the cot, sitting down and resumed her earlier position, leaning back on her arms, leg swinging casually.

"Wow, you really are an idiot, sister of ours." Kyle shook his head.

Sam, Max. We need you at the council meeting. Now. Bowie pushed towards Max and Sam.

Sam tilted her head to meet his eyes, a concerned expression marring her pretty features. "Are we going?"

"As much as I swore I'd never step foot on their land again, I'm afraid it's essential that I do so now." Max looked at Kyle. "We have to go. Will you keep an eye on things?"

"Of course, I'll be more than happy to hold the fort, brother." Kyle mock bowed.

Max chuckled. "Thanks." He glanced at Nadine briefly before waving his hand, creating a pure white portal. He pulled Sam snuggly against his chest and they stepped into the blinding light, vanishing in an instant.

SAMANTHA

Sam swallowed the dry heat that rose up her throat, the moment Max pulled her through the portal. "This doesn't look like a simple council meeting," she whispered to him.

It's not.

You've got that right, Bowie replied, joining in.

Sam looked around the ancient fortress where the damp, moss-covered stones stood crumbling and decaying. Thousands of Soul Keepers had assembled, wearing disquieted expressions; amethyst capes fluttering in the breeze. She'd never seen so many Soul Keepers at a council meeting. Her heartbeat happily for a moment when her eyes met Tom's,

Jess's, Michael's and Angel's. Jane and Red stood beside them and she felt the love they pushed towards her and Max.

Family. She pushed towards Max.

Max's arm tightened around her momentarily at her thought. *Our other family.* He responded.

She nodded, looking out into the crowd, spotting two familiar faces she hadn't seen in months. A small cry of joy escaped her lips as she spotted her mother and father and slipping out from under Max's arm, ran towards her parents. A sea of amethyst capes parted before she launched herself into her father's arms.

"Daddy," she cried, wrapping her arms around him.

"Hello, my darling." Crow Storm hugged his daughter tight, dropping a kiss on her head before her mother, Johanna pulled her into her arms, whispering, "My baby girl, it's so good to see you."

Sam hugged her mother hard before pulling back to smile at her, sad to see tears on her face.

"What's wrong, Mama?" She wiped the tear off her mother's soft cheek, startled to see a worried look on her father's face.

Johanna sighed as Crow put his arm around his wife's waist as they both looked over Sam's head. Sam turned, to see Max walking towards them, her heart filling with love at the sight of him.

He smiled softly at her for a moment before reaching to shake Crow's hand, then dropped a kiss against Johanna's cheek. "It's good to see you both."

"It's good to see you too, Maxwell." Crow nodded.

"What's the verdict?" Max nodded around the fortress.

"The Light Accords have had a visitor and they are currently off having a private conversation," Johanna said as Red headed across to them, smiling as she put her arms around Sam, then Max.

"Hello, Nana." Max kissed her soft cheek.

"Hello, my boy."

"I'm guessing the visitor is someone pretty important to take the Light Accord members away from their own council meeting?"

Red smiled up at him. "Indeed."

Methuselah? Sam asked Max.

It has to be, he replied, placing his arm around her waist once more as the fortress filled with hushed conversations.

It was. Bowie joined in.

There was plenty of arguing before he arrived. Angel shared with Sam.

Sam looked across at her sister, raising her eyebrow in question. *Yeah?*

Angel nodded. *Too many dip-sticks in the mud who didn't want to hear anything to do with collaborating with Max's clan.*

Idiots. Sam snorted. She felt a light pat on her bottom and looked at her mother, whose eyes twinkled.

Behave, darlings. Johanna looked between Sam and Angel.

She was about to say something to her mother when she felt Max stiffen beside her. She looked around the fortress and saw nothing out of the ordinary when a blinding flash of pure silver, fading to the brightest white, washed over the crowd before falling towards the middle of the assembled members.

Amazed gasps replaced the hushed conversations as Uriel, one of the oldest Light Accord members, stood along with Fletch and several other council members which Sam knew held high positions. The one who stood taller than all, shinning lustrous silver, was Methuselah.

Here we go, show time. Bowie brushed against Sam's mind, earning a stern look from Crow.

Bowie unsuccessfully tried to hide his grin as Uriel's speech began.

"My good Soul Keepers, as discussed earlier, we face grave times indeed. There is no other way to save the pure-souls or Mother Earth unless we are willing to collaborate with the Father-of-all's child and his Veins."

Sam glanced at Max before meeting Methuselah's penetrating gaze.

Hello Princess. His silky voice brushed against Sam's ears alone.

Please, stop calling me that.

He smiled handsomely, tilting his head.

Uriel nodded to Fletch, who stepped forward. Dressed in his usual black attire, he looked formidable.

"There are some of you, many of you, who are hesitant to work with the Veins. For this, I cannot blame you. But the imminent demise of Mother Earth has been revealed to us, if we do not join forces immediately."

"So, we are expected to make an ally with our enemy?" A voice in the distant crowd called.

"We are." Fletch nodded, looking about the crowd as whispered questions were strewn around as quickly as rice confetti fell.

Sam stiffened slightly, hoping the Soul Keepers would not let her down with their narrow minds.

Fletch stepped forward before raising his voice ever so slightly. "And those who have aligned with Maxwell Obsidian's cause are our enemy no longer."

Fletch looked at Methuselah. "Would you be so kind as to share your vision with everyone?"

Sam watched in awe, as always, when Methuselah's wings spread out behind him with a snap, spanning six feet either side of his shoulders. They created a gale that had many Soul Keepers stumbling back. He truly was spectacular and despite the gasps and startled looks upon the Soul Keepers' faces, it was clear as day they thought so too.

"What you are about to see will occur in under a month's time. You have the power to stop this *if* you follow my grandson, Maxwell

Obsidian's orders. If not, your fate is already written. And not only your fate, but the fate of those you were born solely to protect." He spoke softly, yet his voice reached the furthest corner of the fortress as his steel cold gaze fell on each of them. "All will perish."

Sam shivered, wondering what would come next, when Methuselah's wings slammed together making a thunderous clap, snuffing out the light of day, sending the fortress into complete darkness.

Max must have sensed her unease as he placed her in front of him, holding her back against his chest, wrapping his arms about her waist. Before she could thank him, the area lit up, revealing a scene. Every single Soul Keeper had vanished from view and there was nothing else around her, bar Max's arms and a sight that made her heart break.

Mother Earth wasn't just on fire – she was crumbling into ashes. Giant chunks of earth falling in slow motion, floating about the galaxy; eerie in her demise as the screams and forlorn cries of the innocent filled every eardrum.

Sam's heartbeat thumped miserably, sending her blood to rush like a tsunami against her eardrums. Pure-souls, animals and humans alike ran to escape the chaos there was no escaping from. Her protective instincts as a Soul Keeper to save them all had every inch of her aching. Tears fell down her face as she watched as bombs were released into the atmosphere. Then, she watched as children burned and animals fell to their death. Watched nature disintegrate and history vanish, as the Veins and not the good kind, revelled in their victory.

Before Sam fell to her knees in utter grief, the scene shimmered, then changed. Soul Keepers and Veins, the good kind, fought together, working to heal the diseased and destroy those Veins who worshipped nothing but chaos. She watched as they located several bombs and gasped as they were sent straight into Max's open arms, where he absorbed every atom. She slapped her hands over her mouth to prevent the scream that wanted to escape, certain the impact would kill him. A warm cheek pressed against hers.

"It's okay, my love, watch." He whispered against her ear, sending shivers down her spine. Max in the scene before her, spread his silver vein-wings wide, and shot a billion silver stars out and across Mother Earth as if sprinkling fruitful seeds upon the earth.

Sam blinked as Angel appeared beside Max, looking as exquisite as ever as she placed her hands upon Mother Earth. Bowie stepped beside her, opening his arms wide to send a gentle rain to drench the earth. New growth burst in every which direction, covering the earth in bountiful nature. Mother Earth was flourishing in ways in which she had never before.

Impressive, as always. Sam pushed towards Angel, not certain she would hear her with this scene playing out.

Thank you. Angel replied warmly before asking. *Who's that?*

Sam focused on the scene, watching as an ethereal figure, her back towards the viewer, approached Max, Angel and Bowie. Shiny, silver waist-length hair brushed her hips as she walked, an amber glow illuminated from her palms. She turned and Sam was taken aback as she watched *herself* smile up at Max, then Angel and Bowie, who nodded.

The other Sam launched those amber balls of light outwards and the scene changed once more. Every dilapidated building, earth's-crust-depleting-bitumen, which stopped Mother Earth absorbing moisture, was sucked into the vortex of amber light, along with unusable materials, garbage and toxic waste alike. Every useless, man-made object, which choked Mother Earth, was absorbed and destroyed, leaving nothing but the purest of resources behind.

Sam was stunned speechless.

Is that all it takes? Bowie joked, although Sam detected a small amount of bewilderment in his tone also after what they'd all just witnessed.

A blinding burst of light forced her eyes shut before the afternoon sun fell over the assembly once more.

Sam blinked, confused as too many emotions swamped her and it was clear on the hundreds of faces she could see, she wasn't alone.

Methuselah folded his glorious wings behind him as he slid one hand casually into the pocket of his silver suit pants.

So like Max.

Methuselah smiled in her direction before addressing the crowd. "As you can see, the future truly is in your hands. Decide what you will but do it soon. I assure you; the enemy isn't dilly-dallying around. You have those who were always destined to lead you." Methuselah opened his palm towards Max, Angel and Bowie. Sam flushed when she realised he was also indicating her.

"I only hope you are wise enough to follow." *It's almost time,* he addressed Sam privately, in his usual, cryptic way.

For what? She raised an eyebrow.

For what you were created for. Be strong.

Before she could think another thought, he slammed his wings together once more, sending the wind to gush around them and a deafening clap of thunder followed as he soared towards the sky, leaving a trial of stardust to rain down upon them below.

Eyes wide, with both awe and disbelief, were burning holes in Sam's, Max's, Angel's and Bowie's backs. Yet no one dared utter a single word.

Sam pushed her private conversation with Methuselah away, as Uriel stepped forward, looking pale, as did the other Light Accord leaders. He bowed his head briefly before addressing the assembly.

"Things are dire indeed and now we know what we must do. What we were created to do. Maxwell Obsidian of Noorat and our dear Soul Keepers of Glenormiston South, you have our full support and co-operation. Mother Earth thanks you, for all you are about to do."

Sam turned to look at Max, waiting to hear what he'd say to those who had made his life a living hell and now, ironically, they needed his help to heal and save all.

His eyes met hers and she swore she saw a forest of green trees sway in the depths of his before he blinked, revealing nothing but his soulful gaze. He then turned towards the council members and spoke in quiet reverence as Methuselah had.

"For all *we* are about to do." He pointed to the assembly. "This cannot be done by any one group and it shouldn't just be up to the most powerful of us. That's where the world has gone wrong, why it has failed. Every single individual has a purposeful role to play, no matter how mundane it may seem." Sam noticed he looked meaningfully towards Fletch and the other high council members.

"Those in power have the responsibility to protect every single creature alike and I for one, will not take this responsibility lightly."

"Nor will we." Crow nodded towards Johanna.

Red placed a small hand on Max's back. "Nor will I."

"Nor I," chorused a thousand soft oaths around the fortress.

This was how things should be done. Advocacy in its most powerful and just form. Where their actions would matter and make the most influential impact.

Sam felt a sense of pride in the Soul Keepers for the first time in a long time and forced the prickling of tears back as she heard Angel sniff. She smiled across at her sister. *Softy.*

Couldn't help it. Angel smiled before Fletch broke their moment.

"There's much to be done in the coming days if we're to be successful. Maxwell, if you and your team will co-ordinate our plan of attack, we will be ready to assist you immediately."

Max nodded but remained silent.

"An apology wouldn't go astray right about now, don't you think?" Sam said boldly, feeling the council's earlier disregard and disrespect towards Max should have been addressed already. She would not back down and met Fletch's unblinking stare.

"Maxwell Obsidian, please accept the council's sincerest apologies in which we have treated you in the past. May this day and every day moving forward, mark a new beginning for Veins and Soul Keepers alike."

Sam met Bowie's gaze as Fletch and every amethyst caped body bowed before Max in apology.

"Apology accepted," Max said in return. "May we keep the souls safe."

"With every breath that we take." A thousand voices echoed around the fortress. Harmony flowed in the breeze that was sweetened by blossoms.

Fletch turned to Sam and raised an eyebrow as if asking her if the apology was acceptable. She was about to make a clever remark when she felt a disturbing shift within her as every hair on the back of her neck rose. Her skin felt icy-cold, yet her insides felt as if they were boiling. Her head ached terribly. Something weird and slug-like, was moving around her stomach, creating severe discomfort at every turn. What the hell was happening to her?

Something's wrong. She reached for Max's hand, gasping in pain as she doubled over, clutching at her midriff.

What is it? Bowie demanded.

We have to get out of here. Now. Max waved a hand and before Sam knew what was happening, her loved ones were snatched through a portal and whisked away before her eyesight was lost to a frenzy of pain.

CHAPTER TWENTY-EIGHT
MAXWELL

Max leaned over the bed, running his hand over Sam's damp brow as she cried out again. He forced himself to remain calm, and passed a hand through the air above her body, trying to locate where the source of her pain was stemming from. When he found it, his gut clenched in anger as she moaned in agony.

"What's happening to her?" Angel asked, folding her arms tightly as she stared helplessly down at Sam, who was clutching at her stomach.

He frowned, not liking what he suspected. "I believe Sam has an engorged Leecher inside her."

"A *Leecher*?" Angel raised an eyebrow in confusion.

"What the *hell* is that?" Bowie snapped.

Max shook his head. "It's when a Vein inserts a leech-like parasite inside a pure-soul, which then integrates itself throughout the body as it feeds."

"I'm confused." Angel shook her head. "Who did this and why?"

"A Vein did this. And there's two reasons why. It's a way of feeding off a host multiple times without killing them immediately." Max took Sam's hand as she cried out.

"And the other reason?" Michael asked.

"The parasite grows and becomes a part of the host. The one who placed it inside of Sam could eventually use his connection within her to control her."

"Oh no," Angel whispered.

"Would Sam not have realised it was inside her?" Bowie leaned over Sam and took her other hand.

"It's undetectable to the host."

"But wouldn't she have felt it when the Vein put it inside her?"

"Whoever inserted this Leecher would have done so in a way that she wouldn't have noticed it. It may have felt similar to a mosquito bite."

"So, why does a Vein feed from it?" Michael asked.

"The parasite extracts pure essence and the longer it's left inside the victim, the blood becomes raw energy. When the Vein taps into it to feed, he receives a potent hit."

"Sounds like a drug problem." Bowie scoffed.

"It is. Unfortunately, for the host, if the Leecher is left in for a time without being fed upon, it becomes septic to the host."

"Septic…?" Michael placed his hands on his hips.

"Yes, similar to a pure-soul's appendix bursting and going gangrenous I'd imagine," Max said, as Sam cried out once again, sweat pouring from her pale flesh.

Bowie hissed in frustration. "Can't you get it out?"

Angel placed her hand on his arm in a soothing gesture, pulling him away from the bed.

Bowie blew out a breath, releasing his sister's hand as he brushed a kiss on the top of Angel's head.

"Can you get it out without it hurting Sam?" She asked.

"I'm certainly going to try." Max leapt onto the bed, straddling Sam's twisting, tortured body, his vein-wings snapping from his shoulder blades, through unseen slits in the material of his clothing. He sent four of his veins to wrap like vines around Sam's ankles and wrists, holding her as still as possible. He placed his hands upon her shoulders, frowning when he felt her burning up beneath his touch.

"Don't panic," he said to the room in general when the flesh along his left wrist split open, releasing an obsidian vein to slip under the waist band of Sam's tee shirt.

He ignored Angel's small cry of dismay before he pushed the head of his vein into the sweet, soft flesh of Sam's stomach and focused on locating the filth causing his love such agony.

He instantly sensed who had placed the Leecher in Sam and fury surged through him. How could he have missed this? He wanted to rip the culprit's head off.

"Max?" Bowie said, his sharp tone jolting Max from his haze of anger. He opened his eyes, alarmed to find his vein-wings had reached out around the room, filling almost every corner.

"Sorry," he whispered, pulling them back closer to his body before he concentrated on the task at hand. He found the Leecher, engorged with her Elemental blood, ensnarled and twisted around inside her body. He froze, terrified of how much damage it had caused.

"What's happening in there?" Bowie stepped forward.

"It's attached itself to her organs, muscles and spine." He continued his search, disturbed and concerned with his findings. The Leecher had punctured every precious part of Sam's anatomy and it was taking over. "It's going to cause severe damage when I remove it," he said, sounding calmer than he felt, as Sam wrestled against her restraints, releasing a tortured scream.

"Shh, love."

"I'm here to help," Angel whispered.

He nodded, closing his eyes, searching around Sam's warm body, as she moaned in pain.

"Sorry love," he whispered as he directed his vein towards the main body of the Leecher. He knew the moment the parasite realised it wasn't alone and before it could rip its multiple feeding arms out of Sam's vital organs, to defend itself, which in turn would kill her instantly, Max sent his vein's razor-sharp teeth to attack it.

His vein bit into the Leecher, and began sucking it dry, gasping in surprise as Sam's blood-essence flowed into his vein and slammed into his body. Any toxicity causing Sam's pain wasn't evident for the sweetest taste flowed within him. How could he have possibly thought that a heavenly soul's essence was the most sublime thing he'd ever consumed?

Within seconds, his wrists on both forearms split open, and he sent several more veins inside to penetrate Sam's flesh and feast upon the Leecher, deflating it in every way possible. He only hoped it wouldn't tear her insides to pieces as he killed it. Several minutes passed, and he sighed in relief as the Leecher became nothing more than a dried, empty tube.

Something else stirred within Sam's body; a powerful, almost familiar force reaching out and towards him. It wasn't dangerous to Sam, yet he felt as if it *could* cause her severe pain? It slapped at every one of his veins, like he was being shooed out.

"What *is* that?" he whispered to himself, shaking his head.

"What's what?" Bowie demanded, sounding frustrated.

Max bit his lip, eyes firmly closed as he whispered. "Hang on."

A small moan had his eyes opening in a flash and he saw Sam

staring up at him; a frightened expression marred her pale features, yet he didn't withdraw despite the look of horror on her face. He wasn't done just yet.

SAMANTHA

The excruciating pain throbbing like an adamant drum, stealing her every thought and breath, was receding. Along with the niggling headache that had persisted for weeks. She sighed, grateful her body was feeling more like her own again, except the unusual weight pinning her down along with the sensual feeling gliding within her before that too, become painful, yet weirdly in a pleasant way.

She opened her eyes to a sight that was both glorious and terrifying. Max was straddling her, his impressive vein-wings spanned the bed and beyond. Several of his obsidian veins were spilling from his wrists and were inserted inside her body. She gasped, feeling them sliding within her, searching for the thing that had caused her pain, destroying it. Each attack on what she presumed was a Leecher, helped ease the pain within her, yet something else was going on inside her. Pleasure rolled into pain, twisting and crashing around her insides like a rogue wave.

"Max?" Her eyes widened as every molecule felt as if it were drowning and burning at the same time. "Max, *something's wrong*!" She screamed, struggling to free herself for his shackles.

"Hold still," Max whispered. "I'm going to pull the Leecher out."

"Be careful," Angel begged.

Max nodded once, concentrating on the task at hand as he extracted the destroyed Leecher.

As Max extracted the parasite, its barbs inserted in her muscles and bones, ripped her insides to pieces. She screamed in agony and white pain filled her vision.

Bowie groaned. "*What* are you *doing* to her?"

"It's feeding barbs are shredding her organs."

Why did he sound so calm when she felt as if she were dying? She screamed again as vessels exploded, muscles tore and every molecule felt as if it were melting in molten lava. And not the good kind.

"Don't let me go, Max," she pleaded, knowing if he released the restraints, she would set the room on fire. She couldn't control the pain eating her insides alive.

"I won't, love. I've got you." He soothed while wearing the most worried expression she'd ever seen. She grit her teeth when Max's veins left her body, pulling out a long, insipid looking thing, which resembled a dead snake.

"Ugh," Bowie spat in disgust as Max tossed the Leecher on the floor. He threw a bolt of lightning at it, incinerating it.

Sam wanted to say something profound, but the pain was too intense. She gasped as she felt something else moving within her invading her broken body.

"We have to *do* something!" Angel snapped. "Sam, Max, tell me what to do?"

Sam opened her mouth to reply when tears of fright fell from her eyes. Something truly weird was happening inside of her. Something *else* was inside her.

"What the *hell* is happening to me?" she choked out. "Max?"

"What the *hell* is that?" Bowie yelled, rushing to her side to wipe a tear off her cheek. He held his fingertip up, and Sam stared at the pure white teardrop before pain claimed her once more.

"Angel's above," Max whispered.

"*Max?*" Her eyes widened in fear. She gasped, terrified as fire swept through her body, disintegrating everything in its path. She screamed before cement-like lava flowed into her lungs, creeping up her throat, blocking her airway, consuming her in its entirety. Hot tears burned her cheeks as she threw her head from side to side, trying to dislodge the suffocating substance and escape the excruciating pain destroying her insides, obliviating her essence, her soul.

Please don't let me die, she begged them.

We won't let that happen, Max promised.

She was grateful they could hear her. *I love you all.* She hoped the terror she was feeling did not mar her words of love.

She wanted to scream, but could not as her lungs, throat and mouth continued to fill with what felt like boiling cement as it solidified. She desperately wanted to see Max, but her vision was filled with hot white light. She felt it then, the moment her world stilled and her heart fluttered once before stopping.

It was then, that she felt herself evaporate into nothingness.

She didn't know how long she'd drifted, floating in the soothing arms of silence and pain-free tranquillity as every nerve ending tingled in ultimate pleasure. She sighed, wanting to cry in relief now that the pain was completely gone. She'd been certain it had sent her mad with its sheer intensity, but no. She seemed okay.

Hang on a minute… am I still alive? She was too frightened to open her eyes but wiggled her fingers and toes to see if she still had them.

"Open up, love." Max's sweet voice reached her ears, sounding velvety smooth before warm flesh brushed her cheek.

"I don't want to," she whispered, afraid if she did the pain would return. She liked her dark little nest of pain-free peace.

"Can you please?" Angel asked, sounding excited.

"Yes, we want to see what the *hell* you've become," Bowie sounded impatient.

"Become?" She raised her hands and covered her face. "I don't want to know. I'm just happy the pain has stopped." She knew she was being a coward but couldn't help herself. She was just damn grateful to be alive.

"Sam," Max whispered, taking her wrists and stroked a thumb along the flesh where her pulse beat, sparking goosebumps. Then, he tugged her hands away from her face.

She squeezed her eyes shut tighter.

Someone chuckled. "Samantha Storm, you are one of the bravest Soul Keepers I know. What are you afraid of?" Michael asked.

"Everything. That I'm not me anymore," she said, feeling lighter, stronger and older than ever before. She could sense something unusual within her.

A featherlight kiss brushed across her lips, sparking a rush of warmth to stroke every inch of her flesh. She gasped, surprised that a single, simple kiss ignited such a deep level of intense feelings. She opened her eyes to meet Max's.

He was leaning over her, watching her. She returned his all-encompassing gaze and took her time staring into the depths of his eyes, feeling like she was looking into his soul. He wore a pleasant smirk upon his lips.

"What?" she whispered, reaching to trace a finger along his five o'clock shadowed jaw line. *My stars but he is so beautiful.* His scent wrapped around her. She raised an eyebrow, when the corner of his lips turned up, smiling wider.

"You said you wouldn't hear my thoughts again unless I gave you permission?"

She wasn't upset and knew he knew it too.

"Come." He stood, reaching down and wrapped his fingers around her wrists, pulling her to her feet. "It's time."

She'd always been agile on her feet, but felt lighter somehow, as if she were walking on air. She glanced down, surprised to see her bare feet were touching the floorboards.

"Weird," she said before looking at Bowie, who, like Angel and Michael, were looking at her in awe.

"Stop that." She frowned.

"Stop what?" Bowie smirked.

"Looking at me like I'm an insect." She scoffed.

"There is absolutely nothing wrong with insects," Angel said as Bowie snorted.

Max circled his arm about her waist and turned her towards the mirror. She swallowed as her eyes met his in the mirror, not daring to focus on herself. She knew something within her had changed, but she wasn't sure she was ready to see it.

"You are love. Look." Max nodded, his breath stirred a few strands of hair across the top of her head and, taking a deep breath, Sam turned her eyes towards her reflection.

The air whooshed from her lungs and she felt lightheaded at the transformation staring back at her. It *was* her, but it wasn't? Her once honey-blonde hair had turned stark white with silver highlights and hung like a silken curtain to her waist. What could have looked washed out, or drawn, only made her appear regal, taller even. Although, she knew she wasn't. Max still loomed at the same height behind her.

She raised a pale eyebrow, noticing her warm amber eyes looked a deep orange, with swirls of forest green within them. *No way.* She breathed, running her fingers along defined cheekbones; her skin radiant, almost pearl-like. She moved her head from side to side, trying to figure out if she looked beautiful, or like an alien?

Beautiful is an understatement, but then, it always was with you. Max brushed against her mind.

She met his gaze before exclaiming. "How is this possible?"

"Let me help you out." Bowie folded his arms as Angel placed an arm around his waist, leaning her cheek against his shoulder, staring wide-eyed at Sam.

"According to Maxwell, Trent, the bastard, inserted a Leecher in you, not long after he arrived here."

Sam shook her head. "I would have known if he'd done that."

"No, you wouldn't have, it would have felt like nothing more than a mosquito bite."

She frowned. "But, surely I would have known something was growing inside me as it fed off me?"

"Because of your Soul Keeper gifts and strength, you wouldn't have felt the debilitating impact of the feeder as severely as a pure-soul." Max stepped back, folding his arms.

"The niggling headaches and cramps?" she whispered, turning to face them all. "But *how* would he have inserted it inside me without my knowing?"

Max shrugged. "He obviously has skills."

Sam frowned, thinking back to the time when the clan had arrived and she had been in the kitchen, placing the bakery goods in the fridge when Trent had startled her and she'd felt a tingling on her neck. "Yeah, I think I know when he might have done it," explaining the morning in question.

Max nodded before Bowie continued. "And as for the other... thing."

"Not a thing," Max interrupted.

"Righto." Bowie swept his palm forward. "Take it away then."

Max nodded, turning back to Sam. "The night you met Methuselah; do you remember everything that was said? What occurred between the two of you?"

Sam placed her hands on her hips, and dropped her gaze to the floor, nibbling on her lower lip as she thought back to that night and the landfill of information she had to process.

Don't do that. Max brushed over her mind.

Her gaze met his in question.

I can't concentrate when you're looking so damn sexy.

Sam snorted. *Please.*

"Have you two finished? I want to see the finale," Michael interrupted.

Max chuckled before continuing. "The night Methuselah wrapped his wings around you, and said you were created for one specific purpose."

"Yeah." Sam nodded. "I remember and I told him I was created to protect Angel."

She smiled across at the one female she loved most in this world.

Angel returned her smile, saying, "Can we please hurry up and get to the good part?"

Sam frowned. *What the hell are they going on about?*

"That night, Methuselah also bit you." Max angled his head, waiting for her to remember.

"Yeah, that sneaky bastard's vein-wing-thing bit-kissed me," she said. "What was that all about?"

Max nodded before answering. "He injected a part of his essence within you, to merge with your essence, and to protect you as much as he could from the parasite Trent had inserted inside you. That parasite was a part of Brendan."

"Like the black entity that was trying to consume you?"

"Exactly like that. Brendan was trying to hurt me by turning the thing I loved most, into something he could control. Methuselah always knew you were going to be mine but had to act that night to ensure the toxin Trent had inserted didn't consume you. And along with your Elemental essence, he knew you would become... this." He waved his hand towards her.

"And what have I actually become?" she asked, hesitant.

"Just an incredibly sublime creature." Angel beamed. Michael nodded in agreement.

Sam frowned, knowing her sister was softening her for what must be a blow to be delivered.

"Maxwell?" She begged as a weird energy flowed through her, increasing with her unease. "What's happened to me?"

"*Kyle.*" He called towards the door.

Sam turned as the bedroom door crashed open and Kyle stepped aside, allowing Nadine to walk in ahead of him. She gasped when she saw Nadine had fashioned a solid spear from her veins and launched it straight towards Angel, who made no move to protect herself.

Sam cried in dismay, leaping towards her sister's aid, confused why Bowie, Max and Michael weren't making a single move to shield Angel.

A hot rush of energy ran along the flesh of her back and burst through her shoulder blades, propelling her forward with such speed, her head spun. When she rushed forward to protect Angel, she felt a power she didn't understand. Whatever it was, it disintegrated Nadine's weapon in seconds and sent Nadine smashing back against the wall. Sam cringed as plaster cracked and bricks crumbled behind it. Panting, she pushed a hand through her hair, marvelling at the softness of it before glaring at herself in the mirror, her eyes widening in surprise.

"What the *actual* hell?" she cried. Behind her, light as feathers, were an army of pure white, vein-wings, scattered with the brightest of silver, rising three feet above her shoulders. "Angels above!"

"I'd say, sister of mine." Bowie smirked.

Vein-wings on a Soul Keeper? What does this make me?

"Beautiful, Sam." Angel crossed towards her, running her hand along the tip of Sam's wing. "It feels like liquid silk," she whispered, sounding bewildered.

She swallowed, feeling completely overwhelmed, but knowing they didn't have time for her to be so. She turned, putting her arms around Angel for a brief hug, needing to feel some sort of normal before turning to Max.

"What was that with Nadine?" she said, nodding to the crumpled figure as Kyle bent to scoop his sister up.

"That was a test that our sister was only to happy to assist with." Max answered, nodding to Kyle.

"And what if I *didn't* pass the test?" She knew she sounded pissed off.

"I knew that wouldn't happen," Max replied.

"Oh, you knew, huh? Well what if these, wing-things hadn't worked and my sister was injured, or killed?" She jammed her hands on her hips as she glared at him.

Max sighed as he stepped towards her, allowing a gap between them. She tipped her head back to look at him and noticed his handsome features were lined with concern for her, always.

"As if any of us would allow that to happen," he said softly.

"Why did *this* happen?" she asked, feeling anguished in that moment. *Who was she now?*

He curled his fingers around her upper arms, holding her as he gazed into her eyes.

"Methuselah said you were created for me, the moment *I* was born."

Sam raised an eyebrow, not wanting to interrupt with a question, so remained silent.

"And so, you were, from an elite, pure line, which carried warrior's hearts, courage like no other, a selflessness and pure power that would always equal mine."

"Sounds about right." Bowie sounded impressed and proud.

Max looked at Bowie before saying to Sam. "You would only ever truly be mine, if it were your heart's desire, too."

"Free will, huh?" She attempted a smile.

He grinned, eyes sparkling with mischief. "Of course. We're not monsters."

Her smile faded then, and she blinked. "Monsters." She whispered, sounding fearful. "So, I was born a Soul Keeper and now I'm... *this*. Am I going to have the sudden urge to suck on...?" She couldn't finish the question as she looked across at Angel, who was snuggled under Bowie's chin, looking as pretty as ever. Then she glanced at Michael, who was standing near a window. Her two favourite Cloud siblings, whom she loved as much as she did Bowie. Would she get the urge to drain their essence? *My stars, I'd rather die!*

Max pulled her under his chin. "No, you won't, because *you* are who you are," he said, assuring her, wrapping his arms around her, holding her close.

Sam squeezed her eyes tight, and pushed her face into the warmth of his chest, taking in a deep lungful of his scent. Every breath stilled the pressure building within her, yet, even with her eyes closed, she felt the world spinning about her. She gripped the front of Max's tee shirt, pushing her face against her fists, refusing to give in to the overwhelming urge to pass out and escape the past few hours. *What now?*

"You need sleep," Bowie said. "You've been through too much in a short amount of time."

"We don't have time for me to be napping." She turned to her brother. "I'm fine."

"No, you're not," Max said, bringing her eyes back to his. "When I transitioned, it took me the full week for my body to adjust and then mentally come to terms with what had happened. Just rest for a little while, okay, love."

"You'll need it." Michael said. "The Soul Keepers will be arriving shortly."

"How do I tuck these wings away?" she asked Max, as he ran a hand along her cheek.

"Just like that?" he smiled.

She was startled to find that, with thinking how to fold her wings away, they folded into her flesh, with nothing more than a whisper of air running a cold finger along her spine. She shuddered once, wondering if she'd ever get used to that.

Max bent and dropped a kiss against her lips.

"Sleep," he whispered.

And just like that, she fell asleep. The last thing she remembered was him catching her in his arms as her head lolled against his chest.

CHAPTER TWENTY-NINE
MAXWELL

Twilight settled around them as they eased into the second day working together in the healing and restoring of Mother Earth. Some of the Veins had been hesitant to collaborate with the Soul Keepers at first, but not after Max shared the 'near-future' scene Methuselah had shared with the council. Everyone acknowledged this was their only choice.

Red instructed Fletch to get them all into groups of four, where two Soul Keepers and two Veins were to work together. Bowie and Angel had been invaluable in the training sessions, as they demonstrated their skills alongside Rick and Gemma. They worked together like a well-oiled machine and the benefits of working together as allies were clear to all watching.

Max was relieved things were running smoothly and because of their joined forces, several global disasters had been reversed. Veins and Soul Keepers alike were respecting each other, their individual abilities, strengths and together, they were saving Mother Earth again the way Methuselah intended.

Brendan and his army were consistently infecting the earth with disease at an alarming rate, but despite this, they seemed to be staying ahead of any irreversible destruction, because they were working together without historic bias.

He'd left Sam to her healing sleep as her body was in the final stages of transitioning. Methuselah had stood watching over her for the first twenty-four hours and had only returned to his place of watch amongst the stars once he'd been certain she would be well.

Before Methuselah left, Max had asked him, "Why did you never gift nana with the same essence-transformation as Sam?"

"You are the beginning of an entirely new species."

"What about nana though?" he'd asked.

"What about my beloved?" Methuselah had answered, never once taking his eyes from Sam.

"When her time comes, and she passes from this world, won't you miss her?"

Methuselah turned to Max then and walked towards him, placing a large hand on his shoulder. "My Red will pass, but not as you think. She will return to me in the form when we first met and fell in love. The best of Souls will always be rewarded when they pass from their realm." He smiled down at Max.

Max nodded as he looked into the wise, cool gaze of this exceptional being before asking, "If we can cure the world from Brendan once and for all, why do Sam and I need these extra abilities? Why do we need such power?"

Methuselah sighed then and crossed back to look down at Sam.

My sleeping beauty. Max waited for Methuselah to answer.

"I've informed you about the other worlds out there, Maxwell, have I not?"

"Yes."

"Then you have your answer. For what may be well just now, will not always be so. And now, you and Samantha will be prepared to lead your own army, to cure the other worlds if necessary. That is why."

As easy as that.

"Indeed." Methuselah smiled at him then before waving his hand over Sam, sprinkling white star dust from his fingertips to fall upon her before penetrating into her skin.

Before Max could ask what Methuselah had done, he disappeared in a blazing silver trail out of the window. Max shook his head as he wondered about the past decade of his life and curiously anticipated what the next decade would bring. As long as he had Sam by his side, he was certain he could manage anything that came their way. His love's voice snapped him from his thoughts and back to the present.

"So, apparently I'm this new, 'thing,' yet I can't even summon a portal. What's up with that?"

Sam's question had him turning, and he watched her and Angel leaning against the back deck railing, a steaming mug in both of their hands.

Angel shook her head. "Stop calling yourself a 'thing.' You're still the same Sam to me."

"Pfft." Sam took a swallow from her mug before her gaze wandered across the yard. He felt the punch in his stomach as soon as her gaze met his. He knew she'd felt it too, as her cheeks filled with a becoming pink.

Angel's gaze followed Sam's and she smiled when she spotted him. *We need a celebration drink, don't you think?* Angel asked Max.

He was silent for a moment before nodding. He wondered with this many Soul Keepers and Veins, if they shouldn't head into Terang and hit the local pub. His cellar was running low.

Wheatsheaf, or Middle? He raised an eyebrow.

Yes, Wheatsheaf. Angel beamed before turning to Sam. "Let's go, I need a night of dancing, a game of pool and a few drinks definitely would not go astray."

"Sounds good to me." Max heard Kyle who had joined them. "Let's get out of these battle clothes and sexy ourselves up a bit."

"Best idea ever." Angel linked her arm through Kyle's and they headed inside.

Sam stood, waiting for Max to join her.

"Are you up for a night out?" he asked, standing on the grass looking up at her. Her hair fluttered softly in the breeze and he had to admit, her amplified beauty stole his breath away.

She nodded. "Sure. The question is, is now a good time to go and dose ourselves in alcohol?"

He tilted his head, thinking she still had so much to learn about their new 'abilities.' "I hope you won't be too disappointed to find out that we won't be able to get drunk anymore, Sam."

She sighed. "Oh? Well, it's not like we were big drinkers anyway, I guess." She shrugged, sounded slightly disappointed.

He thought this was the perfect moment to give her a little boost and, walking around the deck and up the steps, he reached for her hand. As she took his, he squeezed her hand, passing a small burst of energy into her palm. Her eyes diluted and a soft gasp escaped her lips as she swayed.

He put his arm around her shoulders, chuckling. "Steady now, I've got you."

"What the *hell* was that?" She glared up at him, but there was no anger in her eyes.

He smiled, dropping a kiss to the top of her head. "*That* was my own form of elixir, blended just for you."

"Well, I think I like it." She tilted her head back, gazing at his lips.

He grinned and cupped the back of her neck, marvelling again at the sheer silkiness of her hair as it brushed against his fingers. Max brought her flush up against him, and his male ego beamed as a small purr of anticipation escaped her lips before he covered them with his, kissing the air from her lungs.

She wrapped her arms around his neck and he thrilled as she moved against him, trying to close any small gap that remained between them. She drank from him like a dehydrated soul, her tongue sliding against his with perfection. He pulled back as he could feel the rest of his 'male bits' reacting. They were, after all, standing where one-hundred-and-fifty sets of eyes could see them.

"Time to get ready, love." He ran his hand over her hair.

"Phew." She blew out a breath before nodding.

He smiled. "You okay?"

"Sure. Max, who have you got guarding Nadine?"

He was wondering when she would ask about his sister. "Michael volunteered."

"Okay."

"Michael wanted to ask her questions about her childhood. He believes he can get her to open up, to see things in a different light. Maybe help us out where Brendan is located."

"Well, if anyone can do that, it's Michael. He has always been the most patient of us all."

Max smiled, taking her hand as they headed inside. "Truer words were never spoken."

"Why can't we locate Brendan's hideout? It really shouldn't be that hard, should it?" Sam placed her empty mug on the counter as they walked by the kitchen before heading upstairs.

He shrugged. "No. But then, he has untapped powers, kinda like we do Sam. This is all new territory, even for us."

"Understatement of the year." She muttered before they came to a stop at her bedroom door.

He could hear Angel's laughter from behind the closed door before it flew open and Kyle stood there, dressed in fish net stockings, black denim shorts and one of Sam's midriff tee shirts. Max raised an eyebrow.

"Well, hello there, your *Highnesses*," He mock bowed, causing another light laugh to slip from Angel's lips.

Sam whacked his arm before saying, "You look better in that tee shirt than I do. Keep it."

"Why, thank you." He walked past Sam, offering her a high five, which she returned. "Come on brother, let's get you, loosened up," he said before continuing upstairs to Max's room.

Max bent and swept a light kiss across Sam's lips, noticing there was a slight worried gleam in her eyes. "Everything's going to be all right. I'm with you every step of the way."

She continued staring up at him for a moment, not answering before she nodded. "Sure."

He laughed. "Don't sound so convinced."

Sam smiled. "Everything is going to be just dandy." She tiptoed up to brush a sweet kiss across his cheek.

Crisp air, eucalyptus and Sam's pure scent sent a spiral of lust and love to slam into his gut. When she went to step back, he grabbed the nape of her neck and brought her flush up against him in a blinding fast move. Her eyes, wide for a split second, looked up at him in wonder before clouding as his lips descended, capturing hers for an all-consuming kiss. She was the sweetest thing, and he wished he had time to sip from her all night, grateful they seemed to have a lifetime. When he released her, he delighted in seeing the tip of her pink tongue sweep over her bottom lip as she seemed to gather her thoughts, which she was shielding.

"Don't want to share, huh?" he asked as he tilted his head, pushing his hands in his pockets.

She stepped back then through the open doorway, shaking her head as she grabbed the door and smiling before shutting it firmly in his face.

He stood there for a moment, running his hands through his hair as he blew out a breath. Samantha Storm had always been one magnificent being, but now? He didn't have the words himself. He headed upstairs to see what his brother was doing and hoped that the night ahead would gift them all with a few hours of fun and peace.

SAMANTHA

The Princess Highway ran though the main street of Terang, stretching from Melbourne to Warrnambool; its avenue lined with beautiful English Oaks planted prior to the 1890s. The Wheatsheaf Hotel, which had been established since 1862, sat proudly along the highway, along with the newsagents, IGA, bakery, and the Rusty Spanner, where Jess Fowler's award wining paintings were often sold. Friday night at the Wheatsheaf was packed to the rafters and Sam was pleased to see it was no different tonight. The locals enjoyed a yarn while they watched the footy and bet on the horses. A few truckers passing through were more than happy to share the pool table with their crowd and a few entertaining games had already taken place.

She spotted Mr Kemp, their primary school teacher and Mr Kidd, the town's favourite bus driver, greet Max and Bowie with enthusiasm. Max gestured across the pub towards Sam and Angel, who returned their hello-wave with smiles.

The atmosphere couldn't have been more perfect for the night they all needed, to sit back and relax after all they'd been through of late. The vibe was high and the shots easy to consume, thanks to the talented and cheerful bar staff, Skye and Tahlia.

A light nudge at her elbow had Sam turning to Angel, who nodded across to the pool table where Rick and Kyle were competing against Bowie and Max.

"It's nice to see everyone getting along." Angel leaned against the bar.

"It is."

"For now." Jane chuckled as a familiar voice yelled out, "Shots on me!"

Sam turned as Angel laughed before dashing across the room to where their oldest friends, Kylee, Joanne, Lisa and Kim were walking in from the dining room. Sam's heart lifted as she watched Angel hug the girls they'd known since primary school before they joined her and Jane. She wrapped her arms around each of them, feeling the most like her old self than she had in what felt like a long time.

You deserve to be happy, my love. Enjoy tonight, let your hair down while you can.

She looked across to see Max hit the white ball, sending two of his balls into a corner and side pocket, earning an enthusiastic roar from Bowie as Kyle rolled his eyes.

Max's calm eyes lifted to meet hers and she replied, *I love you.*

A slow smile spread across his face. *I know.*

"Ha," she said, laughing, feeling euphoric. She shook her head, grinning at him before turning back to her friends.

"Christ Almighty, not that he needed it, but has Maxwell Black had work done?" Kim asked.

"Shit, he is beautiful." Kylee agreed, causing Jane and Angel to laugh their heads off.

"Not that I know of." Sam chortled as Angel flung her arm around Lisa's shoulder.

"Ah, Sam, your brother is as spectacular as ever." Joanne ogled Bowie.

"Shit." It was Sam's turn to mutter as Jane screamed with laughter, causing many heads to turn towards their cheerful group. Sam was grateful their friends hadn't commented on any of her 'apparent changes.' Maybe to them, she looked the same?

"Bloody hell, I only had a few drinks at dinner." Kim tilted her head. "But I swear I can see two Maxes at the pool table?"

"You're not wrong." Kylee squinted her eyes and Sam laughed, shaking her head.

Jane answered. "No, you're not seeing double. That is Max's long-lost brother."

"Brother?" Lisa raised an eyebrow.

"Sweet baby Jesus, I want one," Joanne whispered, sending their group into hysterical laughter.

Sam met Angel's gaze.

I know. It feels good, doesn't it? Angel smiled.

Yeah, so normal. I've missed... normal.

Normal's overrated. Just enjoy the now, sister.

Sam returned Angel's smile and nodded before Kylee clapped her hands together, breaking their private conversation.

"Come on girls, get these into you." Skye had lined up several shot glasses and filled them with a few different liquors that Kylee enthusiastically announced were 'bubble-gum-shots.'

"Thanks." Sam nodded to Skye before shooting Kylee a wink and together, their happy group did a 'cheers,' then tossed the shots back, followed by another round. Inappropriate conversation mingled with laughter flowed as they caught up on all the gossip from the past few months. Kylee and Kim shared information about the new men in their lives. Sam was thrilled to hear that Lisa had plucked up the courage to date Jess after she had crushed on him during lectures for the better part of last year. The night rolled along in a carefree bubble of laughter and mingling.

"I'm going to the loo," Jane announced.

"I need to go." Joanne grabbed her purse, and they headed off.

Sam tuned into some of the surrounding conversations, glad to note that many of the Veins and Soul Keepers were sharing stories of their past experiences. They discussed views on how they'd been brought up to unquestioningly follow the path of their elders. Their trust in one another and their honesty was refreshing and gave her much hope for their united future.

She'd noticed Max had been trying to make his way across to her for the past several minutes but had been stopped by many Veins and Soul Keepers alike. No doubt they had questions about the next few days and needed his assurance they could get on top of the impending doom.

And here you were thinking we could have a fun night out and escape it all for a while? Sam felt for him and wished she could whisk him away for some peace.

Without breaking his conversation with the group he was addressing, he returned, *I'm fine and as long as I have a few quiet hours with you at the end of this day, before tomorrow begins, that is all the peace I need.*

She flushed, wanting *that* moment to be here soon too and sipped her glass of water, attempting to wash down the gallon of sugar she felt she'd consumed in the various shots and shouted drinks from her friends. She looked at her reflection in the bars mirror, grateful to see she didn't look as 'sugar-high,' as she felt.

Joanne returned several minutes later without Jane.

"Jane still in the ladies?" she asked her.

"No, she left with an extremely sexy looking guy with a blue streak in his hair."

Sam froze. *Trent*. "Bastard." She hissed.

"Uh, no. Hottie." Joanne winked before turning to something Kylee was saying.

Sam looked around the room, trying to locate Max or Angel. Even Bowie had vanished. She frowned, meeting her reflection's eyes in the bar mirror as the hairs on the back of her neck stood on end. Brendan stood right behind her. Huge, grotesque and sending warm, foul air to wash across the top of her head and surround her. She nearly gagged.

Sam spun around, confused to find no one behind her. She looked around for Max and was about to reach out to him with her mind when Brendan's voice whispered, "I wouldn't do that if I were you."

She swallowed, turning back to the mirror, frowning when she saw he was behind her once more. He waved his meaty hand, and the mirror turned into a screen where she could see every area of the pub clearly and everyone within it.

She froze, fear stealing the breath in her lungs as the bar began to vibrate, glasses rattled, then exploded as every pure-soul in sight turned towards her. Their heads became a blur as they unnervingly spun about before becoming still and they blinked as one before their eyes became devoid of colour, turning ink-black. Their teeth turned to pointed shards of glass, looking rotten. Arms elongating, they became limp noodles that hung to the floor.

"What is this?" she whispered.

"This is what is about to happen if you don't do precisely as I say," he answered.

"What do you want?"

"I want you to release Nadine and bring her to me. She'll show you the way. My people tried to get to her, but they exploded into pieces when they got too close to your boundary spell."

"I won't do that," she said, sounding braver than she felt.

"Oh yes you will." He nodded, gesturing around the pub.

She gasped in horror as every pure-soul who'd been turned into instruments of evil, wrapped their vine-like arms around the necks of every Vein and Soul Keeper. They struggled against the surprise onslaught, but to no avail. Six-inch glass thorns protruded from the instruments' pale flesh, cutting into the necks of their victims, hacking and sawing until the heads rolled off everyone she loved.

Sam cried in despair, screaming as Bowie's head hit the floorboards and rolled towards her. It stopped at her feet as his once soulful, amber eyes, stared unseeingly up at her with empty eye sockets.

She swallowed bile as she searched for Max and her world tilted as she spotted him. Sam leaned against the bars counter for support, watching him struggle against the turned-souls, his forest-green eyes pinned to hers.

"Max…" she choked.

He shook his head.

Three men were restraining him as two others were sawing at his neck. A flood of tears fell from her eyes and she blinked them away, not wanting to miss a second of holding his gaze.

His magnificent, silver vein-wings burst from behind him and she cried once more as a beastly man attacked them with the axe that stood beside the pubs roaring fireplace. Silver blood splattered everyone in the pub. She could not stop the sobs that racked her body as she watched Max's wings fall. The world around her moved in a sickly slow pace as his head joined his wings with a thud in a puddle of silver blood.

Her scream of despair shattered every window in the pub and the Princess Highway beyond split open like angry jaws from hell, screaming along with her. All-consuming fires burned and flames shot out of the cracked earth, blazing high towards the night sky. The Elms shook to and fro as the earth rolled and heaved, their groans filling Sam's soul with desperation and horror as she watched them fall into the deep crevices of cracked, burning earth, along with every building along main street.

She cried, pulling at her hair, shaking her head in utter disbelief of what was happening. The pain of tortured, terrified life stock bellowing as screams of the districts pure-souls filled her ears with unbearable humming, like a swarm of furious wasps trying to eat through her ear drums.

She wanted to throw herself into the burning earth to escape it all, but fell to her knees instead, trying to figure out how she could kill Brendan. She dropped her face into her hands and sobbed, trying to make sense of her world without those she loved most in it.

"You can stop it all, if you bring me my beloved Nadine." Brendan's voice broke her from her shocked trance.

She blinked then, to find herself standing at the bar, facing the mirror. Conversations and laughter resumed. Everyone was all right. She heard Bowie laugh and Max joined in. Her knees went weak with relief then and she gripped the counter for support, wiping tears off her face.

"If you want them to live, leave unnoticed. Do it now. You've three seconds."

She didn't hesitate and waved cheerfully to Angel, pointing towards the female toilets. Angel smiled, nodding as she continued her conversation with the girls.

Sam shielded her thoughts with the strongest shield she'd ever created, and ran through the back dining room, out the back door and headed to the white, iron gate. She got in Max's car and starting the engine, churned gravel beneath the tyres as she turned the car out of the Wheatsheaf's carpark and towards Noorat as if the devil himself were on her tail.

CHAPTER THIRTY
SAMANTHA

Sam headed down the cellar stairs, feeling guilty already with the lie she was about to tell Michael. He was sitting in one of the chairs opposite Nadine's cell, arms folded, wearing a calm look across his handsome, steadfast face. How she loved him.

"Hey, you." She forced a smile as he turned to her.

"Hey." He grinned. "Couldn't handle the fun, huh?"

"Well, actually, I was having heaps of fun but Angel was missing the fact that you weren't a part of it all, so she asked if we could trade places for a couple of hours."

He blinked once, tilting his head. "Really?"

"Absolutely." She nearly choked on her forced laugh, feeling sure he would sense her lie. "Max agreed, otherwise I wouldn't be here."

He looked across at Nadine, who was lying on the cot with her back to them.

"Well, I wasn't getting anywhere, really. I'll go pick up Beth and join the others for a bit." He met her gaze. "You sure?"

"Oh yeah, positive. To tell you the truth, I'm relieved. I'm still a bit exhausted after... well, everything." She knew that would work and her guilt multiplied as he stood and crossed towards her, folding her in his arms.

"I'm so proud of you. I always knew you and Max were something special."

She hugged him tightly, forcing the recent horrid visions and threatening tears at bay and smiled up at him. "We're all something special. Every one of us. Now, go get your wife and have some fun, please."

He laughed and kissed the top of her head before turning towards the stairs.

"Yeah, you twisted my arm. I'll see you tomorrow."

"See you," she said, relieved when she heard the door close behind him before releasing a loud, pent-up sigh.

She ran shaking hands over her face before looking towards Nadine to see her standing at the cells door, arms folded, staring at her with cold eyes. She returned Nadine's stare, feeling a flood of fury wash over her, wishing she could snuff the life out of her and not give it a second thought.

Nadine smirked. "Conundrum?"

Sam shook her head. "If you weren't Max's sister, you'd be dead already."

"If I were dead already, so would you all be. Trust me on that."

"Trust this. If I didn't have any other option right now, other than to take you to Brendan, I would gladly make your life a living hell." Sam mirrored Nadine's stance. "As it is. I am releasing you from this cell and you are taking me with you to Brendan."

"Just like that? He must have shown you something spectacular."

She laughed.

"Yeah, he showed me he's an absolute psychopath."

"Whatever. He would only have shown you truth for you to betray Maxwell and your precious *Soul Keepers*." She spat the words out as if they left a foul taste in her mouth.

"You're betraying two men, *your* flesh and blood and for what? You know what, don't even answer that. Just come on," Sam said before shooting a bright white spark of lightening towards the lock. It snapped off instantly, the door popping open.

Nadine stepped through, a pretty smirk on her face. "Prepare yourself, you are about to enter a world of pain."

"Been there, done that. Now shut the hell up and take me to your demented Uncle." She tossed Nadine the car keys, and pointed to the tunnels exit.

"Sure." Nadine turned on her heel and strutted out like she was on the cat-walk.

Sam followed her along the cellar corridor and out the back exit that led to the old horse carriage house where she'd parked the car. She was curious to see where Brendan had been hiding all this time. Wherever it was, it wouldn't be a secret for long. As soon as she had the location, she would reach out to Max and Angel and they would have the upper hand to destroy Brendan once and for all.

MAXWELL

"Hey Michael, Beth." Max hugged Beth, thinking Michael's wife looked more beautiful every time he saw her. Tall and slim, she had a sweet face and raven hair that hung to her waist. She was the first pure-soul to live with the Soul Keepers of Glenormiston South and who had been gifted with the knowledge of all things, 'Soul Keepers,' and the world in which they lived and protected.

"Max, it's so good to see you." Beth returned his hug.

Max smiled as he asked Michael. "Who's guarding Nadine?"

"Why, Sam of course, like you said." Michael stiffened instantly. "You didn't say, did you?"

"No, I did not." He spun around to search for Bowie, hearing Michael curse behind him. *Sam, what are you up to?* He pushed out towards her, waiting for a reply. Nothing.

"What now?" Bowie asked Max and Michael has they approached him, wearing twin expressions of worry.

"Your sister," Michael said.

Bowie looked around the pub. "What about her?"

Angel left her friends to join them. "What's going on?"

"Apparently Sam has relieved Michael to watch over Nadine, but she didn't tell me she was leaving." Max looked Angel. "Did she say anything to you?"

"No." Angel shook her head. "She went to the toilet, but that was a while ago." Angel flushed, looking guilty. "I'm sorry, I've been so caught up with the girls, I thought she'd gone to hang with you for a while." She looked up at Bowie, who ran a comforting hand over her back.

"It's okay," He said before asking Max, "Are we presuming something's wrong?"

"She left without telling any one of us," Max said, one eyebrow arching to emphasise his point.

"And she lied about it," Michael finished.

"Enough said." Bowie nodded in agreement. "Well, let's head off and see what's up. Can you reach her?"

Max shook his head.

"Shit." Bowie clenched his fist.

"Let's not jump to the worst conclusion just yet." Max turned to the crowd and spotting Kyle, waved him over.

"This is supposed to be a fun night," Kyle grinned as he joined them. "Why the anguished looks?" He leaned against a full wine barrel decorated with bottle top lids, which sparkled under the lights.

"Sam's gone rouge," Michael said.

"Fun." Kyle's eyes gleamed wickedly.

"No, actually." Max frowned at his triplet.

When he sensed the seriousness of the situation, Kyle straightened. "What do you need me to do?"

"Get everyone together and meet us back at the mansion." Max ran a hand over the back of his neck.

"Jane went missing earlier," Angel whispered.

"When?" Max asked.

"Um." Angel shrugged. "About twenty minutes before Sam did, I think."

"On her own?" Bowie asked.

Angel shook her head. "No, Joanne said she left with some hot guy, but that's all."

"We need to go. Now," Max said and headed out the front door of the pub, the others two paces behind.

I hope you've got a good reason for this, Samantha. He pushed towards her, feeling frustrated with her and concerned for her at the same time. He couldn't wait to hear what her reasons were for leaving them in the dark.

SAMANTHA

Sam kept her shield firmly around her thoughts; hearing Max clearly, but not daring to respond. Not yet. She wanted to know the exact whereabouts of Brendan to help her clan defeat the bastard once and for all. She had a plan. Kind of. She watched as the headlights lit up Blacks

Drive, better known to the locals as 'Lover's Lane.' Its gravel drive ran from Glenormiston road, through to McKinnons Bridge Road, lined with ancient English Oaks, and fenced off by dry stone walls.

It was as beautiful to look at by night, as it was by day. Her curiosity intensified. Where were they going? She didn't have long to wait, and a scream lodged in her throat as Nadine ripped the handbrake up, sharply spinning the steering wheel left, releasing the handbrake before slamming her foot on the accelerator, heading between two elms and straight into the dry stone wall.

"What the hell!" Sam yelled as the car speed towards the wall. She reached for the handbrake, but Nadine made a fist and punched her in the face. Although she dodged the blow, it landed on the side of her temple, causing pain to burst around her right eye.

Before Sam had a chance to retaliate, they sailed through the stone wall. Sam cringed, waiting for the large rocks to damage the car, but instead, the world around them lit up and her heart accelerated. They were going through a portal? Veins had never had any authority with portals, but maybe Brendan's new abilities allowed him that power? The light ebbed, liquorice black, and she knew they were headed to a dark place indeed.

She dropped her shield, hoping she wasn't too late and pushed two words towards Max, Bowie and Angel before her world vanished and she was sucked into a new one.

MAXWELL

Lover's Lane. Max's head jerked up as Sam's voice brushed against his mind. Bowie and Angel reacted instantly. "You heard that too?" he asked.

"Yes," Angel said.

"Let's go then." Bowie sat forward in the front seat, as Max drove at a fairly high speed along Glenormiston road.

"Shouldn't we notify Red?" Angel sounded worried.

"Already done." Max replied, sounding calmer than he felt as he turned down Lover's Lane.

"I can't see Sam anywhere." Angel peered through the windscreen between the seats.

"There, look!" Bowie cried at the same time as Max slammed on the brakes. They'd both seen the skid and gravel marks heading off the road and towards the rock wall.

"Those rocks haven't been disturbed," Angel whispered.

"Which can mean only one thing," Max said, shoving the gear stick into reverse and slamming his foot down on the accelerator, taking them back down the road.

"Wonderful." Angel sat back.

Bowie turned in the seat and reached to take her hand. "It's okay, baby."

"I know."

Max heard the smile in her voice and slowed the car to a stop. "Angel, I think you should get out." She met his eyes in the rear-view mirror and he sighed at her hurt look. "I just want to keep you safe."

"And she will be, because she will be with two, make that, three of the most powerful Soul Keepers there ever were. Got it?" Bowie nodded to Max.

"Sure. Hold on tight. I'm not sure if this is going to work."

"Yet, it will be fun to find out." Bowie grinned.

Max chuckled. "If you say so," he said before slamming his foot on the accelerator, following the path of the tyre marks down the road before turning sharply and heading straight towards the rock wall.

Before the front of the car collided with the ancient stones, a black orb vibrated around them, sucking them into nothingness. They moved in slow motion, with the feeling of the air in the car being squeezed out. Max fought against an unfamiliar dizzy wave as it rolled over him and looked to see Bowie and Angel slumped in their seats; their seat belts the only thing keeping them upright.

He frowned and focused on staying awake, relieved to see light ahead before they popped out of the portal and bounced as the car's tyres thumped on concrete before rolling to a stop.

Silence greeted him and he unclipped his seat belt, seeing his car parked on the side of the road. They were on the corner of the Princess Highway and Swanston street in Terang, but there was not one living soul around. No cars or trucks drove by. Stillness. Nothing. He nudged Bowie's shoulder before reaching back to drop a hand on Angel's knee, squeezing lightly. They stirred simultaneously, waking fully in under a minute.

"What was that?" Bowie ran a hand over his jaw.

"A dark portal," Max said.

"Where are we?" Angel groaned, unclipping her seat belt.

"You all right, my baby?" Bowie snapped off his seat belt and got out of the car, opening Angel's door and tugging her out and into his arms.

Max got out, closing the door with a click as he looked around. "It looks like we're in a multiverse."

"A what?" Bowie kept his arms around Angel as he raised an eyebrow at Max.

Angel looked up at Bowie. "It's like a parallel dimension, an alternate reality to ours. Does that make sense?" She looked at Max.

"Shit." Bowie looked around them. "Please don't tell me we are stuck in a 'Stranger Things' scenario?"

"I wish." Angel smirked. Bowie shook his head, running his hand over her hair.

"Not quite," Max said as he stepped into the middle of the road. "Stay here, I'll be back in a second." With that, his vein-wings snapped open, and he sprung into the air, vanishing from view.

He flew above the alternate Terang and once high enough, could appreciate the dark energy Brendan had used to create the mirror image of the town. At last, he felt what he was looking for; a vibrating, foul energy pulsed from Thompson Presbyterian Church. He headed towards it, seeing a dark matter swirl continuously around the church as if protecting it. The energy was filled with sickness and rage. Max shook his head, sending a message to Red before snapping his wings together and was back with Bowie and Angel in under five seconds.

"What could you have possibly discovered in two seconds?" Bowie asked.

"That we are in for a battle unlike any we've ever faced," he said.

"Bring it on." Bowie's eyes narrowed as he cracked his knuckles.

"Angel, do you need Mother Earth's assistance to charge you?" Max asked.

She shook her head. "I'm fine and ready for whatever is waiting for us," she said in a confident tone.

"Great." Max nodded. "They're holed up at Thompson Presbyterian." He pointed his thumb over his shoulder.

"Are we going to wait for the others?" Angel asked.

Max shook his head. "They're on their way and won't be too far behind us. Let's see if we can't get by their barrier."

Bowie and Angel nodded and together, they turned towards the highway.

SAMANTHA

Sam followed Nadine through the grand double wooden doors of the church before they slammed shut behind her. She scowled at a Vein who stepped forward and spat at her feet.

"Charming, *pig*." She hissed, waving her hand, sending a gust of wind to slam into the unruly female, sending her crashing against the wall before falling hard on her backside.

"Watch yourself." Nadine glared at her.

"*She* should watch herself. Have you got any idea how much disease is spread by filthy, uneducated vermin who haven't learned that spitting is a no-no?" Sam scoffed. "Seriously." She shook her head as Nadine turned on her heel and continued down the seemingly never-ending aisle of the church.

She looked upward as they continued along and was amazed with her ability to appreciate the church's stained glass windows and architectural beauty despite her current predicament. If she remembered from her history class, back in the days of learning about the town's 'holy places of worship,' this church had been erected in 1893. She only hoped whatever Brendan had planned; this building would not be amongst the carnage.

After what felt like five minutes of walking along the endless isle, Nadine stepped up onto the altar and turned to Sam. "Hurry up."

"Pfft." Sam raised an eyebrow. "What's the rush, no one's waiting?" Apart from the spitting pig at the door, there was not another person anywhere to be seen.

Nadine folded her arms. "Just get up here."

Sam hesitated before stepping up onto the altar beside Nadine, and that's when the floor shifted beneath her feet and the church spun around her as if on revolving floor. She reached for the pew to steady herself, annoyed Nadine stood still as the church blurred around them. Sam squeezed her eyes shut to block out the unnatural movement of the building and tried not to throw up.

Her eardrums filled with a hundred voices and booming laughter had her blood boiling in fury. With hesitation, she opened her eyes, her blood turning from boiling to cold in an instant at the sight before her. They were standing in a cave with stone walls that disappeared into vast blackness; the chill of damp fingers brushed against her flesh. Veins, as terrifying as the ones in the vision that Brendan had shown her earlier and others, who had been altered; limbs fashioned into weapons, faces unrecognisable as human or animal stared back at her.

Alien could be a close enough description.

Veins, openly feeding on pure-souls, eyes as black as a moonless night, the pure-souls in their arms, as pale as Sam felt.

Sam straightened and scanned the room for two things: Jane and an escape. Escape looked doubtful. No door were visible. She pulled in a deep breath as she turned, her gaze falling on a familiar face and her arms snapped to her sides. She was going to *rip* his face off!

Trent's eyes lit up when hers met his. "At last, it's on." He laughed.

"Like you wouldn't believe," she said with a snarl, stepping towards him.

"I see, by your glorious transformation, something's been stirring inside you?" Trent's gaze was filled with lust.

Sam shot him her most hateful glare.

"Don't be like that, my *stella,* our union will be sweet, after the pain recedes of course."

"Union?" Sam scoffed. "Whatever. And the only one in pain, will be you. I promise you that."

As Trent opened his mouth to reply, Brendan held up a meaty paw.

"Hold that thought, son. Thank you, *Samantha.*"

Brendan sneered her name, bringing her attention straight to him. Her head was reeling. Son? *Trent?* No way! *Play it cool, Sam.*

"Thank me for what?" she said, sounding bored.

"For bringing my darling Nadine back to me, of course."

371

Brendan did what Sam presumed was a smile in Nadine's direction. Her stomach rolled, and she had to look away.

"Where's Jane?" she demanded, ignoring Brendan and directing her question towards Trent.

He shrugged as he made his way towards her through the feeding bodies who were watching, waiting. He stopped and tilted his head when he was ten feet away. His ash blonde hair shifted, the bright blue streak falling into what she'd considered attractive eyes when she'd first met him. If only she'd seen him for the despicable snake he was.

"Where the hell is Jane, you *bastard*?" She hissed the words.

"That is a unhanded way to speak to your betrothed." Nadine laughed slyly before adding, "That's not a good sign."

"Indeed," Brendan said, taking in the scene.

Sam laughed. "You're kidding me right? That is never going to happen."

"Oh yeah?" Trent folded his arms. "And who is going to stop us?"

Sam turned to face him straight on. "What century do you think you're in?"

"That doesn't even come into play. My father has promised you to me, so that's all there is to it." Trent raised an eyebrow. "I *own* you. My Leecher has been consuming your essence for weeks."

"And you wonder why we call you parasites?" Sam shook her head. "FYI, your *Leecher* no longer resides in me." She had the pleasure of seeing a panicked look cross his pretty-boy features.

"What! How?" He rubbed his arm, frowning.

"Yeah, Max removed it and then fried it. Thought you'd like to know." She grinned.

Trent folded his arms.

Sam placed her hands on her hips before turning to Brendan. "I'm pretty much going to give you one more chance to tell me where Jane is?"

"Oh, you're going to give me one more chance. That's hilarious." Brendan folded his meaty, repulsive looking arms. Sam was sure she saw a maggot creep into a small hole in his neck.

Don't you dare barf. She sensed threatening movement around her, placing her on high alert. She snapped her fingers and bright lightning sparks fell from her fingertips as she turned in a slow circle, keeping her eye on anyone who might decide to take her on. An unfamiliar, protective energy swirled within her, but she wasn't certain how to use it, so stuck with what she knew: her elemental energy.

Nadine snickered as she moved towards her, opening her arms wide, sending a vein-whip straight towards her face. What would have blinded her if it connected, was burnt instantly as Sam hit it with a blast of searing white heat. Nadine screamed as her vein fell to the floor like a wet, burnt noodle. The air filled with the stench of it.

"You *vile* creature." Nadine screeched in pain.

"I've always disliked this shallow saying, but it seems appropriate for this situation," Sam said, tossing a mile of silver, silken hair over her shoulder. "Sorry, not sorry."

Nadine roared, hissing out an order before another Vein hit Sam from behind with a thud to her lower back. She gasped when searing pain flooded her system as a sharp 'thing' wormed its way inside of her.

She cursed, throwing up her shield, which electrified her attacker immediately. To hear him scream in pain helped alleviate hers. The foul object wormed its way deeper inside her. Sam kept her shield in place and closed her eyes, startled to clearly see an image of the slug-like blob inside her body as it ate through her muscles, making its way towards her bones. She gritted her teeth, sweat trickling down her back as it moulded itself to her spine.

She sucked in a deep breath and sent the air through her body and *watched* as it formed into a sharp, silver blast of ice, slicing the slug in half. To hear it scream in pain, as too, did the Vein it came from shocked her as she forced it out of her body.

When it fell with a sickening thud to the floor, her shield liquefied it instantly. She wiped the sweat from her brow, feeling breathless for a moment, tired of being amongst the putrid Earth eaters.

She turned to Brendan. "I want Jane, *now*."

He stood staring at her with a startled look of awe on his face. "By all the Black Priests that ever lived and every disease they created, you are the most beautiful creature to behold."

What the hell… Sam frowned. What was he on about? She glanced down at herself, then over her shoulder. Sam discovered her vein-wings had burst out behind her, sending a halo of the brightest white that dripped with sparks of silver to shield her.

So, that's what my shield looks like now? Cool.

"I'm sorry, son, but I believe I will take Samantha Storm for myself."

Brendan started towards her; the crowd of bodies moved silently.

"I would literally rather vomit in my mouth, swallow it, then repeat that action until I choked to death before I ever let that happen." Her wings spread wider, her new power sending a warm, pleasant tingle throughout her. The same pleasant feeling she felt whenever Max was near.

I wish.

Is my command. Max answered her.

She spun around; a cry of joy left her lips before she could help herself. He stood, with Bowie and Angel either side of him. Every Vein within five feet of them crumpled to the ground and curled in balls of pain as they clutched at their stomachs.

Max was a vision of power with his magnificent wings spread wide. Bowie's elemental energy glowed brightly and his and Angel's shields were firmly in place, protecting them from any Vein.

"Max," she whispered, relief flooding her. She hadn't known she'd been feeling so anxious until he stood before her.

He held her gaze and she could see a frustrated, although relieved look in his forest-green eyes, speckled with silver. She knew in that moment he had something else to say to her, but it would have to wait.

And it will.

She swallowed, begging her thought of him being too hot in this moment, not to escape her shield.

"*Nephew,*" Brendan said with a sneer, snapping her out of her lust-ful thought.

"Please, you're no *uncle* of mine," Max said calmly, breaking his gaze with Sam to send an icy stare in Brendan's direction.

"You're too late. As you stand before me, your precious Mother Earth is doomed, just as you all are." He chuckled grotesquely.

"Anything you've done to Mother Earth, can be restored. Veins and Soul Keepers alike understand that working together is the only solution for any future. As for us, there's nothing you can do to harm us," Max said.

Trent sneered. "If you think we are going to let you walk out of here alive, you're stupider than I thought."

The mass of Veins cheered at Trent's comment.

"Yes, I thought you had at least half a brain, Maxwell," Nadine sang, sugar-sweet. "But it looks as if you're as dim-witted as those arrogant Light Accord twits."

"And to think you're related," Bowie said to Max. "You must have received the other half of her brain, because she sure hasn't got one."

Max chuckled as Brendan cried impatiently. "Bring the *Soul Keeper* in."

"Finally," Sam whispered, as they turned towards the crowd that parted. Every ounce of blood drained from her face.

Jane was hanging from her wrists on a square, metal frame, which bumped along as it was wheeled over the uneven cave floor before it was brought to a standstill in front of Brendan.

Her wrists and ankles bound, wearing only a skimpy, black bikini. Her once thin, tall frame now revealed a swollen belly too large to be conceivable. Jane's skin, translucent, revealed Mother Earth beneath, spinning within her; the blues, greens and whites, pulsing ever-so slightly.

Sam swallowed hard, feeling Angel's anguish as Brendan cried, "Meet, the destroyer." Throwing his arms wide, the crowd of a thousand Veins sent an eerie chorus to fill the cavernous pit.

CHAPTER THIRTY-ONE
MAXWELL

"What have you done to her?" Max demanded as his wings burst ten feet either side of him, sending every Vein within that distance flying through the air to topple against their brethren. Those who'd fallen to the ground in pain at his proximity earlier had crawled away. He frowned, grateful Jane was alive, but more than concerned for her state. Terrified would be a better word.

Goosebumps covered every inch of her flesh and he felt it the moment Sam pushed warm heat towards his cousin. He glanced at her from the corner of his eyes, appreciating her grace before coldly meeting Brendan's dead eyes.

"I wouldn't do anything rash if I were you." Brendan sat down on a pile of rocks fashioned into some kind of throne as he waved a hand towards Jane. "She is now what we consider Mother Earth. Trent, a demonstration, if you please."

All eyes were on Trent as he moved forward, releasing a thin vein to move towards Jane's engorged stomach.

Sam cried and took three steps forward, her eyes only on Jane.

A shiver of fear spread through Max as Brendan launched a vein-spear towards her. Before it could slice through her, Max leapt in the air, his wings taking him across the fifteen feet that separated them in a second. His arm wound around her waist as he spun them about, his wings forming a cage around her. His shield vaporised Brendan's spear. Sam's body shook in his arms and he turned her about to face him, his wings shielding them from everyone's eyes. Her wings folded against her back.

The worry filling her eyes didn't do a thing to mar her beauty. He ran his thumb over her bottom lip, which trembled. Her cheeks pinkened.

"You're in trouble coming here on your own, you do know that, don't you?" he whispered.

She blinked, as if trying to focus on what he was saying while she watched his lips. He smiled. "Samantha?"

Her gaze met his before she shrugged that cocky Storm shrug he loved so much.

"No harm, no foul," she whispered.

"Like that, is it?"

"Yep. Now, let's kick some arse shall we?"

He nodded, dropping his head as she tiptoed up and they gifted themselves with a brief kiss that shook him to his core, making it hard to focus. He shook his head.

"We need to get Jane clear first."

"Of course."

Have you two finished? Bowie sounded concerned and as Max kept an arm firmly around Sam's waist and his shield strong, he pulled his wings back behind him and saw why. A ring of Veins had closed in on them. Each had their veins inserted into the arms of the Vein beside them, forming a dense barrier around them. Any pure-soul they'd been feeding on, now lay trodden beneath their boots. Behind them, another layer of Veins stood, doing the same.

That's odd. Angel said, inching closer to Bowie.

They won't get to us, Angel. Max assured her.

I know, but what about... Jane's scream cut Angel off and they turned to see Trent thrust his thin, needle-vein into her stomach to pierce Mother Earth. Angel paled, then swayed as around the cave, Mother Earth herself, grumbled and heaved.

Max was surprised when the cave didn't collapse in around them.

"What the hell are you doing?" Sam screamed at Trent.

He turned calculated eyes towards her and grinned. "Why, destroying the earth, of course." With that, he released another thin vein from his wrist and sent it slicing into Jane's stomach, his eyes not leaving Sam's.

Bowie caught Angel as she fell, looking as pale as Jane herself. Tears ran down her face. She clearly felt Mother Earth's pain.

Maxwell, what's going on down there? Red called to him and the others. *We can't get through the barrier.*

Jane is... pregnant with Mother Earth and she and it are being attacked, he said.

Yes, Earth is being destroyed as we speak. Cities are burning, the country is crumbling. You must end Brendan and every single Vein down there as soon as possible!

Max had never heard Red sound so stressed.

Bowie cursed as Jane screamed again. Max looked across and saw how desperately hard Angel was fighting against the pain of Mother Earth being destroyed. Of all the Soul Keepers, she was her true protector and had always been aligned with the planet.

Trent is setting the bombs off within Jane. Max informed Red and the others.

You need to stop him. Obsidian Souls and Soul Keepers are working together up here and will do everything in our power to put things right, but you need to hurry Max. Good luck.

Together then. Max nodded to Bowie as Red's voice faded.

Always.

"I have to help Angel," Sam whispered.

Max nodded, eyes on Jane. "Be careful, love."

She left his side in a flash. By this stage, Trent had twenty veins inserted inside Jane. Her screams were now pitiful mews.

"It's all right, Jane," Max said. "It will be over soon."

"Hell, you are deluded, *fratello*," Nadine hissed.

He turned his attention towards her. "I am no brother of yours." He ignored her to assess the Vein activity.

The ceiling, fifty feet above them was now crawling with what looked to be a mass of wriggling veins. They formed into glistening stalactites with pointed ends that dripped down towards them like sharp daggers. He sensed Sam pour restoring energy into her soul-sister and Bowie's energy was on high alert as he guarded their girls.

He turned to Brendan then. "Are you that much of a coward you'll remain behind your wall of Veins?"

Brendan rose, shaking his meaty head. "Always such a disappointment."

"The God who created you thought the same."

"God? Well, if he's a God and I'm the first he created with some fine amendments, what do you think I am?" Brendan raised his hands, palms facing upwards before turning them over and slamming them towards the ground. As he did, a whooshing sound vibrated in the air above Max's head. He looked up, but before he had time to call out a warning, every vein hanging over their heads dropped like iron spikes. They trapped Max in one cage, Bowie in another and Angel and Sam together.

Brendan roared with laughter. Nadine joined in, setting Max's blood to pump against his eardrums in anger.

"Nothing but children." Brendan scoffed.

Max grabbed at the bars and hissed as the slime coating burnt his flesh. *Acid*.

Great. Bowie returned.

Max raised his eyes the moment Jane hung limp and her crying ceased. Blood seeped from the twenty large drains from her stomach as Trent removed his veins.

He met Max's eyes and grinned. "Mm, yum. I wonder what you'll taste like, Sam?"

Sam gasped.

"You wouldn't *dare*." Max hissed, as the earth vibrated, then stilled.

Trent pointed to Angel. "I'm going to drain her, and then feast on her." He pointed to Sam.

Bowie cursed.

"Nadine is going to feast you." He pointed to Bowie. "Then you." He stood in front of Max. "And then, I'm going to kill you and make Sam my wife and feast on any living Soul Keeper for the rest of their days."

Max tilted his head. "I'd like to see you try all that and live to tell the tale."

"Would you? Nadine, come here."

Nadine crossed over and stood, flicking her hair over her shoulder. To think Max had once thought her beautiful. He shook his head.

"Eat." Trent ordered.

Max stepped away from Nadine as she opened her arms wide. He hissed again as his wings brushed against the acid bars.

"Oh, there's nowhere to hide, darling *fratello*." Nadine leered as she sent several veins to slip through the bars, reaching towards him, their tiny mouths opened revealing razor-sharp teeth.

"Max?" Sam cried in concern.

"It's okay, *Bella*, she won't hurt him… much." Trent laughed as Nadine's veins lunged forward and sliced into Max's chest, throat, arms and legs.

"Feast with me," Nadine begged Trent, who, after a second's hesitation, released his veins to join hers inside Max's body.

He'd meant to groan silently, but released one filled with pain.

Max?

He could hear Sam's desperate plea as if her lips were pressed against his ear.

It's going to be okay… He hated lying to her but needed to calm her somehow. Being worried about Sam was almost as painful as what Nadine and Trent were doing to him. He forced his eyes open, to see Nadine's had turned pitch black. Trent's were closed. He felt their hot, piercing, greedy mouths extracting his purest Soul Keepers' essence along with his elite Vein essence. He grew weaker as the minutes ticked by and slumped against the bars, unable to stand a moment longer. The acid burning his flesh seared him back to consciousness, but he struggled to stand.

"Come on, *brother*," Bowie yelled. "This is a walk in the park. Don't let the dirty parasites suck you dry!"

Nadine gasped at the insult and Trent cursed, pulling his veins from Max and headed for Sam and Angel.

"You can shut up and watch this after that comment, wise guy." Trent smirked at Bowie as he released his veins to slip through the bars and brush against Angel's radiant flesh. Her startled cry had Bowie gripping his bars before cursing as the acid burnt him.

Hang on, Bowie. Max closed his eyes, sensing Bowie's frustration from here.

Hang on? To what? The bloody bars are burning.

"Max," Sam cried.

The desperation in her voice had his eyes opening in a flash. Brendan stood before him.

"Feast," Brendan commanded and Sam's scream of terror had Max staggering to his feet as a meaty vein the size of his arm punched straight into his abdomen.

He groaned as agony stole his vision, his breath, then, his hearing. The last thing that lingered was Sam's plea to stay awake.

SAMANTHA

Sam's heart felt as if it were going to rip straight out of her chest as she watched Max fade before her eyes. How could that be happening? He was superior in strength and power to everyone in this hell-hole. She gasped as another vein stabbed into her back and she felt her life being sucked out of her.

We have to fight this, she implored her loved ones weakly, squinting in pain and fury as she watched Bowie fall to his knees

Trying, little sister.

He sounded weak, and that infuriated Sam more than the filthy blood suckers slithering around under her flesh. Angel sagged against the bars. The acid burning her flesh hurt Sam as much as it did Angel.

She had an idea and as hard as it was to concentrate as agony swept along with her essence, she closed her eyes and focused. Sam placed her hand on her obsidian choker; feeling Max's silky vein gifted her with a sense of calm. She pulled in a deep breath and felt its power pulse beneath her fingertips.

I need you, she begged it. Warmth spilled under her fingertips, then seeped into her skin, sending a glow throughout her body. She wasn't sure how it was going to help her but concentrated on what she wanted to achieve.

She closed her eyes, looked inside her body, and focused on her essence. The very essence the Veins were sucking up into their greedy mouths without a single care the world around them was about to implode. That they were destroying a royal family whose main purpose in this life was to protect the innocent, if not, life itself. Their crimes made Sam's elemental blood, boil.

She concentrated on becoming one with her essence, feeling herself slide up and into their veins, feeling slightly ill as she reached their putrid, toxic bodies. She swirled around their blackened hearts, penetrating their organs and brains before sparking her elemental energy to a deadly level. Every vein inside her body and those Veins still attached to their brethren, became jerking puppets on her string, spasming before they exploded like they'd been microwaved for far too long.

Fearful screams echoed around the cave as the other Veins were splattered in pulpy, bloody body parts.

Nice one, Bowie called.

How did you do that? Angel whispered before completely passing out.

"What *have you done?*" Trent roared.

She grinned, wiping a piece of scalp from her cheek, flicking it towards him.

"Wanna find out?"

He dislodged himself from Angel and reached through the acid bars for her throat. She let him wrap his fingers around her, even acted frail, uselessly hitting his hands away. She saw his eyes light up the moment he thought she was weak. He signalled to someone in the crowd and the bars in front of her evaporated allowing him to drag her against his body.

Ew, she pushed towards Bowie, hoping Max and Angel would be okay until she had this situation figured out.

"Wanna taste?" she whispered.

He frowned. "Why so easy now?" His breath was too sweet coming from someone so rotten.

"Oh, you know." She angled her head towards Max. "I don't want to be on the losing side. I thought he was stronger," she lied, shrugging.

Surely he would not be so arrogant to believe this line? She swore she heard Max laugh weakly.

Trent looked across at Max as Brendan continued to consume his essence before meeting her gaze. She held his stare, raising a perfect eyebrow, knowing with her new 'look' he would be unable to resist her.

She shrugged, making to step away. "But… if you don't want to, I guess Brendan will do." She nearly gagged at the thought.

"No, I think dear old dad has had enough benefits of late." Trent wrapped his arms around her as several of his veins caressed her body.

She nodded. "I agree. Let's do this." She tilted her head, waiting before all his veins penetrated her body simultaneously.

She gasped at the brutality in which he fed from her. His tiny vein-mouths weren't just thirsty, they were angry, greedy and vicious. She watched him moan in pleasure, closing his eyes in ecstasy. This was it. She opened her wings and focused on shooting a small, silver vein-arrow out towards Max, Bowie, Jane and Angel. She felt it the moment they pierced her loved ones' flesh, moving within them, gifting them with her new energy.

We can't hold on much longer. Red's voice was filled with pain and fear. The cave rumbled around them.

Red, hold on, please! Sam begged and poured her lightning essence into Trent, penetrating his vitals. His eyes burst open and he released her body, staggering backwards.

"Father!" he cried, clutching at his stomach.

"Hurts, huh?" Sam narrowed her eyes. "Try this one then." She flung her hands to her sides, crackling electricity sparked off her fingertips as she stepped towards Trent. "I'll save you for Jane, and Nadine for Max," she whispered.

Awe mingled with horror filled his expression as her wings burst out sending searing white sparks to eject from each tip, shooting a thousand poisoned arrows straight into the hearts of every remaining Vein in the cave. They dropped like mosquitoes hit by Mortein on an Australian summer's night. All bar one.

Brendan roared in fury, then confusion as Sam watched him try to eject his thick vein from Max's stomach. He pulled once more before gathering it in his ham-like fists, to tug at it.

Bowie chuckled weakly, making his way over to scoop Angel from the cave floor.

"Hey, baby, how you doing?" he asked.

Angel wrapped her arms around him, as her eyes met Sam's. "Thank you." She smiled through her tears.

"You're welcome."

Sam whispered to the air in the cave and within seconds, Trent and Nadine were swooped up in an air pocket, held ten feet off the ground, trapped, and unable to cause any further damage.

"Wish we'd done that earlier." Bowie shook his head, but like him, Sam knew they wouldn't have had enough air in the cave to lift the mass of Veins and continue breathing.

"Angel…" Jane called, her voice light, as if she were about to drift off to somewhere from which she'd never return.

"*Jane!*" Angel cried and ran towards her, untying her and pulling off her jacket to wrap around Jane's shoulders.

Brendan cursed again, bringing Sam's attention back to Max. She walked closer, not wanting to get close to Brendan, but needing to be closer to Max.

Are you still with me?

Of course. His voice held a smile to it.

"Then, what are you waiting for?" she asked aloud.

"Almost there," he whispered, clearly concentrating.

Before Sam could ask, "For what?" Brendan gagged, his ham-hands giving up on tugging at his vein inserted inside Max, and clawed at his throat.

"Son!" he cried desperately before coughing. "Nad..." He choked before getting her full name out.

"What are you *doing*?" Nadine cried. Sam waved her hand and made the air bubble soundproof.

Thunder shook the cave above them, stones shifted and fell as Mother Earth groaned beneath their feet, swelling, then receding.

"It won't be long till this area collapses," Bowie said, concerned.

Sam bit her lip, hands itching by her sides to throw a force at Brendan and see if she couldn't just blow him up. But she knew this was for Max to do and she wouldn't take that away from him.

Brendan staggered back as far as he could away from Max, the vein between them keeping him in proximity. The gagging noises he was making as he withered in agony and confusion, made Sam feel nauseous.

"Just die already." She heard Bowie mutter the words, and from the tilt of Max's lips, so did he.

Suddenly, Max's wings flew out either side of him and Brendan's vein fell with a wet splat to the dirt floor, flopping around like a fish out of water. Brendan grabbed his monstrous head, starring in disbelief at Max, his huge mouth gaping open as saliva dribbled out, along with a gurgled cry.

"What's happening to him?" Sam wasn't sure if Max had used a similar technique as she had, but it looked like more was going on here.

Max looked at Brendan as he answered her question. "Karma."

The ground lurched and the rocks and earth holding the cave together began to crumble.

"Max, we have to get out of here," she cried and watched as he leapt ten feet into the air, slapping his massive wings together, shooting a silver flame to blast through one hundred feet of stone and earth, creating a wide tunnel.

He flew down and wrapped his arms around Jane's and Angel's waist and said to Sam. "Get Bowie, follow me." Boulders and rock wall continued crumbling around them. Sam nodded before Max flew like an arrow out of the tunnel.

"I can fly too, little sister." Bowie grinned and called to the wind and was lifted off the ground in an instant. "Let's bring them with us."

Sam nodded and created a soundproof bubble for Brendan, glad to cut off his grotesque sounds of agony as she sent him through the tunnel, followed by Trent and Nadine. As they soared higher, leaving the mass of Vein bodies behind, the cave toppled in on itself before falling into a grave of despair. As soon as Sam was surrounded by fresh air and the dusk sky, her soul filled with healing energy, ready to do what she was born to do. Heal and restore.

CHAPTER THIRTY-TWO
SAMANTHA

The healing and restoring of Mother Earth, had been no easy task. It had taken every Soul Keeper and remaining Vein on the planet months to reverse the damage done to Mother Earth. Six-point-eight billion lives were lost, decreasing the population to one billion. Cities had fallen, destroyed beyond repair. Then the cleansing needed to be done before the healing could begin.

It had taken Sam two months to do what she was created to do according to Methuselah. She evaporated every man-made 'thing' that no longer benefited Mother Earth. Landfill and ruined buildings, damaged roads, cars, trains and buses. Every toxic material that caused harm to earth and air. The list was endless and the work exhausting. Her new gifts astounded and frightened her at times as she turned the ruined cities of Russia and China into nothing more than a bag of litter within seconds. Then she burned it to pure ash to scatter in the wind and out into the galaxy. Pure-souls who lived to see the devastation were humbled by their surviving numbers. They watched the earth spring abundantly under their feet, the land greener than they'd ever seen it before. It gifted them with appreciation of what they had, and excitement for a simpler, more wholesome future.

If that was one thing Sam could appreciate after so much death, was that one fact that the pure-souls had caught on. Whilst Sam cleansed the earth, Angel restored it like only she could, along with Bowie, but it was Max who cleansed the oceans and rivers, along with his Obsidian Souls. Veins and Soul Keepers worked side by side, tirelessly, until Mother Earth was healed.

Jane, too, had been healed by Methuselah before he returned to his realm. Jane, Kyle and Max spent a solid week with Red, getting to know each other as a family unit before Max and Kyle returned to the Mansion. Max assured Jane she had a room if she chose to stay with them, which she would do.

That same week, Sam stayed at the homestead, enjoying spending time with Jess, Tom, Michael and Beth, along with Bowie and Angel.

"Just like old times," Bowie said one night after a prime meal cooked by Mrs. McGoldrick.

Everyone else had gone to bed, leaving her alone with her brother.

"Almost." Sam stared into the flames of the crackling fire, thinking it would have felt better if Max were here.

"When are you going back to him?" Bowie grabbed another log to add to the flames.

"Soon. I just wanted to give him time with his family after all the healing." She'd slept a solid twenty-four hours when she'd returned home, followed by hours in the bath, then days nestled in this lounge, or horse riding with Angel. They'd lost many of their pure-soul friends in the devastation. It was a hard time for them all.

"You are his family, Sam." Bowie sighed.

"I know, it's just… now he has a *real* family. His Obsidian Souls, Kyle. Red and Jayne. I want him to absorb that. He deserves it."

"Well, we all need to support him tomorrow."

"Why?"

"He's executing his own sister, along with Brendan and Trent."

The air whooshed from Sam's lungs and she fell back into the settee. "How did I not know this?"

"You've had enough to deal with and he didn't want you to know until last minute."

"Hang on, the love of my life… my…'immortal partner,' has a major, life-altering event occurring tomorrow and I'm only just finding out about it now?"

"Looks like someone's got there energy back." Bowie grumbled.

She threw a cushion at his head, which, of course he threw back at her.

"Life-altering how?" he asked.

"Bowie, how can you ask that?" She shook her head before standing to pace in front of the fire. "I honestly don't think Max will recover if he has to be the one to kill his own sister."

"He doesn't *have* to kill anyone, he needs to."

"What?" She stopped to look down at him.

"Max is the only one, apart from Methuselah of course, who can kill Brendan, Brendan's son and his own sister. The blood that flows in their veins is powerful and can cause disease and mayhem with a single thought."

"Poor Max," she whispered.

"For the continuous greater good of Mother Earth and all who reside on her, he must do it. The sooner the better."

"It isn't fair. Why didn't Methuselah do it when Max was off healing Mother Earth?"

Bowie shrugged. "That grandfather of Max's sure is a puzzle."

"He sure is something," Sam said as Bowie leapt to his feet.

"Look, let's get some sleep." He opened his arms, offering her a hug, which she gladly stepped into. "I'm super proud of you," he mumbled into the top of her hair.

She sighed against his jumper, hugging him hard. "I'm proud of you too." She looked at him. "Everything's different now."

He smiled. "Better different? No evil Veins influencing seven Billion pure-souls to wreak havoc?"

Sam grinned. "Yeah, well, there is that."

"It's a lot for us all to process. But we still have five thousand Soul Keepers and Veins to care for, along with one billion pure-souls, Mother Earth and her animals… so, don't think you can just go on a vacation," he said, teasing her.

"Point taken."

"Always." He placed the grill in front of the fire, slung his arm around her shoulder, and together they headed up the Pretzel carved staircase to their rooms above.

The following afternoon, in the crumbling fortress, those five thousand Soul Keepers and Veins stood as one. Obsidian and amethyst capes fluttered in the breeze as they watched the three culprits of disaster silently stand in the middle of the arena. A silver chain as thin as cotton bound them, preventing them from moving or speaking.

Sam stood between Bowie and Red, looking through the crowd to find Max. It had been two months since she'd seen him. She missed him terribly.

"Hey you," Kyle whispered from behind her.

She turned. "Hey Kyle." She gave him a quick hug. "It's good to see you." She smiled, thinking he reminded her of her love.

"I bet." He grinned.

Murmurs rang throughout the assembly and Sam followed their gazes. She looked sky-high, spotting a winged figure flying towards them. Bowie teasingly nudged her and her butterflies nose-dived as she watched Max land, as graceful as ever, folding his massive wings. His expression was serious, giving him an untouchable, stately appearance.

Sam reached around Bowie for Angel's hand, who gave hers a reassuring squeeze.

It's going to be all right, Angel said, soothing her.

In that instant, Max searched the crowd before his eyes found hers. She swallowed, thinking he had never looked so handsome as he did in that moment and he was about to kill his own sister. She'd shielded her thought, but from the narrowing of his eyes, she guessed he must have heard her.

I did.

She swallowed again, not blinking. *Sorry.*

Don't be, love. I've missed you.

I can guarantee I've missed you more.

Max eyed her up and down. *Not possible.*

Let's move along, shall we? Bowie chimed in.

Sam felt Angel laugh silently as Max held her gaze for a few moments longer before turning to address the assembly.

"Murder is not our way. Yet, forgiveness and pardon will not work on those who relish destruction, chaos and death. I hereby am charged with ending the lives of Brendan Black, Nadine Black and Trent Holland Black." He paused, facing each of them as he said their name.

Sam released Angel's hand to fold her arms, feeling anxious with what was about to transpire. Yes, they deserved to be destroyed. She just didn't know if she could watch it.

Close your eyes, love. It's okay. I don't want you to see this. Max brushed against her mind at the same time as addressing the assembly. "This is to keep every Soul safe."

"*With every breath that we take,*" the Soul Keepers returned.

Sam pulled a in deep breath. If Max had to kill for the greater good, than she could bloody well keep her eyes open. She watched as he reached behind his back and plucked a silver vein-feather from his wing before slapping his hands together.

Thunder rumbled in the late afternoon sky and a single bolt of lightning zig-zagged down towards him. He opened his palm, and the bolt zapped the silver vein-feather into star dust. Max stepped towards Brendan, Nadine and Trent and blew the dust towards them.

Within seconds, the silver dust flew around each of them, increasing in speed and size before forcing its way into their mouths, eyes and ears. What started off as star dust soon formed into liquid before becoming a solid matter, choking their airways and cutting off the blood to every organ. Max wasn't cruel and Sam noticed he waved his hand before them, hurrying their end rather than allowing them to suffer for longer than necessary.

"I would have dragged that out a bit longer if that were up to me," Kyle whispered in her ear.

She ignored him as she watched Max propel the three figures, that now resembled statues, into the sky to disappear from sight in mere seconds.

Fletch stepped through the crowd, looking more like a Vein than a Soul Keeper, adorned in his usual black suit. He turned in a circle as he addressed the entire crowd.

"And so it is done. Justice prevails." He stopped then to face Max. "We thank you, Maxwell Obsidian, for your service this day."

The crowd cheered. Their clapping filled the fortress with sounds of thunder before Fletch raised his hand, calling for silence.

"This bloke's the fun police," Kyle whispered again.

Sam shot him a quick smile as Fletch continued.

"Red has a few words."

Sam watched as Red stepped forward, noticing that she moved a little slower than usual. She wore flat ballet slippers with her jeans and a blue and white striped long-sleeved shirt. Around her neck sat a black scarf with an obsidian butterfly, hanging off an ornate silver clasp. Red smiled at Max before turning to address them all.

"Quieter days have resumed and for that we are grateful. Let's be mindful in every moment possible and assist the pure-souls to be the same." She ran a shaky hand through her thick, cropped auburn hair as if thinking about what she wanted to say next. She remained silent for a minute.

Max stepped forward, placing a large hand against the small of her back. "Are you okay, Nana?" Sam heard him whisper. Red didn't react.

She's just watched her Granddaughter, who was the spitting image of her beloved daughter, be put to death. I'd say she's not okay. Sam shared with Max.

Of course. Why didn't I think of that? Max cursed himself before putting his arm around Red. "Mindfulness. Kindness. That's the message for today. Let's do all to be more." He said, before he pulled Red into his arms and together, they disappeared in a flash of silver star dust.

"Well, let's get the party started, shall we?" Kyle put his arm around Sam's shoulder as Rick approached them.

"Party?" Bowie asked, as Angel smiled at Gemma, who arrived with Daniel.

"Yeah." Gemma nodded. "We've been organising it for when all of this was over and we knew Sam was coming back home."

Sam smiled. "That is so thoughtful."

"And a great idea. I think it's just what everyone needs right about now," Angel said before turning to Bowie. "Can we go home first? I want to dress up a bit."

"Of course, but first, we have to collect a little visitor."

"Oh?" Angel raised an eyebrow.

Bowie nodded. "We're looking after Alana."

"How lovely. Moonie is going to have a friend." Sam said.

"Yep, for a few weeks." Bowie nodded.

"Wonderful." Angel beamed. "They've always gotten along."

"Come on. Who's creating our portal out of here now that starman took our ride away?"

Sam chuckled as Fletch waved his hand and a portal opened up in front of them. "Off you go," he said.

"Thanks," Bowie said on their behalf before they all piled in, disappearing in an electric blue swirl that had Sam's stomach spiralling as laughter and cries of, "Fun times!" rang in the air.

CHAPTER THIRTY-THREE
SAMANTHA

The night flowed like a calm exhale, strewn with shared stories of their joint victories before conversations turned to lighter topics. Platters filled with mouth-watering Italian cuisine went down a treat and the light-hearted laughter filling the night was music to Sam's ears. She enjoyed watching Veins and Soul Keepers alike form deeper connections. Kyle and Rick seemed to be developing their own dance, and she was thrilled to see Gemma and Daniel holding hands, finally looking like more than 'just friends.'

She sipped her coffee while swirling the end of her ponytail in her fingertips. She'd given up on the champagne thinking it was a waste of time chasing a bubble-fizz if it wasn't going to work.

Sam scanned the yard, finding Max. She knew what would give her a lift, and that was being in his arms. A space she'd been missing for way too long. She drained her mug and left it on the patio railing before heading down the steps and out across the lawn to where Max stood. Hands in his jeans pockets, a black, turtleneck sweater hugged every inch of muscle and definition as he stared into the water.

Always so bloody beautiful, is our Max. She cringed as soon as he lifted his head, his eyes meeting hers.

"We really need to work on that," she said, sounding husky before clearing her throat.

"We will." He offered his hand, palm up.

She stepped towards him, sliding her palm over his and he pulled her towards him, closing the distance between them in a flash. She laughed lightly as she bumped into his chest. His scent of sandalwood and orange filled her nostrils and her laughter died with the intense way he stared at her.

"I'm sorry you had to endure that task today. Are you okay?" She watched his eyes darken as he nodded.

"Is Red?"

He smiled then and ran a finger along her jaw. "She is. Methuselah is with her now."

"Why won't he just make her young again and gift her with forever, beside him?" She frowned.

"It won't be long now," he whispered, his tone sad.

Her heart ached for him. "Oh Max, I'm sorry." She ran her fingers over his shadowed jawline.

His eyes stirred with lust as he replied, "Don't be. We'll still see her, just not in the form we're used to."

Sam nodded, dropping her gaze to his lips. He ran his hands across her waist to slip over her hips, pulling her against him, then wrapping them around her, sweeping his fingers up and down her lower back.

He sighed, dropping his forehead to rest against hers. "I can't be without you ever again, Samantha Storm. I won't."

She slid her hands up his chest and over his shoulders to wrap around his neck, to play with his silken strands. "Now that the *root of all evil* is gone, I don't expect you'll ever have to." A conversation with him right now, as his fingers swirled over her flesh, his breath sweet upon her face and his groin notifying her of what he wanted to do to her made it near impossible.

"There's so much we need to talk about," he whispered, brushing a kiss across her temple.

"We don't need to figure everything out tonight, do we?" she asked as he swept another kiss against her cheek.

"I guess not." His voice dropped to a husky whisper as she moved against him.

"I mean… if we have forever, I guess there's a few things we don't have to do tonight?" She stepped back, teasing him. "I mean, I didn't see you eat. I can fix you a plate of food?"

His wings burst out and wrapped around her, bringing her up against him, his hands cupping her face as his wings held her to him.

"Now that's more like it," she whispered, desire sweeping over every inch of her flesh.

"You're not going anywhere."

He dropped his head and swept his lips over hers and that desire burst into a stream of delicious, molten fire that flowed fast and furious.

"Maxwell Obsidian, take me to our room now."

"My pleasure."

He slid his arms around her waist, holding her closer than one could be held by another. In one push of his wings, they sailed into the air, towards the mansion and through his open bedroom window, leaving a trial of stardust and pleased spectators behind them.

THE END

ACKNOWLEDGEMENTS

Writing the second book in the Victoria Collection visually enabled me to return to my childhood home, Glenormiston South. Along with towns Noorat, and Terang, they are exemplary examples of the Western District's beauty. *Soul Keepers of Glenormiston South* prompted enthusiastic readers to explore the region, and I was delighted when they shared with me when they drove through Terang, then Noorat, to arrive in Glenormiston, they felt as if they knew the area already and could imagine the Soul Keepers, and Veins tucked away behind stoned walls, iron fences on grand properties going about their roles unseen.

Why did I choose to make Noorat the location in the second book of the Victoria Collection? After all it's only a one-minute drive from where book one is located, Glenormiston South. I can graciously thank my fabulous readers for that. Readers who were in raptures with Maxwell Black, and who wanted a complete story dedicated to him. The why and how Maxwell Black came to be, and where he was going. I was in complete awe (and slight terror) at the prospect of drafting an entire story based on a character, solely because my readers asked me to.

In saying that, *Obsidian Souls* is for all Max lovers, and all things

Soul Keepers related. Kelly Clark, and Sue Croft, I accepted your challenge and was grateful for your support along the way. Thank you. Sally Taylor, Taylah Manna, Sonee Singh, Jessica Fowler, Danielle Hughes, Danielle Aitken, and every other Max fan with which I've yet to communicate with. I hope you enjoy the ride.

Karen McDermott, you wonderful woman and darling friend. There will never be enough words to express my sheer love and gratitude for you. The joy you give me in our communications, the stability as one of your authors, and the confidence to simply be myself as I cruise along on my writing journey is such a privilege. Thank you.

To the MMH Team – You are phenomenal in every aspect and I am so grateful for your passion, dedication and talent. Thank you.

To my writing community who encourages, supports and celebrates with me. I am so very honoured to be a part of your lives, and grateful for your authenticity. There are so many of you, and some whom I have just met - Naomi Fryers, Stacey Webb. Kelly Clark, Sue Croft and all my PWC writing sister's. I treasure you all. Liz Hicklin & Juliet Marllier – you inspire me with your endless creativity and effortless grace. Because of you, I know I will be writing and creating worlds for people to escape to, for as long as I live.

To my Soul Sister, and fellow consumer of Piss-Tea, Sonee Singh. I have cherished our conversations over the past seven months. Our rekindled friendship has meant everything to me. The laughter, D&M's, and mutual respect for life itself and all things fantasy, has added such colour to my kaleidoscopic life. Thank you for sharing you, with me. Who knew a swing could take on such meaning when shared with a kindred spirit?

To my gorgeous friend, fellow local of Glenormiston South and incredible talent – Jess Fowler. Thank you for collaborating on another worthy project as we celebrate our stunning area. Sharing in lively, complex, and diverse conversations going on close to *two years* now, has been just delightful. I'm so lucky to call you my friend. Now, I wonder… can I muster up a children's book for you to illustrate?

To my editor, Velvet Tea – working with you round two, has been as effortless as round one. Thank you for your support and guidance, and equal passion regarding Maxwell's journey.

To the man who now resides in my childhood home, and calls it his sanctuary – Patrick Caruana, your heart is as big as your generous nature. From that first moment you offered to take mine, and my friends' photograph under the Blacks Road sign, I knew you were a kind-hearted spirit who deserved Mum's home. Thank you for your enthusiasm, and great eye in capturing the chapter heading photographs of our gorgeous area. And thank you tenfold, for opening your home to Leah and I, and our families when we come home to visit. It means the world to us.

To my high school family, I love and appreciate you all so much – Ashley Quick, Kylee, and Brendan Clark. You make coming home a real celebration every time. Thank you for being mine, and Leah's Breakfast Club!

To my hero, my love, my absolute everything – Jade Weitering. Thank you for your devotion and support with everything I do. And to our beautiful boys, Jesse, Zane, and Thomas. I'm so proud of you, and the steps forward you've taken in life. You are incredible men with so much potential. Keep reaching for those stars. I love you all to Methuselah and back.

To Louise Josephine Manna – You've battled a human disease, and won, like no other could. You've turned dreams into reality this past year. I'm so very proud of you, and because of your actions I'm now living the dream too! Frankston will never be the same again!

To my Soul Sister's who make every celebration big, or small

- totally sublime. Girls weekends – eventful and hilarious. A simple back yard game of pool, with loved ones - grounding. A visit to the Coolart nursery - relaxing. Conversations and cuppa's in the Manor – therapeutic. Standing in your paddock with your horses - exhilarating and terrifying. Sitting in your century old Church, talking for hours – priceless. You fill my soul-cup with such joy and because of each of you, my life is all the richer, and entertaining. – Leah Martin, Louise Manna, Sally Taylor, Kym Stante, Nadine Mendoza, Rachael Hecker, Nicole Sirianni, and Siobhan Collins.

To the beautiful young women in my world – watching each of you move forward so bravely in this life makes me so proud to be in yours. – Ireland Turner, Ella Whitford, Taylah Manna, Hannah Hecker, Eden Mendoza, Caitlyn Taylor, Kiralee Hecker, Ava Mendoza, and Emily Taylor. Keep shining darlings… you've got this!

To all the phenomenal journalists who help promote new books as they launch into the world, and celebrate the bigger 'why' behind each of them – Thank you so much. Trent Holland – Terang Express. Monique Patterson –The Warrnambool Standard. Nikki Fisher – Mornington Peninsula Magazine. Chris Earl – Loddon Herald. You may just be doing you 'job'… but I'm appreciative all the same. You all rock!

To the team at Collins Booksellers in Warrnambool. Thank you for reaching out to me when Soul Keepers launched into the world. Your support has meant the world. Thank you.

To Melbourne L'Arche! Thank you for welcoming me into the team with such grace, and supporting me in my other career! Namaste. And to all the core-members, thanks for making every shift rewarding.

As always – Lynette Martin. Xx I've recently been told that you are watching over me, along with Aunty Dorothy and Nana. Thank you for not scaring the hell out of me. I'm grateful for your gentle presence.

ABOUT THE AUTHOR

Mickey Martin is a romantic writer at heart who feels it is important to leave the reader with messages of hope and healing. Her books are filled with casts of colourful, resilient characters who thrive and survive hardships and trauma, allowing the reader to draw endless inspiration from memorable faces who have backbones of steel and hearts of gold as they go in search of their 'happily ever after.'

Mickey is also a non-fiction writer under her married name, Michelle Weitering. Here she seeks to write and make a difference, inviting the reader to question what more they can do to make our world a better place, with acts of kindness. As a mental health support worker, and advocate, she uses her writing to become a voice for those living and dealing with issues such as anxiety, depression, and other important social issues surrounding mental illness in order to raise awareness for mental health.

Mickey is celebrating her love for her home state, Victoria - stretching from the Western District, The Golden Triangle and The Mornington Peninsula, with her new series; The Victoria Collection.

Soul Keepers of Glenormiston was the inspiration behind this series, along with Obsidian Souls. This is her way of celebrating the beauty of Victoria, and the memories she has made within each town. A Chilling Summer in Inglewood set in the Golden Triangle, where her family have lived for five generations, and Sweet Water Creek, in Frankston, along the Mornington Peninsula, where she resides with her family now. Mickey is hoping to do for Victoria Tourism, what *Outlander* did for Scotland, with this collection.

Mickey is a multi award winning author, and shareholder with MMH PRESS, and is a member of the Romance Writers of Australia, Writers Victoria, and the Peninsula Writers' Club, where she adores connecting with, and supporting others, on their writing journey.

Mickey appreciates hearing from her readers, and you can connect with her on the following links.

www.instagram.com/mickeymartinbooks

www.facebook.com/michelle.weitering

The Victoria Collection

Noorat

Inglewood

A Chilling Summer in Inglewood

Glenormiston South

Frankston

Sweet Water Creek

Mickey Martin